MIRROR SECRET MIRROR

MIRROR SECRET MIRROR

Jessica Seaques

Copyright © 2023 Jessica Seaques

The moral right of the author has been asserted.

Apart from any fair dealing for the purposes of research or private study, or criticism or review, as permitted under the Copyright, Designs and Patents Act 1988, this publication may only be reproduced, stored or transmitted, in any form or by any means, with the prior permission in writing of the publishers, or in the case of reprographic reproduction in accordance with the terms of licences issued by the Copyright Licensing Agency. Enquiries concerning reproduction outside those terms should be sent to the publishers.

Matador
Unit E2 Airfield Business Park,
Harrison Road, Market Harborough,
Leicestershire. LE16 7UL
Tel: 0116 2792299
Email: books@troubador.co.uk
Web: www.troubador.co.uk/matador
Twitter: @matadorbooks

ISBN 978 1803135 854

British Library Cataloguing in Publication Data.
A catalogue record for this book is available from the British Library.

Printed and bound in Great Britain by 4edge Limited
Typeset in 11pt Adobe Caslon pro by Troubador Publishing Ltd, Leicester, UK

Matador is an imprint of Troubador Publishing Ltd

For Him

CONTENTS

1.	Red Rose	1
2.	The Proposal	26
3.	Pet Names	48
4	Love Heart	66
5.	Sweet Nothings	89
6.	Those Three Little Words	114
7.	No, You Hang Up	150
8.	Classic Romance	171
9.	One True Love	189
10.	Kissing	212
11.	Just Between Us	237
12.	Our Song	256
13.	Romantic Rhapsody	287
14.	Love Me Tender	310
15.	You and I	354

ONE
RED ROSE

'So, I'm fucking your husband. I assume you know this.'

Katya stated it with a casual lack of emotion – harsh, Slavic tongue effortlessly cutting cold. Charlotte's blue eyes widened in shock. Obviously she knew, but she hadn't expected her husband's mistress to just say it, out loud. Now dropping, her focus landed on the model motorbike sitting on the desk between the two women. One of few personal effects to adorn Katya's otherwise spartan office: concrete floors; high ceilings; three windowless, white walls; one wall entirely sheeted in a giant mirror. Charlotte floundered, still staring at the motorcycle ornament. She knew Katya rode a bike – had seen her in riding leathers before. Although the mistress currently wore a slender business suit.

The wife had avoided looking at the red rose craning out of the glass beside the bike, but the mistress called attention to it.

'He gave me that, today.' Her sly smile never touched her lips. 'It's my birthday.'

Charlotte's gulp caught in her throat. She didn't want to raise her head and make eye contact, but it was pathetic just sitting there.

'Happy birthday,' she found herself saying, sounding forlorn rather than bitter.

The mistress poised gracefully in her executive chair, sitting back from the desk but leaning forward slightly, fingers steepling loosely over neatly crossed legs. Her dramatic beauty always striking. Sharp, statuesque facial features – dark, sorcerous eyes. Jet-black hair matched the suit and contrasted fresh, white skin. Deep red lips and painted nails shocked like blood on snow. Glancing a reflection of the scene in the mirror-wall, Charlotte couldn't help comparing herself unfavourably to her husband's other lover. Shorter and more rounded – conspicuously normal-looking. She regretted her boring choice of clothes: white top and tights with a light-blue skirt. Her soft facial features and curly, hazel hair seemed childish and plain in contrast to the mistress' exotic splendour.

'Do you know what is he like? What is he really like?' Katya's eyes fixed on Charlotte with the icy sadism of a toying cat.

For a moment, defiance blazed up inside the mistreated wife. She wanted to stand and shout: of course she knew him. They'd been married for years – he was her husband, for Christ's sake! She knew all his little foibles and eccentricities. The habits and routines he ritualistically went through before going to bed. The anecdotes he liked to repeat about his worldly travels, or his time living in Japan. The silly voice he used to playfully mock her own (supposedly ditsy) inner dialogue. She knew so many things about him that no one else in the whole world knew. But then she thought about the part of him she didn't know: the part she'd never known... and always wondered. But maybe better not to know. This wasn't why she came here. Her brief surge of passion fizzled and dimmed.

'I don't know.' She shook her head feebly, then her well-spoken voice adopted a prim tone. 'I should go. I really have to be getting on.' Charlotte stood and made towards the door but lost the headstart, flustering back for her bag. Katya rose and moved around the desk, cutting off her lover's wife's escape. Eyes narrowed, as if ready to pounce.

'Don't you want to know? What is he like?' The Russian was advancing: a tall woman, even without those heeled boots. Pursuing as the wife backed away… drawing up nice and close. The distinctive smoulder of Katya's perfume was painfully familiar to Charlotte; it smelled like her husband's affair. The mistress loomed down to whisper in her ear. 'Because he is not like that with you. He told me this.' Lifting her hand to twirl a lock of hazel hair by Charlotte's cheek and pausing to let the humiliation sink in. The wife imagined her tormenter pinching that round, white cheek until it reddened rose. Although in reality the mistress' fingers just brushed against her, the skin flushing pink of its own accord. 'Not like that with his sweet, little wife. No, not like that with you. But I will tell you what is he like. What he does. What he enjoy. He is bad man. Your husband is very bad man.' Relish tickled in her husky voice.

'Tell me.' Charlotte's murmur was low, but the curiosity twinkled as her eyes flicked up to meet Katya's. She did want to know. Of course she wanted to know. Had always wanted to know. (Maybe that was why she came here?)

'Where to start?' The mistress made a show of flicking through various memories with her eyes, off-hand nonchalance deliberately offensive. 'One day, your husband and I… take little, student girl – twenty-ish, geeky glasses, cute. We take her here… and we fuck her.' Charlotte felt numb, but sensed some kind of discomfort in her gut – like getting stabbed under anaesthetic. 'Well, not in here. Through there… behind the mirror.' Katya gestured over her shoulder, body slanting, so the wife could see past more easily: the mysterious mirror-wall.

'What's behind the mirror?'

'What did he tell you?'

'That it was a storeroom. He said the old building had to be rented as a whole. That there was too much space. But it was cheap, for London, so it didn't matter. Said the mirror was always there. That the place must've been used as a dance school or something. I always thought it was… I always found it…' Katya was staring intently. Charlotte gulped out the words, 'A bit sinister.'

The mistress smiled with her mouth for the first time. An alluring smile, but not a pleasant one, the wry curl of red lips drawing attention to the self-satisfied arrogance permanently chiselled into her expression. 'This was never a dancing school. And that was never a storeroom.' Pointing through the mirror. 'That is our playroom – where we play with our toys.' Still twirling Charlotte's coil of hair, Katya drew back slightly, getting a better view of the tormented wife's face. 'We met this girl at one of his drinks things. She thinks he is great man. Wants to please him… very much. And she must please me too. And we come, all three of us, back here. So little, student girl can see "where the magic happens".'

She laughed sneeringly. 'We take her in there and play games. Make her our plaything. Make her into our bitch.' She snarled the word bitch with extra contempt. 'We strip her down, put collar on her… and leash. Stick plug in her asshole, with little doggy-tail. Make her wag her butt as she lick your husband's come out of me. Little puppy-bitch!' Spitting the word again. 'We play many games with her. Tie her to chair and I whip this bitch's ass. I laugh even more watching him do it. She crying and squealing. Tell us she do anything. Want to be our slave. And he fuck her little pussy, very brutal. She love it.' Pausing to savour the memory. 'This little, student girl find out lots about her dark side, this night. No one show her where to look before.'

Charlotte could feel the goosebumps, her body quivering as the sensation tickled up her spine. She believed the story – knew it was true – could imagine the scene clearly. A bewildering excess of emotions racing and spinning. She still felt numb, like how all the colours mixed together appear white… and feel blank. Pain and anger, hatred and humiliation, defeat and despair, curiosity and desire… a hundred swirling shades of jealousy. She couldn't really pick the individual feelings out as distinct from the general melee. Except (perversely) the envious rage she felt towards the little, student girl. Charlotte's husband had never fucked her with that kind of brutality.

'And what about you, little wifey? You have a dark side?' Katya's tone was mocking.

The wife composed herself, looking the mistress in the eye and speaking softly. 'Show me.'

Before releasing Charlotte's kink of hair, Katya gave it a little tug, tweaking the skin as the lock pulled taut. Her eyes sparkled, tasting the wince. She turned and strode around the desk towards the door at the far corner of the room. Charlotte recalled seeing her husband gazing at his lover after the three of them small-talked during one of his drinks events. He'd watched her turn away and then groped his eyes up those long legs before settling them on those perfectly-shaped buttocks… for a protracted period of time. Even more humiliating because the woman from the gallery noticed him doing it as well.

Katya beckoned with a sharp flick of the wrist, jolting Charlotte to follow her lead. She turned off the office light as she pulled open the corner door. The wife followed into a gloomy storeroom: cluttered high with boxes, but with space for the door leading through to the secret chamber. Katya closed the office door decisively, so they now stood in the dark. Charlotte's heart was racing. Could the mistress hear it thumping? Seemed so loud in the silence. Katya clicked a lighter and held the flame between them. Fire writhed in bewitching eyes. A blood-red smile spotlighted against the darkness. The wife suddenly realised she was in too deep. Maybe she didn't want to see. Didn't want to know. Didn't want to go any deeper. But she stood transfixed as the mistress pulled open the inner door.

The secret room was darker still. Katya lit a trident of crimson candles standing on an iron frame by the doorway. Hard heels clacked on stone as she proceeded into the chamber and began to ignite other similar torches. The candelabras stood ominously, like men waiting in the shadows, before the mistress kindled their flames and shed light on the darkness. The room was very large. One wouldn't have thought there could be this much space left over in the building. It felt even more expansive because the wall adjoining the office was mirrored on this side as well. The ghostly reflections of the candle flames flickering in the echoed gloom.

Obscure objects and pieces of furniture loomed and cluttered haphazardly. Most of the items were concealed under drapes – deliberately hidden… horrors waiting to be ceremoniously unveiled. The room was dominated by a grand, oaken four-poster. The bed overflowing with regal-red curtains and spilling with silk and velvet. The surrounding floor skinned with thick, fur rugs. This was her husband's secret place! The exhilaration tickled.

A slinking swagger as Katya moved over to the bed, flicking legs beneath her body to sit. She cocked her head and patted the mattress in summons. Charlotte shuffled into the room, the musky aroma of old incense itching her nostrils. Excitement tingling as the tops of her thighs brushed together. The sexy ghost of that evil, blood-red smile spotlighted in her mind. She placed herself on the bed. Katya sat diagonally behind, staring with unnerving intensity. The mistress seemed entirely immune to social awkwardness. The wife was definitely not. Charlotte began turning to face the other woman, but stopped halfway – freezing in the glare.

'It is comfortable bed, yes?' The boasting was relentless. 'I insist on this.'

God, she was so unbearably smug. Deliberately smug. Sadistically smug. Charlotte felt the hatred flare up, bright and distinct. But only for a second – too hot to hold onto for long. The burn felt cold afterwards. Shaking her head, she noticed the chair, facing across from the foot of the bed. A metal skeleton of a swivel seat without cushioning, the steel armrests joined by a semi-circular pole looping around the back. Handcuffs dangling ominously from the arms.

'You want see.' Katya sprang to her feet, pulling the wife along with a flicking finger. So the two women stood side-by-side, looking down at the sinister item of furniture. The low seat was a mesh of thin, metal wires. Not designed to be comfortable: a macabre device. The dread clutched up as the mistress allowed Charlotte a few moments to muse. A little thrill of fear wriggling through the sexual tension. Katya must surely be able to hear her victim's heart pounding now.

'Sit!'

The mistress' command was issued with absolute confidence. The hiss of the 's' conveyed menace, whilst the abrupt finality of the order demanded obedience without hesitation. Charlotte turned and sat down, a sharp spike of excitement prickling up her spine… and dissolving into the bloodstream like poison. The chair was as uncomfortable as it looked. Even through her tights, she could feel the wires pinching and biting around her buttocks. A crooking broken point needling against her thigh. The wiry seat was small and didn't go all the way back. If Charlotte was to lean on the narrow backrest, then she'd have to stick her ass out to overhang the rear edge of the seat. So she perched awkwardly, looking up to check whether she'd done anything wrong.

Katya made a brusque shooing movement with her fingers: an instruction to sit back. The wife winced as she shifted to sit with only her thighs on the mesh, her bottom spilling over the back of the chair – through the gap between the wire seat and the cold strip of backrest. She placed her arms along the rests and stopped moving. A shiver running through her bones. A shock of cold sweat on her skin. A gulp in her throat that wouldn't swallow. The hissing rush of escalation.

The twisted chair had forced her into a highly undignified posture. The sitting equivalent of standing bent over with hands on knees and sticking her ass out in exaggerated submission. She didn't dare look up – the humiliation of eye contact with the mistress would be excruciating. Yet part of her wanted to feel that – all of it. And all those repressed emotions swirling around in the depths: pain and torment, desire and frustration, love and hate.

Intense passions crashing in and out – a kicking from an anonymous crowd. But she could sense the submission-lust rising out of the emotional chaos – riding on it. Intensifying as the other feelings submerged into it. A delightful warmth kindling below the ears and then tingling through her body… goose bumps bristling as the energy rumpled under the skin. She was soaking wet – a flash-flood – loins lush and vulva throbbing with hot blood. Why did he have to choose such a ravishingly loathsome mistress? What a beautiful bastard! She felt her big, blue eyes lifting up, impaling themselves on Katya's icicle stare – so cold, so hard, so strong… so wonderfully irresistible. She could feel the respect and esteem pouring out of her, spilling out of her eyes, floodgates splayed open.

It must've been the most pathetic thing Katya had ever seen. Her lover's wife – ridiculed, insulted and humiliated – now abandoning any pretence of dignity to dissolve in submission. The mistress didn't feel a tinge of pity for her victim's wretchedness. How could she be so resolutely cruel, so unflinchingly vicious? Charlotte couldn't help but admire her – it was impressive. How could anyone not be impressed? No wonder he loved her. He was right to. Beautiful, obnoxious, pure, loathsome, adorable, evil. She deserved it.

The mistress leant in and reached down, the grate of the cuffs scraping up the right arm of the chair, stony-faced as she snapped the manacle around her victim's wrist. The tight metal sent a chill through Charlotte's bones. She was being restrained – becoming powerless – entirely at the mercy of the hateful woman her husband loved. What would the mistress do? She could do anything she liked! A few moments of silent panic as Katya paced around the back of the chair. Once the next cuff locked, the wife would be defenceless. But when the shackle clicked closed, the panic evaporated. The helplessness was perversely reassuring. A warm flood of relief as she was liberated from the possibility of escape. Totally at the mistress' mercy – the totally merciless mistress.

The spiky protrusions in the wire mesh dug into her thighs, but the captive remained still. Katya took something from a hook on the back of the chair and held it out on show: a ball-gag. The victim wouldn't even be able to scream for help. The mistress took the wife's face in her hand, pushing thumb and forefinger into the middle of the cheeks on either side and squeezing. Sharp, pointy nails digging into soft, plump flesh: forcing the jaw open. Charlotte gawped as the rubber ball jammed in through the teeth. Face puffing out, mouth intoxicated with the chemical taste of embittered plastic.

The mistress pulled the cords biting tight into the corners of the lips and fastened the gag around the back of the head. Looking pleased with herself as she took a step back. Slow paces around to the rear. Gripping Charlotte's shoulders and then swivelling the chair to face the nearby mirror-wall. It took a moment for the captive to realise what she was seeing. Despite the reflections of the candles, the wall was not actually a mirror on this side. It was a transparent pane of glass looking directly through to the office: a mirror on one side, see-through on the other. The office was dark and vacant, exactly how they'd left it.

The mistress lowered her body into a tall crouch behind the chair. Warm breath tickling the back of her prisoner's neck. Then grabbing the lower rim of Charlotte's skirt and pulling it up, exposing the tights and panties. The wife gave a stifled gasp as the bottom of the skirt was tucked into the top. Oh God, no! What was she doing? The mistress put her thumbs back to back and pushed them between the buttocks. Nails tearing into the fabric of the tights, ripping the material open from the middle. Peeling back to expose the bare flesh of the thighs… and the little, white knickers. The violation dizzying. The exhilaration of alarm. Oh God! Please, no! Charlotte's head lolling in faint. Katya's finger hooked into the underwear. Pausing to savour the shock… before ripping the panties down.

The wife cringed red-rose. Eyes shuddering shut as she visualised the mistress sneering down at her big, bulging bottom. Charlotte didn't realise how beautiful she looked in all her glorious submission. Pretty, round face dewed in sweat and blossomed in blush. Little springs and coils of hazel hair bouncing around overhead. Body curled into a voluptuous 'S'. The well-sculpted delve and dimples at the base of her spine puckering as she kinked her lower back. Pointing her breasts forwards and jutting her tubby, little belly to kiss onto her lap. Shapely curves undulating up her calves and thighs before welling into wide, womanly hips. Buxom buttocks bursting out of the bitch-chair's metal frame and out into the air behind. Like strangling wires around the waist of a juicy, ripe pear… and hanging it up in the darkness.

The mistress inspected her lover's wife's body, for a few long seconds, before leaning in to whisper, 'You have a big, fat fucking ass.' Charlotte flinched, screwing her eyelids tight. 'All the better for beating.' A whisk of a slap, so the flesh wobbled. 'You know your husband like to beat big, fat, sexy ass like this. You look just like… how he like… his submissive to look. But… he don't let you play.' Husky voice dripping with mock-pity and then sharpening. 'Because you are so fucking sweet: cutie-pie; nice girl; good, little wifey; goodie-goodie-two-shoes.' Her evil chuckle scoffed. 'No wonder he is so fucking bored of you: frigid, vanilla, dull, domesticated. A good girl like you can never fulfil a bad man like that.'

The pain rolled and bounced as the Russian strolled around to the front of the chair. Such an evil bitch! Yet, in this moment especially, she looked stunning, the most attractive woman Charlotte had ever seen. Long, sleek body curling like sexy smoke. Sadistic, smiling eyes delighting to note the lonely tear trickling down her victim's cheek. She took her phone from an inside jacket-pocket.

'Nearly seven. I have a date at seven.' Pouting her lips playfully. 'He is taking me for romantic birthday dinner.' Katya searched for an expressive response and correctly interpreted the flash of a question. 'He going to Vancouver tomorrow, not tonight. Whatever he told you. He spending tonight with me.' Smile glittering as she basked in victory.

Her victim cuffed awkwardly, ball-bloated cheeks, gag-cords cutting into the corners of the mouth, puppy-dog eyes helplessly conveying respect. Tears licking down the face and dripping onto her thighs. Katya paused thoughtfully, an artist musing on a piece that required a finishing touch. After a few seconds, her eyes lit with an idea and she turned to stride across the room, heels rapping on cold stone. Taking a candle from the stand and disappearing through the door into the storeroom. She entered the office a few seconds later, but didn't turn on the light. Charlotte watched the flame wisping along on the other side of the magic mirror. The mistress must've taken something from the desk, because she was now walking back towards the corner door. The torch momentarily vanishing again.

Katya brandished the candle in one hand and the red rose in the other: the flower he'd given to her, as a symbol of his love. She posed in her entrance for a ravishing second before leaning over to blow out the candles on the stand. She kept the other flame in her hand as she slunk around the room, extinguishing the torches one-by-one. An air of ritualistic ceremony. The shadows crept in as the light fell back. Soon the only source of power was the one Katya held in her hands, flickering the darkness across her face. Charlotte loved the feeling of the mistress standing behind her... standing directly overhead. It was terrifying! She could do anything she liked and her victim could do nothing to stop her. The thrill was giddying.

Now lowering into the same semi-crouch position affected when the panties were stripped off. Placing the candle on the floor, so Charlotte could feel the warmth on her left buttock. Although it shivered along with the rest of her body. Katya clasped the rose delicately: the stem twenty centimetres long, mostly silky smooth, but a few sharp thorns menacing. Warm breath on the back of the neck again. Every goose bump standing to attention.

Holding the rose in front of her victim's face, Katya turned it upside down, so the petals dangled towards the floor. The flower then disappeared behind Charlotte's back. A few long moments stretched. Now the clean-cut tip of the stem tickling around her bottom, a moment of exquisiteness as she realised. The end of the stalk pushing up between her buttocks, pricking into her asshole, penetrating her in such a degrading way. Charlotte's feet lifting from the floor, legs straightening out in front. Then paralyzed stone-still, except for the quiver of tension rippling over the surface of her skin.

Katya forced the rose steadily further. More than five centimetres inside before the thorn clawed into the inner buttcheek. The victim writhed as the barb spiked, hooking into the sensitive flesh. A muffled squeal as Katya let go with a twist. The flower stuck firmly into Charlotte's ass, poking out and drooping towards the floor... like a little tail. The wife re-grounded her feet and put her legs together neatly, bowing her head. A complete picture of unconditional surrender – obviously she looked ridiculous. She could really feel it now. All of it.

The Russian picked up the candle, stood to her full height and began to pace. Charlotte sensed her tormentor's satisfied smile and anticipated the laughter. An unexpected type of laugh though: the predictable gloating chortle was there, but also the ring of genuine glee – emotional elation. She was sincerely happy. Why shouldn't she be happy? She was about to go out to dinner with the man she loved, whilst his wife was imprisoned, shackled and ball-gagged with a flower hanging out of her naked ass.

The mistress circled the chair to appreciate the joke from every angle, finally stopping in front to pose imperiously with hand on hip. The single flame flickered between them, electrifying pleasure radiating from the Russian's dilated pupils. In the obscene romance of the moment, the wife had the disgusting urge to tell the mistress how beautiful she looked in the dancing candlelight. Katya knew of course, but Charlotte wanted to tell her all the same. Yet all she could do was waffle incomprehensibly through the gag. The frustration wonderfully unbearable.

The mistress' smile was fading, the joke wearing thin. She was left with a pitiful sight. Her nose snarled up as she shook her head at Charlotte's shame.

'You don't deserve a husband like him. You are boring nobody!'

She spun on her heels, striding away to disappear through the storeroom door, leaving her victim to contemplate in darkness. The Russian was right: he was somebody; his wife was nobody. Charlotte had always been insecure about that. And Katya was somebody as well. It really hurt. Made her feel so… weak. The mistress blew out the candle and switched on the light as she re-entered the office. The wife sat captivated in the shadows of the secret chamber, watching her captor moving around in the illuminated room on the other side of the mirror-wall. Katya tidied a few items away into the desk drawers, including Charlotte's handbag, which she dropped dismissively into the large compartment at the bottom.

She sat back in her plush swivel chair, feet up on the desk, and began to scan her phone. She was certainly more comfortable than her prisoner. The ball-gag fastened fully taut and the skin at the sides of the mouth red-raw. The handcuffs didn't constrict blood-flow, but were tight enough to chafe abrasively against the bones in the wrists. The wiry seat prickling and pinching at her thighs. A drop of blood had been conglomerating on the rose thorn hooked into her buttock. It was now heavy enough to creep down the stem of the flower.

His lovers waited in their respective positions… for only a few minutes. The secret room was bigger than the office and the mirror-wall was continuous, so Charlotte could see the unlit reception area leading through from the building's front door. The lights flickered on as her husband entered. His expression relaxed and confident; deep, brown eyes hazed in daydream. Dark hair, wind-ruffled and unruly. She always liked it when he wore a suit. He didn't often, but today he'd been for a meeting, so Charlotte had ironed his slickest black jacket and trousers. He'd refused to wear a tie, as usual, even though she'd left one out as a suggestion. His travel backpack didn't go well with the smart clothes and his wife was pleased to see him swing it under the coat-stand. Also glad that he left the jacket on as he strode through to the office. She smiled fondly at the familiarity of his distinctive walk and noted the spring in his step. He was happy. Of course he was: he was due to spend the evening with his beautiful mistress. What a total bastard!

Katya looked up as the office door swung open, a twinkle in her eye and a cute, little smile for him (very different from the way she'd been smiling before). She rose and circled the desk. His hands clasped around her narrow waist and they kissed… passionately. Charlotte's heart shuddered to witness how good they looked together, both tall and slim, both with dark eyes and dark hair: a strikingly attractive couple. Gazing into one other after the first long kiss, smiling intimately before their lips came together again. They swayed and circled in caress, shifting so that he was closer to the mirror.

    The surge of jealousy heated to boiling point, turning Charlotte's body to steam. She seethed to rise from the chair, but the metal cuffs clenched around her wrists and pinned her down. The blistering fury had nowhere to go – straining, spluttering and writhing around – before collapsing back in on itself… and taking all the other emotions with it. Liquefying and sploshing into the broiling cauldron inside – rage, hate, pain, despair, defeat, envy, resentment, humiliation, betrayal. And the sheer frustration was absolutely excruciating. But she could feel the submission-lust consuming all of it. Her masochistic arousal feeding off the suffering… and growing stronger. A demon devouring souls. All her pains and passions twisting up inside. Sick pleasure pulsating in her pussy. She was crying again, one tear of perverse joy for every tear of honest sorrow.

    Still holding each other loosely, the beautiful couple talked in a relaxed, flirtatious manner. The wife couldn't even hear the muffled tone of their voices; the mirror-wall was completely soundproof. Katya leant back and picked up his phone charger, the forgotten item that'd inspired Charlotte's unscheduled visit to the office today. Oh Christ! She must be telling him that his silly, little wife had come by to drop off the charger he'd need on his trip. What else would she tell him? Surely she wouldn't tell him Charlotte was bound and ball-gagged a few metres away through the mirror. Would she? And what on earth would he say if she did?

    The captive couldn't see her husband's face and Katya was standing behind him, so it wasn't possible to make out what was being communicated. He gestured towards the glass that had recently contained the rose, the romantic token he'd lovingly given his mistress, which she'd (less lovingly) given to his wife. Katya replied with an emphatic hand gesture that was mostly obscured from view. They both laughed. Surely she hadn't told him where the rose was?! She wouldn't have told him that. Would she? He wouldn't have reacted like that. Would he?

Charlotte watched intently, but there was no way of knowing what was going on. What would he do if Katya did tell him? Just laugh and do nothing? Come through the mirror and... Rescue her? Throw her out? Fuck her? Beat her? Like he did to the little, student girl, in this very chair. Charlotte's pussy flushed as the eroticism throbbed. Although what would her husband think to see his wife in this state? Face burning pink and toes curling up. She tried to swallow the thought, but instead it swallowed her. He would be... Shocked? Distressed? Happy? Angry? Guilty? Lustful? Embarrassed? Horrified? Ashamed? Finding his sweet, innocent wife bound into the bitch-chair in his secret place, holding the rose... the mistress encouraging him to laugh along. Charlotte's deep red cringe shuddered.

Katya tilted her head coquettishly, bantering with her lover. Her demeanour had changed dramatically since his arrival. Certainly much warmer than she'd been with his wife. Not softer though: hard edges still sharp. It's just that they were no longer pointing outwards: a cat with claws sheathed. She drifted casually around him, so Charlotte could see both their faces in profile. Admiring the sharp shadow her husband's half-stubble cut across his cheek. Katya was looking into his deep, dusky eyes and saying something that made them smoulder. She advanced playfully, placing a long finger on his chest to push him backwards.

He smiled at first, but she must've said something especially interesting because his expression changed: darkening, brow tightening, teeth gritting behind moistened lips... something burning below. Katya pressed him back to the desk. He seethed, sinking down into the chair, focus transfixed on his lover. No hint of domination or submission between them; she was seducing him. Charlotte's jealous hatred upsurged once more – the erotic arousal riding on top.

The mistress placed her black, heeled boot up on a desk drawer-handle. Long leg poising an elegant right angle. Standing directly between the wife and her husband, facing half-towards him as she curled her body and unzipped the boot, removing and tossing it aside. The same with the other, half-turning away. He tickled his finger up the inside of her thigh, hand searching upwards. But the mistress skipped out of range, wagging a teasing finger as she moved around the desk. Slipping her jacket off and slinging it onto the surface. No bra under her sleek, white shirt. The captive couldn't tell what Katya was saying, but there was something sinister about her off-hand mannerisms, her eyebrows flicking up seductively as she threw away various cruel comments. Perhaps she was mocking his boring, little wife? The humiliation sank deep, but Charlotte's submission-lust consumed it greedily – more fuel for the fire.

The performer continued to walk and talk as she unbuttoned her shirt, parading around the room, head lolling side to side. Enjoying the mesmerised attention from both members of her audience. The shirt fluttered open as Katya flashed one side exposed, and then concealed again. Repeating the mocking striptease a couple of times, before removing the shirt altogether. Her snowy, white skin flawlessly smooth and supple. Beautiful breasts shapely and moderately sized: pert, smoothly curved, perfectly symmetrical.

A tattoo, about ten centimetres squared, etched the lower-right corner of the mistress' back, just above the waistline. Black, red and steel. At first it looked like some kind of devil, but what initially appeared to be horns were, in fact, a pair of mandibles. A robotic ant, rearing up on six metallic legs – gaping pincer jaws aloft.

Katya's body shook in brisk, posing dance. A light bounce in her breasts. He was looking on with wolf-like intensity: eyes narrowed and white-hot, jaw jutting… breathing in silent, lustful sighs. The temptress put hand on hip as she sauntered, moving part way back around the desk before stopping by the mirror, just out of range. The spot she chose was ideal: to the flank of the desk, level with the bitch-chair on the other side of the wall. In between the married couple but slightly off to the side, so she didn't obscure the wife's view of her husband. Charlotte was to watch her perform in the foreground, while seeing his reaction in the background. God, the mistress was so evil and arrogant... and the husband so cruel and callous. But the wife could no longer feel resentment without the encompassing lust. Hatred impurified and entirely subsumed. She loathed herself for it, but that just made it worse. Like fighting fire with fire. Her pussy burning up.

Katya flicked her belt open, unzipping her trousers at the side. Rolling the waistband over her haunches as she gracefully sashayed her hips. The trousers were close-fitting, yet fell away like the breeze. She stepped out of them as they feathered the floor. Long legs elegantly toned, slender yet shapely. Smooth, unblemished skin. Tiny panties: bright red. The performer paused for a moment to let the anticipation build. The wife watched her husband's eyes melting all over his lover's body. Katya began to bend, curving her hips to accentuate the delicious round of her ass.

Charlotte realised quite how perfect the mistress' positioning was as her husband fixated focus on the reflection of that beautiful behind. If he could see through the mirror from that side, then he'd have been looking directly at his wife. A brutal illusion from Charlotte's perspective — a calculated humiliation. Katya gave a cheeky glance over her shoulder, admiring her body in the mirror and allowing the captive to taste the smugness of her smile. The flavour sickeningly sweet... with a bitter aftertaste.

The audience was rapt as Katya rolled down her panties. Such luscious curves for a slim woman: narrow waist shaping into curling hips... juicy buttocks peaching perfectly. Charlotte looked into her husband as he gazed on. The intensity of the desire inside wilting under its own weight. He grimaced with passion: thirsting, unadulterated lust. The prisoner's body wracked — a fireball of jealous rage — but her own monstrous masochism just laughed and wolfed it all down. Katya uncurled and returned hand to hip. His eyes moving to admire her pussy. He was sat back on the chair, but clearly wasn't relaxed. Every muscle in his body bristling with tension, hands gripping the armrests as if holding himself down, cock pushing forcefully upwards to strain against his trousers. The mistress turned to soak up the reflection of her own radiance... and it made her smile.

She winked at them both in the mirror before turning to move towards him, sidling slowly, the pronounced sway in her hips micro-quivering a buttock with each step. Arriving at the chair, she continued to look into his eyes as she sunk down. Haunching cat-like between his legs, obscuring the captive's view as she slipped her hand up to unfasten belt and flies, talking seductively all the while. It wasn't possible to see properly as the mistress pulled out his dick. It was surprising she hadn't ensured the wife a better view. Charlotte could imagine how good her husband's big, hard cock looked lolling around in his lover's hands. A deep, sweltering throb of lusting envy – gag-cords cutting into her mouth as her face convulsed. Katya pushed her ass out to curl, leaning forward to run her tongue up and down the shaft, allowing the wife a brief glimpse of the burgeoning crown. He looked into the mistress' eyes with blissful satisfaction and she spent time licking and kissing, teasing and caressing.

Something she said caused him to sit up. Aggressively pulling off the jacket and proceeding to unbutton his shirt: the enthusiasm of a man promised sex with Venus herself. Katya was taking off his shiny, black shoes, the ones Charlotte had polished for the trip. Removing his socks as well. He pulled up from the chair, rigid cock flailing as Katya drew off his trousers and underwear. The wife admired her husband composing himself as he settled back into the seat. She always loved the way he looked, but she now found him more attractive than ever: enthroned naked on the executive chair, striking a powerful pose, muscular arms resting confidently, strong legs set wide, beautiful mistress kneeling between them. His smooth, hard body rippling with excited tension. Chest heaving as he inhaled lust through half-bared teeth, torso muscles tautening. Coveting eyes dark and fierce. Features snarling desire. Charlotte's pussy sizzled in helpless frustration. If only Katya had left a hand free. What a wonderfully evil bitch she was.

Sitting up, the Russian positioned to put his cock in her mouth. Her whole body waggling as she slipped her lips over the large helmet. Charlotte buckled and swooned at the shamefully sexy reality of her husband's engorged dick filling his mistress' mouth. Katya began to move her head up and down. Slowly at first, but building speed. As the pace quickened she danced her whole body along with the motion: lithe physique writhing in graceful, spiralling movements; hips and torso snaking. Charlotte's husband watched hypnotised: the mirrored reflection of his mistress' dancing buttocks, puckering to pout the wetted lips of her succulent... His coveting wince looked painful.

He was speaking now. Eyes flicking up... and focus shifting along the mirror. Setting his gaze straight towards Charlotte, with the appearance of knowing deliberateness. His expression black: the thunder of Zeus' violent lust. Speaking directly to his wife, the last three or four words of the sentence mouthed into the glass with slow, definite emphasis. She couldn't tell what he'd said, but it must have been something cruel, Katya's body reacting with a bone-shivering tremor of arousal.

Was he really talking to his wife? Did he know she was there? Had Katya told him? Did he know all along? The thought that struck her next juddered so hard it jarred her bones. Did he know because he'd planned this himself? Oh Jesus! What if all this was his plan? What if he and Katya had conspired? Had he deliberately 'forgotten' his phone charger, whilst carefully leaving it somewhere it would be found? Calculatingly exploiting his wife's loyal thoughtfulness and counting on the likelihood she'd bring it to the office? Then Katya insisting that Charlotte 'sit and talk' and conducting this sadistic entrapment as her part of the collusion?

Oh God! What if that were true? He was certainly manipulative enough to do such a thing. But could he be that hard and cold – to his own beloved wife? Intentionally plot her total humiliation at the hands of his vicious mistress? Charlotte's pussy was on fire. The cuffs chafed as she wriggled. She hoped it was true… hoped it was all true: that he'd planned it, as a way of introducing his wife to this secret world of delicious darkness. Because he wanted her to be there alongside him. Or on a leash at his feet. Whatever he wanted. Charlotte swirled giddy as the intense emotions heaved, bucked and tossed. She felt them all – but only as varying flavours of masochistic pleasure. Enjoyed savouring all the tastes at once – sweet and sour, spicy and salty, acidic and bitter.

Her husband's focus hadn't left his mistress for long – her supple body twisting and curling ever faster. It was almost too much, he closed his eyes and grimaced, pulling his head back sharply. The emphatic words easy to lip-read this time.

'Oh fuck!'

Cradling Katya's head in both hands to detach her. He'd almost come and needed to stop himself. It hadn't been long: he never came that fast when his wife sucked his dick. But then, she wasn't Katya, was she? The mistress treated herself a cheeky glance towards Charlotte, gleefully sharing the celebration of her latest victory.

As Katya rose to stand, strong arms clasped her waist: pulling her around, pushing her back to sit on the desk. She began to raise her legs in anticipation. He slid off the chair to kneel, head between her thighs, eyes salivating as they drew into her. A luxuriant lick up the slip of her pussy. She moaned visibly. He repeated the movement, a couple of times, before pushing his face tightly against her, writhing his tongue inside. Katya's legs rose further as he kissed between them fervently. Ballet limbs arcing gracefully, stretching into the air: a flower opening up towards the sun. And then lowering down to clasp together behind the back of his neck. She lolled, gazing dreamily into the mirror, boasting another triumphalist smile before her expression crumpled in pleasure – head falling back with a cry of elation.

The wife admired his rock-hard dick as he pleasured his lover. Wished she could be under the desk right now, sucking her husband whilst he licked his mistress. It just seemed the perfect place for her: beneath them both. God, she so wanted to join in – the desire was agonizing. She wouldn't expect much attention – she could just be a little, dick-sucking fluffer for them. Could learn to eat pussy as well. Oh God! Why didn't they let her in? Of all the emotions swirling into her submission-lust, the extreme frustration contributed the most. The constricted energy collapsing back in on itself in waves. Ever more powerful waves – reeling and spinning. She squealed into the gag, legs kicking out at the knees, wrists twisting against metal shackles. The rose wagging behind as her ass wiggled desperately... the claw of the thorn hooking deeper.

Now it was Katya's turn to remove her lover's mouth. He began to stand as she pushed away. Her posture shifting forward: a stalking cat preparing to pounce. He was already blending with the movement, bracing his body to catch. They crashed back into the chair with gusto. It rolled and nearly tipped, but the entwined couple were moving in unison to rebalance. Locked in a desperate kiss, bodies colliding excitedly. A chaos of hands thrusting, grabbing and clawing. Katya's legs splayed over the sides of the chair. Pushing up against his torso to run her moist pussy down his hardened rack of abs. Sitting back to slot his cobra of an erection along the perfect cleft of her ass-cheeks.

The wife had always loved her husband's cock, but it'd never looked as good as it did now: clamping possessively around his mistress' wetted groin. Charlotte craved to lick her tongue up it, would give anything to do that now. Katya was kissing and biting, impatiently pulling her body up and back: attempting to impale herself. She missed… his rigid erection bending against her leg. She tried again – missing again. They'd lost their practiced coordination in the flaring heat of the moment: his dick swinging about, frustrated, as she jostled to readjust. If only Charlotte had been there, she could have helped place it for them. Oh God! It was so unbelievably unfair Oh sweet Jesus, please! Please!

The beautiful couple were regaining composure. His biceps bulging as his hands set around her slim waist, lifting her back as she curled an arm behind to grab his dick, guiding it in to penetrate. They looked into one another's eyes. Dark smiles as she pushed down onto him, smoothly sliding lips around the shaft. Katya's body twitching in mini spasms of elation as he thrust within. Charlotte melting along in memory: it felt so good as that big helmet drove in like a crowned battering ram, filling up the pussy. Certainly better than having a rose stuck up your ass. She groaned helplessly. The mistress was moving up and down on Charlotte's husband's throbbing erection. Rhythm building as the momentum gathered.

As when blowing him, she writhed and weaved her body in elegant, dancing motion. Scratching at his shoulders, attacking his neck with kisses. Both lovers now lathered in perspiration, skin glistening wet, beautiful bodies shining. He held her middle in solid grip whilst her buttocks bounced up and down on his lap. Thick cock sliding in and out, gleaming with the lubrication of his mistress' juices. If only the wife could get closer. All she wanted was to sit between her husband's legs and watch his lover's spectacular butt bobbing up and down above. Maybe she could dab her tongue on his shaft between every thrust: taste the mistress on her husband's dick. Hold her tongue there so it flicked the rim of Katya's pussy as the dominant woman's ass bounced on her upturned face. How deliciously shameful to desire such degradation. She hated herself.

The chair had been rolling around in the gathering force, but was now shaking violently as the turbulence escalated, wheels taking turns to rock off the floor. Katya threw back her head, crying out as he bit around her neck and shoulders. The seat was going to tip. At the last moment, he clutched hands around the peaches of her butt and drove down into his legs. Lifting his lover as he stood, the chair clattering onto the floor behind. Holding her fully in his arms, cock still deep inside. This was getting too much for the prisoner to take, the sexual frustration unendurable. Her pussy screaming and pleading. This torture was too terrible! She tried to screw her red-raw wrists out of the cuffs for the hundredth time; all she needed was to touch herself, just briefly. It would only take a few moments to reach the most profound orgasm ever. Burning up; a series of hot flushes overwhelming. Passing out for a second as everything went blank, her head caught flopping forward.

Her husband still hammering away inside the beautiful woman twined around him, teeth clenched tight and fully bared, sweat pouring from his face. Her soaking body slipping about in his grip. She waved her head back and forth as the powerful motion of his hips battered upwards, shouting something and swinging her arm towards the mirror. He steadied his hold underneath sweat-slick ass-cheeks before stepping forward, driving his cock up inside as he moved, incorporating the striding motion into the rhythm of his thrusts. Another lunging step, forcing himself upwards into her. They were moving towards the mirror, step by fucking step. Charlotte shook, exhausting thirst building towards fever pitch, head spinning in dizzying droop. It was too much. All of it.

They were nearly at the wall now. He swayed, clutching his lover fanatically tight. Likely they'd smash straight through the glass. The wife watched through bleary eyes as her husband staggered the last few steps to ram Katya's body into the mirror-wall. The glass flexed, but held. The mistress crying out ecstatically. Surely they'd crash right through on the next attack. Charlotte sobbed dry tears as she prayed to all the gods for her husband and his lover to break through onto this side of the wall… so that she could be with them when they came. The next strike even harder, the barrier shivering but holding firm. Katya's behind looked amazing pressed up against the glass. A dripping drench of the lover's sweat on the mirror as her body peeled away. He banged her up against the wall again, rooting feet securely for the last few drives.

Bang!

Katya barely had control of her head as the orgasm built. Managing to twist her neck to snarl into the mirror. No longer able to muster the coordination to properly gloat in the penultimate moments of total victory.

Bang!!

His eyes flashing with a glimpse of the coming climax, breathing spit through his teeth to steam the mirror around his lover's ear.

Bang!!!

Charlotte wished she could come with them. She could explode – needed to explode! This was so unfair: so twistedly sadistic. How could she be tortured so ruthlessly? She just wanted to be kneeling there, with mouth wide, ready to clean up when they finished.

Bang!!!!

On the final strike, the bodies of the two lovers reeled together in the euphoria of mutual orgasm, limbs shuddering out: blood, bones, hearts, minds, souls, beings – alive and electrified. They embraced the long moment with passion that trembled.

Charlotte felt the blank swallowing everything as she passed out, the dizzying pain of sexual frustration finally overcoming. Wilting and fainting, head drooping towards the floor – a red rose.

TWO
THE PROPOSAL

Writing that story had to be the single most stupid and embarrassing thing Jess had ever done. She tutted out loud in self-reproach. Lucky there were no other pedestrians around to think she was mad. She was mad though! What on earth had she been thinking? Actually submitting the story? By all means, write it. But obviously never show it to anyone… ever. Oh shit! Why, oh why, oh why? Must've been insanity, brought on by lack of sleep, that made her do it. It'd been 5am when she finished writing, typing for twenty hours straight on the last leg. She was obviously in no fit state to judge whether it should actually be submitted.

Why even send it then – right after finishing? Could've waited until morning, had a good night's sleep, woken up, re-read it, and decided definitely not to send it… to anyone, ever. Oh shit, shit, shit! Such a stupid thing to do. And yet somehow, at the time, it'd seemed like the most brilliant thing she'd ever done: a great victory – a bold statement. Demonstrating to him that she could write something dark and twisted – that she wasn't just a soppy little innocent. And through impressing him, also proving something to that evil bitch, Katya.

Oh fuck! Jess flinched at the mind-boggling reality that she'd actually sent it to Katya. Had really sent her an email with the 'Red Rose' story attached. A fiction in which the Russian herself played a leading role. The writer had changed the name to 'Natalya' in the version submitted. But it was obviously about Katya; she'd been described exactly as she was in real life (seriously!) and it was clearly the same office. Oh shit! What would that horrible woman think if she read it? And Charlotte, as well (the 'Penelope' pseudonym was equally transparent) – what if she read it? What would she think to see herself portrayed like that? As a pathetic submissive, who got a rose shoved up her ass... and loved it. You couldn't get much more offensive than that. However tightly Jess screwed up her eyes, it still remained a fact that she'd done it. She'd never normally do anything like that. A strange context, of course, but even still. What was she thinking?

The writer jolted to a stop, catching herself nearly walking out in front of a car. She paused to let the long, grey vehicle slide past. Maybe she should've kept walking? Then she wouldn't have to go to the meeting. Just send an email instead: 'Hi Katya, sorry to cancel at the last minute, but I got run over on the way to the office.' That would be good – just a broken leg or something. She looked around vaguely, but there were no other moving objects in sight. The east London neighbourhood was quiet and still, an unseasonably-sunny winter afternoon. She really needed to calm herself down.

They probably hadn't read the story. It wasn't for them, anyway; it was for him. Likely, they were just go-betweens and never even opened the document – just forwarded it on. Jess tried to compose herself, yet couldn't help shuddering at the realisation she'd nearly arrived. Just a hundred or so paces down the street and she'd come out facing the office, at the junction of another unassuming, residential road. Oh shit! But it was too late to change anything now. She just had to live with it. She'd done it... and couldn't undo it. Time to face the music – like a grown woman.

As the unusual building came into view, Jess marvelled again at its weirdness. It would be her third visit to this strangely-shaped, converted warehouse... or whatever it was. The structure was single-storey, but tall because of the high ceilings. One wouldn't have thought there'd be any kind of business inside. If that's what it was – some kind of business? Fifteen minutes early: 13:45. Why was she always so early? Even to get somewhere she really didn't want to be. She'd paced fast the whole way, lost in a daze of relentless self-scolding. She would have to walk around the block before going in. Couldn't be fifteen minutes early. Five was good, but fifteen was annoying. Didn't want to annoy Katya... who might already be angry because of the story. Oh shit! Why did she do it? Her own behaviour seemed unfathomable. How did this happen? Jess went over the events of the last few weeks in her mind as she began a slow circuit of the block. Trying to understand why she'd done what she had (so irreversibly) done.

Understandable to enter that writing competition. A £500 prize for the best erotic short story, along with the possibility of further work in the future. Why not enter? The peculiar online advertisement was intriguing and the prospect naturally of interest to an aspiring writer. An ambitious young woman who'd moved to London recently, but who was already fed-up with working fifty-hour weeks, waitressing in a busy central café. Why not do something exciting, like try her hand composing erotica? And £500 could go a long way right now, given that a depressingly large portion of her wages went on renting a small room in an over-populated house-share.

The initial story submitted had been considerably less sordid than 'Red Rose' – sexy, of course, but without any hint of domination games. Jess had been ecstatic when she found out her piece had won. The email was bland and unemotional, but clearly stated she'd secured the prize. It made her so happy... she spent the rest of the day fantasising about her future life as a writer: Jessica Seaques the famous author! She had virtually skipped all the way to the office, where she'd been told to collect her reward.

The happy winner had tried to strike up jovial small talk when first encountering Charlotte behind the funny little reception desk of the anonymous office. She'd not let the receptionist's stiff and awkward reaction dampen her mood and instead cheerfully waited for Ms Stilenskova, idly admiring how good her own shiny, brown hair looked in the bizarre mirror-wall. Actually meeting Ms Katya Stilenskova for the first time had totally taken the wind out of Jess' sails. The Russian swept into the building, twenty minutes late, greeted the writer with an irritated scowl, and then proceeded to ignore her whilst barking orders at the receptionist for a few minutes. Katya spoke to her subordinate with all the manners of a prison guard in a Stalinist gulag and Charlotte responded with fearful obedience: 'Yes, Ms Stilenskova'. The formal surname address seemed completely out-of-place in a trendy, East London work-hub, especially as both women were in their early thirties.

When Katya finally ordered Jess into her office, the prize-winner went with an air of trepidation. She found the severe Russian highly intimidating. On first glare, Katya made a show of moving her eyes up and down the writer's body with an exaggerated expression of contempt. A crudely simple (and yet irritatingly successful) strategy, designed to underline her own superiority. Sitting in the office, and glancing a reflection of the scene in the mirror-wall, Jess felt totally inferior. She'd later transposed the experience onto Charlotte's character in 'Red Rose'. Jess and Charlotte looked quite similar in some ways: both short-ish brunettes with slightly plump, pear-shaped figures. Although Jess wore glasses, had straight hair, and brown eyes.

There was only one chair in Katya's room, so Charlotte had scurried off to fetch another, Jess being reinstalled on the embarrassingly small folding-chair from the waiting area – not really appropriate for a fully-grown adult. As the two women sat facing each other, the difference in their heights seemed to reflect the balance of power.

Katya kicked off with, 'So you the little, student girl who want to be an erotic writer.' Jess floundered right from the start of what turned out to be a strange interrogation. The waitress did try to explain that she'd finished university a couple of years ago, but apparently she'd already been marked as a 'little, student girl'. For some reason, the interrogator needed to fill in a form about the prize-winner that involved recording a detailed physical description. Jess had squirmed when her tormentor openly doubted whether she was really size 14. 'I'll put 16,' she said with a sneer. Katya had quickly picked up on the writer's habit of quivering her nostrils 'like a bunny-rabbit' and strongly implied that the behaviour was irritating. Jess had never perceived this mannerism in herself and no one else had ever pointed it out (although maybe everyone noticed, and found it annoying, but most were too polite to say?).

However, the most humiliating thing was when Katya brazenly asked, 'You not a virgin, are you?' What a question to ask someone who'd just 'won' an erotic writing competition! She wasn't a virgin, but the query did tickle Jess' insecurity that, in truth, she wasn't sexually experienced enough to be an erotic writer. She'd blushed uncontrollably after that particular exchange. Her horrible habit of blooming bright pink when embarrassed: an exaggerated physical reaction, that was, of course, painfully embarrassing in itself. And Katya hadn't flinched – not even a shadow of empathetic awkwardness – her eyes cold with the sadism of a toying cat as she continued the relentless bullying.

It became clear that the £500 wasn't really a prize. The prize was, in fact, a £500 contract to write an erotic short story – i.e.

Jess wouldn't see any money until she wrote another piece, which apparently had to be quite different from her initial effort.

'He wants you to write it differently.' Katya had stated as she handed Jess a brown package: a sealed, A4, unmarked envelope, weighty with papers. 'He make notes. Read them and do as he says.'

'Who's he?' the writer had asked, wide-eyed.

'The Patron. The man who will pay you.'

Jess couldn't recall what it was that first gave her the idea – perhaps Katya had glanced into the mirror in a peculiar way as she referred to 'the Patron'. Whatever the reason, the writer began thinking that the strange mirror-wall might not be what it seemed. She imagined a tall man, standing in the darkness of a secret room on the other side of the glass. Could feel his predator's eyes watching her as a wolf stares from the shadows of the forest… on naïve prey grazing in the open. Jess had always had an overly vivid imagination and, for the rest of the meeting, hadn't been able to shake the feeling of being watched from behind the glass.

Although she obviously knew it couldn't be true. Well, it wouldn't be true. It (almost) certainly wasn't true. The rest of the meeting didn't last long, however. A couple of Jess' hesitant questions, about the Patron, were swatted off. Before Katya outlined the specifics of the deal – the writer had two weeks to write a short story, to be submitted to the mysterious Patron via his 'agent' (Katya). A couple of days after that, Jess would return to the office to obtain feedback and payment. Having received her orders, the writer was dismissed with an irritated shoo of the hand.

Jess dwelled on that bizarre first encounter all the way home. The strange, dominating relationship between Ms Stilenskova and her receptionist appeared extreme: more than just your average bossy manager / weak employee type situation. The writer found her own reaction to Katya even more bewildering. Jess had never been an especially assertive person, although she wasn't usually a total wimp (she'd been proud of her own fierceness when she told that creepy guy in India to 'Fuck off'). But she'd totally gone to jelly in the face of the overbearing Ms Stilenskova. Had spent most of the time with eyes lowered, looking at the model motorbike. Imagining Katya, dressed in leathers, just walking right over her prone body... trampling with hard heels. The striking image evoked a peculiar spark of excitement. Which was strange. Jess didn't usually feel so sexually attracted to women... and she didn't normally like it when people were nasty to her.

And obviously, Katya was exactly the type of person Jess hated: arrogant, bitchy, bossy, actively unpleasant... the type of person everyone should hate. But there was something infuriatingly desirable about the harsh Russian's powerful beauty and aggressive confidence. Jess had found herself not even wanting to fight back, adopting submissive body language from the outset, meekly weathering insults and agreeing to give personal information about her appearance, which was clearly inappropriate to demand. Actually, probably illegal to demand. Couldn't quite catch-in-the-act the part of herself that enjoyed the masochism... but could feel it was there. Her response was intriguing.

Even more intriguing was the mystery of the Patron: the man observing from behind the mirror-wall. Jess had to keep reminding herself that the secret room was (surely) just a figment of her imagination. Yet she'd sensed his eyes watching her intently and persistently... and this continued even whilst walking home. Almost as if she were being hunted, repeatedly looking over her shoulder. Although obviously there was no one there. A strange excitement pervading the atmosphere.

The envelope had been torn open as soon as she got home. Inside was a printed copy of her manuscript: the initial story about an executive having sex with his PA in an office. It had markings on it! He'd written over the document in a red pen – crossing things out, ticking things, and writing occasional comments. On closer inspection, it seemed he'd cut most of it out, slicing away whole paragraphs with a brutal cross of pen strokes. The parts that hadn't been removed didn't really hang together as a story and it wasn't easy to see why he'd cut some paragraphs out whilst leaving others in. The most passionate deletion was a couple of sentences describing the gifting of a red rose – the whole section of text angrily scribbled out in an emphatic manner.

Later on in the story, the word 'romantic' was also deleted with a vengeance. One paragraph had been almost-entirely crossed out, line by line, with the exception of two words: the last word of the sentence, 'she'd kept it a secret'; and the second word of the sentence, 'The lust was all-consuming'. He'd ticked in two places: the first seemed to indicate approval that the liaison was adulterous; the other rewarded a respectful compliment made by the PA to her boss. Elsewhere, the word 'torment' had been double-underlined. There were two hand-written comments scrawled on the manuscript. The word 'Personal' floated without context at the top of a page, midway through the text, and the confusing instruction 'DEEPER' was written boldly at the end.

Jess had been thoroughly perplexed, searching text and envelope for the feedback she must surely have missed. But it seemed that really was all she had to go on. She pondered a long time, deciding that all the clues together suggested he wanted an erotic story without romance: a meaningless adulterous affair perhaps? Something purely physical? A domination-themed fantasy? The sinister atmosphere in the office had already put that sort of idea to the forefront of Jess' mind. She interpreted the 'DEEPER' instruction as meaning 'DARKER'. What to make of the word 'Personal'? Could mean a few different things.

She got totally carried away trying to imagine the man she was writing for. There wasn't much to go on, but the task of attempting to work out what he wanted was fascinating. What was his plan anyway? Why would he want to hire an erotic writer in this way? If he'd just wanted to read a sexy story, then surely there were plenty of already-written texts to be getting along with. So he must want something specific and personal. Was that what that comment referred to? But if so, why hadn't he given more information? How could she make it personal to him when she had no idea who he was? So what was it then? Was it more about the writer? More about her? Was he getting some kind of kick out of establishing this weird, anonymous Patron-artist relationship? What sort of kick? And how was he planning to go forward? What were his plans for Jess? The mystery tingled.

She became convinced that it was he who decided that Jess should be made to sit on the little chair. He'd deliberately arranged that she should be put in that position. Did that mean he knew what it meant to her? How could he know? Jess had never told anyone about her weird fetish for uncomfortable seating. In fact, despite masturbating about it for years, she'd never properly admitted it to herself... until he forced her to.

This was a strange game he was playing. What a delightful proposal he'd made to her. Jess realised the picture of him building up in her mind was based on a strikingly attractive man glimpsed over her shoulder, just before entering the office for the first time. There'd been a brief moment of eye contact as she looked into the eyes of a predator, before losing her nerve and glancing away. He'd walked on, long coat swooshing as he turned the corner and disappeared down the street running along the side of the building.

She'd later fantasized that he must have been going inside from another entrance to watch her humiliating interrogation from a secret position of power. She'd surely exaggerated those intense, hunting eyes, imagining them burning out of the shadows. Every time she pictured the image, it made her feel like a carefree bunny rabbit dreamily looking up, to suddenly see the wolf right there! Her heart fluttered. She had to keep reminding herself that, in reality, she'd no idea who the Patron was... or what he looked like.

Jess had felt highly motivated, but writing the second version of the story proved tough-going. She never really managed to get into the flow properly: typing haltingly for hours whilst pondering the mysterious desires of the Patron. She had plenty of ideas but it was impossible to know what he really wanted, considering the sparsity of the instructions. A messy process as she repeatedly went back, chopping and changing the narrative, trying to work in various ideas that might pique his interest. The first story had flowed much better. She barely slept that fortnight amid waitressing and writing. Really had to force the narrative out… grind out the words. The plot involved the same characters as the first story, the boss and his PA, but there was an added domination element – things like spanking. She wasn't particularly pleased with the text finally submitted, but it was hard to judge. It was amazing that she managed to get it done at all really, given the harsh deadline and her long hours working in the café.

It was with a sense of apprehension that she'd made her way to the second meeting with Katya. The encounter was, in some ways, similar to the first: Charlotte had been shy and socially awkward on reception; Ms Stilenskova had been late and brought her aggressive demeanour along when she finally arrived. But the second meeting was short. Katya only had one thing to state: 'He says this is not what he is looking for. You are not up to it.' A harsh bombshell! Jess was taken aback. She tried to ask why exactly… attempted a few times. But the agent wasn't inclined to elaborate and acted as if the meeting was over.

Apparently it should've been obvious that Jess wasn't going to be paid, given that she hadn't delivered the desired product. The agent's expression didn't communicate anything further than the general contempt she'd always displayed. The reject had tried to compose herself and do something to save the situation, but the Russian's phone rang. Taking the call, Katya dismissed Jess with a waft of the hand. It was crushing! The failed writer had trailed out of the building with her tail between her legs.

It'd made her angry... with herself. She'd disappointed him. And as she re-read the second story, she understood why. It was soft – too soft – not nearly dark enough. She'd pulled her punches, been cowardly. The domination described was superficial, mechanical and emotionless. It was a bad story... and not in a good way. She wasn't 'up to it'. What on earth had made her think she would be? Didn't have enough experience: only seven sexual partners... never even played a domination game in real life. How could she write about it? She'd been stupid and he'd been right to discard her.

Jess hadn't been able to sleep that night, dwelling on the rejection. How she'd managed to fall at the first hurdle, despite being so enthusiastic and excited by the adventure. It kept tossing and turning over in her mind... writhing in torment. She ignored the obvious fact: that her perspective on this whole situation was completely perverted. Actually she did know how she should feel. It's just that she didn't feel that way... at all. Instead turning all the anger inwards.

Although as the sleepless night stilled on, the shapeshifting emotions drew different forms. From her dejection, shame and sense of failure rose determination, motivation and the resolve to put things right. She was no coward. She wasn't afraid of the dark... and could prove it. He hadn't offered another attempt at the assignment, but she'd show initiative and take one anyway. Jess reinterpreted the instructions and decided to take a bold approach this time. Would go deeper and make it more personal. Show a bit of cheek as well. Typing began at 3am and 'Red Rose' flowed so easily. She wrote for a week, pretty much solid, calling in sick to cancel her shifts at the café.

Actually the excuse hadn't been her own sickness. For some reason, she told Pablo she needed the week off to look after her mother in Guildford, who'd developed a mysterious paralysis down the right-hand side of her body. Where the fuck did that come from? Jess wasn't very good at lying; she tended to go over the top and say something ridiculous like that. So now she'd have to worry about future elaborations to cover the lie. And what if her mother really did develop paralysis as some sort of karma for Jess' deceit? No, the universe didn't work like that... don't be ridiculous.

She'd had to cancel another shift to attend the meeting today. Pablo had been understanding about it and asked after her mother's health – the guilt-tripping bastard! So now she was properly bunking off, walking around London whilst supposedly in Guildford. She didn't normally bunk off anything, was usually a good girl. But obviously, she had to attend the meeting. After all, she'd asked for it, by sending off the story last week... in that fit of delusional triumph. The replying email had been typically curt, literally just: 'Come to office – Monday 2pm'.

Jess had nearly completed her meandering circuit of the block, the office now coming up on the left. She struggled to match the exterior of the building to what she knew about the interior... and to what she'd imagined about it. There were funny angles and a jostle of other structures, so it was hard to tell whether there was space for the large, hidden chamber she'd visualised. Perhaps the secret room was smaller? She also looked for the side entrance the attractive stranger must've used if he really was the Patron, watching through the glass. There was a bin area leading into an alleyway, possibly to another entrance? Difficult to tell. Jess had to shake her head and remind herself that the secret room, and the involvement of the man with the predatory eyes, were just figments of her imagination... almost certainly.

It was 13.57. Shit! She was now standing in front of the building. It was time – time to face it. Fuck! The summoning message had been ominously devoid of information. What if she was in trouble? What if Katya was angry? The thought tickled with seductive dread. Jess had really landed herself in it this time. Maybe she should go back and tend to her mother's imaginary illness? No!

No, she'd come this far and was going to see it through. She was a daring person and this was a brave thing to do – an adventure! Katya hadn't read the story. The agent was just a go-between. She'd implied she didn't read the stories... sort of. Had certainly communicated a high level of disinterest in Jess, generally. And Charlotte definitely hadn't read it – she was just a receptionist. Only he'd read it... and the only question that mattered was: did he like it? And probably, he did. Why else would he have summoned her back? Other than to see his agent give his naughty little writer the reward she so deserved.

Deep breaths... should she press the entry buzzer? 13.58. Shit! Exhale long and slow – you're a calm and confident person. It's easy to stay relaxed... deep breaths. Jess watched her finger tentatively reaching out to touch the button. The hesitant, nasal beep seemed an appropriate signal of her arrival. A pause... a long pause... Perhaps they weren't there? Maybe she should go? Just turn around, go home and forget all about this? No! She was brave and bold. This was an adventure and she was the heroine! Her forefinger pointed to press the buzzer again – assertively this time.

She was strong. Just stay strong. A few seconds ebbed away before a mechanical click indicated that the heavy, metallic door had been unlocked. Jess drove in to push it open, stepping into the building: head high, shoulders square, stiff upper lip. A few concrete paces to herself behind the partition wall, before coming out on the reception desk. She used the time to consolidate the façade: a confident stride... a good imitation of a confident stride.

'Hiya...' her greeting tone bubbled over with implausible assuredness. The receptionist looked up furtively, her welcome smile half-hearted and embarrassed. She must've read the story! He must've shown it to them both. Oh shit! No. No, that wasn't what'd happened. Charlotte was always like this: a shy person. She hadn't read the story. Why would she have done?

'I've got an appointment to see Ms Stilenskova... at two.' (And did I mention, I really am super-confident right now.)

'Oh, yes... ummm...' Charlotte flustered. The deliberateness with which Jess ignored the building awkwardness proved counterproductive. 'Ms Stilenskova is just on a call right now, but she'll be with you when she's done.' A coy touch of eye contact.

Had she read the story? Why was it so hard not to think about that question? And why was it so obvious, to the whole world, that she was specifically trying not to think about it? She was standing at the desk. Was she supposed to be at the desk still? Or was she dithering here? Floundering?! Had her mask slipped? Catching her own glance into the mirror-wall, over Charlotte's shoulder, Jess immediately realised she'd blown it. Had allowed him to see all her anxiety stripped bare: spread-eagled in the stocks. His eyes saw through her like the glass, and now she was wavering. Anything she did to take control would come across as trying too hard.

Surprisingly, Charlotte actually saved the situation. 'If you just...' she said, gesturing towards the waiting chair on the other side of the reception area. Jess swung around enthusiastically. Able to point her face away from the mirror for a few steps as she approached the ridiculous, almost-child-size seat that was always hers. Impossible to maintain one's dignity on such a small chair – so low to the ground. Still... at least it was better than the bitch-chair on the other side of the mirror! She caught herself nodding through the thought as if it were a sensible, real-world comparison. Her own silliness made her want to laugh; it was all so delightfully preposterous. What a wonderfully strange world.

As she turned and sat all the way down, he'd note that the amused smile in her eyes was sincere. Although the innocence now affected, looking into the mirror, would obviously be spotted as fraudulent. After all, he'd definitely read the story. So he knew that she knew about the magic mirror-wall and the secret, watching room. She sparkled in reflection. Hair pulled back in a casual ponytail. Light-blue jeans, subtle-green top and chestnut overcoat. A good choice of clothes. Her red, fifties spectacles looked cool, as always. This was fine. She removed her jacket and folded it neatly across her lap, resting her handbag on top. Everything would be fine. She indulged a little wriggle of erotic excitement, pressing her soft ass against the hard plastic of the chair. He'd specifically instructed that Jess be made to sit on this uncomfortable embarrassment of a seat. She loved that.

The reception was bare, white and windowless. Despite the lingering odour of paint, all the walls were dirty: ancient paintwork crusted with thin cracks. On one side of the room, Charlotte sat on a swivel chair behind the desk, staring at an open laptop. Jess could see the reflection of the screen glowing in the mirror behind. A couple of metres beyond, the wall cornered into a room that ran at a right angle along the other side of the secret chamber. Jess tried to visualise the inside of the playroom, to recall whether the mirror continued along the other internal wall. Did it corner into two mirror-walls, L-shaped around the secret room? She couldn't remember – perhaps it'd been concealed by drapes on that side?

Catching her imagination running away for the umpteenth time, she again reminded herself that 'Red Rose' was just a fiction. An entirely made-up back-story created as an eccentric explanation of the weird atmosphere in the office. In the real-world reception, the only other piece of furniture was the coat-stand a few metres to Jess' left. Alongside Charlotte's thick green duffle jacket, Katya's long black trench coat hung ominously. She was just on the other side of the wall... doing something. When she'd finished, she'd deal with Jessica. Shit! The anxiety prodded and pinched. No, don't dwell. No point in dwelling now. Whatever will be, will be.

This chair was preposterous – totally inappropriate for a professional environment. But was this really a professional environment? If so, what was the profession? Katya was acting as an 'agent'. A literary agent? It was a writing job, of course, but certainly a bit of an odd one. There were no signs or logos anywhere. The buzzer on the front door was unmarked. What kind of place was this? Whatever kind of place it was, there must surely be another chair somewhere. The seating was definitely a calculated humiliation. Buzz tickling again as she micro-wiggled surreptitiously.

Obviously, Ms Stilenskova kept her waiting… five minutes… ten minutes… fifteen minutes. The wait threatened to sap Jess' spirits, but she mustn't fall back into worrying mode. She had to stay strong; she couldn't just let herself go to pieces as soon as Katya summoned her in. Deep breaths. Think about something else. Charlotte was focused intently on her computer screen. She looked quite good today: sensible brown skirt, smart white top, dark heeled boots, baby-blue eyes, hazel curls all lush and springy. And yet she came across as an unconfident woman with low self-esteem. Jess congratulated herself on definitely being more confident than Charlotte, in general. She had to remember that when coming up against Katya's frightening self-certainty. Don't crumble this time. Best not to think about it.

The receptionist was reading something on the computer. Not typing, just scanning down with the mousepad. Jess could see, in the reflection, a body of text without images. A Word document perhaps? Not 'Red Rose'… surely?! Imagine if she was reading that now, with the writer sitting just across the room. Visualising herself cuffed into the bitch-chair and knowing Jess had crafted that image. Holy shit! It didn't bear thinking about. Anyone watching through the mirror would have seen the writer micro-cringing… and then her feet squirming as she concentrated on stilling her tell-tale face.

Holy fuck – what if Katya was reading it now?! How would she interpret it? Some kind of grovelling tribute to her own beauty, no doubt. It was painfully obvious the fictional Charlotte had been used as a vehicle for Jess' own feelings towards Katya... and not in a subtle way. The writer was as pathetic as Charlotte had been when she sat in the bitch-chair. More pathetic: Jess had invented an imaginary bitch-chair, put it at Ms Stilenskova's feet, and climbed into it... wearing only the skimpiest pretence of a disguise. A strange thing to do. Was it perhaps the most embarrassing thing that anyone had ever done in the whole history of humanity? She imagined herself in the position she'd put the fictional Charlotte in: cuffed and ball-gagged with Katya standing, hand on hip, looking down with disdain. She loved the feeling of the mistress standing behind her, directly overhead. It was terrifying! Jess tingled where she felt she shouldn't, imagination leading her astray again.

But then it was actually mortifying in real life. The fantasised visual image did kind of reflect the position the writer had put herself in. Oh shit! Katya had read the story. What the fuck had Jess done?! She wanted to be sick, physically sick. Struggling to keep her composure. Imagining him sitting back and watching from his secret lair, enjoying her squirm, reading every thought betrayed by her treacherously expressive non-verbal communication. Relish tickling in the darks of his eyes: a fire in the cold. A predator waiting. Oh shit! At least she hadn't blushed yet. She mustn't allow Katya to make her bloom this time.

There was a jolting alarm as the mobile on Charlotte's desk rang: an intrusive siren of a ringtone.

'Hello... Yes, it's done, Ms St... Yes, Ms Stilenskova... Yes, she's right here, M... Yes, Ms Stilenskova... Yes, Ms Stilenskova.' (Three bags full, Ms Stilenskova.)

The receptionist put the phone down and gestured towards Katya's office door. 'Ms Stilenskova will see you now. If you'd like to... Oh, maybe you should...' She mimed carrying the chair. Jess picked up and folded the flimsy little thing. Her reflection looked nervous as she walked across the room. Oh shit! Should she knock or go straight in? She'd been told to go in – it would be silly to knock. Confidence! She pushed open and bustled in, trying not to bang the chair as the door swung back. Cringing as the slam echoed under the high ceilings.

Ms Stilenskova barely looked up from the document, gesturing for Jess to sit opposite. Oh shit, she was reading it: reading the story right now! No. No she wasn't. The sheaf of paper she held was too thin to be a print-out of 'Red Rose'. The agent wore close-fitting black trousers and a tight white top. Dark hair pulled back in a sharp ponytail. Lips and claws blood-red as always. Legs crossed tidily, curling posture relaxed but alert. An open laptop, a mobile, and the model motorbike on the desk… no glass for a flower. Jess clumsily unfolded the chair and sat. The seat was only a few centimetres too short, yet the childish perspective made the writer feel silly. She realised she was still holding her folded coat. Why hadn't she hung it on the stand?

A few seconds of silence before Katya spoke.

'So… you write another story. Who tell you to do this?'

The agent's dark eyes pounced. The writer was able to hold her gaze for a second and search for a clue – a knowing look! She had read the story! She'd read Jess' uninvited tribute and thought it was pathetic. Of course she did: it was pitiful! And now the writer was going to be totally humiliated. Just don't blush. Please don't blush. Oh no! She could feel herself beginning to bloom, face reddening uncontrollably. Mask stripped off, like a little pair of panties… red-rose cheeks expressing all her nakedness. She didn't dare look towards the mirror. That fucking motorbike!

'Well, I… it's just that…' Deep breaths, calm down. She hadn't necessarily read the story. 'I just wasn't happy with my last submission… so I… wrote him another one.' She touched Katya's glare to offer an apologetic half-smile.

'This was not instructed.' The agent's eyelids fluttered with peculiar rapidity as she inhaled. A few menacing moments stretched themselves out. 'But, I send to him…' Katya had an unpleasant taste in her mouth. 'And he says you will be paid.' The agent picked up her mobile.

Jess tried to digest. She was going to be paid? Paid! That meant she'd done well, right?

'Bring now.' Ms Stilenskova snapped the order into her phone whilst hanging up. A second later, Charlotte hurried into the office clutching a couple of brown envelopes: A4 and A5. The respectful nod towards Katya almost bobbed into a curtsy before the receptionist turned and offered the packages to Jess. The larger one was sealed and unmarked – it must contain an annotated print-out of the story, as before. The smaller envelope was full, unsealed and labelled '£500'. She'd been paid. She was a writer: a paid writer! This could cover the rent for a month (nearly). Real money for real writing work... well, sort of. Jess looked directly into his eyes (through the looking glass) to express gratitude, revelling in the glory of her first moments as a professional writer.

A flash of Katya's eyebrows dismissed Charlotte from the room. 'So, you will have twelve days. The deadline is Friday next week, 5pm. Come for meeting here 2pm following Monday. Same deal as before.' Katya hired Jess bearing the exact same facial expression and tone of voice she'd used to fire her the previous week. But who cared? This was amazing, brilliant! Jessica Seaques was a professional writer! And also an agreeable maniac, judging from the way she was nodding.

'Thank you. Yes, thank you. I'll get it done by Friday next week.' Her eyes beamed although she managed to straighten her mouth, to be less incongruent with Katya's cold indifference. It was clear the Russian now wanted her to leave. That was fine, although maybe...

'Did he say...?'

Ms Stilenskova cut her off with a pointed nod towards the large envelope. Jess flashed a closing smile and gave a little bob of thanks as she stood. She struggled to bundle the packages along with her coat and handbag… and realised she should probably take the chair as well. She apologised for the kerfuffle as she blundered out of the room. The agent was sending a text and ignoring the irritation. Charlotte also ignored the writer's halting exit, keeping her timid eyes fixed on the computer screen. After setting down the chair, Jess laid her stuff on the seat to organise it.

He was paying her attention: she could feel him watching! He was pleased… and wanted to see her enjoying the reward he'd bestowed. The writer turned away from the mirror, bending right over as she squeezed the small envelope inside her handbag. Plumping buttocks towards him, waggling them slightly as she moved. If this was the forest, then this was the bunny rabbit inviting the wolf to pounce, to sink his sharp teeth into her soft flank and take her down. It took a while to reorganise things in her bag, conscious that she had left herself vulnerable to attack from the rear. A warm buzz tingled below her ears and prickled down her spine. But there was no attack. She put on her coat and left.

The street was quiet, except the big-city hum of distant traffic all around. The glare of the winter sun was striking; the air crisp and cold, breeze stiff enough to chill as Jess buttoned her coat. She had to get out of sight and open the envelope at the first opportunity. How was it she'd managed to wait until getting home last time? She crossed the street, remembering a low wall under a tree close by – that would make a good spot. No point wondering what the feedback was when she was about to find out. It must be positive; she'd been paid £500! Okay, not a lot if you remembered the whole month of intensive writing. But not bad if it was considered payment for just one week's work. More than her weekly wage at the café.

She sat on the wall and ripped open the A4 envelope. A printout of 'Red Rose': papers stapled together at the top corner and the document rumpled with perusal. A red tick on the first line! She bubbled with pride. Skimming through, more ticks leapt out.

Counting them greedily: a couple of dozen. Usually symbolising approval for the nastiest parts of the story, with clusters celebrating especially dark moments. Flicking red dashes also rewarded instances of curiosity, courage, subservience and high emotion.

Throughout the document, various words and phrases had been underlined. Never full sentences – only specific parts of sentences. The phrases: 'she didn't know', 'knew it was true', 'you want to know' and 'all true' were each highlighted in this way. The words 'very bad man' and 'instead it swallowed her' had been emphasised, but so had more reassuring sentiments like 'strong arms clasped her' and 'holding her fully in his arms'. The word 'help' was underscored wherever it was used, including the variations 'helped', 'helpless', 'helplessly' and 'helplessness'. Was he chiding her for using it too often?

The terms 'daydream', 'dreamily', 'dizzying droop', 'hypnotised', 'passed out', 'bleary eyes' and 'wilting and fainting' had all drawn attention. She traced her finger around the looping line cradling the phrase 'wilting and fainting'. Looking through, it seemed there were different styles of underscore: some curved around the bottom of the words, whilst others were drawn especially straight. She noted the expressions related to knowing had all been highlighted using clean, horizontal lines, with the phrase 'all true' apparently deserving a double-dash.

The writer was pleased to note that (unlike with the first story) there were very few deletions. The letters 'e' and 'd' had been removed from the word 'waited' with a tidy box of red scribble. At another point, the words 'even be able to' had been chopped right out from the middle of a sentence. The word 'total' had been cut from the phrase 'total victory' with a neat cross of pen strokes. A row of three small arrows led away from this particular deletion. Arrows also snaked off from the phrase 'find out lots about her dark side'. There were two hand-written comments, both on the last page. Once again, the word 'DEEPER' was capitalised as an intriguing, final instruction, the bodies of the D, the P and the R looping up and around expansively. The three Es seeming to point onwards, stretching their upper limbs to gesture over one another's shoulders. However, the big, red words at the top of the page were the ones that really grabbed attention: 'Your talent is special'.

She swooned dizzy as her whole self swelled to absorb as much of the compliment as possible. This was genuine approval: hard won and deeply meaningful. Her talent was special! She was special. He'd recognised it! He knew it. The flushing warmth reaching up her neck to tickle. Rereading his words, the glow only sweetened to the savour. Emotions fizzing like pink champagne… strawberry bobbing happily. His handwriting was so fucking sexy! It sent shivers down her spine… and up again. His words: assertive, strong, sure, confident… certain, sincere, powerful, flamboyant. The red ink seared, the message burned…

The game was on!

THREE
PET NAMES

She should never have sent it. She'd known it was a mistake, even as her finger hovered over the send icon – flashes of regret trailing in advance. Oh Christ! What had she done? Why had she done it? What a fool she'd been! A shudder ran though her body as the anxiety engulfed. But there was no point dwelling on it all night. What's done is done. No taking it back now. Besides, it wasn't that bad really; perfectly reasonable in the circumstances. Although the empty bottle of wine on the coffee table might imply that something may've been misjudged.

Charlotte huddled back into the sofa to reread the text she'd sent her husband earlier in the evening. Was it too direct? Too indirect? Surely she was just trying to help their marriage. She shouldn't have mentioned Katya; that was probably a mistake. But what she'd actually written could be interpreted in various different ways. The text was very carefully worded. Had she betrayed a shared secret, been 'disloyal' to the woman who'd shown her the part of her husband she'd always wanted to see? Maybe. Although the woman who'd imprisoned her, stuck a rose in her ass and made her watch her own husband's adulterous sex show obviously didn't deserve loyalty.

But Christ, what a show it had been! The vivid image of the mistress bouncing up and down on her lover's big dick had proved a haunting memory. And the erotic ghost of that evil, blood-red smile remained spotlighted in Charlotte's mind. So shameful that she'd spent the last few days masturbating over those memories. Surely that must prove some kind of deep character flaw or psychological defect? The adulterer's actions were cruel and callous, but at least they kind of made sense. It was the betrayed wife who should feel most ashamed. She was a disgrace! She hated herself! Why was she like this? How could anyone enjoy something as horrible as that? It was unnatural. It was sick. She was sick... and it really turned her on.

She'd consumed many hours tormenting herself... and spent plenty of time pondering the big question: whether her husband knew. He may well have done. He might have planned it all from the start. Stood over his unconscious wife after the performance. Got his mistress to un-cuff her before they went out for the evening. Would that make Charlotte's message tonight just another part of his plot? Those were surely sentiments he'd expect her to express... that he'd manipulated her into expressing. How could she have done anything wrong, if this was all part of his plan? But then, what was his plan? She hadn't been able to find out.

Her gaze drifted towards the desktop computer sitting on the far side of the living room. No incriminating messages in any of his email or social media accounts. Her pang of guilt was quickly followed by a surge of anger – directed at herself. She shouldn't feel guilty about spying on him. It was pathetically weak to feel remorseful about that. He was the one who should feel guilty. And anybody would say she was well within her rights to read the correspondence of her philandering husband. That was true, whether or not he'd deliberately orchestrated the sex show.

But of course, if he didn't know what Katya had done – if he hadn't known that he and his lover were performing in front of his imprisoned wife – then the text might've come as a bit of a surprise. Charlotte hadn't said anything explicit. Even so, the mention of his mistress' name could cause alarm. Although would that necessarily be a bad thing? The considerations were complex. And of course, if he didn't know, then what'd happened was all down to Katya. In which case, what was her scheme exactly? What was she trying to achieve? Was she trying to break up the marriage? Or hoping to make the relationship some kind of weird three-way affair? Maybe it was just an opportune bit of sadistic fun?

She'd certainly enjoyed it a lot. Charlotte recalled the happy darkness in the mistress' dilated pupils as she laughed at her humiliated victim in the chair. What an evil bitch! Perhaps what'd happened was entirely the mistress' cruel caprice? A mad whim? Maybe there was no long-term plan at all! Oh Jesus! What if no one was properly in control? That would turn Charlotte's actions into choices that genuinely impacted what ultimately occurred. Surely not! In that worst-case-scenario, what should she do? She couldn't just carry on as if nothing had happened. Could she? Surely Katya would know that things had changed irreversibly. There were obviously going to be repercussions.

Charlotte had even tried to find the other woman, so they could discuss things. Returning to the office the day after the ordeal was perhaps the bravest (and weakest) thing she'd ever done. But the mistress hadn't been there. Instead the wife had to post a note under the door – her mobile number and the request 'Please call me'. That was two days ago. Katya hadn't responded. And it'd now been two hours since Charlotte had messaged her husband. Sent at 8.22pm. No reply yet… It was nearly 10.10pm – 2.09pm, Vancouver time. Why hadn't he responded? She knew he wasn't busy today. Had she done something wrong? But then he wasn't generally very quick at returning texts. So she shouldn't read too much into it… yet.

She should probably just put it out of her mind and think about something else. Charlotte pulled her plush, pink dressing gown snug around her body and stood to begin clearing the coffee table. She'd leave Puggle there, for now. She didn't normally seek out the company of soft toys, but had been drinking about her husband all evening and fetched Puggle down because of his symbolic significance. Actually, perhaps she should take the little pink creature back upstairs – she really didn't need encouragement to obsess about her marriage anymore tonight.

Maybe watch something on TV to take her mind off things? That Scandinavian thriller he kept going on about? She needed to watch it on Netflix before the new series started on the BBC. What was it called again? 'Killer' something? Actually, probably best not to watch something scary. It was a big house to be alone in… and if she managed to get herself worked up then the quietness of the West London neighbourhood tended to resonate the eeriness – make her feel small, isolated, vulnerable. She definitely wouldn't watch that thriller now. Perhaps something lighter?

Few cars pulled into the close at this time of night. Although, obviously, hearing one would be no cause for alarm. But that wasn't a car. That was a motorbike. A motorbike! Turning into the driveway now, engine growling, gravel crunching. Jesus Christ! She was here! Charlotte froze stone still. The bike pulled around past the living room window, towards the parking area outside the front door. The glaring headlight flashed menacingly across the outside of drawn curtains. Katya was here, had come to get her! What should Charlotte do? Hide! Could her silhouette be seen through the curtains?

She dropped into a low crouch, clutching the bottle, glass and toy to her bosom like a mother shielding a baby from a bomb blast. The bike had stopped. It would be obvious to the mistress that someone was in the house; the lights were on all over the ground floor. Sweet Jesus! Charlotte's heart was pounding, a cold plunge of adrenaline flooding her body. Why was Katya here? Why now? She must know about the text. He'd told her? What'd he said? What had made the mistress drive all the way over here… to…

Charlotte set the bottle, glass and toy back on the coffee table. Sinking onto her knees, she crawled across the soft carpet. At the living room door, she could poke her head out and see the front entrance, a few metres across the hallway. Katya must be closing in… inevitably. A shadow fell across the portal-pane of frosted glass in the door. The shrieking bell pierced an exaggerated silence. Jesus Christ! The long blast was intimidating enough on its own, but was immediately followed by a succession of loud, snapping knocks. Angry knocks! Katya was pissed off!

Charlotte stared at the door of her besieged home in horror, hands shaking. She should run away! Where? Quickly crawl down the hallway to the basement and hide? The bell was howling once more – a furious banshee – and again came the aggressive raps of a closed fist, muttered swearing in raging Russian. How could she be this angry? Charlotte hadn't done anything… hadn't really said anything. This was ridiculous, crazy. Katya was crazy… and she was at the door!

Shadows flickered dramatically across the portal-pane as Charlotte stared up with eyes wide, tensing on all-fours like a frightened animal. Katya's silhouette suddenly disappeared: she was crouching down. Charlotte whipped her head out of sight and sat back on her knees. Just in time, as the mistress pushed open the letter-flap to peer in. The wife was hidden from view, but she could feel furious, dark eyes glaring in… invading her home. It wasn't safe here anymore. The flap snapped shut and the mistress resumed her assault on the bell and door. Jesus Christ! What could Charlotte do? She couldn't just cower here indefinitely? Could she? What if Katya smashed her way in? Jesus Christ! A pause… The sound of the letter-flap opening again.

'I know you in there. Open the fucking door, right now!'

The fierce voice sent a shiver down the spine. This was absurdly unfair! How could the crazy bitch be angry with her? In what universe could the mistress possibly think she had the right to be angry at her lover's wife – for sending a text to her own husband? And the message's content wasn't at all unreasonable. This reaction was ludicrously disproportionate. This was just… so… unbelievably unjust.

'Open the fucking door! I know you in there.'

It was true. Katya did know. There was no escape. But perhaps if Charlotte just stayed still and quiet… what would the besieger do? Remain outside and wait it out, like a cat with a cornered mouse? She surely didn't have the patience for that.

'Let me in, you little fucking bitch!'

The tone struck cold. In her panic, the householder found herself staring up at the samurai sword mounted on the living room mantelpiece. What a ridiculous thought. She couldn't fight, couldn't run, couldn't hide… not indefinitely. This really wasn't fair. She should feel angry about it, but instead she felt scared. What a pathetic weakling. A jagged saw of frustration, followed by a shameful spike of moist between her legs – visualising the mistress sticking the rose up her ass. Oh God! Why couldn't she feel emotional about this without provoking sexual arousal?

It was all so unfair. But it wasn't about fairness anyway. The victim was just going to have to face her tormenter, try to placate her, attempt to reason with her. Just do it now, before the mistress worked herself up even more. Charlotte stood reluctantly. Deep breaths. She didn't do anything wrong. She wasn't trying to antagonise her husband's lover. She just wanted to be… more involved. God, was that her only defence: her own pathetic pitifulness? Deep breaths.

The mistress had resumed hammering, but must've seen Charlotte's silhouette approaching. The silence crashed in. Fluffy pink boot slippers slid too easily over the polished, wooden floor. Should she put the chain on? What was Katya going to do? Without the door, there'd only be a soft dressing gown between those sharp claws and Charlotte's naked body. But surely she wasn't going to physically attack? The Russian's slim shadow loomed ominously. Composure. Keep calm. Exude peacefulness. One last long exhalation, before opening…

The palm of Katya's hand was already on the wood. As it began to move, she leant in and pushed. The door swung violently with Charlotte stumbling clear. The mistress burst into the house in a black storm of riding leathers, ponytail swooshing, claws jabbing and pointing, eyes aflame.

'What you fucking tell him?!'

Charlotte staggered back. 'I didn't say anything. I didn't tell him… please…'

Katya's arm flicked up, open hand stinging a sharp slap across the wife's cheek. A squeal of shock. The force of the blow was enough to spin the body part-way around, hands clutching to protect the face. The mistress grabbed a fistful of hair, pulling up and down to rattle Charlotte's head.

'What you tell him, you little fucking bitch?!'

Katya drove forwards, twisting her victim face-to-face; right hand clamping the underside of Charlotte's chin, nails digging into the cheeks, squeezing the jaw tight… muffling pleas for reason. The housewife was forced back across the hallway and slammed against the wall in a dizziness of stars. The mistress held her face and pushed upwards. Charlotte floundered on slippery tiptoes, hands desperately trying to loosen her attacker's grasp. But the grip was vice-like, thumb and forefinger: a steel pincer. How could she be so strong?

'What you fucking say to him?'

'Please… I didn't tell him anything.' Words slurring in the clutch of claws. 'Except that I saw you…'

'You tell him you see us?!' Livid eyes igniting.

'The charger! Just said I saw you when I dropped off the charger.'

Charlotte couldn't swallow; she was welling up. This was so unfair. Why wasn't he here to protect her? Would he protect her, even if he was? The tears were rolling now, her face crumpling pitifully. Katya snarled, releasing the chin-grip and stepping back, pulling her right arm across and preparing to smack back-handed. Charlotte moved fast, darting sideways to escape towards the stairs. The mistress snatched after her, grabbing the billowing gown and pulling, diverting the momentum so the wife swung an arc around her attacker's body. Charlotte scrabbled, feet frantically slippering the polished floor, managing to twist to flee towards the living room, but Katya held tight. The housewife's slippers slid as she wriggled and slipped out of the gown, naked body hitting the floor on knees and forearms. A frantic crawl towards the lounge.

Katya came up behind, leg swinging, the tip of her boot hammering into her victim's ass. Charlotte yelped as the pain skewered up through her middle, the force sending her sprawling forwards. The second kick hooked painfully under the groin with a hollow thump. A face-full of carpet as she found her head against the bottom of the open living room door, body squirming on the cold wood of the hallway floor. She twisted onto her side as the mistress stamped a red heel-print onto the white of the buttock. Rolling onto her back, Charlotte tried to bring her legs up in defence.

A pair of fluffy, pink slipper-boots waggling in the air, inviting Katya to grab hold of each with strong hands and stomp her right foot down in between. The riding boot crushing onto the wife's groin, the short, wide heel hooking underneath, corners digging into the butt-cheeks. Charlotte squealed as her tormentor leaned forward to apply more pressure. The wife on her back: legs spread open, pussy squashed underfoot, face streaked with tears, naked except for a ludicrous pair of furry slippers.

'Please! I'll show you the message. It was just a text… and I didn't say anything bad. Please, let me show you.'

As Charlotte pleaded, the fury in Katya's face began to tickle. Looking down imperiously, she mused on the fate of the vanquished. Noticing the front door agape, the mistress stepped off her lover's wife, ponytail flicking decisively as she turned and strode over to close it. Charlotte had given up; there was no point in resisting… no escape now. She sat up on her buttocks, huddling legs closed. The dressing gown was strewn on the other side of the hall. The naked feeling of defeat flooded through her blood. Such a deep, primal, overwhelming emotion. But the resignation glittered as the energy drained, a warm tingle below the ears, a bristle at the base of her neck.

Katya the Conqueror slammed the door and turned back with purpose. She snatched a clutch of curls and dragged the householder along as she marched through to the living room. Spotting the phone on the coffee table, the invader moved to take Charlotte's former position on the sofa. The wife was now kneeling below, setting hands on thighs as a sign of submission. The mistress kept hold of her hair as she sat back, twisting it so Charlotte's head turned awkwardly against the front of the armrest.

Katya cast a contemptuous glare over her lover's wife's nakedness. It was satisfying to see her totally defeated: on her knees, trembling all over, skin moistened and flush with panic. The queen crossed her legs, a sly smile in her eyes as she picked up Charlotte's phone with her free hand. No need for a password inside the safety of a 'trusted location'. A few casual taps of the thumb and the mistress was reading: perusing the once-private correspondence between husband and wife. The invader's expression was stony at first, then came a flair of the nostril. As she continued to absorb, a micro twitch below the eye hinted that she wanted to bare fangs. Finally, her eyes pounced. She leaned in, jerking Charlotte's head back to fix gaze.

'What you say about me, bitch?!' Charlotte felt a fleck on her face as the final word spat.

'Please, I just said you showed me around the offi—'

'That's not what you say. Liar!' The mistress screwed her victim's hair, tearing-tight as she sat back to read out loud, affecting a cutesy, high-pitched tone as an insulting impression of little Charlotte.

'Hey Hun, hope you enjoyed the exhibition and hope the meetings haven't been too tedious so far. Perhaps I shouldn't bring this up now, but going to the office the other day, Katya showed me something that made me realise there's a barrier between us…' – the mistress cast an accusing glance – 'and I really don't want there to be. Sorry to mention it now. I'm not complaining. I'm just saying I'd like to know more… about you. I'd like for you to trust me more. I'd like to be closer to you.' Katya's expression mock-melting in romance. 'I'd like to be more involved. I want to see the other side. I need to see the other side! Please understand, I don't want to intrude or interfere, I just think that if I knew more, I would understand more about what makes you happy… and surely that would be a good thing… for everybody. Smiley face, kiss, kiss, kiss.' The mistress amused herself, theatrically miming the kisses, before her eyes narrowed again. 'You say, "Katya showed me something". You tell him! You telling tales.'

'No, please… I didn't. I just meant… I just wanted him to… let me in. I'm not asking anything except… let me in.' Charlotte knew exactly how pathetic she was. 'And I just thought, if I mentioned you… it might… get his attention a bit. Not in a bad way. I didn't say anything explicit. I mean, I don't even know what he kn—'

'How sweet – little wifey want to be involved.' Katya's temper was cooling. She was more relaxed, turning back to the screen and scrolling up through earlier messages. Settling in, she released hold of Charlotte's hair and read out another text, wagging her head side-to-side whilst chiming the words, 'Hey Hun' in squeaky impersonation.

'Hey Hun, hope you had a good flight. Yikes, sounds cold there! Don't forget to buy a proper coat :) xxx' Laughing as she turned to Charlotte. 'Smiley face, kiss, kiss, kiss. How cute. You send him message saying if he have good flight. When you know he not on flight yet. You know he still in bed with me when you send this.' The mistress' expression lit with delight. 'But you pretend you don't know this. Aren't you clever girl.' A suspicious eye lingered a moment, before flicking back to continue scanning the message chain. Katya was clearly enjoying herself, feeling quite at home now. Although her expression snarled up in confusion.

'What is Puggle?'

'Puggle?' Charlotte gulped. 'Oh, it's just… it's just what he… sometimes calls me. You know, like… like a pet name.'

'Pet name?' She questioned warily.

'Like a nickname… between lov… between husband and wife. For intimacy.'

'And he call you Puggle?' Katya was disgusted. 'What it mean?'

'Ummm… It just means… Well, it's a baby platypus.'

'What?!'

Charlotte was embarrassed, but pressured to continue. 'A platypus. You know, the Australian animal… like half-bird, half-mammal… or half-marsupial or… lives in the water. A platypus.'

'Platypus.' Katya mouthed it slowly, then began a steady nod of recognition. 'Yes, this Australian animal with duck's nose… and swimming. You are platypus?'

'Well, yes… I mean… a baby platypus – a puggle. A puggle is what you call a baby platypus and…' She gestured sheepishly towards the soft toy sitting on the coffee table. 'That's a puggle: Puggle. Well, a toy puggle.'

'This is Puggle?' Katya loomed over the helpless toy, pinching Puggle's neck between her nails and lifting the small, pink creature to dangle before her eyes. Inspecting it guardedly, as if she might be dirtied somehow. 'Why he call you this?'

'Oh... well, because he said I...' Charlotte didn't want to go into details, but demanding eyes forced her on. 'He just said I looked like a puggle. We were watching some documentary on Australian wildlife... and there were these... baby platypuses, puggles... and he said I looked like one of them. I was tired, so I had kind of sleepy eyes... and you know how baby animals have... sometimes have... sleepy eyes. Well, he said I looked like a puggle... and started calling me Puggle... and it just kind of... stuck. And then when we went to Aus... Well, part of the reason we went to Australia, on our honeymoon, was to see puggles. Kind of... romantic.'

'And they are pink?' Katya nodded towards the toy, which had been contemptuously dropped back onto the table.

'Oh... ummm... Well, the toy is pink. Because they had toy puggles in one of the shops we went to... and I said I wanted a yellow one. But I was a bit sunburnt at the time... and he said... Well, he bought me the pink one... because he said it was the same colour as me. It was kind of a joke.'

Katya didn't seem to get it. Although as the joke involved suffering, you might've thought it would suit her sense of humour.

'Puggle. You are little, pink puggle... like little, pink piggy. This is why he call you this. And now your cheeks are pink like dumb fucking toy. Anyway, this name is fucking stupid!' Katya shook her head at Charlotte's shame and returned to reading through the intra-marital correspondence. The wife sat at her feet, watching helplessly. 'Go get me wine, Puggle-Pig.' The horrible perversion of words elicited a wince. Charlotte backed away to a distance where she could respectfully clamber to her feet. 'And don't put any clothes.' The mistress didn't look up.

Katya was enthroned on the living room sofa, dominating the home. Such a loathsome woman. The helpless hatred constricted Charlotte's body in thin, barbed wires, a disgraceful thrill prickling up her spine as the emotions twisted. There was something so impressive about the mistress just bursting in and taking over. Claiming ownership through primal right – she just took it. An alpha female. A slender, leather-clad Venus... bewitchingly wonderful: so strong, so ruthless, so hard, so pitiless. How could Charlotte not be impressed? She remembered swooning at Katya's beauty by candlelight, pupils dilated with joy. How could anyone not be impressed? She should be worshipped... served. It was an honour. The bitch-girl must fetch the wine. There was a chilled bottle in the fridge.

Glancing at herself in the long, hallway mirror – plump, curvaceous body naked, except for the fluffy, pink slippers – Charlotte realised she'd never walked around the house like this before. It made her feel silly... and yet sexy: satisfyingly humiliated. The fully clothed mistress had specifically ordered the wife to remain naked, deliberately degrading her. Katya had taken charge, so all Charlotte had to do was follow orders. No choices to worry about: she couldn't disobey the mistress. She was still sore from the kicking. The boot-stamp on her buttock was bruising already, but it was the first kick, right between the ass-cheeks, that hurt the most. A numb, hollow kind of pain spearing up into her. She enjoyed still being able to physically feel the power of the mistress. It would tingle later when bending over in front of the mirror and admiring her bruising through dreamy eyes. Would make her want to come. She'd come so many times over the last couple of days.

Opening the fridge, the wave of cool air clashed with the rising flush of heat in her face, the cold nippling her breasts. She wanted to come right now. Just crawl back onto the living room floor and lie at Katya's feet, touching herself... offering worship. Charlotte was feeling woozy, weak at the knees. It wasn't the alcohol – that drunkenness had evaporated in the flash of a headlight. She would fetch a posh glass, one of the expensive, sleek flutes. Maybe an ice bucket? Too much? The mistress was driving, of course. Unless she was staying? Taking over the home until he got back from Canada – reducing the woman of the house to a slave. Katya could easily do that... if she so desired.

Charlotte's posture straightened as she returned to the living room. The mistress was still engrossed in her reading. Smoking a long, thin cigarette and leaning back with feet crossed over the surface of the coffee table. Puggle sitting nervously at her boot heel. Katya gripped the cigarette in her mouth and held out her hand. Looking up as Charlotte handed over the glass – dark eyes gleaming with knowing smiles. It was certainly true she knew more about her lover's wife than she had a few minutes ago.

That smug expression was so infuriatingly alluring – like when the mistress gloated through the mirror whilst fucking her lover. Charlotte loved recalling that treasured image in those melting moments before orgasm, but hated herself for doing so in those shameful moments afterwards… as reality mercilessly re-solidified. The hostess bent forward daintily, cupping the bottle with both hands as she filled the invader's flute. Katya scoffed as she read out another text, this one from a few months back.

'Hey Hun, hope all went well and they accepted your position on the changes. It's a bit stressful here, still lots of tension between Steve and Lisa. But quite interesting apart from that. You'd love Mark's in-laws. They're crazy (and the mother-in-law's personality explains why he gave in on the name). Wish you were here (although I know you're glad you're not). Anyway, have fun at your drinks thing tonight and try not to get too drunk :) Back around five on Monday. Love you lots and lots :) xxx'

'Smiley face, kiss, kiss, kiss.' Katya looked up with a wry smirk. 'You know where he was this night? When you in… wherever… with your family.'

'No,' Charlotte admitted softly, 'where?' She moved to fetch an ashtray from the computer desk.

'We spend the night in the playroom. We find new toy.' Katya boasted proudly. 'One of his fans, from America, visiting for few days. Businesswoman or something. Act all tough: loud and talking… and big laughing. You know, she is the boss in her office,

or whatever. Middle-aged, blonde... and on phone: "da-da-da..."'
Charlotte set the ashtray on the arm of the sofa. A sharp finger indicated that she was to resume kneeling on the floor. 'But she not so strong as pretend. Secretly... she want be weak. She want him make her weak: break her! That's why she want... really she is weak... soft woman.' Katya paused, exaggerating her expression of disdain even more than usual, carefully communicating that she herself would never harbour such shameful feebleness. 'She only pretend be strong and she want him break her.' The word 'break' rumbled in the Russian's brutal accent. 'It is me who bring her. She is surprised at this. First time she shut her fucking mouth!'

'But she want go to him. This time, I mostly watching. Usually I play, but this time, just want watch. I want see her broken. See the moment when she not strong anymore. Not at all... and see she know then that she never was! She is helpless and small... changes quickly, you know, everything comes out...' The expression the mistress assumed was not really an impression, more an attempt to convey the sense of being totally overwhelmed, head circling, mouth wide open in long exhalation. 'Many games with her... this long weekend. He has wicked imagination, your husband. Oh yes, has his fun with this one.' Katya rested her eyes on a fondly remembered image. Glazing over, she allowed Charlotte time to muse on the details.

'I enjoy watch. See pretend-strong woman shown she is weak. See real strong man do this to her.' Katya tapped a finger on the side of her forehead. 'See how she come. Oh yes, like someone been holding the hose long time, you know. Ha! Soft bitch! She fly back home Monday morning. He say he want her think about him on plane. So, take sandpaper... you know, for wood. He take it... put her over his knee. Hold her down and... sand her ass. Rub hard, so white skin is pink and sore. All over her butt... and the nerves on skin burning and raw. You know, when skin is like this, put something citric, acidic, on it: lime juice. He use lime juice this time – because it worse than orange – and wow! It hurt! Look like hurt a lot… and she is loud again.' Katya sniggered.

'And, you know, it hurt for many hours when you do like this. Prepare pain receivers on skin, then put on juice: pain for long time. She don't forget. She think of him, whilst sitting on her sore ass, on plane… and send to him many texts: how much she love it, how much she think of us. She is annoying in the end. But you should see some of the messages. Would be fun I show you these.' The mistress' playful smile almost glinted with sharing intimacy. Perhaps this was her idea of a fun girl's night in. What a giggle!

Katya hadn't finished with the phone yet. She wanted to read the correspondence through all accessible mediums: email, WhatsApp, Facebook messages, etc. Charlotte knelt passively and looked up at her dominator in admiration. Righteous hatred overawed – subsumed by evil love. The mistress smoked deliciously: long pauses punctuated by sharp drags, taken assertively from the side of the mouth. Each inhalation snarling half her face. During the slow exhalations, the smoke wisped out at a smoulder… snakes of tobacco-mist wreathing her body: a goddess in the clouds.

Occasionally, Katya read out a particularly embarrassing text. Often imparting a hurtful piece of related information or indulging a cruel insight. Washing down the pleasure of each further humiliation with a pampering swig of Château Cheval Blanc. The woman's gall was unbelievable – magnificent – truly awe-inspiring. Just sitting there, with her feet up, casually raping her victim's privacy. And all Charlotte wanted to do was curl up on the floor, with her fingers inside herself, and lick Katya's boot.

Puggle still looked worried, cowering in the shadow of that riding boot. So humiliating that the mistress had extracted the intimate story behind the soft toy – even invading the honeymoon. God, imagine that! Katya storming into the honeymoon holiday and taking Charlotte's husband from her, then tying her up on the balcony of her own wedding suite. Making her watch them fucking – like in the office, except him definitely knowing his wife was there. Deliberately ignoring her pleas for mercy whilst enjoying his beautiful mistress. Letting Charlotte burn in the blaze of the Antipodean sunshine. White skin reddening painfully as the adulterer's shouts of elation drowned out the wife's begging sobs. And later, Katya laughing when he bought his wife a red puggle toy instead of just a pink one. Jesus Christ! She was so wet. What a horribly perverted fantasy; it shouldn't make her so excited. What would Katya do if her bitch-girl just started fingering herself right now?

But the mistress was clearly becoming bored. In fact, her facial expression suggested she'd reached the final, stomach-wrenching straw. 'You send him picture of puggle toy wearing sunglasses.' Katya flashed the offending image from an old WhatsApp exchange. The guilty party lowered her head. There wasn't much to add to that statement, although…

'Does he have a pet name for you?' Charlotte was surprised to hear the question popping out of her own mouth.

'No!' the mistress answered sharply. But then she hesitated, a flick of pupils betraying that she had thought of a possible answer… that she wasn't going to give. 'No, this is stupid!' Katya went back to glaring at the screen for a few more seconds. Then abruptly whipped her feet off the table and stood up, tossing the phone onto the couch. A final swig of wine as she looked down at her lover's pathetic wife.

'So you want to be "involved", ha?' The mistress took on an exaggerated, patronising tone. 'You want to see the other side? Well, maybe I help you. Maybe I teach you… train you to be little puppy-bitch. Just the way he like it. Then when he is back, maybe I bring you to him, like this – like little puggle-puppy.' The mistress chuckled. 'See what he say then. Maybe he like you like this. Maybe we let you play. Anyway, he not back for ten days: plenty of time for me teach you how to be good bad little bitch. When he return, I bring you to him.' She mused for a moment. Did her expression suggest she knew what he'd do? Or did it imply she didn't? 'Start tomorrow. You come to office, five o'clock… and…' the Russian loomed, 'you don't tell him nothing. Nothing!'

Katya cast down a scornful glare. She clearly wanted to storm out, but felt she hadn't quite finished yet. One more blow was required to round-off the victory: one more infliction of pain. Her cat's eyes hunted around. The gaze of both women fell on Puggle at the same time. No! Surely not? The mistress moved fast, stooping to grab the helpless toy by the scruff of the neck. She fixed a cruel stare on Charlotte as the fingers of her other hand crept around to pinch the head. The wife was aghast. Surely not! Katya twisted as she pulled. Puggle resisted valiantly for a few seconds, denying his attacker the satisfaction of pulling him apart in one clean movement. But those hands were strong. As the fabric tore, the head popped off in a little burst of fluff.

The mistress smiled as she tossed the corpse of her decapitated victim back onto the coffee table. She clearly enjoyed flicking her ponytail behind to mark a dramatic exit, the brisk slink of her hips rolling so her perfect bauble-buttocks ground around one another under the tight leather. The windows shuddered as the front door slammed shut. Charlotte remained on the floor as she listened to Katya rev up her bike and leave. She looked at little Puggle's staring dead eyes.

The long silence was rudely broken by the perky chirp of her phone. A message. It was him.

Hey Puggs, yeah, the exhibition was good. A few interesting novelties. Not sure what Katya said, but she can sometimes be a bit rash/insensitive. Or a bit misleading. Let's talk about it when I get back. Off for an afternoon stroll in the snow now. Love you lots :) xxx

Smiley face… kiss, kiss, kiss.

FOUR

LOVE HEART

A flood of self-pity as Jess made eye contact with her reflection in the mirror-wall. Sodden hair straggled around her wind-blasted face. Her clothes were soaked right through – tight jeans, the last thing you want to get wet… soggy denim clinging to the skin. That good-looking chestnut jacket, not really waterproof against a heavy shower, now drooped limp from the coat-stand. Obviously the storm only lasted the twenty-five minutes it took Jess to walk here. Typical! The world loves kicking you whilst you're down. Welcome to homelessness – it's pissing with rain.

Now sitting on this absurd insult-of-a-chair, enduring Charlotte's silent waves of awkwardness, waiting for Ms Stilenskova's summons. No doubt Katya would make some unpleasant comment about the bedraggled appearance of the writer – call her a wet rabbit crawling out of a ditch or something similar. Jess had to admit, she did look quite a state. What would he be thinking, watching from behind the glass? She smoothed her hair back and tried to regain some composure. Although there was no point trying to pretend everything was alright. It definitely wasn't alright.

Honestly, how did Charlotte always manage to make the atmosphere so painfully unsettled? A real talent. The woman radiated nervous vibrations like a leaking social-tension reactor. It was hard to describe how she did it exactly. Instead of just not looking at the waiting visitor, the receptionist was, somehow, actively not-looking at her. As if deliberately holding her eyes in place, avoiding any possibility of a chance glance. Instead of just not talking, Charlotte was, somehow, actively not-talking. Making a conspicuous effort to maintain the rigidity of her lips. Her whole body bristled with stillness: continuously not-moving… relentlessly not-moving. The tautness in her posture made it seem as if she was hovering just above her chair, rather than actually sitting on it.

Of course, the visitor was now complicit in the negative atmosphere, reflecting the awkwardness back in an ever-escalating feedback loop. Jess was normally quite capable of sitting in a waiting area in comfortable silence, so this must definitely be Charlotte's fault. Unless, of course, the receptionist had read the stories, in which case this level of social tension would be entirely proportionate. Holy fuck! That was obviously what'd happened: Charlotte had been reading the stories and was finding it increasingly difficult to disguise her natural reaction to them. Oh shit. Shit!

No! No, that wasn't how it was. That wasn't what'd happened. The receptionist had always been like this, had had something stuck up her ass long before the writer poked a fictional rose up there. No one had shown her the stories. Why would they? Don't think about it. Best not think about anything right now. Just need to break out of this suffocating silence. Talk! Just talk. Jess jostled around in her bag conspicuously, expressing a few disapproving murmurs as she pretended to find a text message on her phone (presumably somehow relevant to the impending conversation). Charlotte ignored the charade, keeping her gaze fixed resolutely away, but she couldn't prevent the writer from speaking.

'So, I'm a bit worried at the moment.' Leaning forward to catch the receptionist's eye. 'In a bit of a pickle – just been kicked out of my house. Well, been given notice. The landlord's selling. Got to be out in five weeks.'

Charlotte looked shocked. Not by the news, just by the unanticipated demand for her to engage. 'Oh dear,' she managed sincerely. During the pause that followed, the receptionist could have commented that five weeks didn't allow long to sort everything out properly. She didn't say that, but the faint purse of lips at least indicated general concern.

'Five weeks,' Jess emphasised, 'to find a room in a shared house. Could be hard to find somewhere decent in that time. You know how these things can be... and on my budget and...' she stopped herself. Best not to mention the mistake she'd made in quitting her café job, a few days before finding out about the house. That was embarrassingly stupid: resigning her salaried work in a daze of optimistic naivety. To say it was too early in her writing career to safely quit the day job was an understatement. And of course, fate saw to it that her bold positivity should immediately be punished. House-hunting was going to be especially fun this time around. Do you have employment that provides a regular income? Yes... well, sort of: I write erotic stories for a nameless man, who pays me in cash via intermediaries, and works out of an anonymous warehouse (or whatever this place is). Oh fuck!

Charlotte was nodding in solemn sympathy. 'That's unfortunate.' She could've asked what Jess intended to do now.

'So now I'll have to start looking for a room... in a shared house or something. I don't really... Well, it's not that I don't get on with my housemates. It's just that I'm not really friends with them. And none of my friends here are looking, at the moment...

for rooms. So I won't really be moving "with" anyone.' Eye contact always glanced off Charlotte's sliding pupils. 'It's just such a pain, you know. It was such an ordeal sorting something out last time… and I really didn't think I'd have to be trailing around places and it's, like… you know when the viewings are kind of auditions… like a personality test or something… with the housemates judging you. And, well, it's just… a lot of stress.'

'Yes, it can be…' The receptionist's intonation implied that this was only half the sentence. But the words were now drifting off on their own, dissipating… with Charlotte just nodding absently.

'And I really want to stay in the East… like, somewhere round here. I'm down by London Fields at the moment, so anywhere between there and here. Or around Bethnal Green… maybe Dalston.' This conversation had always risked turning into a monologue. Jess could see she was going to have to push a little harder. 'What about you? Whereabouts do you… errr…' She abruptly realised her words might be misconstrued as a hinted request to move in with Charlotte. Fuck, imagine that!

However, there were a number of possible explanations as to why the receptionist looked so alarmed. 'I… yes… I'm just round… out… errr…' – darting blue eyes – 'on the other side of the city.' Her hands were resting on her lap, crossed at the wrists. Jess realised she was onto something, quite an obvious strategy really: the weakest link. As long as she pretended to be 100% sure that Charlotte hadn't read the stories.

'So you're out west, then?' The writer leant further forward, symbolically closing the space between the two women. Her questioning poise would've appeared impressively stylish, if she hadn't been sitting on such a credibility-crushing chair. 'This side of the river?' Jess' encouraging body language made it difficult for Charlotte to avoid nodding along.

'West London,' the receptionist stated, looking as if she was trying to remember something important.

'I don't get over to West London much. My friend lives in Fulham. Says it's really nice around there. Expensive though. What about you, whereabouts in West London?' Charlotte couldn't prove that Jess was doing anything other than making casual conversation.

'Errr... yes, this side of the river.'

'Oh... must take a while to get over here. How d'you come?'

'I... errr... commute.'

'And do you... live with anyone? Housemates? Boyfriend? Husband?' Jess gave a brisk tut of a laugh to underline how offhand and innocent the question was, casually removing her rain-specked glasses for a slow polish. The receptionist floundered, caught in the headlights.

'Ummm... errr...'

The mobile on the desk now buzzed into life, both women startling at the piercing ringtone. Charlotte then smiled primly, her whole body exhaling back into the chair as she answered. 'Hello.' The expression on her face was almost confidence.

'Yes, it is looking like that.' A twinkle of unexpected humour conspired in the receptionist's voice as she turned away, hugging the phone to her right shoulder. Jess was frustrated, firing an accusing look directly through her own reflection.

'No, right... yes.' Charlotte's face dropped, then contorted, becoming serious again. 'Yes, I'm sorry... yes.' Professional tone. 'Yes, she's right here. Yes, Ms Stilenskova.' The name especially pronounced this time. 'Yes, Ms Stilenskova.' Charlotte set the phone down and looked up.

'Ms Stilenskova will see you now.' Helpfully pointing out the door. 'You'll need the... errr...'

Jess knew the drill, flashing a curt smile as she folded the little chair. In the mirror, she noticed her eyebrows were raised and her tongue was pushing playfully against her inner cheek. She had a knowing look. Although she didn't really know anything.

She especially didn't know what the others knew – Katya, for example... Oh shit! The writer remembered anxiety as she pushed open the office door. Ms Stilenskova was lounging back, her feet up and crossed over the surface of the desk. It somehow looked as if she'd only just put them there, which could mean a number of things. Her right arm draped languidly over the armrest, phone held loosely in the dangling hand. Jess couldn't see the mobile screen, but it didn't appear to be emanating any light.

The office was the same as always, except for a single green apple sitting on the corner of the desk. The fruit was perfectly crisp and shiny (Charlotte had presumably polished it earlier). Jess eyed Katya's long heels: the same beautiful black boots she'd stripped off during 'Red Rose'. Perhaps the writer should make a compliment about them? Although there were good reasons not to focus on the footwear. In any case, it was the agent who kicked off.

'You are wet.' The tone implied the rain-drenched woman was somehow at fault.

'Totally soaked through.' The writer agreed. 'The sky just opened up the moment I left the house.'

A pause... Was Katya searching for an insult? Or carefully choosing from a selection of potential insults? Jess kept her nose rigidly still and moved to set up the chair.

'No, you wet. You don't sit. You make everything wet.' The seat was already soaked, but the writer wasn't going to argue. 'There's no need anyway. Charlotte will give you money and papers. You just carry on as before. Deadline a week Friday and review meeting, 2pm, following Monday. Five hundred. Same as before.'

The agent had clearly decided on the best insult: making the meeting last less than thirty seconds, after Jess had walked for half an hour through the pissing rain to attend. Actually, that was quite a good one – simple but effective. In any case, relief at the promise of continued employment was at the forefront of the writer's mind. Katya was now looking at her mobile, preparing to terminate the meeting with an uber-nonchalant dismissal. Jess hadn't really planned on mentioning it, but...

'Oh...' the word popped out as if the writer had been poked unexpectedly. 'It's just... I've got a problem.'

'Yes,' Katya agreed, raising her eyes to read through a series of visible problems.

'It's just... well, I've been kicked out of my house... given notice to leave, I mean. The landlord's selling. Got to be out in five weeks. So, well, it might be difficult for me to... I mean, I can definitely get the story done on time and everything. So, I'm not saying I... it's just...' Where was she going with this? What exactly did she expect the agent to do? 'Well, I'll have to be going around house-hunting... which is always time-consuming and... I will still be able to get everything done, by a week Friday. But... well, I'm just letting you know.'

Katya's eyes had sharpened, gripping the writer in narrow focus. She clearly thought the subject was relevant. She was thinking, weighing something in her mind... was maybe going to suggest something? Surely not something helpful? The agent's phone lit up and began to vibrate. She continued to eyeball Jess thoughtfully as the mobile slid to her ear, letting the other person speak first.

'Yes, I know.' A smug smile. 'Yes, I know.' A more serious expression as she listened. 'Yes, exactly.' Agreed emphatically. 'Haha, I always do.' A sly smirk complimented the self-congratulatory tone. 'Well, that because of who in the boat.'

Katya looked pleased with herself as she finished the call, returning attention to the writer in a regally unhurried manner. At first, her expression suggested the conversation with Jess had been forgotten, but she appeared to remember a few seconds later. 'You don't need worry about this. You will live here.' The agent gestured through the mirror with a lazy flick of the wrist. 'There plenty of space.' Jess felt her jaw literally dropping. Surely she didn't mean the writer was going to be kept in the playroom? Perhaps there were cages hidden under the drapes? 'There is bed… water… cooking… bath.' The Russian nodded her head to underline each facility, although the movements became less unwavering as the list progressed. 'So there is no problem. You will live here. No charge.'

So that was that: the decision was made. The agent was back on the phone, summoning Charlotte to 'Get in here'. The writer was stunned, just standing transfixed, still holding the little chair. It apparently hadn't occurred to Katya that Jess might have anything to say on the matter of where she would live. You had to marvel at the audacity of the woman – just taking control of the writer's life and expecting unquestioning obedience. And you had to admire how amazing she looked, sitting back and giving orders with her feet up… even better than imagined.

'She is moving in here,' Katya stated as Charlotte shuffled in. 'You sort out back room. Make it nice, with all things she needs. Do today, instead of… other thing.' There was the hint of a secret in her tone. Jess realised she should be paying more attention to what was going on. She hadn't even noticed how Charlotte's face had reacted to the headline news. 'She move in tomorrow. You meet here in morning. Sort out money and papers then. Meet at… 8am.'

The abruptness with which Katya finished sentences gave her orders a strong air of finality. Her tone certainly didn't expect any questions. A few moments of silence… (And a few sliding glances towards the mirror?) Katya surveyed her inferiors with fading satisfaction. So that was decided then. Why were those silly bitches still loitering? And that fucking bunny-rabbit-girl was twitching her annoying little nose again. The agent crunched her face and widened her nostrils in a nasty, caricatural impression of Jess (who immediately stilled any nasal movement). Katya's face continued to snarl up as if something stank, her glare unambiguously pinpointing the dual sources of irritation… and the underlings were dismissed.

Jess held the image of Katya's exaggeratedly contemptuous facial expression as she and Charlotte bustled out of the room. The agent's non-verbal communication was always so absurdly over-the-top, her features contorting into cartoon caricatures epitomising disdain, disgust, arrogance, smugness, bitchiness. Still, at least you knew what she was thinking. But did you though? There were certainly times when a more ambiguous thought or emotion appeared to lurk beneath a blatant, pantomime-style expression. Subtlety concealed within extreme crudity, perhaps? Complexity pretending simplicity? Overstated displays of sincerity implying there were no lies to look for, but actually the assured mask used as an effective disguise? It was important to watch more carefully from now on.

Preparing to leave, Jess' parting small talk involved a few pessimistic predictions regarding the weather. They turned out to be well-founded: this part of the world was, indeed, due another twenty-five-minute downpour, starting the moment the writer stepped outside. As the deluge began, Jess realised she hadn't actually requested a viewing of the room. Hadn't even asked any questions about it. Had barely said anything at all. It was her life and yet someone else had just decided where it would be lived, with Jess submissively standing by and accepting her fate. She wasn't normally this passive. She really wasn't! And now the decision was made. What the fuck was she doing?! What was she letting herself in for? Was she really going to be kept in the playroom? In a cage? On the floor, leashed to the frame of that big bed? Oh fuck, please!

This was crazy though. Totally crazy! No sane person would go through with this. What if they kept her? What if they abducted her against her... What if they abducted her? And who were they... really? Who was he? Would she meet him? Find out his name? Find out his game? What was his game? Why would he do this? Do what exactly? What just happened, just now in the office? What had been said over the phone? Who was in what boat? What the fuck was going on, in general, and with all the specifics?

The questions whirled around Jess' head as she went back to the house and began sorting out her things. She didn't have much stuff to take. The room she was leaving had been rented pre-furnished and many of her possessions were still back at her mum's place in Guildford. After a few hours of packing, she ended up with a number of boxes filled with books, several bin bags stuffed with clothes and bedding, and a few travel-bags containing electronic gadgets and other bits and bobs.

She was moving out with minimal fuss... and no need for fond farewells. The house was surprisingly unsociable, considering the youthfulness of the tenants and the vibrancy of the neighbourhood. Jess had never worked out exactly how many housemates she cohabited with. There were eight rooms, but considerably more regulars than that. It wasn't always clear which familiar faces belonged to official residents and which belonged to girlfriends/boyfriends/cousins-from-Bolivia-sleeping-on-the-floor. The turnover of tenants was high, with multiple changes in the six months Jess had been living there. It always seemed that at any one time, there was at least one phantom housemate whom she'd never actually met.

She didn't dislike any of them, but Tomas was the only one she actively liked. As far as Jess was concerned, one had to be favourably disposed towards anyone who could be so amusingly self-deprecating so soon after crushing their own finger under a pallet of garden gnomes. Tomas wasn't in, so the writer didn't bother telling anyone she was leaving. Anyway, she'd be keeping hold of the keys for the remaining five weeks of the contract... just in case.

As night set in, it seemed impossible to sleep. A passionate mob of worries and questions jostled to elbow their way into the foreground of consciousness. What would happen tomorrow? What was she letting herself in for? What'd she done? Was she crazy? This was definitely a crazy thing to do. She was allowing herself to be manipulated, her vulnerabilities and weaknesses exploited. She was being led into a trap! Why did thoughts like that provoke so much excited pleasure? Jess couldn't shake the image of herself, happily skipping along, dress flouncing, pigtails bouncing, through the dappled sunlight of the forest… straight into the wolf's lair. Please don't hurt me: I'm innocent! Her insides squirmed. So many aspects of that visualisation conspired to arouse her: the hunting, the trap, the exploitation, the doomed naïvety, the violation of innocence, the injustice of the predator's reward.

Moving into the office was so obviously a bad idea – a completely mad thing to do. Mind you, at least it was an interesting thing to do. Exciting! And she needed an adventure. Moving to the big city hadn't worked out to be as much fun as she'd hoped. She spent most of her time working and commuting. And in her free time, she was generally exhausted… from all the working and commuting. A few of her friends had also moved to London recently, but they were dispersed across the metropolis and were all relentlessly busy themselves. She did have fun; some of the girls from the café really knew how to party. But she craved much more in the way of stimulation. Say what you will about putting your head inside the wolf's jaws, at least it got the adrenaline going. And she was going to be a writer… and storytellers require a wealth of interesting life experiences to draw upon.

But most importantly: he had chosen her! That was enough on its own. He was hard to please: a discerning man with high expectations. Yet ultimately, she'd won his approval and earned exceptional praise. 'Your talent is special' was such a special way of putting it (much better than saying 'you have a special talent' or 'you're especially talented'). Emphasising that her talent was both special to the world, as well as special to him. What a special game they were playing together. He clearly had special plans for Jessica because he'd seen something in her.

He had probably noticed it the first time he'd looked into her eyes, outside the office on her first visit. At that stage, he'd already picked her initial story as competition winner. But thinking back to the encounter, Jess realised there was so much more he had seen, looking inside her, in that moment. Like he saw everything… right the way down – even things she herself didn't yet know about. She had learned a lot about herself since then. He'd taught her so many things… and there was so much left to discover. His deep, dark eyes holding everything… so much of the world… so much experience… so much of all life has to offer. And he was the perfect teacher as well, making her bite into the carrot sideways as the stick drew up behind. A man who could show her the whole world. All of it! And this was his choice. She was his choice. That was her choice. Their choice.

Jess twitched restlessly all night. Well, not quite all night. She must've got to sleep eventually, because at 6.30am she awoke to the intrusive bleating of the alarm clock. Usually she'd hit the snooze button and grab another fifteen minutes, but today the energy was coursing through her veins as soon as her eyes snapped open, immediately deciding she'd wear jeans and t-shirt for the move and then change into her vintage, floral dress for the rest of the day. She just wanted to get going and get on with it.

She arrived at the office early. The Uber driver helped with her baggage and received a generous (pre-promised) tip for his trouble. It was a grim morning: overcast skies and depressing drizzle. The light but persistent precipitation posed a threat to the pile of bags and boxes now stacked outside the building. 7.46am. Charlotte probably hadn't arrived yet, but Jess pressed the buzzer just in case. What a miserable morning. Why did they have to do it so early, anyway? 8am implied there was a specific reason to do it before nine. Perhaps the receptionist normally started work at 9am, but had been made to take on this additional responsibility during her own time?

From Katya's perspective, the early start was also a good way to be sadistic to Jess, who was definitely not a morning person. The horrible bitch was probably at home in bed right now, dozing comfortably, her dreams warmed and sweetened by the knowledge that, somewhere across the city, her inferiors were both up early and suffering in the depressing rain – just because she made the spur-of-the-moment decision to say '8am'. Jess prickled with frustrated hatred. Last night, in an unsuccessful bid to steam off some of the boiling tension, she'd actually orgasmed whilst thinking that very thought. How erotically irritating!

There was a mechanical click and the heavy door pulled open. Apparently, Charlotte had arrived earlier. She now offered a guarded greeting smile alongside a polite (although not particularly friendly) 'Good morning'.

'Morning,' Jess chirped – warmth aimed to shame. Probably best to just start talking right away and keep going – not give that awkward silence a chance to set in. 'Well, at least the rain is not quite as heavy as yesterday. Oh, and I did get soaked on the way home, by the way... just as predicted.' An amiable roll of the eyes and then a gesture towards her belongings. 'So I brought my stuff... obviously. Errr... I didn't actually look yesterday. I should've asked more questions really. But I can be a bit... you know...' She wagged her head to communicate she meant 'ditsy'.

Charlotte was stony-faced and already getting down to business, pushing the door fully open and heaving a large paint can over as a doorstop. She'd clearly been instructed to physically help with the move, joining Jess on the pavement to review the workload.

'We should probably just get it all inside first.' The writer added a question mark with her eyes and Charlotte nodded in affirmation. The two women began shifting the baggage, starting a new pile, just inside the entrance. 'So, I'm sorry if you had to get up early, especially for me.'

'No problem.' The receptionist replied without discernible emotion.

'What time do you normally start work?'

'Ummm... nine.' Charlotte sounded unsure about this.

'Oh... Well, thank you. I guess this is outside your normal job description – removal work.' Jess waited until Charlotte had put down the box and turned, so her face was visible. 'Unless you often have writers staying here?'

The receptionist looked into the distance over Jess' shoulder. 'No, that's fine.'

The interrogator was annoyed with herself. Should've framed the question better. Now she'd lost the element of surprise. Although perhaps it could be turned to an advantage? 'Oh? So it's normal then: for writers to stay here?'

'Nobody normally lives here.'

'Ha! Well, like I say, sorry to be the awkward one of the bunch.' She paused but there was no reaction. 'How many writers are there?'

'No one else lives here. It's just Ms Stilenskova and I working in the building.'

Charlotte looked pleased with herself. She was operating a classic 'no comment' routine and had kept her poker face intact – hoping a blatant lack of cooperation with the conversation would make Jess feel too socially awkward to continue. But the writer already knew the only alternative to an awkward conversation with Charlotte was an even more awkward silence. So there was nothing to lose by being annoyingly persistent. She opened up another line of enquiry.

'I hope you didn't spend too long yesterday sorting things out on my behalf. It sounds like you're quite busy at the moment.'

'Oh, no. Well, yes. But that's okay.'

'Oh, I am sorry. That obviously means you do have a lot on. What is it you're busy with?'

'Just normal stuff... you know: reception, admin, emails to send and... so on.'

'And there was something Ms Stilenskova told you to put off doing because of me. I am sorry about all this – you probably have to do it later today.'

'Oh, yes... just a little... marketing thing. It's... I really can't discuss it, actually.'

'Ha, sorry to be nosy. It's just... well, to be honest, I don't really know much about the... business. I mean I'm, like... new to... everything. I haven't worked in this kind of place before... and, I mean, I don't even know what this... What is this organisation actually called?'

'What organisation?' Sharply.

'This organisation. I mean, I haven't seen any logos or business cards or anything.'

'We're independent. It's a private pr... operation. I work for Ms Stilenskova.'

'And she's a...?' Jess smiled apologetically.

'Ms Stilenskova works in the publishing industry. She's a literary agent. She's independent at the moment.'

'Oh okay. So the company has no name? There's no website or anything?'

Charlotte was staring directly at Jess now, smashing a personal record for length of eye contact as she endeavoured to work out what the writer was thinking. 'No. There's not.' The preceding pause had emboldened and highlighted the quick-fired words. The receptionist then rattled off the information she was allowed to give again. 'Ms Stilenskova works in the publishing industry. She's an independent literary agent.' (Name, rank, number, nothing more!)

They'd finished bringing Jess' belongings inside, giving Charlotte the opportunity to symbolically underline closure of the discussion. The paint pot was removed and the door's heavy slam echoed through the building.

'So where am I going to... errr...'

'I'll show you.' The receptionist grabbed a bin bag of clothes. 'Might as well take a load through with us.'

Jess plucked up a bag and followed. An uneasy mixture of eagerness and apprehension. Were they going to the playroom? Surely that would be weird, just going with the receptionist? Unless the others were there now, sleeping in the four-poster bed. Waiting... for... breakfast. Jess wasn't breakfast in bed, was she?! Oh fuck! Charlotte veered left past her desk, leading the writer into a part of the building not seen before. The area was spatially identical to the reception, at a right angle to it. There was a door on the far wall, symmetrical to the door that led through to Katya's office from reception.

The mirror-wall turned out to be L-shaped as it continued around the corner, meaning this part of the building could also be overseen from the secret room. The space was white, windowless and empty, except for a row of low tables arranged against the wall opposite the glass. Only one surface was in use, boasting a scruffy kettle, a microwave, an assortment of tins and packets, and a gleaming silver coffee machine. Still the concrete floors and the lingering smell of paint.

Charlotte marched through briskly, opening the far door. 'This is where you'll be staying.'

The room had exactly the same proportions as Katya's office. A plain, single mattress lay on the floor in the corner. A stout, lamp-bearing filing cabinet crouched alongside. Several shelving units were pushed up against the walls. A small desk sat in the middle of the room, positioned sideways from the door. And he'd ruthlessly ordered the incorporation of Jess' favourite little chair. Fuck! That really turned her on! The seat's placement meant the workstation faced directly away from the mirror-wall, but pointed towards another large mirror – tall and about three metres wide – set on the opposite wall. The confronting mirrors reflected one another endlessly. There was a door on the far wall, like the one that led from Katya's office to the storeroom/secret chamber. The receptionist dropped the bag on the bed as she wordlessly pointed out an electric radiator sitting by the desk. The heater looked antique, but did seem to be producing a decent amount of warmth. Charlotte bustled through to continue the tour.

'This leads through to... errr...' Jess' attention twinkled as her guide pulled open the far door. They entered a dark corridor-type space. To the right, the mirror had stopped, and instead there was just an ordinary wall – conspicuously lacking an entrance to the secret chamber. To the left, a flight of stairs... descending down into the shadows. Opposite was another door, which the receptionist now pushed open. 'The bathroom...'

The hesitation surrounding the noun did not bode well. And indeed, it was the most unpleasant bathroom Jess had encountered in a long while (since the latrine beach-hut in Goa). Oppressively dank, grotty and malodorous. An ugly, old toilet protruded from the side wall like a misshapen fungus. A battered sink hung off the far wall. Sitting next to it was an old, free-standing, metal bathtub. Jess had always romanticised the idea of a free-standing bath, but this one was grim and appeared not to have been used in decades. Everything looked horrible, even though it had been thoroughly cleaned yesterday. Charlotte pointed out the short hose attached to the hot tap in the sink, clearly designed to enable filling the bath.

'It only attaches to a single tap at a time. If you want a Y-shaped one – that connects to both taps – then you'll have to get it.' Charlotte eyed Jess resentfully, emphasising the word 'you'll', as if the writer had just demanded the receptionist immediately provide her with a Y-shaped... whatever-it-was. Pulling the door closed, the guide continued, 'About the bathroom... ummm... It's actually the... room that I use. So, I do... well, actually need access, during the day. So, if you could... just make sure I can access the facilities, during office hours.'

'Yes, right, yes, no… fine, no problem.' The writer bobbed her head as if she wasn't horrified. So much for being able to organise her own timetable, indulge her natural night-owl inclinations.

Charlotte was now leading Jess back through the building, pausing to draw attention to the 'kitchen area' on one of the tables. Alongside the microwave, kettle and impressive coffee machine sat a camping stove with an old-fashioned hob and pan. A rusty, red-chequered tray bore an assortment of tins and sachets: teabags, coffee, sugar, etc. There were three drinking vessels clustered in front: a tall, thin, red coffee-cup; a wide, shallow, white teacup; and a large green mug spiralled with hypnotic whirling patterns. There were three bowls and an absurdly large supply of Quaker Oats porridge: six full-size cartons.

'The stove works fine. You'll have to get water from the bathroom… for cooking and washing up and stuff.' Jess tried not to visibly recoil as the b-word was mentioned. Charlotte ducked to point out the mini-fridge squatting under the table. 'This needs to be kept on the lowest temperature setting.' She pulled it open to reveal a carton of skimmed milk and a sleek box of blueberries. 'It shouldn't be turned off.'

The receptionist was up and walking again, clearly impatient to get the move done as fast as possible. The two women began ferrying belongings through the building, Charlotte leading, Jess keeping close behind… and reopening the investigation.

'I guess we need to get this stuff out of the way as soon as possible? Might look a bit funny… if a client came by.' Charlotte didn't reply. 'By the way, what should I do when there's… visitors or… clients around? I don't want to… get in the way. Or make things look…'

'It's fine. I'll let you know, if there's anything… you need to know.' The receptionist sounded quietly pleased with her own evasive eloquence.

'Are any clients coming by today?'

'No.'

'Ha! Not trying to be nosy, it's just...' As Charlotte set the box down by the glass wall, Jess could see her face in the mirror. 'Well... it's just you have some interesting clients... I mean, we have some interesting... client.'

The receptionist had no expression, turning and walking back past Jess in an automated manner. At first, it seemed Charlotte was just getting her face out of sight before responding, but apparently she was simply going to leave the statement hanging – not respond at all.

'I mean, I'm not wanting to... obviously it's great for me. But I can't help wondering... What's his... motivation for... What's his motivation?'

Charlotte was walking stiffly, pretending to be a robot. 'Whose motivation?'

'His motivation! My client's... the Patron's... Your...? What's his motivation, for doing... all this?'

As they bent down to gather more boxes it seemed as if Charlotte's face was expressing a great deal – in a quiet, not-telling kind of way. There was some sort of emotional response, but Jess couldn't work out what it meant. Her words were equally confusing.

'Just because he's... It doesn't mean there has to be some kind of...' Resolution hardening and a rare moment of deliberate eye contact. 'Either you make the world, or it makes you.' Charlotte underlined the statement with narrowed focus and a pointed nod. Although, a moment later, she seemed to realise her poker face had dropped and the explanation abruptly restarted and veered off. 'I mean... you know, discovering new... talent'. The receptionist whisked up a box with a brusque, pulling-away movement. But her interrogator was right on her heels, hovering around the ear like a persistent wasp.

'So you know him! You know the Patron?' She couldn't prevent the excitement squeaking through.

'Well, I've…' Tone beginning to fret. 'I think maybe you should ask Ms Stilenskova about this. I'm not really… I don't know exactly. You speak to her about it… maybe.'

'But I want to know, what you know… about him.' Jess affected the manner of comradely collusion. 'Anyone would be curious.'

'Well, I don't… You need to speak to Ms Stilenskova. I'll tell her you asked.'

The last words were clearly intended as a threat. Jess pretended to be silenced by them. Really she was just waiting for another opportunity to use the mirror's reflection… when Charlotte set down the box of books.

'I saw him!'

The receptionist definitely looked shocked this time, although she erased the expression quickly. She swung around to confront her interrogator: square shoulders, defiant eyes, defensive lips. 'I can't talk to you about him! He… The… A confidential… client.' The receptionist's jaw was trembling. The two women stared at each other for a few moments, before Jess moved to diffuse the situation, politely shuffling past to set down her box (and noting that Charlotte's deep inhalation of air was accompanied by a rapid flutter of eyelids).

'Sorry, I didn't mean to…'

Okay, so the receptionist had won a brief respite – she'd earned that. They continued to move the belongings in silence as Jess reflected on what she'd learned. Not a lot of solid information, but a decent number of vague clues. Charlotte definitely knew him… for sure! That much was certain. Not a lot else was, though. What was all that about making the world? What was that supposed to mean? 'Make' as in create, or 'make' as in force? (What was the difference?) Were those the receptionist's own words? Or were those his words, that she was repeating? And what did her facial expression mean, when her defences were down? Were her defences down or just pointed elsewhere? Defensive lines inside herself? What did that even mean? She clearly felt conflicted about things... but don't we all...

Try not to over-analyse, Jess – just use your intuition. What feelings were sensed in those moments? Justification. Charlotte's tone had been one of justification. What did that mean exactly? The detective was obviously going to have to ask more questions... it was just a matter of waiting for a good opening. They continued to work in silence for a few minutes, marching back and forth mechanically. Jess snuck a few glances towards the receptionist's left-hand ring finger, trying to assess whether there'd usually be a wedding ring... but there wasn't really any way to know. After putting down a particularly heavy box, Charlotte took a moment to adjust her hair in the mirror. Jess pounced.

'That's a cool mirror. I didn't have a full-body one in my last place. But no need to worry about that here, eh.' The writer gestured expansively and gave a little tut of a laugh. 'What's the story with the mirror-wall anyway?'

'Oh... I think this place used to be a dance school or something.'

Charlotte said it casually, completely dead-pan, as if the statement meant nothing. She didn't even appear to register the horror flashing across Jess' face. A dance school? No way was it ever a dance school! The writer had considered this question. The rooms were obviously the wrong shape. The theory clearly wasn't true. In the 'Red Rose' story, the fictional Charlotte hadn't really believed the dance-school explanation. She'd merely gone along with it out of convenience. But now the real Charlotte was repeating the exact same thing. She must've read the stories! Oh shit! Reading detailed accounts of her own abject humiliation and brutal degradation, penned by the woman she now had to help move boxes. Fuck! This was excruciating!

Jess felt the blush rising, her whole body heating up with prickling embarrassment. Fortunately, the receptionist had walked off to fetch another load, ignoring the fallout from the bombshell she'd just exploded. Although perhaps that meant it wasn't really a bombshell? Maybe it was just a coincidence she came out with the dance-school idea? It was quite plausible... probably the first thing most people would be reminded of, on seeing a mirror-wall like that. However, most people would then realise that the room's the wrong shape. But the fact that Charlotte had said it at all did actually suggest she hadn't read the stories. Surely she wouldn't have the nerve to calmly quote her fictional self and deliberately reveal her knowledge of the content of 'Red Rose'? She wasn't brave enough to do that. If she had done it knowingly and proceeded to brazen it out like this, then the woman deserved an award. She wasn't capable. She hadn't read it. She didn't know anything.

Despite rationally persuading herself that what'd been said was coincidental, the writer still felt shaken. The flushing heat in her body took a considerable time to ebb away and the rest of the move was completed in cringing silence. The largest carry-bag had been left until last and Charlotte decided to let Jess deal with it. Instead, the receptionist went over to her desk and started taking things out of the drawers: a large, unmarked envelope; a smaller one marked '£500'; a keyring with an electronic fob attached. She laid them out on the workstation surface, next to her open laptop. Jess could see, in the mirror's reflection, that the computer screen was dark.

The final bag bulged with heavy, awkwardly shaped items. It had been overfilled in a way that made the short straps impractical. As Jess heaved it up, with both hands, an assortment of clumsy protrusions jammed into her shin. She advanced without grace, leaning over in an inelegant shuffle. It looked as if there was just enough room to steer clear of the furniture, but as she went past the bag clipped against the desk leg. The impact was minimal; just enough to shudder the surface of the workstation. The computer mouse quivered, the Bluetooth device interpreting the movement as an instruction to wake the sleeping laptop. The screen flashed into life, illuminating an image...

The background was pitch-black. A voluptuous white love heart floated in the middle of the screen. The top of the shape was dramatically rimmed with a thin, red outline.

Charlotte leant forward and snapped the computer shut.

FIVE
SWEET NOTHINGS

The move hadn't taken long, so Charlotte was able to start work early. Obviously Jess needed to read the much-anticipated feedback from the second story before unpacking. She sat down to contemplate the unmarked envelope lying square on the desk. It didn't feel as if he was here… yet. Although if he was, then he'd certainly be watching now. Jess opened the package and delicately removed the print-out of 'Pet Names'. There was clearly nothing else inside, but she pantomimed an attempt to search for bonus material.

As before, the papers were covered in feedback: white surfaces lined and dashed with bright red streaks and strikes. Her heart danced to celebrate the numerous ticks bestowed. Again, the marks rewarded nastiness, submission-lust, emotionality and courage going deeper. Clusters of ticks evidenced his favourite parts of the story. He clearly appreciated the physical violence and the kicking. Also the bit when the mistress told the wife to remain naked whilst serving… and gave the order without looking. Apparently, he even enjoyed the demise of poor little Puggle. Five ticks surrounded the phrase, 'feeling of defeat', in recognition of her efforts to follow his instructions and escalate along this theme.

The range of phrases underlined was eclectic: 'haunting memory', 'This was just', 'Aren't you clever girl', 'keep calm', 'no point in resisting'. Also terms such as 'sleepy eyes', 'dreamy eyes', 'woozy, weak at the knees'. How boastful and teasing it was to emphasise the expressions 'planned it all from the start', 'him definitely knowing', and 'maybe we let you play?'

'Yes please!' She spoke out loud, sparkling expression rebounding in the surrounding mirrors.

Once more, the word 'help' and its derivatives had been repeatedly underlined. Similarly, the words 'safe' and 'protect'. As before, some of the underscoring was straight and linear, whilst some curved and looped to cradle the highlighted terms. This distinction clearly meant something.

There were only minimal deletions from the text. A question mark and the words, 'What if no one was' had been smugly sliced from the sentence, 'What if no one was properly in control?' In another sentence, 'the message' had been deleted to leave the tantalising promise 'I'll show you' burning out from the page. Little rows of arrows led away from the words 'bring you to him' and also extended from the phrase 'help their marriage'. On the last page, the word 'DEEPER!' was again emboldened as the encouraging final comment. He'd also drawn a smiley face and three crossed kisses. She beamed sunshine at their first joke properly shared and raised her eyes to look into the mirror. Communicating her gratitude… just in case.

But in truth, she was disappointed with the feedback overall. He'd entirely ignored the key text. He must've noticed, but he hadn't acknowledged the message as a personal communication from the writer herself. And there was no positive comment comparable to the butterfly-tumbling phrase, 'Your talent is special'. Did that mean he was less pleased with this story? She'd done exactly as she'd been told. Unless the story wasn't as good as last time? Perhaps she'd fallen short? Maybe it was the lack of sex? Although he'd definitely enjoyed the violence and domination. It seemed harsh to withhold such a simple reward as a positive comment. But then, he was supposed to be harsh.

Jess fondly traced her finger over the bold, red letters he'd inscribed. 'DEEPER!' The thought that his hand had been on this very page made her twinkle glitter. What sort of man makes the world like this? What sort of mind envisions a game like this? What sort of character makes it a reality? What sort of confidence just invents his own rules and plays by them? She'd never met such a man. He was just so… unbelievably… Oh God! The electrifying thought tickled all over. And here she was – his naughty little writer – right here where he wanted her. Making the world. She was making the world. He was making her. A whole new world. Their world.

She looked at herself in the facing mirror, sitting with a hint of a squat as the short seat forced her knees up at an abnormal angle. The mirror-wall surrounded, so she could see herself from behind as well. Reflection echoing in endless replication. A line of doppelganger writers, sitting at identical workstations, stretching off into the vanishing distance, in both directions. Strange conditions to work under: engulfed in her own image, with him able to observe from every angle. Certainly a recipe for over-self-consciousness. And perching unnaturally low on the seat rounded her buttocks exaggeratedly… and made her bottom look bigger. At least the mirrors made the room seem expansive: important, given the total lack of windows.

She watched herself in surround-sight as she stood and turned with a dreamy expression, sidling up to the mirror-wall. He probably wasn't in yet. Likely there was no one watching now. Unless he was observing from the four-poster bed? She mused on that a moment, toying with her hair as she attempted to stare through the glass from the wrong direction. She couldn't feel his eyes. But then, would she really be able to feel them? She had definitely felt his presence before. Although obviously, that could simply be her imagination. She just felt like she'd felt his presence?

Hand on hip, Jess blew a playful kiss into the glass... just in case. Best put on nice clothes, something appropriate for a first day in the office. And of course, she had the perfect thing already selected: the flowery, vintage-style dress, acquired online for the thrilling price of £9, thanks to the calculated exploitation of two special-offer discounts combined. She'd bought it with the money he gave her for the 'Red Rose' story. Kind of like he bought it for her? Okay, probably not like that. Actually, it was her who bought it for him. Also a pleasant thought. She couldn't help but prance flirtatiously whilst undressing, even though there was no one around to impress.

A pity, because the new outfit was definitely impressive. The classic, floral-pattern dress was pleasingly colourful. The upper part was loose, narrowing to hug close around the middle, before billowing out along sharp diagonals around the hips. The flowery collar and charming cherry-buttons finished it off quaintly. Somehow, it made Jess think of a child's drawing of a dress: pencil-sketched in two dimensions. She smiled and twirled coquettishly in admiration of the design. It was cute and quirky... and went so well with her red fifties spectacles. Rounded red shoes and a dainty pair of white socks completed the look. Like an old-fashioned secretary. She'd done her make-up this morning, but the lipstick could use a touch-up – the bright colour matching the shoes and glasses. Maybe put her hair up in a loose bun? That would fit perfectly.

Jess pouted into the glass as she beautified herself. She really did look like a fifties/sixties office-girl. The fresh-faced, enthusiastic kind whose ass the boss just couldn't resist slapping. She wiggled her buttocks into the mirror and imagined him giving them an encouraging little pat. Or a forceful smack! Perhaps pulling up the circle-rim of the dress so he could spank a rosy handprint directly onto the soft, white cheek. Maybe hold her skirt up and sit back, in the executive chair, to admire the view. Her posing with buttocks plumped invitingly. A sly smile at how eager-to-please she was. Gritting his teeth and squeezing powerful hands around the curves of her hips, pulling her body back onto him. Long legs swept wide as he sits her directly between them. Feeling his big, thick dick pushing up against her vulnerability. Throbbing as the shaft begins to engorge. Surely he wasn't going to brutally fuck the youthful innocence out of his new office-girl?! Not on her first day of work?

Jess could imagine herself held tight around the waist, being bounced up and down on top of him. The boss thrusting his greedy cock in and out. Her squealing louder and louder. Him pounding her harder and harder, having his fun before pulling out to spray come all over her ass, warm spunk splashing across the cheeks. Then just dumping her exhausted body over the desk: face down, make-up streaked and smudged, hair scattered and splayed, steam-clouded glasses barely hanging from her nose, sticky streaks of come dripping down her thighs. Oh fuck! Maybe she should touch up her make-up regularly throughout the day? Surely that would tempt him to come out and ruin it. Come out and ruin her!

But first things first: a cup of tea. Jess was an avid tea-drinker and intended to use the habit to keep an eye on what was going on in the building. If Charlotte regularly heard the writer using the kettle, then she couldn't reasonably assume it was anything other than a coincidence were it to be used when something interesting happened to be occurring nearby. For example, if someone came to the door just before Jess popped out for another cuppa. Shared tea-runs might also be a good way of breaking down barriers with the receptionist, although Charlotte turned down the offer of a hot drink with an almost-offended-sounding, 'No, I don't.'

It was disgusting filling up the kettle in the bathroom. The sink was too small to get it under the tap, so Jess had to use the little hose. She would need to stock up on bottled water, to avoid ever doing this again. Of course, eventually she was going to have to use that horrible toilet. It definitely looked like the kind of seat one should hover above rather than actually make physical contact with. Surely Katya didn't use it. She must have a fully refurbished lavatory behind her own office, located on the diagonally opposite corner of the building. Jess somehow hadn't noticed the door when passing through during 'Red Rose'. But then, it'd been dark and all her attention had been focused towards the secret chamber. Which cup to use? It was obvious whose was whose. Best not use the red one! She brewed the tea in the swirling green mug and flashed a cheeky smile towards the mirror as she carried it back to her room.

She decided to keep her door, eyes and ears open whilst unpacking, as it was important to monitor any comings and goings. All the doors in the building liked to slam themselves shut, so Jess propped hers ajar with a carved wooden elephant. Heaving Eloy into place, the writer remembered, with fond irony, how much trouble it'd been to lug him thousands of miles around Asia. Backpacking Rule Number One: don't buy a super-heavy ornamental elephant on the second day of a ten-week trip.

Her bronze touch-lamp replaced the gangling office-light on the bedside table and she unpacked a few other electronic items into the desk drawers. Two large, triangular, flat-panel speakers were carefully positioned in the corners of the room, opposite the mirror-wall. Jess wasn't usually particularly into technology gadgets, but she'd fallen in love with these speakers the moment her dad unveiled them on her twenty-second birthday. The gift didn't fully make up for him eloping with a junior colleague from the planning office, but they were definitely better than the shitty little speakers she'd had before. She looked forward to getting the chance to try them out in here. The high ceilings and reflecting mirror-wall would surely make for good acoustics. She could set herself up on the mattress at the audio focal point, turn the volume up and flick through songs on Spotify. Maybe dance for him?

There was a decent amount of space on the shelves for books and clothes. Also plenty of surfaces on which to array her random collection of ornaments, trinkets and knick-knacks. The painted oriental dragon got pride of place, leading a procession of pottery ducklings across the top-centre of the desk. The mattress had been positioned in the corner, against the mirror-wall long-ways, so he'd be able to see her whole body were she to sleep naked with the covers off. There was no bedding in the room, but Jess had brought her own. After fitting the sheets and duvet, she provocatively sat Rupert the squirrel right in the middle of the pillow.

The unpacking took up most of the morning. Katya still hadn't arrived when Jess headed to the shop for bottled water and a few basic foodstuffs. It was great news that the local store sold high-quality vegetable samosas – almost as good as the ones from the corner-shop in Guildford. She bought three large triangles: the first of many such batches, no doubt. Charlotte was again snippy when offered a warm beverage, gravely informing Jess that it wouldn't be necessary to ask in future. Sitting at her workstation with a fresh mug steaming, the writer realised she was now actually going to have to start writing… here! A difficult place to work, caught in the infinite reflection of the opposing mirrors.

The desk clearly wasn't supposed to be moved; it had been carefully positioned where it was for a reason. She liked the idea of him standing behind and watching her type. Invisible save for the looming shadow of his presence. She loved working for his pleasure. And she loved that he made her sit on this ridiculous little chair. The possibility of secret supervision was tantalising… but distracting. Maybe she should read 'Pet Names' again and really absorb his feedback properly. Actually, she should probably reread both stories to lead into writing Part Three. The process was a long one and the writer couldn't help fiddling around making edits, even though the stories had already been submitted. She ate a sandwich and samosa at her desk as she mused and dawdled around with the text.

Ms Stilenskova didn't arrive until 2pm. Jess heard the front door slamming as Katya stormed into the building and immediately began verbally laying into the receptionist. The writer couldn't make out what was being said, even with ears cocked and pointed intently out of the door. The tone was biting; Charlotte was certainly getting an earful. The receptionist's responses (if any) were totally inaudible. Maybe she could get a bit nearer by making a cup of tea? No, it would be too risky. And the agent's angry voice was moving now… drawing closer. Shit! She was coming! The writer scrambled back to her desk.

Katya burst in without knocking, flashing hostile eyes around the room and then frowning emphatically as she settled her glare. Jess nearly said 'Good morning' but stopped as she remembered it wasn't morning. Did 'Good afternoon' sound a bit critical, given that the agent had apparently only just showed up for work? 'Hiya,' she found herself chiming over-enthusiastically, cringing to realise that she was using the exact same tone Katya had mocked when reading out Charlotte's intra-marital texts. She continued bubbling to disguise the discomfort. 'Got myself settled in okay. Love the mirrors!'

The agent's expression concisely communicated that she thought someone who looked like Jess should actively shun mirrors. Nevertheless, she decided to emphasise the point with a couple of thought-provoking observations. 'Why you dress as old woman, eh? This old-fashioned stuff looks stupid – out-of-date.' Jess slid her eyes down the agent's body. As usual, a sharp suit and killer shoes. She looked amazing. 'And you shouldn't wear this dress anyway. It's too small for your body.'

The writer concentrated on Ms Stilenskova's feet as she struggled not to try, not to blush. She could feel the tingle though, a frustrated excitement prickling the hairs on the back of the neck. Fuck! The Russian was so wonderfully mean. Jess glanced up to notice Katya's eyes had fallen on Rupert the squirrel, sitting on the pillow.

Surely not?!

Of course not.

'Don't lose the keys.' The agent turned to march away. A whiplash of a ponytail-flick.

Jess twisted to look into the mirror-wall. Had he come too? Was he here? Could she feel him? Not sure... maybe? The receptionist was clinking about in the kitchen area. Perhaps it was time for the writer to grab another cuppa. Charlotte appeared especially cowed and sullen, still reeling from the scolding and even more desperate than usual to avoid eye contact. She was using the gleaming silver machine to make her boss a coffee (in the thin red cup). Measuring out precise quantities of mineral water and ground beans. As meticulous as a Nobel-winning chemist, carefully putting the finishing touches to a life's work.

The receptionist currently looked particularly unreceptive, but Jess had been angling for another chance to ask about the love heart image on the laptop. At the time, Charlotte had ignored the writer's questions on the subject and tried to distract attention by reeling off a load of information about the living arrangements (modems, internet, light switches, electricity fuse boxes, key-fobs, etc.) Jess had ignored the attempts to fob her off with trivia and decided to re-raise the love heart question as soon as possible. The arresting image was playing on her mind, slightly disturbing. And the receptionist's secretive reaction had confirmed it was somehow significant... somehow relevant.

'Oh yes...' Jess mused, as if only just remembering. 'What was that image on your screen earlier?'

Charlotte kept her eyes down as she huddled preciously over the coffee. 'What image?'

'The love heart. The white and red love heart against the black. What was that?'

'I-don't-know-what-you're-talking-about.' The words dashed into each other as they scrabbled to arrange a defensive line.

'The image you were... The picture on your screen. You were working on something?'

'No. I don't know what you're talking about.'

'Oh, right. Well, I just thought... it looked nice, is all. Not nice, I mean... it looked, kind of... sinister. You know, in a good way.'

Charlotte blanked the comment, cupping the coffee carefully with both hands as she turned and left. She truly was fucking annoying, one of those irritating people who love keeping secrets. Always that tell-tale hint of triumphalism in her not-telling near-expressionlessness. Bitch!

Oh well, back to work. It was easy for Jess to spend hours perusing her own writing, unable to resist the urge to make edits and ponder possible alterations. Vaguely planning the next stage, absently scribbling notes, trying to work out what was going to happen next. Daydreaming about... him. How could she write under these conditions? Forced to sit on this wonderfully humiliating chair. Centre-stage in the reflective focus of these gargantuan, surrounding mirrors. Illuminated in a spotlight she couldn't escape. Him able to observe from every angle, reading her face and body as easily as her stories. She'd exposed herself, showed him so much already. Surely it was time he showed her a thing or two? He'd promised! Distracting thoughts. Just try to concentrate: Part Three. Need to be productive on the first day in the office. But where did all the time go? How long had she been fiddling about? Need to start actually writing now. Maybe fetch another tea and then get straight down to it.

Charlotte didn't share her new colleague's passion for hot beverages and only made one drink for herself during the day.

However, she did manage to eat an enthusiastic three bowls of Quaker Oats. She must have a bladder made of steel, because she only used the toilet once. Of course, it was excruciatingly embarrassing as the receptionist hesitantly knocked on the ajar door and awkwardly shuffled through. She looked especially ashamed trailing back on the return journey. Jess didn't see Ms Stilenskova again until the agent left, around 5pm. The Russian came by the writer's office to check that she was alright... and not feeling too intimidated about spending her first night alone in the strange building. Not really! Katya just swung open the door, stabbed a claw and two eyeballs towards Jess and snapped the instructions:

'Don't touch anything! Don't nose about!' She snuffled her nostrils in mock-mimicry of rabbit-girl and stalked off.

Charlotte finally made to leave around seven, coming through to check that Jess had absorbed all the important information about modems, lights, doo-dahs, etc. The writer assured her everything was fine, except she didn't have a contact phone number in case anything went wrong. The receptionist wasn't keen to impart the data, but Jess was persistent and her case logical. Charlotte eventually agreed to scribble some digits on a piece of paper. There was the suspicion that the number was fake, but that theory couldn't immediately be tested.

As the front door slammed shut, Jess was supposedly alone in the building. As if! This was surely the time he'd be most likely to watch. Obviously she was going to have a snoop around after the others left. He'd know she'd do that. So what would he do? Perhaps he was waiting for her? For her to come... and find him... in the secret room – in his lair. Waiting for her to walk into his trap. She'd been told not to 'nose about', so surely there'd be trouble if those instructions were disobeyed. What would he do if he caught her snooping around in his den? Maybe that was exactly the plan? Maybe she'd meet him tonight? Oh fuck! But she obviously couldn't start exploring immediately. Give it at least ten minutes. Got to play the game properly... even if you want to lose. Her feet twitched relentlessly, however she managed to give it a whole fifteen minutes before allowing them to go anywhere.

Charlotte had turned off all the lights outside the writing room and the building was cold beyond the modest range of Jess' sturdy, old radiator. In the gloom, she watched her own shadowy reflection ghosting along the mirror-wall. This place was definitely going to get spookier as night drew in. What did the receptionist say about light switches? The writer used her phone-torch to locate an eccentric-looking box of controls on this side of the entry-partition wall. The old tube-lights along the ceilings flickered into life. Several of them strobe-spluttering, one audibly fizzling in a desperate effort to keep up. The intense, artificial glare was unpleasant, but Jess decided she'd leave all the lights on constantly. Not great from an energy-saving perspective, but if she was going to sleep alone in this big, empty building then it sure-as-hell wasn't going to be in complete darkness. The door-entry button was located next to the light controls, meaning every time it was used, the receptionist must have to leap up and then quickly sit back down.

Jess swung open the front door just to catch a glimpse of some natural light. But the sun had set and night already fallen. The writer double-checked the door was secure after it smashed shut. Although of course, the predator that stalked her was inside already. A reflected expression of blank innocence as she padded through the reception area. A deep breath before pushing the door to Ms Stilenskova's office. Oh? Oh shit! Locked! Jess hadn't previously noticed the lock set below the door handle. Actually, it looked recently fitted: shiny, new brass. That's irritating. She'd known there was a good chance the secret room would be inaccessible, but was still hoping to get further than this. Might as well give him the satisfaction of seeing her cartoon 'damn-you've-foiled-me' face.

It was never going to be that easy anyway. Plan B was obviously the stairs, the ones by her bathroom, descending to… Satan-knows-where. She made her way back through the building. The corridor area at the top of the steps was dark and cold. Eloy the elephant gatekeeper changed doors, so the glare from the room improved illumination out here. Jess searched for switches or controls, but there didn't appear to be any. Shining her phone-torch towards the ceiling, it seemed there were no lights fitted in this area at all. Pointing down the stairs, the modest wisp of torch lost itself in the shadows. She couldn't make anything out. The only sound was the intense beating of her own heart – a drama queen who'd suddenly decided to seize centre stage.

Jess didn't realise the stairs were metal until feeling the clank of her shoe on the first step. There wasn't a handrail either side, so she leant against the wall for security. Hesitantly proceeding one measured step at a time, carefully scouting ahead with the feeble beam of her torch. The staircase was hollow, with no vertical axis (i.e. they were the kind of steps where someone hidden below could reach out to grab your ankle). Oh shit! But the good news was they didn't go down as deep as first feared. There was a wall ahead, with a square platform at the corner of the staircase. Only a few further steps after that. Reaching the corner and entering a cluttered storage area, a narrow passageway that looped back on the stairs to run underneath the bathroom. Various strange shapes huddled in the shadows, whilst towering shelving units loomed above, garbed in cloaks of black tarpaulin.

Deep breaths as the explorer ventured onward. Down the last few steps… into the under-passage. On closer inspection, the strange shapes were an eclectic mix of mundane items: a broken guitar; a Henry hoover; a bicycle's skeleton; pool cues; spades. The below-stairs area stored decorating materials: long-rollers; a couple of ladders; fragrant stacks of paint cans. Jess poked her head behind the covers on one of the shelving units, the ancient dust hitting her face like a swarm of undead locusts. She discovered badminton rackets, shuttlecocks and some rolled up tangles of net.

Pushing on deeper, she drew level with the top of the stairs. The passage narrowed as it passed underneath the bathroom on the floor above. The tall, hooded shelves leant in overhead. One uncovered metal unit was filled with boxes of old magazines. Jess wondered how many cases of National Geographic crouched in dark places all over the world. Deeper and deeper… A shattered pool table propped up against the wall. A burial mound of obsolete landline phones. A pile of chairs…

'Chairs! I knew it. I fucking knew it!'

Obviously there were other seats in the building. Although on closer inspection, all the furniture was broken. Actually, it had been decisively destroyed, the wood snapped and splintered. Or even cut? Some of the breaks seemed to be clean. Sawed? No. Jess wouldn't claim to be an expert in this area, but it appeared more likely that the wood was sliced with one swift blow. An axe? Saw or axe? Jesus Christ! This was neither the time nor place for a question like that. She looked around anxiously. Courage! DEEPER!

Coming to a turn in the passageway, a jumbled fuse box hung off the wall directly ahead. The corridor must turn right behind that final set of shelves to pass under the forbidden chamber. Or perhaps there'd be stairs leading up to it? Would he be waiting? The anticipation tinkled. However, as she approached it became apparent there was no corner: just a solid brick wall. A dead-end. Shit! Although one of the bricks jutted out conspicuously. Obviously it wasn't a hidden lever operating a secret door. Jess pressed the brick quickly several times before her rationality had a chance to catch up. Nothing happened, of course, but it was worth a try. Actually, she did attempt to push a few other potential clandestine levers. They also turned out to be ordinary bricks.

Imagine there was a hidden lever. The kind where the wall suddenly rotates and you end up on the other side. In the place below the secret room. Beneath it! Perhaps even worse things happen down there?! She visualised being transported to the other side, naked flames dancing with shadows… torches on stone columns… the silhouette of a tall man, standing silently across the chamber. Facing directly. Watching… fierce eyes burning out of the darkness. Too gloomy to see anything else… just the outline of a muscular figure, unclothed from the waist up, standing and waiting patiently. His posture changing now; only a slim movement, but startling. The head dropping minutely, brow sharpening, shoulders angling forward. The body language of a predator, in the moment before moving in on cornered prey.

The expression on her face in the moment she realises she's gone too far… been drawn in too deep… and now suddenly wanting to escape. Escape! Panic gripping hold, hands scrabbling at the wall's lost levers. Nothing there! Just normal bricks. Him advancing, slow stealthy paces… slinking. No need for him to rush; there's no escape for her now. Relishing the scent of her fear. Sadism salivating… building an appetite. Desperate attempts to reverse the rotating wall, frantically clutching at the brickwork, fists beating hopelessly against stone… helplessly. Screaming. Pleading. The predator moving slower and slower, drawing closer and closer. Really wallowing in the suffering of anticipation. The terrified prey unable to bring herself to turn as he looms up behind. Face against the cold stone, eyes tight-shut, arms spread and palms flat against the wall, whole body quivering, voiceless-ness shuddering. A dark shadow falling. The warm breath of a red-blooded carnivore on the back of her neck. A long pause…

Oh fuck! Snap out of it. Jess was allowing her imagination to run away with itself as usual. Those kinds of thoughts were for writing time and this was investigation time. She gave the wall a tentative knock, tilting her head to listen for hollowness. Was that the sound of hollowness or solidity? It wasn't actually that easy to tell. Oh well, lucky there was a Plan C: finding another way in from the outside – a back door. After all, if there was no internal route to the secret room, avoiding Katya's office, then on the day of the first interview he must've used a side entrance. It would probably be locked, but maybe the key fob would work?

It was a relief to get out of the passageway, up the stairs and back into the light. She snatched the key as she marched through her room and out past the kitchen area. Embarrassingly startled as the room door crashed closed behind, but composure quickly regained. The winter evening bit cold as soon as the front door cracked ajar. It hadn't rained since morning, yet stepping outside, Jess could sense that was about to change. There was a tension in the stillness of the air, the atmosphere anticipating a storm. Crossing her arms with a resolute shiver, she hurried along the face of the building and around the corner.

Soon she was peering into the alley that separated the office from the residential buildings behind. It was dark down there too. Her phone-torch was getting a lot of use tonight. She edged past a couple of large bins. No windows overlooked the winding passageway. Following around the route dead-ended, the buildings coming together as if by surprise, like drunks bumping in the night. There was an entrance though: an oversized, rusty door that must lead through to the secret chamber. It was locked, of course. The keyhole demanded a large, old-fashioned, iron key. A metallic rumble as Jess pushed against it impatiently. He would hear that. She stopped and listened… Nothing. And no windows or anything. Shit! Jess tilted in to knock a graceful rat-a-tat-tat, stooping so her mouth hovered around the keyhole. A polite, little voice.

'Please, let me in.'

He didn't reply. Bastard! Was there a Plan D? Go through the bins? Jess screwed up her face at the stench. Maybe another time. What else could she do? Try and sneak into Katya's office during the day, perhaps? That would be risky. And would there even be an opportunity? Charlotte was probably irritatingly conscientious about all of her responsibilities and locking Ms Stilenskova's office was likely one of them. Shit! Jess left the alleyway and trailed back into her strange, new home.

Okay, she would have to do some actual work now. She hadn't really done any proper writing today. What the fuck had she been doing all afternoon? She could get some done now though. It always seemed more natural to write during the night anyway. Especially this kind of thing. A quick Pot Noodle, return Eloy to his post at the kitchen-bedroom door, then back to the workstation with a brimming mug of tea. How to begin the next story? What had she decided again? She couldn't really think, but needed to write something. Just write anything. Jess placed her hands on the keyboard and they began to move.

About fucking time! He sidled up to the mirror-wall. Leaning on the glass to watch over her shoulder as the letters popped up on the screen. He smiled at her enthusiasm. She was a good girl. A good little bad girl. His good little bad girl. He'd shown her her own beautiful weakness and now she would do anything for him. She was his, to use however he pleased. Look at her... sitting on that silly, little chair, slanting forward and curling her lower back as she types, presenting him with that peachy, round butt. Her whole body curving and shaping at him. Posture pleading with him to just come and get her.

COME AND TAKE WHAT IS YOURS!

He didn't need to read her body language anyway. She was begging for it. Literally... explicitly... begging for it! And he was growing impatient. Muscles tightening, mind pacing aggressively, fingers flexing to grip. It was becoming hard... to remember why... he was still holding back? Why not just storm out, burst in, grab that little bitch and slam her over the desk. Pin both arms behind her back, rip those panties off... stuff them into her mouth to muffle my screams. And you can fuck me any way you want to... or beat me... or whip me... whatever you want!

I AM YOUR TOY!

The distant rumble of thunder added to the drama, so she wrote it in.

She was just so isolated and vulnerable here: such an exposed target. Foreseeing the silent attack of a calm predator. Hunting her down, cornering her, subduing his prey with ease. Just slinging her over his broad shoulder, locking a strong arm around the thighs and carrying her off like booty from a slave raid. Marching through the building with purpose... abducting her... taking her... back to his lair. Where he could do anything he wanted with her. Tear that nice, new dress to pieces, slap those cheeks pink, hurl her onto the bed like a rag-doll... a sex toy...

FUCK HER LIKE THE FILTHY FUCKING SLUT THAT I AM!

A patronising smile from behind the looking glass. Her eagerness was very sweet, but her immature ploy wasn't really that clever – not nearly subtle enough. It was never going to be that easy... and the writer knew it. He watched her shoulders sink as she stopped typing. A heaving sigh and a forlorn expression longing into the mirrors. She stood, ostensibly to check the cable attachments on the back of the laptop. Bending over the desk to adjust the cords. A tickling wiggle, her hand drawing back to pull up the rim of her skirt. Cheeky little bitch! He'd a good mind to go through there and teach her a lesson. Mark that white skin red like a bad story.

The rain was falling heavy now, hammering down on the corrugated iron roof. The thunder rolled closer.

He could see what she was thinking. She was still writing her thoughts directly onto the screen. Wondering whether she should take off her dress? Stand in front of the mirror and strip down to her underwear? Return to the desk and carry on typing in just her little white panties and matching bra. Should she actually do that? Or just write about doing it? Which was the better tease?

Or she could write about it and then do it for real? The thought of undressing for him made her want to touch herself.

The writer stopped. He watched her fingers stroking up the inside of her thigh. She was wet. Clasping herself now, head lolling back, eyelids shuddering shut, vulva throbbing, pussy drenching with thirst. She held her eyes closed, imagined opening them into the facing mirror and seeing his reflection behind her. Waiting… silent stillness. Muscular arms folded over bared chest. Eyes gleaming like knives in the dark.

Not just looming up behind – all around her, echoing, surrounding the writer infinitely… fantasy reflecting reality reflecting fantasy… mirrors within mirrors… stories within stories. She was becoming lost… and yet charging on, headlong through the darkness… fingertips moving faster and faster… rattling on the keyboard like bullets from a Gatling gun. Writing continuously, fervently, manically… on and on… time drawing into the zone… minutes becoming hours. All the while, her own seductions rebounding back and turning against her. The atmosphere was laden, but the sexual energy still gushing, spilling, flooding out… bouncing off the walls and mirrors… reverberating inside with ever-escalating intensity.

And the epic storm raged on, the building a metal drum as the chatter of keystrokes drowned in the clattering rain. The thunder seemed to approach from every direction, booming closer and closer.

Jess fell from the chair as if struck by lightning, rolling onto hands and knees – electrified. Facing directly towards the mirror-wall, pupils wide and sparkling with energy. Staring upwards: straight into his eyes as if there were no barrier at all. She scuttled over on all fours, clutching the glass and using it to pull herself up. Pushing back off to stand before him. Swaying – too much energy to remain still. Melted-plastic knees bending under the heavy weight of lust. Looking directly into him with wild, desperate, grasping eyes. Cheeks blossoming in the monsoon of desire. She bit her bottom lip. The gesture was intended as coy and flirtatious, but she bit so zealously the skin nearly broke.

    She used a cooling tremor to try and capture some composure. Squeezing a hand around her waist and pushing down into the curve of her hip, posing for him. She wanted to perform a slow striptease… as Katya had done. Seduce him gracefully: a heavenly temptress… elegant and demure. But who was she kidding? She didn't have the patience for that now. Her left hand flicked backwards to unzip, her right simultaneously grabbing the circle rim of the dress and pulling it up and over her head. Imagine him doing that to her, violently tearing the dress off in one sweeping movement. And then ripping her underwear to confetti. Him fully clothed in a slick, black suit as she blushed before him in glorious nakedness. Fingers tweaking around a tickling nipple. Reaching down to skitter playfully around her clit. She wanted fingers inside her.

    But looking down, her hands were still moving frantically over the keyboard. She was sitting fully unclothed on the chair, buttocks rounded, back straightened, head high, breasts pushing forward… straining to keep up with eagerly pointing nipples. Soft ass-cheeks pressing against the hard plastic of the seat. Typing away enthusiastically, head bobbing to keep rhythm with the raining keystrokes. Working hard… for him, her Boss… her Big, Bad Boss! He was so mean! Humiliating his writer by making her sit on this comical little chair. Forcing her to work all day… all night. Exploiting her weakness. Her pussy was soaking.

    Imagine getting summoned into his office for a supposed misdemeanour, knowing he just wanted to indulge his lusting love of power. Sitting behind a big desk with legs crossed wide, insulting her, belittling her, reprimanding her, chucking orders about for her to run around catching, fetching and picking up. 'Yes, Sir!' Punishing her, unfairly, even though she'd been a good girl.

Ordering her to strip off and work the rest of night stark-naked: a proper dressing-down! Toiling away for his pleasure. All part of his evil masterplan... his villainous scheme. He was the bad guy and she wanted him to win. Jess would do anything she could to help him... whatever he told her.

Oh God! Why didn't he just come and get her? His bad-girl writer performing her servitude naked. How could any red-blooded predator resist? Surely it was against the rules for her to touch herself like this? Surely this was professional misconduct? She should be disciplined, severely punished. What does it take to get a beating around here? How could he let her get away with all this? Playing her devious games – she deserved to be put in her place. If he was really strict, then he'd surely know this was the time to stamp his boot down... hard! His writer was being overly mischievous... getting away with all sorts... needed to be brought back into line...

MAYBE YOU AREN'T THAT HARSH AND STRICT AFTER ALL?

The sentence she wrote after that one was deleted immediately. But he still had time to read the words before they scurried off the screen. Had she gone too far?

A pause...

The full fury of the tempest was directly overhead now, relentless rain pummelling and panelling. Jess sat back and looked up at the roof, listening as a sprawling loll of thunder broke itself open and shattered across the sky, growling echoes resounding in the aftermath.

Bang!

Jess jolted in shock! That wasn't the storm. The reverberating bang was one of the doors in the building slamming itself shut... being slammed shut! The writer sat bolt upright. Someone was here! Someone was inside. Which door was it? The front door? The door to Katya's office?

A loud clap of thunder struck the building and everything plunged into darkness. The lights went out, both inside and outside the room. Just an eerie glow emanating from the computer screen as the real world vanished into the shadows, the laptop using its own battery: the power had totally gone... been turned off! Holy fucking shit! Fuck, fuck, fuck! He was coming for her... really coming for her now! She'd gone too far. Shit, shit, shit! She'd pushed her luck, crossed the line... and now she'd really get it. Her mind was spinning. An endless line of writers shuddered in the cold, dark glass. She had forgotten how to exhale... or inhale... the breath sticking in her throat. It was too much! She'd thought she wanted it, but it was too much. There's a difference between fantasy and reality! She'd gone too far – too deep – deeper and deeper... Now she wanted to go back... wanted to take it all back. She didn't mean it. Not really. Not like this. Oh fuck. Oh shit. Oh fuck!

But it was too late. She'd asked for it – wound him up, provoked him. There was no going back. She was being hunted! A little slither of excitement stirred in the tension, but nothing else did. She couldn't move... apart from the trembling. Couldn't hear... except for the rain. Darkness surrounded as she sat in the computer screen's ghostly spotlight... and waited... for him... long moments dragging into torturous seconds. Those seconds then placed on the rack and stretched into agonising minutes. She sat and listened... but he didn't come.

It'd been at least five minutes now. Perhaps he wasn't coming? Maybe he hadn't turned off the power? Possibly he wasn't even in the building? It could just be that the electricity was outed by the storm? That did actually make perfect sense. Charlotte had said something about it being important for Jess to listen to the information regarding the fuse box, because... What was it she said again? Well, presumably the fuse box info was significant, precisely because power failure wasn't so improbable. It was a funny old building after all. And at least Jess knew where the fuse-box wa...

Oh fuck! That was the last thing she needed: having to go down those spooky stairs again… through that creepy tunnel. Oh shit!

But fuck it! It was only a bit of gloom, and she'd already proven she wasn't afraid of the dark. Courage. DEEPER! Pull yourself together and stand up! Jess put on her dressing gown. She decided proper shoes were a requirement for this mission, although the clumpy walking boots might've been an overkill. She didn't like the idea of the room door slamming shut behind, so Eloy would have to switch posts again. A deep breath before pulling open the door leading to the stairs. She was quite glad to have Eloy for moral support. They'd travelled across Asia together, after all – an emboldening thought. She yanked open the door and set down the elephant gatekeeper. The phone-torch's beam jabbed around quickly, checking that she was indeed alone… at the top of the stairs. DEEPER!

Her heavy boots clanged on the metal steps. It was even darker than before, only a faint hint of laptop-light emanating from the room. Just her piddling phone-torch against the pitch-black. Don't imagine grabbing hands from under the stairs, no point thinking about that. On the corner platform now, turning to make the last few steps… into the under-passage. Remember, the dark shapes are all just mundane objects. The shelves simply filled with piles of old stuff. There was no one hiding behind the shadowy, tarpaulin cloaks. There was space for someone to hide between the towering shelving units. But there couldn't be anyone hiding there… wouldn't be anyone there. Although if there was, then they had the perfect place from which to launch an ambush. Numerous spots ideal for a surprise attack, from either side of the tunnel. Oh shit! Courage. DEEPER!

There was no one lying in wait. Just a load of now-familiar objects: an old guitar; a Henry hoover; a bicycle's skeleton; a graveyard of old phones; a pile of chairs hacked to pieces by a man with an axe. Oh fuck! Courage! Keep going. Coming up to the fuse box now: a strange contortion of wires, boxes and sticking-out bits. What did Charlotte say about it again? Why hadn't Jess been listening? Oh, wait a minute: a row of those little levers, all facing the same way... except one. This was recognisable. Just flick the odd lever back in line with the others, right? She could feel the reaction as soon as she pushed it: humming and buzzing back to life. There was still no light down here, of course, but she could sense a faint wisp of illumination from the floor above. Job done. Success!

Turning around, Jess saw movement at the far end of the passageway – a figure! She gasped in panic, hands flying up, legs twisting on the spot, caught in the headlights – totally cornered! But the other person was panicking as well, hands flying up, legs twisting on the spot... Hang on a second. That wasn't another person. That was her own reflection. There was now a tall mirror at the other end of the passage. It hadn't been there before, for certain – she'd definitely have noticed. Someone had just put it there! Oh shit! But it was large, so wouldn't be easy to move around stealthily. It couldn't have been put there just now – impossible. Although why hadn't she spotted it before? Maybe it'd been covered by a tarpaulin... which had now been removed? Someone had removed it! Why? Why do that? More likely that the cover had just slipped off. Probably she caught it whilst passing and it slid down without her noticing. Don't worry about it. Don't be such a wimp.

Her reflection approached as she walked back along the passageway. She could definitely sense the light from the room. And look: there was a crumpled cover lying at the foot of the mirror. A blanket so thin she wouldn't have noticed it slipping off. Nothing to worry about. Although looking at it another way, a light covering might've been used especially because it could be removed quietly... deliberately. Her nerves bristled into a faint jangle, a wind-chime in the breeze. A wind-chime that was about to be smashed to pieces... by a projectile hurtling from nowhere.

It happened as Jess put her boot on the first step. Music! Loud music! Speakers roaring into life: sound exploding from her room at full volume. Violins, a piano, a romantic ballad, a familiar tune. Her sound-system blasting full-pelt. Someone had turned it on… someone was up there… in her room!

Aghast, she took a step back… into something… something behind her… standing behind her… someone standing behind her! She caught her scream whilst it was still in her throat. His arms came around, scooping her off the floor, cradling. She twisted frantically, body straightening, legs shooting out. Boots hitting the wall and pushing hard, with enough power to springboard back. Him moving with her and holding tight as they span around. Seeing their reflection in the magically appearing mirror for a second: a tall man calmly holding a terrified young woman whose heavy boots swung towards the glass. The image falling away in a shatter of jagged shards.

Embracing her solidly now, folding her body into his strong arms. His chin on her forehead… the graze of stubble. Him saying something. Whispering something. Words in her ear. She could hear them without remembering them. She was good at that. His voice very deep… deeper and deeper… It was okay. No need to worry about anything. He was here now. He was here and everything was okay.

Sweet nothings whispered in her ear as he carried her up the stairs.

SIX
THOSE THREE LITTLE WORDS

Charlotte's knees had grown accustomed to the cold stone, but it was still painful to maintain this rigid posture for so long. At least the mistress hadn't sprinkled grains of rice under the kneecaps this time, as had happened, more than once, during 'training'. Such brutal disciplinary practices had helped hone an impressive 'puppy-pose': head up, eyes fixed ahead, back curling to accentuate rounding buttocks and perking breasts, begging-dog arms bent up in the air at chest level. Bottom hovering above the ankles... never allowed to rest on them, even for a second (Charlotte winced). She was naked, except for the thin, leather collar buckled around her neck and the fluffy, plug-in doggie-tail tickling the soles of her feet. Hair secured in tight, girlish pigtails. Slutty make-up exaggerated to an appropriately undignified level. Face powdered white, cheeks rouged red. The mistress had added a shiny, black puppy-nose in a final humiliating flourish.

After forty minutes of waiting, the stress of anticipation ached worse than the physical discomfort. Katya seemed on edge as well.

Charlotte could feel the tension rippling in the chain stretched between the two women. From this side, the mirror-wall reflected no better than glass, so the wife could only make out the mistress' transparent silhouette enthroned on the tall, mahogany chair behind. Katya's statuesque pose overstated calmness, but she'd chain-smoked the last three cigarettes without pause and couldn't stop fiddling about with her phone. It was hard to tell whether she was more nervous… or more excited. She was often difficult to read under that un-melting mask.

Nevertheless, Charlotte had learned plenty of interesting things about her husband's lover during their recent time together. Especially noting the little affinities that she and the mistress shared because of him. For example, on several occasions, Katya was observed restraining her temper using a deep breath accompanied by a tell-tale flutter of eyelids: a 'calm spell' as he called it. He'd also taught his wife this technique (although she generally used it to cool anxiety rather than anger). These touching intimacies somehow helped Charlotte grow close to the mistress, giving their strange, new relationship a twisted kind of romantic depth. She loved that Katya showed no fondness whatsoever – a sharp-cut ice-sculpture of Venus, totally impervious to warmth.

Charlotte hadn't told her husband anything about what had gone on during the fortnight he'd been away. The texts exchanged had been entirely innocent and (unusually) they hadn't spoken over the phone or Skyped. That didn't necessarily mean he was unaware of what was happening, of course. On the contrary, his wife had undertaken the training in the firm belief that he did know. She'd envisaged her husband secretly pulling the strings from above – manipulating everything. Whenever the mistress hurt her, she felt his hand steering it. She visualised him setting tasks and training regimes from behind the scenes, musing on appropriate punishments and humiliations; conspiring with his lover, against his wife; cooking up inventive torments together.

Katya had described herself as 'being restrained' in the way she treated Charlotte: keeping that white skin largely unmarked and unbruised. 'Saving it' for him. Did this comment (and the particular intonation used) suggest that he was directing things and actively restraining his lover? The wife could imagine her husband soothing the fires inside his passionate mistress – tempering them – using them to forge something exquisite. An expert craftsman, his creations always so decadently beautiful. She loved being part of his masterplan – being led along in such supreme confidence.

But kneeling here, in the dreaded moment, Charlotte had finally found true doubt. What if he didn't know? What if this really was Katya's own plan? Katya was clearly mental! A certain kind of goddess: the kind with the legendary reputation for destructive caprice. Mad impulses always destined to devastate the lives of the innocent mortals huddled below. Although Charlotte wasn't really that innocent anymore. After all, she'd taken the initiative by failing to text her husband before bringing his charger to the office that fateful day. If she had, he may have told her not to worry about it, that he'd buy a new one at the airport or something. She'd deliberately decided not to give him the chance to do that. She had gone because she wanted to go – wanted to find out more.

She'd got more than she bargained for, of course. But really, the wife had encouraged the mistress... gone along with her... a long way. A very long way to end up here, unclothed, vulnerable and doubting everything. In an absurdly weak position. She used to have the moral high ground, but that'd been decisively abandoned. And it wasn't about morality in any case. At the end of the day, she was the one who was naked, on a leash, with a pom-pom doggie-tail sticking out of her ass. And whatever she did, he and his mistress would still have each other... and their special, secret world. She was the one with everything to lose. Oh Jesus! What if he didn't know? What if this was a mistake? A big mistake? Her big mistake? She wasn't supposed to speak, but had to ask...

'Does he know?'

'Shut the fuck up.'

His lovers waited for him in their respective positions… only a few more minutes. A creaking clink in the tautening leash as they watched him enter the reception area. His expression light and casual – like he had no idea what was about to happen. Oh God! But maybe he was just playing it cool? Backpack in hand, dark cloak of a long coat swinging from his shoulders. Approaching the stand, surely he'd spot there were two coats already hanging. Although he'd not seen his wife's new cream jacket before. Pretending to notice nothing, he balanced an even triangle between the three coats and six hooks. He breezed through to the office and entered as if expecting to be greeted in there, eyes beginning on Katya's empty chair, before swooshing steadily around towards the magic-wall. Mock innocence as he sidled up to the glass. A knowing look… but that didn't mean he knew everything.

He always insisted on wearing that same dark t-shirt whenever flying. The 'travel top' had visited over forty countries, so was now worn and weathered. It looked especially faded alongside the fresh, black jeans. Charlotte had pointed out (numerous times) that he could take it with him without actually wearing it, but apparently the shirt had 'earned character'. And in any case, her husband wasn't 'one for pretending everything has to have a rational reason… most "reasons" are just invented afterwards'. He regularly deployed different variations of this typically abstract (and profoundly hypocritical) argument as a strategy to transform light nagging campaigns against him into gentle chiding operations against her.

She did like the way the top fitted though. It hailed from a time when his slim body had been less muscular, so the shirt was now quite tight. Not overly-so, just enough to shape a faint fossil of the well-defined chest and abs below. Tongue in cheek as he casually adjusted his hair in the mirror – a few streaks of grey rustling amidst the lush tangle of dark. His bicep flexed as thumb and forefinger stroked up the shaded carve of stubble under his chin. Such an attractive man; facial features and contours angled the perfect balance between sharp and smooth. Strong brow, chiselled cheekbones, full lips. His current expression was flirtatious. Mouth held straight to emphasise the knowing smile twitching in the corner of an eye. But how much did he really know? If he knew, then this was masterful composure: a temperate coolness even more impressive than Katya's icy cold. But maybe he simply didn't know. Oh God!

He turned towards the corner door. Katya was standing now, her slender slip of a little black dress beautifully disproportionate to those oversized biker boots. The leash dropped from the mistress' hand and slapped the floor.

'Go hide.' An air of anticipation in the husk of her voice. 'And don't let him see that fat fucking ass sticking out.'

Puppy used her teeth to pick up the lead's loop-handle and scuttled behind a nearby clutter of drape-laden cages. One final glimpse of her husband strolling through the office, gait exclaiming, 'What a lovely day for a riverboat ride. Yes, of course I'm sure there's no waterfalls ahead.'

Some very long seconds...

All the candles shivered as the inner door swung open. The light pad of trainers on stone. The strutting clack of Katya's boots. She could sense the adulterers coming together in the darkness. Pushing against one another, embracing, kissing, not saying anything. The smell of desire in the air... the first scent of raw flames licking against the flesh. Katya was pulling away though, tease and tense in her voice.

'Don't you want to see? I have present for you... special present...'

Oh...

My...

God!

It's happening now. This is happening now!

The mistress' footsteps rang out decisively, swaggering across the room, drawing closer, coming around the drapes. A twang of reflexive alarm amidst the pounding panic: Charlotte ensuring an unimpeachable puppy-posture. Katya standing over her now, expression narrowing before widening theatrically.

'Awwwww! Don't you look frightened.' She leant over to pinch a rosy cheek between sharp nails – eyes sugared with supermodel sincerity. Mocking tone building a slow rhythm. 'Scooby-Doo… doobie doobie doobie doo.' The mistress plucked the leash handle from puppy's mouth, coiling the chain around her hand until taut. 'Come, bitch.'

Oh my God! Crawling forward… watching her own hands moving over the stone: left hand… right hand… left hand… right hand… Katya's steps sadistically slow – as if further dramatic effect were required. He would be looking down on his wife at this very moment. He could see her! If he didn't know before, then he definitely knew now. Charlotte kept her head lowered: left hand… right hand… left hand… right hand… If the atmosphere above was biting, it was doing so silently. The mistress came to a halt. He was standing right in front of her. The wife could see the tips of her husband's shoes. Oh God, oh God, oh God!

The hiss began to build behind Katya's teeth.

'Sit!'

Charlotte jolted into position quickly, but experienced it in slow motion. Back and torso unfurling, arms bending up, neck straightening, head rising. Eyes moving up his body: his shoes, his shins. And up: his thighs, his groin. And up: his torso, his shoulders. And up: his neck, his chin. Looking up at her husband's face now… and him staring all the way back down. Masculine eyes deep, full and intense. Heavy glare holding so hard she couldn't gulp. Expression stalking still – nothing moving on his face. Although the jut of lower jaw suggested his tongue was pushing forcefully behind the teeth. What did he see in the world before him? Beauty? Madness? Chaos? Order? Love? Despair? Desire? Disaster? Charlotte dipped into the darks of his eyes, reaching out... reaching in. But he reacted, focus vanishing and dissipating in the mist; awareness expanding, taking in the whole field, spreading over the room, deflecting any attempted insight. Jaw settling, posture relaxing, stance readying in subtle ways.

Katya's tone was a little too confident. 'Look what I bring... for you.'

As the Russian reached out to touch her lover, the edge of his palm rose to cut off the advance. His eyes refocused on the mistress now, the wife locked in peripheral vision. Were the adulterers silently communicating in the stillness? Were their lips nearly moving? What was the exchange? Was he going to say something out loud? What was he going to say? He needed to say something... now!

But he didn't say anything – nothing at all. Instead he took a step back. He was turning... and walking away. Just turning and walking away! They watched gravely. Neither moved. He shielded the potential slam of the first door with a touch of fingers. Likewise, with the second as he emerged into the lighted office. Striding through in long, deliberate paces. Just walking away! The third potential slam also cushioned and he returned to the reception area. The stand wobbled as his coat was removed, a brusque air pulling it over his shoulders and picking up his bag. A last swoosh of cloak and their lover disappeared behind the partition... and left the building. He'd just walked away!

Charlotte was numb, her mind cold and blank. Katya inhaled with menace. Her next words stated with minimised emotion, but the tone betrayed a hint of the explosion to come. 'Useless bitch.'

The chain pulled tight as the mistress burst into action, veering and marching towards the exit. Yanking Charlotte sideways, collar choking around the neck as puppy scrambled on all fours, trying to keep up. A skittering tin-can strung to a motorbike. The door flung open… the wife tumbling through as it slammed shut. Heaved past the second crashing door as well. Katya storming through the office – sizzling with energy, furious piston-hips, sparks flying as thighs gnashed together. A fierce wrench to pull Charlotte into the reception area, door smashing behind. Making towards the building's exit. The mistress was going to throw her out, naked except for the puppy attire! Oh Jesus!

The wife had a chance as they tore past the stand, able to grab the bottom of her cream coat and cling on as she was dragged the last few metres. The stand toppled. Katya ripped open the door and swung around to prop it with her back. Both hands on the leash to haul the unwanted bitch onto the precipice of the threshold… into the dizzying daylight. The wife flailing frantically, managing to hook a single arm inside her jacket. The mistress stepped away from the door, placing her boot high on Charlotte's back and pushing. Puppy paws hit the pavement as the reject sprawled onto the street, half-rolling as she scrambled to find her feet, cold air biting nakedness, desperately chasing the tails of her flapping coat. A couple of whirling seconds before the knee-length jacket was fully around and covering her.

A dizzying scan to check the street was empty, before Charlotte found herself shocked in eye contact with the mistress. Katya snarled as she wiped her boot on the step. Although the amusing pitifulness of the rejected puppy raised her spirits a little. Regaining composure, her expression sneered into a smirk.

'Aww, poor little puppy. But you not wanted. So you can just fuck off now.' Exaggerating a smiley face as she mocked and mimed… 'Kiss, kiss, kiss.'

Hand on hip, the mistress curled her body playfully, touching fingers to pouting, red lips as she overblew the final kiss with theatrical flourish.

The door slammed shut.

Charlotte stood blinkering in the daylight. The street was totally still. No one was around; nobody saw. Unless someone was watching from an upstairs window? Better not to check. Sudden eye contact with a witness would be absolutely excruciating. Not that she could blush any deeper. Oh Jesus! The rouge cheeks, the doggie make-up! Her hands clutched up over her face. The wet wipes were in her bag. Everything was in that bag: phone, purse, keys, money, cards. Her clothes were inside the building as well... even her shoes. Oh God! At least the green scarf had bundled its way outside along with the coat. She quickly wrapped it around her neck and lower face, covering her painted nose and cheeks, also pulling off the hair-bands and taming down a few crazed shocks of curl.

What the hell to do now? She obviously couldn't go back in there, meaning she couldn't get her stuff. Oh Jesus! Where had her husband gone? Driven home probably. How was she going to get home? No card, no money, no phone... not even any shoes! Try to sneak onto the train without paying? What if she was caught? Dressed like this – a stranded stripper. Beg for money first? At least she looked pitiful enough to deserve charity. Maybe ask to borrow someone's phone and call a cab? Or hail one on the street? She could worry about paying for it later. But in that scenario, she'd have to interact with the taxi driver. What would he think of the shoeless woman with the half-covered, over-powdered face? Probably think she was a junkie whore unable to pay her fare. Although if he did stop, at least her posh, polite voice could persuade him to upgrade his situational diagnosis to dizzy harlot in sexual misadventure gone epically wrong. An analysis that would be pretty much on the money, to be fair.

No, she couldn't face any human interaction. She'd just have to walk... all the way to West London... with no shoes on. Jesus Christ! What if she stepped on broken glass or something? There were lots of nasty things lying around on the streets. And it was cold. Not freezing, but certainly not appropriate weather to be walking without footwear. The wind was already drafting up under her coat. It must be about three hours hike from here and she didn't know the best way. Was there a quiet route with fewer passers-by? Whatever way she went, there'd certainly be other pedestrians around. And some of them would inevitably notice her conspicuous lack of shoes.

But what the hell. She could just keep her head down and walk quickly. Rely on Londoners' legendary lack of street-empathy to ensure she got home with no awkward questions or humiliating offers of help. And at least the long journey would give her lots of time to think. Charlotte decided to leave her tail between her legs as she began the marathon walk of shame. It seemed appropriate. She left the collar on as well, under her jacket, the metal chain cold against the skin, snaking down the front of her body.

So what'd happened then? He didn't know? It was a complete surprise to him? Although he didn't really look that shocked, given the extreme circumstances. He was generally an expressive man, exuding a magnetic field of animated energy as he interacted and communicated. Where desired, he could disguise his real thoughts pretty well, but there was usually something given away, especially when taken by surprise. Unfortunately, Charlotte had given him at least ten or twenty seconds between the time she was revealed as a puppy and the time she'd finally looked up. Plenty of time for him to consolidate a mask.

Of course, it wasn't necessarily a black and white, did-he-/didn't-he-know question. There were other shades and shadows of possibility. What if he sort-of knew, but sort-of didn't? Maybe involving his wife was something the adulterous pair had discussed, but without ever confirming a specific plan? Possibly they'd previously fantasised about it as a sex game? Perhaps regularly? There was certainly a lot of chat during foreplay in the office. Maybe they liked talking dirty on the subject of humiliating his silly little wife? A game they'd played with scandalous relish, but that Katya had now, opportunistically, taken too far? Quite a plausible explanation. Or maybe it was his plan, but it didn't work out? Perhaps he thought he wanted it, then changed his mind when fantasy actually became reality? Although surely, if it were his scheme, he wouldn't just have walked off like that. He wouldn't do that. So was it simply that he didn't know... at all? Hadn't even guessed anything was up? A total surprise? Jesus, what a surprise!

It was just so agonisingly embarrassing. Whether he did know, didn't know, or sort-of knew, the fact remained that Charlotte had been emphatically rejected. What a nightmarish humiliation! Begging her husband doggie-style on his mistress' lead and being turned down. What mortifying shame. After everything she'd done. And she'd done it all for him; for her husband, for their marriage. Obviously Katya was attractive in her own right, but it was his love for the mistress that truly motivated his wife's desire to be close to her. To be close to her love's lover.

During the harsh periods of training, she'd inspired herself onwards with the thought that she was doing it for him. Holding that gruelling stress position for another half-an-hour, proving her love and loyalty to her husband. Fondly imagining him chatting on the phone to his mistress, telling her to tighten his wife's nipple clamps a couple more notches. Charlotte went through this whole ordeal for him, because she thought that's what he wanted. What more could he ask from her? And how could he blame her for trying? It certainly wasn't the worst thing a betrayed wife had ever done to her husband. She should be furious with him – any self-respecting woman would be. But she was too demoralised for anger, couldn't muster the energy. Where do the strong get their strength anyway?

The brutal truth was that he didn't want her like that. So now she'd ruined everything. How could they go back to playing the normal happy couple after such a catastrophic encounter? The last thing she'd wanted was to destroy what they already had. Was it destroyed? What would he do? Leave his wife for his mistress? Run off with her? Or just throw Charlotte out and move Katya in? Oh God, no! Please no. She needed him. She was weak with love and couldn't do without him. He was special – irreplaceable – her heart would never heal! She would have nothing... and he and Katya would have each other and everything the world owed them. Perhaps this was what the evil mistress wanted all along – to break up the marriage? Charlotte's shattered heart adding a tang of sadistic spice to every future orgasm the evil goddess enjoyed... and nothing more than that.

Although surely the difficult situation must've caused tension between her husband and his lover? If it was a total surprise to him, then he'd surely be angry with Katya. After all, between the two women, it was visibly the mistress who'd taken the lead. Yet she was so infuriatingly forgivable. He'd think 'what a crazy bitch... but she's stunningly beautiful!' He was obviously going to exonerate Katya and abandon Charlotte. Was probably packing up his stuff right now. Please no! We can work it out. Please, let's just somehow work this out.

How the hell had this happened anyway? How had it happened to them? They had a good relationship in most respects, didn't they? Together for five years, married for three, and few real arguments in all that time. They talked, laughed, had fun, treasured each other's company. And the sex was decent enough, wasn't it? Charlotte certainly enjoyed it, generally, and it seemed as if he did. He came, at least. The image of her husband and his mistress sliding and writhing together loomed up in her mind. Obviously the sex with Katya was better, but he surely got something out of making love with his wife. The intra-marital copulation was fairly regular and it was an even split as to who initiated. Sometimes he was very enthusiastic, although nothing compared to how passionately he ripped off his clothes when the mistress seduced him. Don't think comparatively! Don't try to compete with Katya in that area. Can't win that one. Charlotte already knew that nobody competed with his alpha mistress.

Katya gloated like the villain from a Bond movie, so the wife had learned many details regarding her husband's philandering. The adulterers had been together for eighteen months now. They loved each other. It seemed that three-way sex with various other women played an important part in their relationship – 'because we both dominant', the mistress explained… as if the behaviour were perfectly normal. 'Unicorns' (single women adding themselves to an existing couple) were 'hard to find, for most', Katya had boasted. 'But, we find lots and lots.' Apparently the hunters had seduced around a dozen different 'submissives' together, with a couple of these affairs becoming semi-regular. Their success was based on a winning combination of his renown, her beauty, and the harmonious melody of their contrasting charismas.

Also, they employed a range of devious seduction strategies. The details were hazy, but many of their ploys sounded complex. And there seemed to be an escalation in this direction, with the most recent game-plans being especially Machiavellian. The predators clearly enjoyed conspiring and working together, like a pair of wolves feeding off each other's energy as they relished the thrill of the hunt. The women they entrapped were subjected to some kind of particular 'treatment'. Katya was mysterious as to what exactly this involved, but the associated memories always evoked an especially evil smile. The puppy-in-training had assumed she was destined to find out the details the hard way. Surely that was the plan, after all? Surely this was another of the hunters' plots – their most audacious yet? Katya had hinted about some kind of grand scheme.

Anyway, the point was: no one competed with the goddess. He only wanted one equal partner in these games. One dominant female. One queen to rule alongside. The rest would submit to them both. Charlotte had been surprised at how integral the idea of dividing people into 'dominants' and 'submissives' was to Katya's way of thinking. She also deployed notions of 'sincerity' and 'purity' as (vaguely defined) evaluation measures. Of course, the mistress' world-view was warped by the spectacular gravitational pull of her own ego, but Charlotte didn't disagree entirely. For example, the fact that the wife herself was defined as a 'natural submissive' seemed accurate. That was undoubtedly her proper place. That was all she wanted. All she was asking for: to be his submissive.

Actually, coming to appreciate the dom-sub duality had helped calm the wife's jealousies and insecurities towards the mistress. From an erotic perspective, the two women offered completely different things… and neither could replace the other. Therefore, they weren't in competition at all. And obviously, Katya was incapable of providing him with the comfortable and relaxed emotional support that Charlotte had always rendered. She was a good wife in that respect.

And she loved being his wife – occupying a special and unique position in his heart. But she didn't want to be his 'good little wifey' anymore. She wanted to be his 'bad little bitch'. Genuinely wanted that, had wanted it for a long time really. Although the idea had only coalesced into tangible form following the inspirations of the last couple of weeks. The vague churn of once-nameless notions now describing themselves excitedly through internally verbalised chains of thought. She'd finally found out what her husband really wanted and, at the same time, happily discovered that her own secret lusts matched his exactly. Why had it taken this long? She should have done something sooner. This must be her fault. Although he could have done something. After all, he was the dominant one. He should have done it really. Just taken what he truly wanted. All of it!

Why didn't he, then, at any point in the last five years? Another of Katya's bragging sprees sprang to mind, where the humiliation angle focused on demonstrating her superior knowledge of his early sexual history. Apparently, he had a well-established system for testing out a woman's receptiveness to submissive sexual behaviour. He started by tugging their hair a bit rough during an early kiss, then gauged from the reaction whether he should push it further. Charlotte had avoided letting on to Katya, but she'd immediately recalled the first kiss with her husband. How she specifically enjoyed the hair-pulling and the fact that he pushed her around. And yet seemingly, she must have failed the test... or else he would've taken it further. With hindsight, there'd been a few other occasions when he may have been attempting to draw her into the dark. The memories were hazy, but again, she clearly flunked the tests. The marital sex was definitely vanilla by his standards, but (embarrassingly) she'd previously thought of it as kind of rough... certainly passionate.

So why had he married Charlotte? Kinky sex was clearly important to him. So why marry someone apparently unfulfilling in that way? It wasn't like he found it difficult to attract women, so why not marry one of the ones who'd actually passed the test? Yet he'd decided to settle with Charlotte and rely on adultery to satiate his darker desires. Why? He did love her, of course. She knew that was true, despite everything. So was it that he married for love, regardless of the disappointing sex? Was that the trade-off he chose? Although there were other possibilities.

Charlotte recalled watching a random Channel 4 documentary where a web-cam girl was interviewed regarding the various kinky lusts of her customers. The woman described how her largely married clientele would routinely keep their dark fantasies secret from their wives – even the ones with supposedly happy marriages. So maybe that was the answer? He wanted a nice, kind, caring wife at home, but needed to keep her away from his dark side? Keeping her pure, like some kind of sacrificial virgin? Maybe because he truly loved her, he only wanted to protect and care for her – not degrade and despoil her? He felt protective over his wife, so couldn't bring himself to dominate and hurt her? Kind of sweet… but very frustrating if true.

Charlotte had never seen her husband being properly violent before, unless you counted martial arts training (or his drunken party trick of cutting up wooden chairs with a samurai sword). His anger was fierce when roused, but that was a rare occurrence and there was never any violence. She'd never felt physically threatened. Okay, so he punched a wall, once, as his wife stomped away from a ridiculous post-flight argument in a hotel room. But that was nothing.

It was only during sex that she'd truly seen evil shadows in his eyes: silhouettes of violent thoughts lurking. Charlotte hadn't previously recognised them for what they were, but she now realised that seeing them flicker had always excited her. What was he thinking in those moments? Was he fantasising about treating his wife wonderfully badly? Imagining 'taking her' instead of 'making love'? Or did he reserve those thoughts and treatments only for others? For women he didn't love? Women he could objectify and treat as sex toys, whilst keeping his love separate from all that wickedness?

That explanation did kind of fit with other evidence. For example, it had always upset Charlotte that her husband hated it whenever she said 'I love you' during sex. Once she confronted him about it, a few minutes after an especially blatant recoil. He denied the charge, but his visceral reaction at the time had been unmistakeably emphatic. Funny, because he wasn't usually averse to the 'L-word'… only whilst actually making 'L'. So she didn't say it at those times anymore. Which was a bit sad.

Basically, he wanted a separation between true love and true lust. With Katya exceptional, of course. He needed a dividing line between his different lives and now Charlotte had ruined it by forcing the two worlds together – like planets colliding. It was bound to go wrong; always destined to be catastrophic. But what else could she have done? Surely she had to try? She'd been right to try! Should never regret trying. Whatever happened now, she shouldn't blame herself for giving it a go.

It was all those years of not trying that she should feel ashamed of. All that time knowing her husband was growing increasingly bored of their vanilla love-making and her doing nothing about it. The different stages of Charlotte's denial regarding his chronic philandering had been ridiculous and her eventual passive acceptance of it was pathetic. She'd been such a coward – from the start... always. He must hate her for it: his prim, proper, boring, frigid wife. But she didn't want to be that anymore. Never had wanted to be that! She wasn't sure exactly how it would work in practice, but Charlotte was definitely sure that she wanted to be part of his secret world. Wanted to play the game – his game. She didn't want to ruin it. She wanted to fit in with it. In whatever role he deemed appropriate.

'Just tell me what to do, God damn you! Order me. Be specific. You're the dominant one. You should expect a natural submissive to be passive. Just take total control, properly, firmly. Do anything you wish. It can't be wrong! I choose to let you choose!'

The respectable old gent walking by wore the expression of someone who'd just witnessed a mad, shoeless woman praying out loud to Satan. Charlotte tucked her head down and tried to compose herself as they hurried by one another. His disapproving face reminded her, in no uncertain terms, that the only civilised place to have a mental breakdown was within the privacy of one's own home. He wasn't the only person to notice something a bit odd about Charlotte during her epic walk of shame. She managed to attract a few other bemused expressions from passers-by... but no one said anything.

The clouds gathered sombrely to brood over the reject's long journey, skies increasingly gloomy and overcast. When it finally began, the rain fell slow and grey, a depressing daze of drizzle. Charlotte trudged on, mostly able to make her way along quieter streets, running parallel to the big east-west artery roads. She ignored London, and London ignored her. Her feet were icy numb, but had hardened to their task and accepted the ordeal as rightful and just. The rain was feeble, although prolonged exposure was gradually drenching. At least no one could tell the bedraggled locks sticking to the side of her face were recently pinned back in high pigtails. Her fancy-dress make-up would be dripping, although there was no way of assessing the damage right now. She could have used the rain to disguise her tears, but she didn't cry at all. She was too dead inside to cry. Draining away the wearying walk… longer than three hours.

The oaks stood either side of the road. Wizened old gatekeepers, guarding their leafy cul-de-sac. Usually reassuring to the home-comer, but presently unwelcoming – foreboding. Through the hedgerow of little conifers, she discerned the metallic claret of her husband's car. Oh Christ! He was home. And now she'd have to encounter him… again. No one should have to experience such insane levels of anxious anticipation twice in one day. Surely social awkwardness on this scale was only possible in nightmares? Just don't think about it; keep a blank mind. Her masochistic feet reawakened to flinch as she hobbled onto the gravel, following the curving drive around to the dusty crescent of shingle in front of the house. The building stood squarely overhead. Its outward expression gave little away, but there was the hint that it knew something she didn't. By the porch, the flowerpot with the painted sunflower attempted to look unassuming, huddling alongside the others, but the key was underneath as always.

Charlotte could see something was wrong from the unusual slant of shapes and colours detected through the door's frosted glass. A little gasp as she entered: the place had been totally smashed up! The floor strewn with broken objects, littered with debris. The vase from the key table was shattered across the hallway: a festoon of fresh flowers. The tree-lamp that usually stood by the entrance had been javelined against the far wall and now lay in a tangled heap of broken limbs. The shoe-rack had also been thrown, contents jettisoned over a wide area. Smashed glass everywhere. He'd trashed the house – their home! She stopped stone-still and listened to the silence… No way of telling where he was now.

Fortunately, Charlotte's Havaiana flip-flops had landed nearby, so she was able to get some protection underfoot before surveying the carnage. The front room had been devastated: chairs toppled, ornaments destroyed, everything showered in glass. Paintings torn from the walls and hurled about in artful wreckage. The giant TV screen – a web-work of spindling cracks – probably struck by a flying ashtray. The sheath hung above the mantelpiece, but the sword was missing. Charlotte moved with head low and muscles tensed as she continued to explore the ground floor. The bar area had been ransacked and bottles lobbed in all directions, the walls dripping with liquor. At least the pot-plants had been spared, although little else had. Even bookcases had been overturned, with no apparent concern for their valued contents.

The white walls of the garden room had fared badly. He'd let fly a whole crate of wine bottles, one at a time. It now looked like the set of a Tarantino movie after a massacre scene. Looping back around towards the open-plan kitchen, Charlotte was shocked to find the slaughtered remnants of her dining table chairs. They'd been hacked to pieces with the sword: a jagged jigsaw of splintered wood. The kitchen was worst of all: every item of food and drink had been removed from the well-stocked fridge and cupboards and flung against the walls, floors and surfaces. Yoghurts, cereal, juice, Coke, milk, meat, cheese, cream… splashed and splattered everywhere. The ground a sticky mulch of garbage. A scatter of jellied egg yolks staring up with wobbling eyes. Only the breakfast table remained conspicuously unscathed. The welcome-home cake she'd baked, in accordance with tradition, sitting miraculously intact. Well, he had always liked her cakes.

Where was he now? Charlotte made her way to the foot of the stairs and peered upwards. Still couldn't hear anything. As she crept up the steps and reached the landing, her ears picked up a faint noise coming from above. She focused in on the sound – a repetitive grunt – a deep, jagged grunt. He was practising swinging his sword, up in the dojo on the top floor. What did that mean? She hesitated. Looking around, this floor of the house hadn't been damaged at all. Charlotte peaked into the bedroom to find it immaculately tidy... and the bathroom sparkled as well. She hovered warily at the foot of the upper staircase. Could see the door to the dojo from here. She tiptoed up the steps with the exaggerated poise of a mime artist, mouth ajar, gaze fixated on the door handle.

Standing right outside, she was able to hear her husband practice. She knew every grunt accompanied a swing or thrust of the blade. This type of measured battle-cry was apparently important for the technique, because... Well, she couldn't remember why exactly, but he'd certainly explained it to her plenty of times. The specifics of Japanese swordsmanship weren't interesting, but she loved the passion with which her husband talked about it. The adorable sparkle when stimulated on a subject close to his heart: allowing one to see the excited, little boy jumping out of the big, strong man's eyes. Charlotte surprised herself in knowing exactly what sort of cut he was performing. The particular grunt indicated the manoeuvre where he stepped back, before moving forward with an arcing, overhead chop of the blade. She could feel the steel in the silent cut of the air. It was unusual for him to practice with the metal blade – he generally trained with wooden ones.

Charlotte listened for a few minutes before retreating down the stairs. She went into the bedroom and sat on the edge of the bed. What should she do now? Go up and confront him? Shout at him? Get into bed and pull the covers over? Pack a bag and leave? Shower, clean the house and just act as if nothing ever happened ('Hey Hun')? What was the normal thing to do in this situation? How was she supposed to react? What did he want her to do? What did his behaviour mean? Did he have a plan? He'd smashed up their home – had never done anything like that before. Did he simply lose his temper with a gale-force never previously witnessed? Why only the ground floor? Just ran out of steam?

But the cake had been left deliberately... very deliberately. That meant something. There was some kind of method in this madness. It wasn't just a tantrum. He was too big for that. So what had happened here was not an act of uncontrolled rage. It meant something. It was a test – he was testing her. He had a plan! Maybe this was always the plan. She had to prove herself and her determination, even in the face of abject rejection. 'Break them and make them.' Katya's self-satisfied voice echoed inside Charlotte's head. That was it – had to be it. This was all still part of the game. Play on!

She rose decisively and approached the dressing table mirror. Her makeup looked like it'd been applied using a clown's cannon – a messy explosion of plastic-pink, black and white. Maybe she should leave it like this? Show him how much he'd humiliated her, how broken she was? No, that was the wrong approach. He hadn't broken her... not yet. If he wanted her makeup all smudged and smeared, then he'd have to ruin it himself. And from a psychological perspective, if she was going to play a new role, it would be helpful to have a mask to hide behind. She set about carefully reapplying the cosmetics, resetting her puppy face, rouging her cheeks and re-shining her nose. She put the hairbands back in as well. Decided to leave her hair wet. Kind of recalled a downtrodden puppy's ears as the bunches of lank curls dangled down her cheeks.

She stripped off the coat and checked her tail in the mirror. A tinkling tremor of arousal as she pinched the fluffy appendage at the top and gently wiggled the butt-plug inside. Being made to wear an ass-plug was such an embarrassing delight. What a mean bastard! She'd bought lots of new outfits over the last week, so had the option of dressing as a sexy maid. But it seemed a pity to sacrifice the stark purity of nakedness. She'd definitely need footwear. Maybe just put on those white, frilly stockings with the suspenders attached to the silky belt… and suitably repressive shoes. She had a particular pair that were much too small, with highly uncomfortable heels – designed by a sadist. They were perfect. She tucked the chain into her collar, curving and pouting to assure herself that this was, indeed, the right look.

A couple of paces back from the dressing table, she could see most of her body in reflection. A little fluster of confidence trilled below the ears: she knew her husband liked the way she looked with no clothes on. The sincerity of his compliments corroborated by the way he gave them, dark eyes narrowing to tug half a snarl up one side of his face. Charlotte weighed her breasts in her palms with a gentle juggle. Modestly sized and slightly asymmetrical, but lush and round with big, blooming, purpling-pink nipples. Pulling her hands away, she curved her spine to thrust her bust up and outwards. Admiring the healthy bounce as her breasts sprung to attention, taut skin quivering. Now sliding the splays of her fingers around the soft contours of her belly.

She had always worried that she was too fat, but her husband described her as 'pleasantly plump'. And said he liked the way her 'tubby little tummy' accentuated the womanly 'S' of her figure in profile – stomach curling away from the dipping delve, just above the base of her spine. Turning side-on to the mirror, Charlotte recalled standing side-on to her sitting husband as he cupped one palm over her belly, whilst pressing the other up against her back… and then sliding them both down to outline the pronounced curve of her ass. He liked to fondle his hands down her sides in the same way, squeezing as he groped over the feisty flare of her hips.

She twisted around to stare back at herself over her shoulder. 'Big, bountiful, voluptuous buttocks... a ripe, juicy pear.' Thick thighs and calves narrowing smoothly around the knees and ankles. She looked good. Eyes glistening with false innocence... and just the stockings, suspenders, heels and collar. Anticipation visibly wriggling under her skin.

She was going to clean the house. That was the task she'd been set. Katya said he liked to make women work for him: exploit them, enslave them, set chores for them. Apparently 'service submission' was important. He must have intended the cleaning as some kind of initiation task. Or even if he hadn't, his wife was going to treat it as such anyway. What did she have to lose? If he was angry about it, then he could beat her as hard as he liked. If he wanted to kick her out of the house, then he'd have to physically stick his boot in her ass himself. He was getting a bad little bitch of a wife now, whether he wanted it or not. This was her choice – her big, strong, powerful choice – to be weak. And there was nothing all his strength could do to resist that – nothing he could do to resist her. It was yin-yang... or something. Sub-power!

The clean-up was a big job. First things first: get rid of the larger debris. Tottering inelegantly on her heels, the floor alternated between sticky, slippery and crunchy as she began putting things in bin bags. There were a lot of broken objects to dispose of and the stack of garbage by the back door grew high. She worked as fast as possible, but maintained a proper posture at all times. Katya specified he liked submissives to 'stick out ass and tits' as a demonstration of eager subservience. Charlotte stuck to this principle zealously, teetering on her wiggle as she walked and laboured. Keeping feet together, legs straight and ass plumped as she bent over. She loved bending over in that fashion – made her skin crawl like a cow-tow. A good bad little maid. Maybe he'd even let her stay on as a domestic servant after he moved his mistress in?

Once the major rubble was cleared and the bookcases struggled upright, the next task was to sweep the sea of shattered glass. Squatting down with dustpan and brush, she could feel the pom-pom tail tickling her ankles. Could hear the faint swish as it tussled the floor like a feather-duster. Imagine he made her clean up like that: just stuck a feather-duster up her ass and ordered her to squat and wag until all the floors sparkled. Her pussy thrummed and moistened. And then his deep voice commanding her to clean the staircase as well. Tickle, tickle, tickle. She didn't take that approach, but it still took ages to clear all the glass and shatter. The lounge was the only ground-level room with carpets, so it got vacuumed. Fortunately, there hadn't been any bottles at hand to throw around in there.

The next stage of the operation was even more gruelling: wetting and wiping the surfaces, scrubbing and polishing the floors. Charlotte didn't want to use a mop. She loved being on her knees with her ass in the air and tail sticking out. It made the hairs on the back of her neck tingle. She felt so small: moving across the floor of the vast garden room at the back of the house. If only he were watching her work, beavering away for his pleasure, sweating for him. The vigorous scrubbing was exhausting, but she didn't use that as an excuse to let her posture slip. Not for a single moment. Not in hours of cleaning.

There was a lot of unpleasantness. It was especially disgusting slopping the eggy gunk from the kitchen floor into a bucket. But the degradation of the servitude made her thirst with lust. She wasn't going to let him down. Wasn't going to let herself down. She'd be the best damn submissive he'd ever seen. The best that had ever lived! She'd toil for him, slave for him, suffer for him. Prostrate herself and worship him… fanatically. Would do whatever it took and never give up. Never!

He stayed on the top floor for a long time – a marathon exercise session. God knows what sort of state he was working himself into. Could be meditative-style relaxation. Could be aggressive psyching up. He knew his wife was in the house; he must've heard her coming in several hours ago. Charlotte didn't know what he was thinking… what he was planning. But surely he'd appreciate how hard she was trying? And how pitifully cute she looked in all her shameful glory. The walls would ultimately have to be repainted, but leaving that aside, most of the cleaning was done. It was drawing dark by the time she finally heard her husband's footsteps rumbling down the upper stairs. Every muscle in her body tightened, but she stuck with the plan: hurrying over to the particular area of garden room that was visible from the foot of the staircase.

Charlotte listened as his bare feet padded down the lower stairs. Crouched on all fours, the leash-chain tinkled the floor as she lowered her face. Needing to concentrate intently on whatever it was she was scrubbing. Curving her back, she was acutely aware of the dinky doggie-tail wavering around in the air like a flag. He would be able to see her now as he paused at the bottom of the steps. This imaginary stain on the floor really needed a lot of attention! He walked into the sitting room, presumably to sheathe the sword. Next he'd go through to the kitchen, to drink chilled water from the dispenser on the fridge. She'd come face-to-face with him in there. She wasn't scared anymore. Just play the game. If she was playing it wrong, then it was his responsibility to set her straight. The fear was fun. It was all part of the game – part of her role. Just play.

She held her head high, straightened posture kinked to accentuate breasts and buttocks. Letting the tall heels guide the exaggerated waggle of her hips. Just an innocent little maid going about her business, playing the role demanded of her to perfection. She came through to the kitchen from the garden room a few moments after he'd entered via the hallway door. Cubes of ices chinked against glass as they slushed into the large, Bavarian tankard. Stepping back from the fridge, he turned halfway towards her and raised the receptacle to his lips.

A big, glugging, manly swig. Charlotte loved the way her husband drank after training, all tough and sweaty. Strong, hard, lean body slick with perspiration. He let the icy water overflow, so it streamed down the jaw, splashing onto his chest. She watched a sparkling droplet trickling down his side, snaking as it traversed the muscular contours of his upper torso, before swerving to follow the pronounced diagonal sculpting from the waist. She adored the defined carve of that symmetrical V-shape arrowing below his hardened stomach. Feet planted a solid, square stance. Black, martial-arts trousers slightly flared. No footwear – he'd obviously felt pretty confident the glass would be cleared by the time he got down.

He placed the empty tankard on the surface of the counter-bar between them. Staring at her now. She held his eye. A resolute flicker and a defiant puff of her jaw. The look firing into her was not a familiar one, his pupils a boiling stew of shadows yet his focus sharp and penetrating. The slight snarl of his nostril indicated something was burning. Their eyes stayed locked as he moved around the counter. The miniscule sticking sound of bare feet treading polished floorboards. She could smell the musk of man as he drew close, stopping to stand a metre away. His eyes searching her now, going through her stuff. She stood stark still, in the blatant hope they'd grope her improperly. He was interested, observing, trying to learn something – learning something new. She should wait for him to speak or act. She waited... but he just kept watching.

The cake on the breakfast table hovered in their peripheral vision. Charlotte carefully detached eye contact sideways. 'I made you a welcome-home cake.'

She tottered over to the table and picked up the dessert, turning back to offer it up with both hands. It truly was a beautiful work of art: dense, spongy chocolate; generous fillings of jam and cream; lathers of dark, rich icing. Swirls and patterns of sculpted flake decorating the surface. Along with a bright 'Welcome Home!' message lovingly drawn in thick, red icing. The silver sprinkles were not scattered randomly. They'd been painstakingly arranged in a particular way: thin, metallic columns criss-crossing each other as they marched busily over and around the cake. It'd taken ages. She'd really outdone herself this time. Her best bake yet.

'I'll cut you a slice.' Charlotte turned away, setting the dessert back on the table.

'No.' A decisive ring in his tone, stepping up behind. Warm breath on her neck. Stilling her movement as she reached for the slicing spade, his palm covering the back of her right hand. The other arm reaching around to encircle, palm sliding over to control her left as well. Drawing her arms now, gently but firmly pulling them behind her back. Bringing them together to hold both wrists light in his right hand. The fingers of the left tickling up her spine – guiding the electricity. His thigh glanced against her tail, nudging the plug inside. Her legs wobbled and she pushed her ass back into his crotch, the heavy loll of the shaft indicating his arousal had already begun. Looming around to whisper in her ear. 'I don't want a slice.' Deep voice lacing. 'I don't like your welcome-home cakes. They're too sweet. Too sickly fucking sweet!' His low growl rose into the cut of the last word. His left hand ran up the back of her neck. A claw of fingers sliding through her hair. 'I've never liked your cakes. You're the sweet one. You can eat it!'

He moved fast, pushing his wife's head down whilst pulling the arms up, bending her body into sharp right angle so her face splatted into the cake. Gasping mouth suddenly filled with chocolate. A muffle of surprise. He held firmly to squish her in, face plunging through icing and sponge, jam and cream. Squelchy, smothering softness.

'Sweet enough?' He twisted her head with his hand to spread the icing, rubbing her face in it. Standing directly behind and leaning over on top of her. Hard dick pushing against her tail. 'Eat!'

He held the scruff of her neck and ploughed her face through the thick chocolate. Swallowing sweetness clogging the throat. She tried to gulp it down, but more was piling in. Releasing her wrists, he used his other hand to shovel cake over her gaping mouth, slapping the creamy stickiness across powdered cheeks. Charlotte was choking on chocolate, but gorging it in. Forcing it down, eating it, tasting it, savouring it. Beautiful, rich, dark sweetness. She gawped her jaws to scoff, teeth grating against the ceramic. Her insides wriggled in the twist, the movements squirming her whole body.

She thrust her ass back to smear generously over his cock. Barely restrained in the loose trousers, his erection jostled and stabbed the back of her thighs, the thick shaft now bending to press horizontal against her ass cheek. She licked her tongue out lavishly, slavering and curling along with the writhe of her hips. He exchanged the grip on her neck for a looser hold around a sugar-coated pigtail, keeping a straight back as he leant forward to suppress her. Only his dick and groin touched her body as he pushed his weight on top. Pinning her solidly over the table, holding her down with his big, heavy manliness. The ass-plug tickled deeper, her inner thighs sweltering, tongue lolling in creaminess.

With a graceful shift of weight, he pulled away and stepped back. A tug reminding that his fingers still held her hair. Flakes and sprinkles and powdery snow as her face emerged from the once-beautiful cake. Blinkering eyelids heavy with chocolate. Body peeling away from the table, turning to follow his pull. Stumbling heels as she twirled around to confront. Feeling her moistness as the top of her thighs slid against one another. She scraped the gooey icing from around her eyes. The rest of her face was caked in sticky chocolate. He was still, except for the straining point in his tented trousers, intense look daring.

'Is that what you want... sweetness?' His whisper was a rusty graze.

Charlotte paused as if thinking. Head cocked, tongue poking teasingly from the side of her mouth, before slowly licking out... and around the top of her lips. Proceeding full-circle, waggling like a burlesque dancer on parade. Eyes melting in syrupy glaze. 'Yes, it's deliciously sweet.' She leant forward to pucker her pout. 'Welcome home. I love you.'

His reaction chinked open, a scoff of breath dropping from his nostrils. Snarl sinking in, eyes gleaming, evil expression now wearing the skin of a smile. 'Always so sweet.' He said with sincere bitterness. 'Always! No matter what.' His strong fingers flexed in frustration: they wanted to crush something cutesy cute... had wanted to crush it for a long time now. Couldn't resist anymore.

He used his pinch on her pigtail to draw her head down and towards him at an angle. She looked up serenely as her body bowed, face full of beaming cheek. The tempo quickened as he released the hair and advanced to draw along her flank. His left arm coming down over her back, looping around the waist to shelve her stomach. His other hand hooking under the fist and lifting sharply, flicking her legs off the ground. The feeling of being plucked into the air, jolting as he launched into stride. Long, blitzing paces to propel his catch across the garden room, brandishing her underarm. Hard, lean muscles controlling pliant softness. She loved having all this strength deployed against her. And the feathery bounce of the pom-pom tail tickling against her thighs. The flush of blood to her face hot enough to melt chocolate: silver sprinkles glittering the floor in their wake.

As they reached the wide, wooden chair without armrests, he stopped and turned to sit. Swinging around to thump her stomach across his thigh: enough force to knock the breath out. Seesawing over his left leg as he stamped his right down to gather in her wriggling, lower limbs: forcing heeled feet together. Palm flattening across her back to tip the upper body downward, her hands trailing the floor. She was now bent double with her chubby, bubble-butt firmly over the knee – doggie-tail fluttering proud. He paused to savour the moment. A carnivore licking his lips, whilst casually deciding what to eat first. A pointing finger tracing along her thigh, following the frilled rim of the stocking, before cornering upwards at the suspender. A teasing mini-twang to test the elastic. He fondled around, whirling her tail in lazy loop, fingers brushing over her pussy. Flipping the tail onto her lower back. Presenting now, lush like a heavy dew… the scent itching in his nostrils.

'I love you,' she taunted with melodious chime.

She could feel the energy drawing as his hand rose in the air behind. A bird of prey hovering – zeroing in – before swooping down with violent speed. Smack! Charlotte squealed as his open palm slapped onto the fleshy round of her buttock. Red handprint scalding onto white skin, painting primal. The claw of fingers pulling off to kite up again… soaring ominously… and streaking back down. Smack! Stinging as the palm whipped away on the glance. She stifled her sob. She wasn't going to break easy. The mistress had taunted that Charlotte would burst into tears on the third blow, but she wouldn't. Fuck you, Katya! This time his hand clapped across both cheeks at once, bouncing back off to rain down the fourth, fifth and sixth strikes in quick succession. The pain blazed. Wild, determined eyes as she bit into her lip.

She used his pause to rebalance and readjust the enticing presentation of her behind. Could feel his hardness against her flank. Fingers skittering over her pussy playfully, before drawing away again. Her buttocks cringing as they tried to pose. He leant back to get a better angle on her left cheek, bringing his palm down vertically to spread the red – a flurry of flicking slaps. One strike thumping square onto her tail, driving the plug deeper with bone-shivering reverberation. His thumb slipping inside her pussy as he repositioned her body at a steeper angle. Her neatly paired ankles viced between the back of his right thigh and the taut muscles of his clenched calf.

His arm swept in lashing motion, hitting hard... again and again. Slapping down on her helplessness. Buttocks wavering like the sea under a furious storm. White skin spanking pink, rosing deeper as the brutal beating battered on. Reddening under the hail of stinging strikes, cheeks burning to glow – a heating ember. A powerful blow jarring the ass-plug again, juddering through her centre. Another vicious spank onto scalding skin. The agonised whelp irrepressible this time. Her sobbing cries unleashed like a panicking fool as his strong hand clapped down without mercy. Charlotte's ass red-raw, the pain consuming, the escalation unbearable. No, not unbearable! She would bear it. Bear it for him! She'd take it all whether she could or not. Whatever he gave, more than the others... any of them. She'd take it. All of it. She was his wife and she loved him!

His hand stopped to hover close to her blazing cheeks, as if warming around the fire. A slim pant after the exertion. Sitting back to admire his handiwork: a nicely roasted rump, succulent meat all soft and tender, juices flowing to marinade. A satisfied sigh whilst idly massaging the flesh, clutching a handful of ass in his squeeze. The suspender cords had flown loose, but the stocking-rims remained neatly circled around the top of her thighs. The pain scorched an inferno, but she wasn't going to be beaten both ways. The hold of his leg around her calves had loosened, so she was able to set her feet on the floor along with outstretched hands. She pushed her butt up atop the arch of her body, thrusting towards him, pom-pom tail twitching enthusiastically – beat me more.

Her posture was delicately balanced... just a little shove and she clattered to the floor. He rose to stand as she picked herself up on all-fours, scurrying around to approach between his legs. The chain had fallen untucked from the collar, so she dutifully collected it up in her mouth. Sitting upright on her knees before him and unfurling the perfect puppy-pose. Along with the ultra-innocent look puppies always have when their nose is covered in chocolate. His glare barbed, sincere anger riding alongside the lust and sadism, as if she'd stolen something of his and now taunted him in triumph. His lips flared as the breath seethed out in continuous exhalation, shadows cutting along the angles of his face. Such a handsome man.

'I love you.'

As he struck, she managed to minimise her flinch to a wincing wink, taking the full force of the slap across her left cheek. A little shock of spittle as the leash handle flew from her mouth. Head spinning, body flummoxing, but going with the movement, bouncing back around like an inflatable punch-bag. Coming from below to nuzzle up the inside of his thigh, pressing into the trouser-tent walls at just the right angle to draw his erection against the side of her face. Coddling for a moment, before he leveraged a pigtail handle to jerk her head back, into the line of another swinging smack, this time across her right cheek. A bright splash of pain as her body twisted, hand steadying against the floor. Coming back around, sweeping low to gobble in the leash and straightening up onto her haunches again. Cheeks blooming, breasts perting, ass hovering, arms begging, eyes shining defiantly.

He couldn't hide his swoon. His finger skewered the loop of the lead as he drew it from puppy's mouth, folding the chain around his left fist as if tightening resolution. Another long expression of unabated breath. Holding eye contact, she darted her head forward in a playful bob, kneeling at full stretch to bite her teeth around the top of his trousers, just below the bellybutton. Feeling the thick root of his shaft through the fabric under her chin, crown nodding around her neck. Staring vertically up him: his abs valleys of jagged contours, chest muscles heaving in the background. All her cheekiness gobbled up by greedy eyes. He held the chain taut thirty centimetres above her head, digging in as it pulled up around the front of her neck.

She secured the elastic waistline of the trousers firmly within her teeth. Snarling like a boisterous puppy, she leant back and pulled down sharply. His dick thumped up against her nose as it leapt free, large, bell-curved helmet posturing aggressively. Thick, pulsing veins clutching his erection hard and thrusting it in her face. A sparkle of cartoon-coyness in her eyes as she drew her head back and opened her mouth. Hands remained begging at chest-height as she tried to catch his throbbing crown between gaping lips. Deliberately missing... and nudging so it swung back against her cheek. Oops-a-daisy. Trying again, this time letting it swipe the other cheek. Already a thread of pre-come clinging to her face. The raw scent of manhood.

'I love you.'

With a cheeky beam, she slid her lips around his helm and pushed her mouth over him. The shake in his head dissolved as his eyes closed with a grimace. She was making his desire hurt him now. Could see it – like Katya had done. The glow shivered as she widened to gobble in the whole head, before closing her lips around the shaft, keeping her focus fixed upward. His big cock filling her mouth. She loved the feeling of being completely full: over-flowing with dick. The taste in her mouth, the smell in her nostrils, the feeling moving inside.

Her mock-innocence was lying offensively as he watched her eyes bulge, beginning to bob her head back and forth, hard dick sliding in and out. Her puppy-posture perfect. And now, moving in a way he'd not seen from his wife before – in accordance with the training handed out by his mistress. Not the way Katya herself moved of course – something more suitably humiliating. A pronounced, side-to-side sway in her hips. A wiggle into a wag and she felt the fluffy-tail pendulum brushing over her ankles, sweeping back and forth and kinking the plug against the ring of her ass. What a total humiliation. After all he'd done to her: betrayed her, deceived her, manipulated her, beaten her. And all she wanted to do in return was suck his cock and wag her tail, just the way he liked it. What a bastard he was! She could now feel her anger, hate and frustration towards him, but they were just playful parts of her subsuming submission… and solemn parts of her love. She detached herself with a mischievous lick of lips.

'I love you.'

He bared his teeth, gathering up the pigtails and leash-chain in his left hand whilst pulling her head back to view his right hand rising. And smacking across her cheek. The tightened grip on her hair prevented the slap from spinning her face, so the returning backhand whipped fingers across the other cheek. The hand clapping down, whooping back and forth… again and again. Stinging, jolting pain. Chocolate cascading in the blitz. Cheeks blushing violently under the flurry of blows, but she didn't raise her arms in defence, instead concentrating the flinching into her face. The whole world consumed in fiery flashes of red.

A cold shock as the assault ended. Stars dizzying, her vision refocusing through the blear of watering eyes. His expression full of brooding darkness. He wanted her – really wanted her. To take her and use her: a sex object that belonged to him. The shrill arrow of excitement, shooting up the back of her spine, had a curved tip to rumple under the skin. His grip on her hair had loosened, so she was able to nestle back into him. His erection swelled full, the tension of a taut rope straining to hold down a surging balloon. She smeared her face against the root of his shaft, his helmet floating up as she pressed the heaviness of the trunk back against his body. Nuzzling lovingly before drawing away. His dick on her nose, timbering down between her eyes. Now halting to posture diagonally above. Desire burning her nostrils.

'I love you.'

She smothered her own words, gaping her lips back around him. Holding his gaze, so he could savour the cream in her eyes, disgusting himself with his own greed. He couldn't hear his own thought, but she could read it: All this, in me, is your fault!

His dick was pinning her tongue to the floor of her mouth, but she nodded her head to signal agreement: Yes, it's me. It's all me!

The hiss hushed – saliva drawing into the front of his mouth, lips fluting as he tilted his head forward. The lovers looked into one another for a long moment. Her big, blue eyes widened as she realised what he was about to do: spit right in the middle of her face. The spittle splatting over her nose and eyes felt like it was sinking through her. The humiliation exploding in the deeps like an oceanic volcano, molten blood sizzling the cold sweat on her skin. Exclamation muffled by the meaty, raw dick filling her mouth. She hated him, but there was nothing she could do – she loved him.

And now a strong hand cupped the back of her head and forced her in. A pinch of fingers closing the nostrils. Bulging helm driving into the back of her mouth, pushing down her throat. Filling her, gorging her, gagging her, choking her. The instinctive explosion of suffocating panic merged into the spiralling elation – crashing together, spinning and dancing – like true love forged in the furious heat of a drunken carnival. He tilted his body back, pulling her head up as he drew her deeper onto himself, forcing her to stumble into an ungainly squat on tottering heels. Whole throat full to bursting with throbbing cock. Tears streaming from popping eyes. Hand clasping her clit. The frantic alarm of the choke buzzing – desperation wriggling. He released the grip on the back of her head and she pulled away, spluttering and gasping for breath. Crouching below and peering up through watery wells. But clearing her throat to manage a whimper.

'I love you.'

Gawping her jaw, she pushed onto him again. Her own force driving that ferocious dick back down her throat. Straining to push as far as possible. Holding her brimmed eyes open as the gag choked. The powerful weakness energising. Heels and knees together, back curling to pert her buxom buttocks up, so he could see her tail as she wagged. Shaking her body from side to side. His long sigh rumbling between purr and growl. The pom-pom tickling delightfully as it swooshed against her buttocks. But the choke became too much and she had to pull back. Her vision was too blurred to see his expression, yet she could feel his pleasure. She was his pleasure. She could feel his weakness. She was his weakness – a mighty weakness!

The leash tightened as he coiled the chain around his fist, drawing her up to stand blinkering beside him. Strong hands over her body, the stubble on his neck grazing against her cheek, breath whispering in her ear. The ground disappearing as she plucks up into the cradle of his arms, body and mind collapsing into all-consuming strength. As he marches she floats through the house, like a bubble wobbling in the water. A dreamy glimpse of her rosy, heart-shaped buttocks as they whisk past the hallway mirror. The romantic image swimming in the daze. Sensation uplifting as they ascend the stairs, him carrying her towards the threshold of the marital chamber. The rhythm of his erection beating up against her ass-cheeks on every step. His whole exterior hard, but her womanliness wallowing in the softness inside… mud-bathing. The power… of love… of power. Drifting tight – all the romance of wedded bliss.

You made the world like this. You did!

SEVEN
NO, YOU HANG UP

The hipster couple in front were taking forever. Who needs to ask twenty questions before deciding which coffee to order? And the chatty, Brazilian barista-girl's sing-song responses were just indulging their vanity. The café was always busy at lunchtime: tables humming with a colourful crowd of fair-trading vegans, basket-cyclists and trustafarians. Jess had seen that lanky guy with the geek-chic glasses in here before – always sat at the same table, tapping away on his Mac. Perhaps he was a writer? Strange how some people prefer working in public spaces. Surely the only sensible time and place for writing was midnight, alone in an abandoned semi-warehouse, surrounded by magic mirrors. She smuggled herself a sly smile.

It was a good local coffee-shop though… aromatic atmosphere lying low, like a rich merchant's ship. She'd been in regularly, during her five weeks living in the area. And now it was officially 'her' area, given that she'd formally moved out of the old house this morning. Of course, in actuality, Jess had moved out of the real-world ages ago… and revisiting today had been weird.

A surreal experience: sitting at the kitchen table, chatting with Tomas. Apart from a few omission-packed phone calls with mum, it was her first proper conversation with anyone since moving into the mirror. She almost felt as if she'd been disturbed from a dream: sitting there, trying to remember what reality was like. The writer had, only clumsily, managed to evade questions regarding her current living arrangements, but fortunately Tomas hadn't pressed the point. Most of the chatter had been light-hearted banter. Yet even that was hard-going – social interaction had become alien to her. It'd been so long since she'd done anything except sit within the mirrors and write. She'd been so totally absorbed in her work... entranced.

'Those Three Little Words' had been completed within the normal fortnightly timeframe. The associated meeting, with Ms Stilenskova, had followed the established pattern, except that the writer had been given four weeks to complete the next story instead of two. When asked what the change meant, Katya simply shrugged and referred Jess to his instructions. It seemed the agent had no idea how sparse those instructions always were... and the latest feedback had been as opaque and non-specific as ever. Jess had received her money as if it was to last the month, but Charlotte handed her another £500 two weeks later and thus the rate-of-pay remained constant.

So the writer just kept going at the same pace. She wrote 'Love Birds' – a fantastical tale where he played the part of a demonic Circus Master with a flaming whip. She finished the story last week, even though the submission wasn't due until next Friday. Unable to stop typing, she was now writing the story of her current life. Kind of like a diary, except told in the third person. The strange tale of the erotica competition and the mysterious proposal of patronage. She aspired to record the narrative accurately and keep everything exactly as it happened in reality. Although that proved to be easier said than done, because it was surprisingly difficult to straighten out what was real and what wasn't.

Ever since that first meeting in the office, Jess' imagination had been running wild. Her fantasies unleashed like excited children, scampering to explore a grand labyrinth of a garden. And when the writer actually moved into the office, it'd been like moving into her own mad, fictional world... where she now lived full-time. The figmental children scattering over the grounds with boundless energy, chasing through the woods, losing themselves in the secret places. Memories amok with imaginings, imaginings lost in fantasies, fantasies teasing dreams, dreams crashing into realities, realities catching daydreams, daydreams playing with memories.

In the chaos of her own creativity, reality and fiction had been tangling, twisting and twining themselves together. Knots are so very easy to tie... and he was tying them deliberately. The strings were invisible, but she could feel herself being drawn. The puppet-master manipulating his toy, pulling her in different directions, exposing her, making her dance, holding her in suspense. And there was no escape; he seemed to have penetrated everywhere. Dominating her stories, her life, her thoughts, her dreams. Jess had dreamt about him every night sleeping in the mirror. And the dreams were so vivid. Felt completely alive – visitations almost – like he was really there. He was really there! Really here. Deep inside now. Powerful presence ever-pervading: watching, whispering, caressing. She knew what he smelled like as well. Can you dream that?

'I can help?'

Jess popped out of her bubble with a startle. That must've been the second or third time the barista had asked, although the girl still wore a generous, shining-white beam. The writer flashed an apology-smile and ordered her Mocha. Retreating a little from the counter to watch the coffee being brewed. The practised crank of the machine's handle, the splutter of hot liquid, the hiss of the steam billowing and drifting off... back into her odd, little world.

Despite the underlying drama, the reality of the writer's current life was actually pretty mundane. A regular routine had settled in. She was up and dressed before Charlotte arrived, having performed a standing body wash over that disgusting bath. She didn't get much writing done in the mornings, just went out for a pastry breakfast and then idled around online. In the afternoons she slowly got going, usually starting with general editing and planning, momentum gradually building, so that by evening she was in full flow, typing well into the night and not stopping until the early hours. She wasn't sleeping enough during the weeks of course. She tried to make up for it with long lie-ins at the weekends, although she wrote through the nights on Saturdays and Sundays as well. It was all she did; she even wrote in her dreams.

Actually, there was one other thing she did: investigate the mystery. Her curiosity focusing around the questions: Who is he? What's his plan? What's his story? There wasn't much to go on though. The feedback from 'Those Three Little Words' had been typically cryptic. Plenty of ticks as usual: he clearly liked the puppy-pose, the cleaning, the cake... and the sexual violence. Again certain phrases had been underlined (with reasoning that varied from blatantly obvious to entirely ambiguous).

His highlights included 'part of his masterplan', 'further dramatic effect', 'silently communicating', 'all for him', 'her own secret lusts matched his exactly', 'prove herself and her determination, even in the face of abject rejection', 'the privacy of one's own home', 'she'd have to encounter him... again', 'she was destined to find out the details the hard way', 'in the house', 'she'd been right to try', 'she was his pleasure', 'just play the game', 'the key was underneath as always'. Jess loved that he'd double-dashed below the phrase 'bad little bitch', clearly intended as a compliment to the writer. She could imagine/remember him gently whispering those very words into her ear. 'DEEPER + DEEPER...' This time the final instruction had been written twice, as if reflecting itself. There was only one deletion from the text: the question mark after the double-underlined phrase, 'fantasy actually became reality'. A promise? Jesus! He was such an infuriating tease.

In all this time, she'd only caught sight of him on that one occasion outside the office, before the first meeting with Katya (unless you counted seeing him in dreams or in reflection). She sometimes spotted him out of the corner of her eye, but those were probably hallucinations – mirages in the mirror. However, the feel of his presence could not be an illusion – it was too strong. And the words she'd heard him speak couldn't have sunk so deep without the gravity of concrete reality. If they weren't real, then how could she have remembered to forget them so completely? She loved it when he leant over and whispered in her ear as she typed. Sweet, dark nothings breathed in his honey-velvet voice: what his plans were... what he would do with her. So many promises she put in his mouth... and he put in hers. She orgasmed a lot, including every morning after dreaming of him.

'Excuse madam, your mocha.'

The writer snapped back to the real world. Again, it had taken the twinkling barista a few attempts to wangle her customer's attention. Jess bubbled an affable mime, mocking her own airy-fairy-ness, before taking her coffee and leaving. Out into the warm, spring afternoon: bright, blue skies patched with dreams of fluffy-white cloud. Drifting as if he were carrying her up through them once more... higher and higher... deeper and deeper... The feeling of profound security: under his protection, within his protection, under his power, within his power. What was his power anyway? How did he take it? How did he make it? What's it made from?

She had to find out about him, but there weren't many good leads to follow. Jess had searched the building thoroughly, inspecting all the junk in the under-stairs corridor without turning up any useful clues. The varied mix of objects seemed to suggest several rounds of dumping over the course of the building's lifetime: lots of badminton paraphernalia, some broken photography equipment, various old office bits and bobs. The 'National Geographic' magazines didn't seem to fit – surely they'd come from someone's house. And the expensive, dining-table chairs as well. Jess had decided these really must've been carved up with a samurai sword. Oh, and there was also a big box of children's puzzles and magic tricks which seemed appropriately misplaced.

She'd been through the bins, a few times, to no avail. It was a paperless office and there was never any post, deliveries or visitors. The investigator was still waiting for an opportunity to get inside Katya's room uninvited, but it was always locked, occupied or protected. The agent did leave it vacant and on the latch sometimes, although only when Charlotte was there to keep watch… like a loyal guard-bitch.

There was nothing about the address online. Nothing about who owned the building, or whether it was residential or commercial. And nothing about the other women who worked there. Jess had ascertained (through ruthless interrogation/polite conversation) that Charlotte's second name was 'Wright'. There were lots of Charlotte Wrights in London of course, but this particular one wasn't discoverable on Google or any of the major social networks. 'Katya Stilenskova' didn't show any relevant results either. Alongside the first-name 'Katya', Jess tried terms such as 'Russia', 'London', 'publishing', 'literary agent'. But nothing came back. So it seemed they were probably both using fake names. Or at least, slightly altered names. Quite sinister when you think about it. No luck searching for their associated phone numbers or email addresses, or with googling the agent's car registration.

Physically spying on her colleagues hadn't yielded any breakthroughs either. As it turned out, Charlotte worked a light, part-time week. 10–4, Monday–Thursday, with a long weekend (she never started at 9am, despite what she'd originally claimed). When unsupervised, she usually took extended lunches, disappearing for two hours to sit, eat salad, drink smoothies and read her Kindle in the café (she'd been tailed a few times). It still wasn't clear what Charlotte was working on. Every time Jess caught a glimpse of her screen she was either sending an email or browsing around on a social network.

On a couple of occasions, the writer had resorted to shamelessly blatant manoeuvres to get a view of the receptionist's laptop. Especially angling to find out what name she was using online. But all Jess had seen was an email inbox full of social media notifications and a Goodreads.com book review (that Charlotte was apparently reading during working hours). One time after work, Jess had followed the receptionist to Hackney Central and confirmed that she did, indeed, take the westbound train home.

Ms Stilenskova turned up most days Monday–Thursday, but never before midday and rarely for longer than a couple of hours. There were non-specific references to external appointments that the agent was attending, but it seemed that Jess was the only person ever invited for meetings in the building. Obviously Charlotte's demeanour hastened and hustled when her boss arrived. The receptionist would be commandeered into Katya's office, later emerging in a hurry: bustling around, making coffees, scurrying off to fetch blueberries. Not much could be gauged from their interactions, except that Charlotte was working on something and Ms Stilenskova was supervising/bullying her. Katya always came and went in her sleek, black car. She never rode in on her motorbike.

Both women ostensibly ignored the writer, as far as possible, although Jess was beginning to realise that Katya actually paid her quite a lot of attention. A number of times she noted the Russian blatantly checking her out – fixating eyes on her ass in a predatory, sexual manner. The writer had even taken to adding a bit of extra wiggle when walking near the boss. Hopefully Katya enjoyed that as much as she did. Jess found it especially satisfying (and flattering) given what a contemptuous bitch the agent had always been. The whole thing was quite a thrill and served to intensify the strange, erotic atmosphere ever-building within the office.

Jess had made attempts to reopen the cross-examination of Charlotte, but unfortunately the receptionist now had a carefully scripted line to parry work-related questions: 'We have a sensitive clientele, so I can't talk about work with you. Ask Ms Stilenskova, maybe she can help.' She also had a prepared phrase to counter personal questions: 'Sorry, I don't like to talk about my personal life in the office.' (A sharp conversation-cutter, even by Charlotte's snippy standards.)

There were no drawers to search on the receptionist's table-desk and she only used physical paper for doodling anyway. When disappearing into Katya's office she always took her handbag with her... and did it so habitually she never forgot, even when summoned during tempestuous, Siberian storms. Her phone and tablet were both biometrically locked. She brought her laptop in every morning and took it home every evening. It was left unattended during lunchtimes, but was password protected (paranoid bitch). Jess tried a few basic guesses: Password1, Pa55word, Puggle1, Puggle1!... But all failed. The writer couldn't get access to Katya's phone, bag, laptop or desk. She often raided her colleague's coats, when they had their meetings, although she never found anything interesting.

The only clues that half-excited Jess' attention were gleaned from eavesdropping on Charlotte's phone conversations. Every time the writer heard her colleague's irritating ringtone she slipped out to sneak up and listen. Mostly it was Ms Stilenskova, calling from out of the office. There'd been a few personal, customer-service-type calls as well. Not much specific information was overheard, but it was significant to note the name 'Charlotte Wright' being used in a formal context.

Also, there was a discussion with some sort of service-provider, where Charlotte felt she'd been wronged. She argued her case persistently, until eventually winning some kind of rebate. It was interesting because the receptionist actually managed to be quite forceful, with her prim tone and determined manner. Not exactly scary, but from the perspective of a telephone customer-service assistant, probably not the sort of complainant you'd want on your case all day. The fact that Jess was so impressed by this reflected how low her estimation of Charlotte had always been. However, the insight made the writer reconsider and re-evaluate her character in various ways.

Of course, it was the calls Charlotte received from him that were the most intriguing. This had only happened, for definite, on three occasions. It was the way the receptionist answered the phone that gave it away. She was trying to sound extra normal (not-not-normal). But her business-like 'Hel-lo' fractured false: the syllables unnaturally conjoined, as if pronounced by a primitive automaton. A secretive manner then huddled around and she hushed, 'No problem. I'll call you back in five.' A few minutes later, she'd march out of the office and be gone for at least half-an-hour. Always returning brandishing a hot chocolate from the café (these were the only times she ever brought drinks back to the building for herself). So it was clear Charlotte was somehow working directly for him, without always using Ms Stilenskova as an intermediary. And it was clear she was fucking smug about it too – indulging in the creamy cocoa with the glazed expression of a spoiled, overfed housecat.

But the really frustrating thing was that none of Jess' investigations had yielded any breakthroughs. And there weren't many leads left to follow. One day, she'd inevitably shadow Charlotte all the way home. Bit creepy, although the writer had long-decided that the agent and receptionist were fair game. After all, it was they who were somehow conspiring against Jess. They didn't know everything, but they definitely knew more than they were letting on. The idea of deploying more sophisticated espionage strategies had entered the writer's increasingly obsessed mind. Actually, she'd already tried the tabloid phone-hacking trick:

calling both women's voicemail boxes, from her own number, and guessing simple pass-pins. But unfortunately, the conspirators' cyber defences were up and operational.

What else could she do? Use hidden cameras? Get one of those covert pen-cameras and set it up to spy on Charlotte's screen? How about dropping tracking devices into her colleague's coats? Or some sort of bugging device? Somehow get a 'key-logger' onto one of their laptops? Hire a team of hackers, from the dark web, and break into their accounts?

Okay, she was probably getting a bit carried away now, but this whole mystery was maddening. She'd tried engaging with him in the most direct way available, yet he'd ruthlessly ignored her pleas. How could he be so hard and cold? Nothing seemed to provoke him. He must have seen Jess sneaking about – witnessed some of her little ploys… but no reaction. He didn't seem to mind Jess using his tea mug either. Maybe she should smash it and see if that stirred a response? Smash it right through the magic mirror perhaps? Might be the only way to get a breakthrough? It did seem as if desperate measures were in order. Why didn't he give her more to go on? Surely he was growing impatient as well. There's biding your time and then there's this! If he wanted to work Jess up into a frustrated lather, then he'd succeeded long ago. There really was no need to prolong the anticipation any further. It was sadistic!

Was that him now?! The writer's focus zeroed in on a long-cloaked figure crossing the street in front of the office. No. No, it wasn't. Similar coat, completely different stride. Jess well-remembered the way he held weight whilst walking. Just like that first night in the mirror. Her hazy gaze drifted upwards… fluffy, white clouds misting blue skies… eyelids fluttering in the bright of the sun. It was okay, no need to worry about anything. Always a flurry before the calm. She knew him. She knew what he wanted. All she needed to do was relax and enjoy the game. She was good at it. She was special – very special. Special to him!

So this was her only home now. Jess hovered the key-fob over the sensor and pushed her way into the building. Wonder whether Ms Stilenskova was in today? It was always easy to tell from the receptionist's posture. Turning into the room, the writer was surprised to find both her colleagues in unfamiliar positions. Katya was sitting behind reception, with Charlotte squatting at her feet, diagonally to the other side of the desk. Was the underling being made to clean her boss' shoes? The black stilettos were certainly shining chic. But no – the receptionist was fiddling around with the modem. The agent was wearing a white jacket with black lapels and linings, alongside a matching skirt and one of her favourite angry faces. Charlotte was sporting a dowdy cream top, a drab navy-blue skirt, and her well-worn fluster of anxiety. It was obvious that the receptionist had just been found guilty of something (likely without a fair trial).

'Internet is kaput!' Katya spat. 'This fucking… Virgin!' Her pointed gesture was presumably aimed at the modem/broadband provider, rather than the receptionist. Charlotte emphasised concern by tinkering with the box a little more (although she must've already pressed the reboot button). A suspicious flicker as the agent crooked an accusing finger towards Jess. 'You touch this?'

'No. No, it was fine this morning.' The writer assured with placating pools. Katya was now trying to think of a semi-rational reason that the problem could be blamed on Jess, but was finding it frustratingly difficult. Probably best for the writer to remove herself from the firing line asap. She smiled innocently and escaped with the promise, 'I'll let you know if I get a signal.'

As Jess hurried through she noted Charlotte moving around the desk to reposition at her boss' shoulder. The new lines of sight would leave a good opening for espionage. Katya might well let something slip whilst in this kind of frustrated temper. Perhaps, in some ways, she was the weakest link? Jess swung her room door wide for an especially cacophonic slam. Dropping her bag on the desk and grabbing the cup, before moving back to the door.

Reopening and slipping through, quietly this time, cushioning the close with earnest precision. She crept along the mirror, positioning herself less than two metres from the corner, three metres from her colleagues. The angle of the wall would keep her out of sight, even if they were to suddenly turn in this direction. She'd be vulnerable if Charlotte was ordered back around the desk to reset the modem. But in that instance, the writer could just start walking at pace, brandish her cup and ask if anyone wanted a hot drink.

'Nothing is happening.' Katya's seethe was palpable, although it'd only been two minutes since the modem was reset. You had to give it at least four or five in Jess' opinion. Perhaps also in Charlotte's…

'Maybe it just needs… It might… It's normally quite reli—'

'No. This is fucked.' The agent stood impatiently. 'You will phone… get this beardy, Virgin man come sort his fucking shit.' Charlotte must've already been fumbling with her mobile. 'No, not now! Now we go to café… use Wi-Fi. You finish show me thees.' The Russian accent left it unclear whether she meant 'this' or 'these'. Katya was now marching towards her room, the echoing clack of heels striking concrete. 'You sort when come back.' The far door slammed heavy. Jess listened, Charlotte wasn't moving to pack up. She must be waiting to see whether the internet came back – very sensible. But it was only a few seconds before Katya's blistering return. 'Come. We go now!'

Charlotte closed the laptop and hurriedly bundled up her stuff. Jess felt a flutter of excitement – this could be an opportunity. Was the office room door on the latch? It'd sounded as if it was, when it last crashed shut. Or was that just wishful thinking? The writer could sense her colleagues coming together by the coat-stand. The receptionist was saying something quietly, the words inaudible, but Jess could detect the intonation of a question. There was a delay before Katya responded: a hissing 'tssssk' to dismiss the subject and the two women hustled out of the building.

A touch of tension: this really might be an opening. She rounded the corner and peered suspiciously towards Katya's office-door. Could be on the latch? Difficult to tell. The writer hesitated before going to check. What if they came back? Realised they forgot to lock up and returned to catch Jess snooping? She looked down into the cup, as if that would help divine the best course of action. It did: she'd take the mug back to the kitchen-area, in order to give her colleagues time to get clear of the building. Don't get too excited Jess – you'll probably be thwarted again. She inspected the invisible tea leaves once more, before setting the vessel down. Arms rigidly by her sides as she slid through to reception. Don't look towards the mirror. Okay, maybe just sneak a peek – her expression looked naughty. Felt deliciously naughty. Coming up on the door now. Was this a trap? Was he waiting for her? It would surely be locked.

No, it wasn't – it pushed open! The adrenaline pumped up a notch as Jess sidestepped through the ajar door and let it slide closed behind. The light had been left on, glaring down on the stark office to wink off the motorbike's curving metal. The writer's eyes narrowed on the far door. It had a shiny, brass keyhole to match the one opposite. Maybe it would be unlocked too? Please be open, please be open, please be open. Approaching with head bowed as she mumbled the mantra. A little push. No! It was locked – definitely locked. Shit! Jess thumped her shoulder against the door in useless protest. Why was she always shut out?

Although maybe there'd be a key? In the desk? The imposing, black bureau had six drawers: three either side. She padded over and began pulling them open. The ones on the right were full of stationary: pens, pencils, post-it notes, hole-punchers, staplers, etc. The drawers on the left were mostly empty, except one filled with magazines – gossipy, fashion mags mixed in with professional journals related to the publishing industry. Jess checked all the drawers again, but there were no keys and nothing interesting at all. Shit! She turned away with a melodramatic tut. What a bitch the world was! It took a few moments to dawn that she'd glanced something at the back of the room… attached to the wall socket in the corner. A charging cable – a phone. Katya's mobile! The agent had forgotten it. What an opportunity! Haha! Knew she was the weakest link. But it must be a trap. Surely it would be security locked. Jess stared at the little device as it lay beckoning on the floor.

The vague awareness of footsteps was half-absent, but the crash of the front door jolted attention. Someone was here! Katya must've noticed the missing mobile. She was steaming straight for the office right now. Shit! Hard heels tick-tocking like a timebomb. Another shrill of alarm as the phone burst into siren. Jess' head flicked back to see the screen lit up and the device quivering over the concrete. Fuck! She was surrounded. Half a crouch as her body shimmied. Where to hide? There was only one place. The chair was rolled back from the desk, leaving an open bolt-hole. Jess shot underneath just in time. The bulky bureau had a back panel, so huddling in, the cover was quite good. The slamming door sent air shaking in Katya's striding wake, marching to catch the call. Long legs flashing past the mouth of the desk. That really was a ruthlessly short knife of a skirt. The agent was out of sight as she answered.

'Hello.'

A sultry lick around the 'l' hinted as to who it might be. Katya swung back after retrieving the phone, her lower half becoming visible again. Pace slowing into a sidle as she admired herself in the mirror. What if he was on the other side of the wall right now? If this was a trap, then it'd worked out perfectly for the predators: their prey had bolted straight into the box, right in the middle of the room. If he'd been watching, then all he'd have to do was tell his co-conspirator to bend down and look under the desk. Cat's eyes pouncing. And what could the writer say? What possible excuse could there be? Jess manoeuvred, so the side of her body was right up against the back-panel, arms clasped around knees.

'Must wait, fucking internet! Router is kaput! We go to café now and finish go through the list.'

Frustrated energy broiled in the agent's calves and thighs, but the honey-velvet words pouring into her ear sweetened the mood: a light wax in her posture. She gave a playful, dismissive tut (probably agreeing with a compliment). Listening further before responding.

'No, it's okay. I'm at desk. Tell me now.'

Katya turned and stalked over to the bureau. Curling her body into the swivel-chair as she rolled it into place. Pulling forward so her lower half drew under the table with Jess, legs ranging perilously close. Shit! There'd be no way of evading if the agent stretched or kicked out with one of her characteristically aggressive body movements. Jess screwed her side tight against the back-panel, rolling up on one buttock and straining toes against the ground to push away. There really was no excuse if she was caught. It must be some sort of crime. More importantly, Katya would be fucking furious! Jess would be roasted alive on a spit! Her heart was thumping up her throat. A silent exhalation attempted to displace the flutter elsewhere, but she couldn't spell calm.

'Wait, wait... I get the...'

The top drawer pulled open. Fingernails scratching against wood as Katya spear-fished out the required stationery. Sounded like a pack of post-it notes slapping down on the surface above. The agent's legs adjusted as her upper body jostled, buttocks clenching to grasp and manoeuvre the seat. Calves pressed together and slanting to form a diagonal barricade across the mouth of the desk. Her skin always so smooth and snowy. Those long legs were focally intrusive at the best of times, but now they were right in Jess' face.

'Mirror... secret... mirror.'

The Russian said the words slowly, with considered deliberation. A twang of excitement underneath the desk: they were talking about the secret mirror!

'Yes, I see.' Curtly cutting off an unnecessary explanation. 'Say again.'

Katya repositioned, withdrawing her legs beneath the chair and crossing them at the heels, toes to the floor, upper body leaning forward to write. Listening and taking notes.

'And the…?'

He'd started answering the question before it was finished – very irritating! What was she writing? 'Mirror secret mirror…' What did that mean? What was the accompanying information? There was enough of it to fill a post-it note apparently. Katya's body swung emphatically as she ripped off the top layer of paper. The notes continued on the next page of the pad. The rhythm of her body movements suggested a phone number being taken, jerking back and forth to note one character at a time. Hopefully she was going to read it back. Jess set her mind ready to record. But unfortunately – no.

'Yes. I know this.'

The Russian's words bristled to cut off information she didn't need or want.

'No, she's in café. I… send her down first… sort out Wi-Fi. I give to her, in minute.'

Did that mean the note provided some sort of instructions for Charlotte? Katya's feet were poising as if preparing to stand.

'Ha!' The Russian scoffed contemptuously. 'Don't know… writing, maybe.' A ticklish thrill sparkled up Jess' spine. He was asking after her. He cared… and he didn't know she was hiding under the desk. 'Or eating, more likely… fucking custard cream or some disgusting shit.'

Oh for fuck's sake! Just once the writer had been caught eating a custard cream tart. She only bought it because of the yellow discount sticker. But apparently Katya considered it a character-defining crime and was now telling him what a greedy, little piggy she thought Jess was. Fucking bitch! Fucking blueberry-eating bitch! The agent's legs suddenly shot out as she stretched her body back. Pointy shoes now centimetres from Jess' buttocks and thighs. The writer was already squeezed and there was no way of getting safely out of range. Maybe she should eat fewer sweet pastries? A smaller body would leave a bit more distance. Fuck – that would be an annoying reason to get caught. Could just imagine Katya interpreting it that way: 'You too chubby to hide there, piggy.' And getting felt with a foot wasn't the only risk – the agent was now leaning back. If she went much further, and rolled the chair a bit, the writer risked getting skewered in her line of sight.

'But she tell me she give back old house-keys today. So now she live… only here.'

The Russian swung her left foot up to rest on the toes of her right and waved it absently. The stiletto heels taunted like stakes.

'Yes!'

The word only one syllable, but she managed to cut it in half with an evil laugh. Her feet stopped twitching, stakes set sharp.

'Whatever way you take her, she take it.'

Holy Shit! Jess' brain buzzed with flashing images. What were they discussing? It couldn't be what she thought it was…

'Ha! This was inevitable!'

Katya was very confident about that. She moved her feet absently, raising the left shoe away from the right and kinking over to touch the side-drawers Jess was leaning against. The agent's legs were now parted and angled so the writer could see up her skirt. It was dark, but Jess could make out her tiny, red panties. Katya's foot idly pushed against the side, enough force to turn the chair and flick her legs around against the opposite set of drawers. Jess felt a spike brush against her buttock as the heels glided past.

'Ha! So you keep saying.'

A bit terse. The left foot clamped jealously back over the right, ankle crossed over ankle this time.

'Fuck off!'

A slightly amused tone. The writer smiled along. Whatever tease he'd levelled at Katya, Jess was sure she was on his side. The agent pushed her legs off the opposing side-drawers to swing back to where they'd been. The writer painted herself extra-thin on the back-panel to avoid getting brushed again.

'Ha! I know you!'

The tone was harsh, but there was humour colluding... and something sexual. Katya straightened her left leg so the heel jabbed the air just above the curve of Jess' flank. If the extension had angled a couple of degrees lower, then the stiletto would be sticking into her upper hip. Tension rippled along the agent's long leg as it held still, calf muscles tautening as the toes curled back and thrust the heel-point into the loose fabric of Jess' top. He'd stopped speaking. Katya had been asked a question and was musing on her response.

Finally, mock-reprimanding with the statement, 'I don't want play this game now.' Her legs folded away, pulling back to slant across the desk's mouth. The drawer was playfully slapped shut and her next words chanted with melodious rhythm. 'I want you... to tell me... what you think. Because I know... that you know... more than you pretend.'

Oh my god! What Jess would give to hear the answer to that question, whatever the exact context.

'Yes.'

Sounded like he'd clarified the query. Katya was attentive again, her body nodding in agreement.

'Yes. Very clever... and what will...'

She was going to ask a question, but he'd already started answering it. Unbelievably frustrating to hear just half the conversation! Katya listened for a while, still approving of what she heard, until...

'Really?! Why should she know this?'

The agent was genuinely surprised. His explanation lasted a few sentences.

'Well, I think this is big risk. She is sneaky – clever-clever this one. She need to be controlled.'

Katya was so right sometimes! The Russian listened for a while and seemed to accept his argument, but had a further question on the matter.

'How will she find?'

His thirty-second answer elicited the intriguing response, 'Everybody love secrets!'

No they fucking don't! God, that was tantalising! What did that comment refer to? How excruciatingly frustrating! Jess reared up a few centimetres and pointed her ears intently, but his explanation continued for Katya's ears only.

'I will enjoy this.'

The agent jerked her leg as if kicking something. Fortunately, her calves were still diagonal across the desk-mouth, so Jess wasn't struck.

'Ha!' An excited scoff of a laugh. 'This is a very good idea. I will rehearse.' She kissed her own hand theatrically. Then her legs settled as he talked for some time. Annoying that Jess couldn't even hear the tone of his voice. Katya's body still nodding along.

'Like finding one of these pages.'

The agent's statement intended to demonstrate she understood what he was saying. Which pages? Story printouts?

'Very cruel.'

She joined in with his chuckle. Were they laughing about something they were going to do to Jess? Must be nasty, if even Katya classified it as 'very cruel'! The amusement subsided and he was speaking again.

'This is so romantic!'

The Russian's statement was ironic.

'You are. This is true, my darling.'

The satire continued, Katya emphasising her merry mood with an exaggerated roll of darling's 'R'. Her posture waxed as light words pitter-pattered into her ear for a while, before the tone switched.

'Yes, me too.'

The agent was business-like. Shoes planting into the floor in preparation to stand, but he was cajoling her back – could tell from her little snicker of amusement.

'Don't be silly.'

She wanted him to continue being silly.

'No, you hang up.'

Her tongue was deep inside her cheek. Body wagging in playful mock-melodrama.

'No, you hang up.'

She repeated the lover's shared in-joke with mirthful glee. What a fucking bitch!

'No, you hang up.'

Not even funny to begin with – sickening... even as a joke. What a stupid, smug, arrogant, annoying, nasty, horrible fucking bitch!

'Okay... we have do that.'

Apparently he'd thought of a solution to their pretend dilemma. Katya was holding the phone in front of her face and laughing along. Eventually she hung up, presumably at the same time as him. As the giggle subsided her body oozed with the warm afterglow of flirtation. She slipped the phone into her bag. The drawer opened and closed as the pad and pen were returned, then she stood and walked over to the mirror. Spending a few moments admiring herself, before concluding that she looked amazing and turning to march out of the room. Jess heard the latch being clicked, so the door slammed locked this time. Although that didn't matter – it could still be opened from this side. The writer exhaled a long expression of relief. That was close. Really fucking close!

After hearing the front door close, she stayed put for about thirty seconds. Give her heart some time to calm down. Then she watched her reflection gingerly crawl out of the hiding hole and pull herself upright. Calming down the tufted hair on her left side. He definitely wasn't behind the mirror-wall now. It looked kind-of empty: just glass. And only her own eyes looking back. She noticed the glint of the plan in them though – a cunning plan. Checking around slyly and cocking her head as she pulled open the top drawer.

The yellow packet of post-it notes sat in the middle of the compartment. The papers just used had been removed, but the fossil of the last page would be imprinted on the next. Picking them up, it was clear Katya wrote exactly as one would expect – as if gouging out the eyes of a hated enemy. Jess could almost make out the characters already. She took a short, bluntish pencil and set the pad down in front. A sneaking tremor of excitement as she scribbled over the page and the message leapt out. Could see everything that had been written on the last note very clearly. Unfortunately, it didn't make any sense…

1) Muriel + Prisi
2) "

EIGHT
CLASSIC ROMANCE

Living between the mirrors… as the weeks turned into months, Jess wrote relentlessly, obsessively, prodigiously. After submitting 'Love Birds', she penned 'Because You're Worth It' – a fictional account of Katya's work as a professional dominatrix. Next she authored 'Choosing the Ring' – a jewellery heist caper involving her favourite dominant couple. These submissions differed from her previous ones, as they were standalone stories, set in fantastical alternative realities. The writer wove all her narratives together by copy and pasting sentences between them, highlighting things that were the same – things that reflected. It felt like piecing together shards of shattered mirror.

He continued marking her work with his sexy red pen. Always giving minimalist feedback and keeping his instructions cryptic… but inspiring. The writer flushed with pride every time he bestowed praise. Halfway through 'Love Birds', he wrote, 'Keep going Jess!' She loved it when he used her name – such romantic intimacy; it made the bottom of her ears tingle with heated excitement. The only apparent changes to his marking approach were that he no longer highlighted the 'sleepy/woozy' words and all his underlining was now sharp and straight. Jess puzzled copiously over all the clues, but still couldn't work out where her story was going.

Her schedule settled so there were always four weeks between deadlines, with £500 paid every fortnight. She consistently completed her submission-stories within two weeks, which left plenty of time to write the autobiographical narratives, recounting her peculiar journey over the last few months. She chunked the writings – chapter-style – and gave each piece an ironically romantic title, in reflection of the fictional stories ('The Proposal', 'Love Heart', 'No, You Hang Up'). She decided not to submit the autobiographical pieces to him… not yet. Wasn't even sure why she'd decided to write this account – surely he'd somehow instructed her to do it?

He also set other tasks. The day after her under-the-desk espionage, Jess returned from the café to discover he'd left her a present. Anais Nin's classic erotic novel, 'Delta of Venus', placed neatly on the corner of the desk. On the inside cover he'd written: 'For Jess :) xxx'. The loving message inscribed with a bold, blue, fountain pen, as opposed to the red one he used to mark her stories. Long, languid, looping strokes rolling into one another. She loved it! Fondly imagining him entering her room to place the gift. He could've simply told Charlotte to place it, but had instead decided to do it himself.

Jess devoured the 'Delta of Venus'. The compilation of short stories was beautiful… yet deeply dark. Wutheringly well-written, but the brutal erotica was too extreme for Jess' liking. He wasn't suggesting she try and write like this, was he? The grim horror-style definitely wouldn't suit her. Although when she finally went back to read the introduction, she realised his point.

Apparently, in the 1940s, Nin was contracted to write erotica for the private indulgence of an anonymous 'collector' – a mysterious man, who only communicated through intermediaries. So presumably, this is where Jess' patron got the inspiration for his little game. But the artist-benefactor relationship had developed differently for Nin, who rebelled against instructions and ended up challenging the collector. This contrasted with Jess' pathetically obedient responses to her patron's commands. Bet he felt smug about that. Although Nin's anger had been roused after her sponsor demanded she 'take the poetry out', whereas Jess' sponsor had always encouraged the opposite.

He hadn't actually specified, but Jess realised she was expected to write a book review. So she did – writing in first-person blog-style, without addressing him directly. She submitted the piece alongside 'Love Birds'. He didn't give feedback on the review, but she soon received another book, delivered in the same way as before. And he continued the routine, leaving a new novel every fortnight. Always inscribing a similar message on the inside cover, which made the books especially precious.

She gobbled them all up. Pauline Reage's 'Story of O' – covering the shocking adventures of a woman striving to become a possession. Anne Rice's deliciously twisted fairy tale, 'The Claiming of Sleeping Beauty'. The perverse story of 'Justine' by the notorious Marquis de Sade. And Leopold von Sacher-Masoch's infamous masterpiece: 'Venus in Furs'. Jess handed in the reviews alongside her other submissions.

On one occasion, he left a print-out of a short story: 'The Secretary'. The accompanying note instructed her to watch the film as well. Jess enjoyed the prose, but preferred the film. So eccentric and quirky… and steaming hot. Edward Grey's hypnotic style of speech reminded the writer of someone… and he marked work using the exact same red pen!

Belle de Jour's 'The Intimate Adventures of a London Call Girl' wasn't really erotica, but there were plenty of interesting stories about sex. It made Jess think: maybe she should write an anonymous blog, detailing her erotic escapades? Although of course, these amorous adventures had only happened in her head... so far. Anyways, she was much too shy to share her stuff publicly... and there was no guarantee she could remain anonymous (Belle de Jour's real identity had ultimately been exposed). Still, a fun idea in theory.

As well as the classics within his curriculum, Jess downloaded and devoured dozens of books via her tablet. She hadn't actually read much erotica, previously, so selected an eclectic range within the BDSM sub-genre: old and new, mainstream and alternative, high-brow and low-brow. She wrote mini-reviews for some of these books as well. Submitting the unrequested additional work with the smug shine of a teacher's pet (who surely deserved to get beaten up for being such a goodie-two-shoes).

Her routine settled, so she read during the day and wrote during the night. As spring blossomed into summer, she increasingly ventured out to enjoy the sunshine. Sitting in parks, under trees, or outside cafés... and reading. Sometimes catching the train across London to settle herself further afield. She loved reading erotica on her tablet, in public – it felt so naughty! Sitting on the train all prim and proper: halo shimmering, perfect cube of unmelted butter posed on the tongue... but reading something dark and depraved and slatheringly smutty. No one around suspecting!

Despite her wanderings, the writer remained psychologically cocooned within her strange, little bubble. Felt like she was only passing through the outside world as an observer – not really interacting with anyone – just dazing along in a daydream. Everything in the real world growing ever more distant, whether she observed it or not. She immersed herself in multiple fictional universes, but never re-emerged into reality. Just merging and submerging, a menagerie of erotic ideas, images and stories swirling around her mind.

It was fascinating to learn about other people's (mostly women's) sexual fantasies and experiences. And reading so intensively within the genre enabled observation of interesting recurring themes, behaviours and psychologies. Jess found that many of the novels followed the classic romance storyline and end happily ever after. These books focused on the male lead, whose role was to seduce the reader and provide her with the book-boyfriend experience she paid for. The heroes tended to be modern-day versions of princes, knights or vampires. Transporting the heroines (and readers) to whole new worlds – the fantasy paradises they always dreamed of! Princes provide wealth and metaphorical promotion to the status of princess. Knights are heroic fighters who promise security and justice. Vampires offer primal, magical BDSM... and can even bestow immortality.

Jess found non-romantic erotica to be more diverse, generally chronicling the protagonist's independent sexual adventures. Often done in compilations of short stories or autobiographical memoir-style. Rather than combining sex and love, these narratives mix sex with all manner of other emotions. Sex and fear being the classic – plenty of shock-horror-style erotica.

Jess wondered what type of erotica hers would be, if it was a novel? An erotic romance of course – just look at the names of the stories! And he'd manipulated things to make himself the central focus of the narrative (despite not physically showing up yet). And surely the whole thing was destined to end romantically? At least as romantically as it'd started! Although Jess had to concede: the hero of her tale hadn't delivered much in terms of wealth and luxury (she visualised her grotty toilet). And he hadn't dispensed any justice... or bestowed any magical powers.

Imagining her real-life story as an erotic novel, Jess realised her characters were deeply clichéd. The writer herself, as the young, inexperienced and enthusiastic heroine. Some may even say a little naïve. What would the reader notice that the heroine (frustratingly) refused to? What doom hung over Jess' head? Best not to think about that – wouldn't want to spoil the story! He was a cliché as well: rich, powerful and mysterious (and really overdoing the mysterious bit). And let's not even get started on Katya – her whole Russian femme fatale persona following the classic 'Venus in Furs' model. Although the stereotypical characterisation wasn't the writer's fault – he chose the cast. And it wasn't an erotic novel anyway – it was Jess' real life. Her writings were just between herself and him... and always would be. How romantic is that?

Staring into the mirrors, Jess reflected on the way erotica reflected on humanity. Not always painting a particularly positive picture. For a start, a lot of popular book-boyfriends are complete dickheads! Arrogant and entitled, aggressive and bullying, possessive and domineering... abusively so. Jess found this irritating, especially when she herself fell for the dickhead's charms... which wasn't so uncommon. Annoying that characteristics, behaviours and attitudes that should rightfully evoke anger and rebuke, can sometimes have the polar-opposite effect. Something that would engender hatred in any other context, suddenly induces shameful quantities of desire. Only in that exact context though. Like finding the frequency on an old-fashioned radio – the noise offensive unless you're tuned in to the precise frequency.

The infuriating appeal of seeing some cocky bastard, jutting out his jaw and confidently taking what he wants from the world. Of course, in real life, it was Katya who provided Jess with the experience of lusting after someone who should rightfully be hated. She had always forgiven the agent's unbelievable rudeness and outrageous insults – had actively enjoyed the humiliation of receiving them. It was as if they'd gone straight into a domination game and remained in role ever since.

Pretty embarrassing to go weak at the knees for some total dickhead who treats you badly. No wonder erotic writers try to give their readers respectable excuses for falling in love with their bad-boy heroes. So many stories randomly sprinkled with undeveloped references to what a nice guy the lead male really is (disabled animals he's rescued or charitable work he volunteers for). These elements of the character often feel tacked on – blatantly designed to help readers justify their lust, without having to question their moralistic self-image. And then there's all the abusively-possessive behaviours supposedly excused by the intensity of the hero's passion… and the admirable sincerity of his love.

Possession seemed a strong theme running through all kinds of erotica. The desire to be owned: made into his wife, his assistant, his servant, his slave. Or further, made into his pet – a little beast kneeling at his feet. Or further still, made into an object, owned by him – objectified into a pure possession. In the 'Story of O', the heroine becomes the possession of any man who happens to belong to the same club she does. And the man she loves gives her away to his friend – for keeps – as if gifting an inanimate object. Most erotic heroines would rather be possessed by one particular man of course. Either way, being objectified and possessed is not generally viewed as a terrible humiliation. On the contrary, most heroines want to be highly valued prizes. Possessions so precious they possess their owner in return – like Gollum and the Ring of Power. Treasures so irresistibly desirable that the hero simply must have her for himself… must take her for himself.

Oh, to be taken! Conquered! By force. Targeted, relentlessly pursued, hunted down, captured… and carried away. Stolen! The beautiful resignation of defeat. The intense relief of resistance broken. The squirming, cringing excitement of submission. And the self-affirming pride that you've been conquered by the best – by a man like that. He can have anything he wants, yet all he wants is you! He chose his prize and took it. But of course, erotica heroines always get taken by the one man they'd have willingly given themselves to anyway. What a happy coincidence that the protagonist gets her own choice forced upon her… and she can even indulge in the delightful pretence of putting up resistance.

In Jess' sexual fantasies, she generally imagined herself being forced into submission: abducted, exploited, bullied... domineered. Yet she always envisaged herself enjoying it – made to do what she wanted to do anyway. The glory of fantasy! All her erotic stories were elaborately constructed fantasies, with the heroines acting as proxies for herself. She could thus imagine her heroine-self being forced into submission, whilst her writer-self enjoyed total control over the whole fictional universe. The Oneness of the Maker and the Made. She even wielded the power to mould her dominator as the opposing mirror-image of herself.

In different fantasies, Jess envisioned herself offering different levels of resistance. Sometimes she put up a real fight. Sometimes she could be dominated with nothing more than a look. Whatever the case, ultimately her resistance had to be 'broken'. And broken meant total surrender – the flooding relief of resignation. The enforced acceptance of submission. Felt so beautiful, but that wasn't the best bit... that was still to come. Even better than being forced to submit – independently choosing to go further than demanded. To delight the dominator with an additional act of submission they weren't expecting. Only after they'd been nasty and dominant enough to truly deserve it of course. Bestowing them a bonus. A reward. A show of love?

Evil... how easy it is to fall in love with a dominator. Like 'Stockholm Syndrome', where abductees become strongly attached to their captors. Or all the timeless tales of peoples who adore their brutal dictators. Why? Perhaps it's just that the mighty can offer so much in the way of protection... security... solidity... safety. And those that live in fear, love safety the most. And then there's the abject liberation of having personal responsibility stripped away – the beautiful simplicity of slavery. Are those who submit doomed to love their dominator? Or to love their dominator's power? Or simply love the power itself?

Jess thought a lot about her own sexual history. She had never done any BDSM in reality, despite always knowing she was interested. She'd lost her virginity, mid-teens, to her first (and only) long-term boyfriend – Pete. They were together for nearly four years. Their sexual encounters were nervous for the first few weeks, then became exciting, for about a year… before they got kind-of boring. There was never any hint of BDSM. Pete was too lovely for that. It would've been embarrassing to suggest… and excruciating to go through with. She wouldn't have wanted that with him – not even in fantasy.

Early in their relationship, Jess regularly masturbated about sex with Pete. Although she began to do this less and less, until she completely stopped imagining him whilst playing solo. And, to be honest, even during real-world intercourse she often thought about something else, especially to get herself 'over the line'. Fantasising about some bad man doing bad things to her (in order to block out the reality of the nice man doing nice things). And experiencing flashes of guilt about this as the two of them cuddled up in post-coital embrace.

The writer had been with half-a-dozen sexual partners since Pete and had a couple of half-assed relationships. None of the guys had shown any signs of wanting to dominate in the bedroom. Jess had offered a few subtle hints, but none were picked up on. Malcolm had been her most passionate lover. His enthusiasm almost felt violent sometimes, the way these things whirl up. On one occasion, she'd tried to coax him to take things further, during a drunken, post-pub roll-around on the bed.

In a confusion of panting and murmuring she breathed the words 'rape me' into his ear. He likely heard exactly what she said, but his reaction was to stop abruptly, look down earnestly and ask, 'What?' She toned it down on the repeat and whispered, 'Take me'. 'Yea, I'll take you all the way' was his underwhelming response and the subsequent sex was standard vanilla. That was really irritating! But Jess had been too coy to bring it up again… with anyone. Much too embarrassing – the terrifying threat of social awkwardness looms so large in life.

Funnily enough, the closest she'd ever come to real-life BDSM was with her school-friend, Carl, when they were both about five or six years old. They used to play-fight a lot. Jess loved the feeling of getting overpowered – being pinned down and physically unable to get away. One game was called 'Wolf and Lamb', where the predator would hunt, whilst the prey would (theoretically) try to escape. It always ended with Wolf wrestling Lamb to the floor and playfully devouring her – gnawing his teeth around on her neck, back and belly. Somewhat morbidly, Jess always insisted the game continue after Lamb's apparent death. She wanted Carl to carry her off, but his childish muscles weren't developed enough to pick her up. So she had to help him place her in a toy wheelbarrow, before he triumphantly paraded her back to his lair (her Wendy House) to spread her out on the table. Thinking about it now, it was a bit of a strange game.

Another secret thrill Jess smuggled out of her relationship with Carl revolved around the way they watched TV at her house. She loved to set him up in her little, wooden rocking-chair – placing extra cushions to ensure his comfort. Then she herself would sit on a metal footrest that'd been liberated from under Dad's desk. Simply a horizontal bar raised 20cm above the ground. She loved to feel the hard steel pressing into her ass, whilst simultaneously knowing that Carl was enthroned in luxury. Also a bit of a strange way to get one's kicks. Is everyone that weird? If they are, they certainly don't talk about it much.

Sitting uncomfortably was Jess' favourite fantasy when she was young. Imagining herself perched even higher up – on an even narrower bar – with Carl sitting comfortably below. The first time she'd sat on the footrest was because he'd told her to. He was just following the haphazard logic of a random game, but Jess loved the feeling of being ordered to sit. He'd given the instruction in a totally innocent way, without seeming to realise the erotic excitement generated. He always acted naïve, so she had to be sneaky and manipulate him into telling her to sit on the bar. Had to trick him into dominating her – conning the kicks out of him, whilst he just followed along unwittingly. Jess was a lot brighter than Carl, so it was easy to perfect the art of 'topping from the bottom'. Was he really that naïve though? Surely, on some level, he knew what was going on? Surely he felt it too?

Surely everybody feels it? How could they not? For Jess, the eroticism of domination had been there for as long as she could remember. Much longer than her 'vanilla sexuality', which had only emerged during puberty. Although maybe not everyone experiences BDSM-eroticism? Everyone's different – each individual has their own unique sexuality. But she still found it difficult to believe that some people simply don't feel it at all.

It was impossible to know, because everyone lies about sex. Everyone has something to hide. Even those who seem open about the subject have secrets they want to keep. People act dishonestly to make themselves look better in all sorts of contexts… but most of all, when it comes to sex. Perhaps it's because their sexuality so often conflicts with their morality? Offending their good character, their virtue, their politics, their religion, their ideology. Undermining the core pillars of their identity. The erotic part of them – an embarrassment to all the other parts – a pariah. Thus, they not only have to deceive others, they have to lie to themselves. Just bury things, ignore them. Oppress. Supress. Repress.

Jess had kind of done that, for most of her life. Ignoring the existence of her submission-lust feelings, except when she actually needed them. Only allowing them into acknowledged consciousness when she was sexually aroused. And the most brutal thoughts and ideas only permitted when she was approaching orgasm. Not as if they just leapt into her head out of nowhere. More like lighting a candle and realising the monster's been there all along… waiting in the darkness.

The escalation in extremity of BDSM fantasies fits so perfectly with the escalation towards sexual climax. Thinking worse and worse thoughts. Nastier and nastier. Deeper and deeper... until God knows what you'll end up with (or Satan knows, at least). Sometimes Jess let her imagination run wild at the last moment... and orgasmed whilst visualising something truly awful and disgusting. Feels so good for those few precious seconds, but the ecstasy ebbs away so rapidly. Then comes the abject shame as the decent parts of herself return to consciousness together – like a group of wholesome housemates walking into the lounge, to find their wayward cohabitant furiously masturbating to violent porn whilst impaled on a giant dildo.

In the aftermath of such orgasms, Jess had always cringed and immediately switched her mind to think about something else. She'd never faced those demons in the cold light of day – not until he made her do it. She just hadn't wanted to properly think about it. Submission lust is so embarrassing. It's humiliating to want to be someone's inferior. To be defeated, downtrodden, bettered, belittled. In this world, you're supposed to strive to be a winner. You have to pretend to be successful. Only losers lose! And no self-respecting modern woman is supposed to let men just walk all over her. It's wrong to want it. It's shameful.

So why did Jess feel this way? Where did these feelings come from? Moulded during her childish play with Carl? Perhaps those games helped shape her particular fetishes for wolves and uncomfortable seating, but they weren't the root cause of her submission-lust. It went deeper than that. Came from deep inside – right from the beginning. Domination eroticism was built into her biology, her genes – hardwired into her body and brain. She was certain of it. But why would it be that way? Why would tendencies towards such feelings and behaviours be coded into human DNA?

The Marquis de Sade offered an implicit answer, using the libertine characters from 'Justine' as mouthpieces to repetitively espouse his views. To paraphrase, he essentially believed that the law of domination is the primary law of nature. The strong crush the weak... and enjoy doing it. It's the most natural thing in the world. Sade argued that God, religion and morality were invented specifically to deny this brutal fundamental truth. They are fake and unnatural: illusions, inventions, delusions... insincere apologies, unconvincing denials, cowardly hypocrisies. Thus Sade contended that humanity should abandon conventional morality and instead embrace the sadistic morality of nature. (If it gives a bastard a boner, it must be 'naturally just'.)

'Justine' is a decidedly anti-moral story. A perversion of the traditional moral tale that children are taught the world over – the goodie is good, so ultimately gets rewarded... and the baddie is bad, so ultimately gets punished. Sade reverses this logic to actively reward the bad guys, specifically for being evil, whilst the innocent heroine gets brutally punished every time she does something good. The book is deeply subversive, because it goes right for the jugular. Attacking the moral story itself – the primary way that humans learn about morality and how they should live their lives.

Jess found Sade's fantasies disgusting, psychopathic and misogynistic. However, from a sexual perspective, she totally got the erotic thrill stimulated by reversing morality. She loved the idea of getting punished for being bad, yet preferred the idea of getting punished for being good. Something so deeply erotic about being tortured when you're innocent – when you really don't deserve it. And Jess wanted her dominators to be rewarded for being evil.... she wanted to reward them herself. A submissive returning good treatment in exchange for bad – the thought made her insides squirm like a bag of excitable snakes. And being evil... can be really sexy. Tragic... but true.

The idea that the law of domination is the primary rule of nature made sense to Jess. A few years ago, when feeling ill, she'd spent a week lying in bed watching wildlife documentaries. Her rumbling headache put her in a dour mood, so she couldn't help but focus on the brutality of it all. So much callous violence in the natural world... and when it truly comes down to it – might is right. Sure, social animals can do heart-warming things to take care of one another, but so much of what they do is vicious and horrible. If a big rodent decides to steal the carefully hoarded food stores of a weaker counterpart, then the victim will die during winter and the dominator will survive to pass on his genes. Likewise, the meerkat who sneakily slaughters her sister's young will be rewarded with promotion to the position of alpha female... and it's her murderous genes that get passed on to the next generation.

Nature clearly doesn't hand out any prizes for being morally good. And Sade's contention that domination is the primary law of nature does seem to foreshadow the theory of evolution, proposed a century later. Darwinian theory suggests there really is one primary rule guiding the evolution of organisms – whatever can survive and thrive wins! There are no other rules: the fight is 'no holds barred'. When it comes to understanding biology, evolution, genetics and life: dominance is the key concept. In this universe, being powerful, aggressive and good at violence is advantageous for survival, thus nature effectively encourages these traits – demands them! Being dominant is incredibly useful, so it's only natural that organisms evolved to find it sexually attractive. All animals find dominance sexy. And higher-level, social animals probably feel the associated primal urges in a similar way that we do. Even aliens must've evolved that way – it truly is prescribed by nature.

It had to be this way: some animals fight for dominance and others become sexually attracted to those that win. Submitting to a powerful dominant can bring many rewards, so enthusiastic submissives thrive in their favour. Jess had read somewhere that people (both men and women) are more likely to be sexually submissive, rather than dominant. That makes sense – leaders need to be outnumbered by the led. And it's easy to see how social cohesion is improved when followers get an erotic thrill out of obeying orders.

Jess didn't believe there was a God… and if there was, then the divine being certainly didn't seem to prioritise morality. So morality must've been invented by humans – starting from scratch. And we devised it in direct opposition to our pre-existing sadomasochistic urges, as a way of trying to control them… attempting to improve ourselves. So it's no coincidence that many of our sexual impulses are immoral. It's to be expected. Morality points us in a certain direction, specifically because we've always inclined to go the other way.

Essentially, Jess agreed with most of Sade's foundational arguments, yet she didn't agree with his obscene conclusion. It's true that 'natural morality' is horrible and sadistic, but it doesn't follow that we should just give up on true morality. By curious coincidence, an inadvertent counter to Sade's philosophical ideas comes from the writer who gave his name to the other half of the sadomasochistic spectrum. In 'Venus in Furs', Masoch also perceives a natural world where might is right – musing that a lioness has no choice, except to go with the dominant lion. However, his conclusion is the opposite from Sade's. Rather than give in to our savage instincts, we should strive to improve ourselves, through moral and political progress.

Jess wholeheartedly agreed with that. Nature is amazing… and beautiful… and sacred. But it's fundamentally brutal and doesn't provide a good example for human morality. If we want a better world, then we're going to have to make it ourselves. Seems obvious that we need to move away from sadistic 'natural justice' and towards civilised 'human-made justice'. Of course progress is slow and difficult, because numerous anti-moral tendencies are hardwired into our biology. So we need to be thoughtful about how we handle these troubling instincts – we can't just wish them away.

The moral of Masoch's story was ahead-of-his-time feminist – explicitly setting gender equality as the priority for progress. Jess found the subject of gender and domination/submission interesting. In almost all cultures, traditional gender roles prescribe: the male is dominant and the female submissive. Although the zealotry with which these customs have been enforced implies that men have always felt somewhat insecure about this. On average, men are physically stronger, which gives them some sort of natural dominance, according to the might is right rule. Most social animals tend to be led by alpha males, although notable exceptions include some of the most sophisticated and impressive species (hyenas, meerkats and elephants live in female-led groups).

Of our closest relatives, chimps and gorillas generally submit to alpha males, many of whom are brutal and authoritarian. On the other hand, bonobos tend to follow a collective style of leadership, often led by a core of sociable females. Judging from the barbarity of recorded history, humans have probably always erred towards following an alpha male. Perhaps that makes it the 'natural' way to be. But as discussed, natural doesn't mean desirable or morally correct. If anything, the opposite is usually true.

Further than thinking in terms of male and female, Jess thought about the timeless poetic concepts: masculine and feminine. Fundamental energies present in all human beings, in varying proportions and temporalities. The masculine as forceful, active, assertive, aggressive, dynamic. The feminine as pliant, passive, reactive, responsive, enduring. That which yields and that which is yielded to. Domination and submission – right at the heart of all things. Yin and yang. Two halves of the whole. Two opposites reflecting endlessly.

Bizarrely, Jess had always fundamentally pictured domination and submission in terms of shape and motion. Domination is hard and pointy – it thrusts and penetrates. Submission is soft and round – it yields and encompasses. That was a deeply ingrained fetish for the writer; she loved anything along that theme. She kept fantasising about her own soft, round buttock with Katya's long, pointy finger prodding in to depress the flesh – poking – hard. And him thrusting his big, powerful cock inside her, of course. Perhaps her ideas on penetration/yielding derived from sex, but Jess felt like it might be the other way around. Maybe the shape and motion of sex derives from the nature of masculinity and femininity as the sacred universal duality?

Okay, maybe she was getting carried away – her obsessive mind seeing the same thing everywhere. Domination and submission at the core of everything. She saw it through all of history. Class-obsessed societies with rigid hierarchies and social norms that seem straight out of a BDSM game. Serfs, slaves, servants… Kings, Kings of Kings, God-Kings. 'Yes, Master. No, Master. Three bags full, Master.' Women treated like possessions, given away and sold… from one man to another. Marriages like BDSM slavery-contracts… except that someone else chooses whether to consent on your behalf.

A hierarchical world, full of hierarchical organisations. All of them riddled with people abusing the system for their own erotic pleasure. Not just sexually, in the narrow sense of the term, most of them getting off on domination-lust alone. Erotically stimulated by the organisational power dynamics and relations. All those bosses ego-tripping as they order their underlings around, belittling them, making themselves feel big and powerful… and pretending it doesn't turn them on sexually. Jess didn't buy the world's false naïvety when it came to BDSM. Deep down, they all knew what they were doing. At least on some level, they felt it too. Domination and submission is everywhere: bosses sitting whilst their employees stand, snobs giving pointless orders to waiting staff, contestants saying 'thank you' after they get fired from 'The Apprentice'.

All these erotic BDSM feelings swirling around the world, unacknowledged, causing so much damage, in so many different ways – abusing, bullying, making war. If only these impulses could be channelled into something less harmful. Maybe if humanity just came out of the closet and admitted we're kinky. Openly recognise our sexuality is fucked up and try to find ways of dealing with that. Accept our primal sadomasochism and attempt to express it positively. Can consenting BDSM games and relationships provide catharsis for our dark side... so it doesn't need to inflict itself quite so negatively everywhere else? Could we keep the evil inside us at bay with a tribute like this? A tribute to Satan. Humanity's tribute to the God of Power!

Or would that just feed the beast... and make things worse?

NINE
ONE TRUE LOVE

The bright, flashing lights of the city at night, the drunken swirl of noises and smells, the blink of a staggering streetlamp. All slipping away as the little door nooks shut. Sounds of the metropolis fading into the distance – vanishing like cries in a chasm. Only the echo of her own footsteps descending. The staircase dark, narrow and steep. The clenching air glows red… and whispers smoke. Hand balancing against the cold mirror-wall as the ground drops away, step by step. Paces plunging in unfamiliar high heels. Momentum carrying downwards. Deeper and deeper… drawing towards his gravity.

The flight leads below to a heavy mirror-door. The weight of the frame pushes back as reflection strains against curiosity. But curiosity emerging on the other side… onto the corner of an L-shaped corridor, at the axis of two ways. The floor is a chessboard of black and white tiles. The walls and ceilings, mirrors… all mirrors. Identical aisles stretch off into the distance, one an angled reflection of the other. But which is real and which only reflection?

Which way to choose? Right or left? Left or right? Right or wrong? Deeper and deeper...

The mirror-door swings from behind and shoves her through the one in front. Passages disappear as the scene slips off and folds into itself. Multiple doors move and mirror back and forth, a kaleidoscope of shifting sheen, reflecting reflections and sliding perspectives. Swallowed selves swimming by in the glass. A full-length image sweeping past – a girl spinning, rotating, turning... right... the way around... left... to vanish into the mirror. Absorbing, immersing, consuming. But the motion settling: scene focusing into one long, tunnelling corridor, winding off into the wabe. Had to be right... was the only way left. Deeper and deeper...

Walking within the mirror-walls, lost in an endless line of reflected selves. Sights, sounds, feelings and experiences echoing along. An infinity of heels chiming on the tiles in snaking ripples of repercussion. Whilst the way is straight they march in rhythm. But when the corridor curves, the line distorts and harmony shudders into discordant rattle. Reflections flitting in a confusion of angled mirrors as the passage arcs and crescents... widening to become a chamber.

Turning to find a young woman standing before twin mirror-doors. Dressed as an angel, in immaculate white: short skirt frilled in rings of feather boa, a bra of downy plumage, a cutesy perk of cherub wings, repressively high heels. A halo of fairy lights attaches to her glittering tiara on a thin twist of dark wire. The masked-ball visor doesn't hide much – a familiar face, but no one can remember who it is. The angel looks down at her pocket watch. The brass shines as red hands creep over the white face – numbers running anti-clockwise, down to minus thirteen. Watch needles regressing at irregular intervals. Deeper and deeper...

They look up together, in time to see one another split in half and vanish as the mirror-doors slide open. Tucking the pocket watch into her feather boa, she steps into the elevator – a mirror-box with a chequered floor. The warmth from below flooding up under her skirt. The sniff of something burning deep underground. The dark cloud of his presence rising. She turns to find the doors gliding to a close and attention drawing to a digital display. A small, rectangular screen framed inside a mahogany panel. A pixelated, red 'G' lolls lazily on its back. No buttons to press, but the elevator knows where she's going. She's going down. Deeper and deeper… The numbers lying on their sides and scrolling upwards…

-1…
-2…
-3…
-4…
-5…
-6…
-7…
-8…
-9…
-10…
-11…
-12…
-13…

Deeper and deeper… The uplifting exhilaration of the descent accelerating. The burden of the body becomes lighter as the weight of the air becomes darker… and warmer and heavier. Sinking into the depths. Immersing into the Underland. The numbers speeding past, faster and faster… −38, −39, −40… Deeper and deeper… Turning towards the mirror on the left, she's unable to see her own reflection directly, but can see herself from behind instead. The first reflection passing right through, as if she were invisible, and yet the rebounding one capturing her… and carrying her off to the infinities… −65, −66, −67… Deeper and deeper…

Swivelling 180 degrees to observe the opposing mirror. Again, she can only see her replication once removed, pocket watch swinging hypnotically from the waist, back and forth, back and forth, back and forth. Turning to look into the glass at the rear of the elevator in time to see herself pull apart once more in the reflection of the opening doors. The wave of heat hitting her back as if snorted from a sleeping dragon's nostril. The lift stopping, but numbers still speeding past... −99, −100, −101... Deeper and deeper... and on and on and on...

And out into the mirror-maze – to wonder the great labyrinth of tunnels and chambers and halls and stairways. Flowers of flame scattering the darkness. Black-stained glass, where torches burn shadows into the walls like torture scars. Mirrors, mirrors every place, lost reflections, lost in space. And the wanderer losing her selves as the images echo and multiply. A radiation of angels reflecting and reflected in the convoluting glass.

Footsteps chiming on the chessboard floor. Tiles ringing like unholy church bells. Stepping on white, her shoe turns black. On black, it turns white again. Half and half is yin and yang. The pocket watch says she's late, but looking up to find her way, there's only the myriad motion of the angels. She pauses, so the mirror-images will freeze. They don't stop all at once though, some taking a few seconds to get the message, as if they didn't hear the music stop. Now waiting... and listening to the smoke creep. She can feel him watching – all the reflecting eyes merely jewels belonging to him.

A single pair of footsteps resound. Gaze flicking up to glimpse the echo of heeled legs disappearing around the corners. Someone else is here! But from where did the reflection emanate? Searching eyes twinkle like stars in the dark, glass sky. A flash of white fluff moving in the adjacent room and the adventurer springs into pursuit. Another angel! Perhaps she knows the way? Rounding a corner to glance her quarry at the end of the tunnel ahead, turning out of view again. Hurrying to catch up in a shower of echoing steps. Following the twists and turns through the great warren, right on her heels, through tunnels and rooms and hallways, chasing down the corridors like a lost shadow. Always a few paces ahead and behind... flashing out of sight... unable to catch up. Deeper and deeper... Triangular chambers, pentagons, a diamond room to hurl the angel's image through the mirror-maze in an explosion of vanishing selves. And gone. Pausing to listen... but only the silence reflecting.

The blaze of the nearby torch tickles her ear. Not many light sources around now... great shoals of shadow swimming in the deep glass. Perhaps take a flame to carry? But reaching up to collect, her fingers slip over the smooth sheen. The apparent fire only a reflection, despite the crackle of its warm breath. So the torch opposite must be real? However, walking over she finds that one just an echo as well... yet also emanating heat and sound. Where's the real one then? The original? Exploring further, all the torches seem the same – no actual physical flames, only mirror-images.

Phantom objects appearing to clutter the corridors. Victorian-era hotel furnishings and amusement arcade novelties: a room-service trolley laden for a tea party; a taxidermy walrus standing stuffed to attention; a seaside puppet-show... wooden frame strung with dead-eyed dummies. All of them merely ghosts in the glass, their reflections chasing on forever. And the hotel-room doors just apparitions as well. Nothing real to the touch except the looking glass itself. The phrase 'Mirror Secret Mirror' scrawled on the glass in red lipstick – the letters reversing back and forth as the words echo endlessly through the maze.

Deeper and deeper... the old clocks ticking and tocking. Table clocks, wall clocks, great grandfather clocks – heavy, swinging pendula – back and forth, back and forth, back and forth. All the lying faces telling different times, but each counting down to minus thirteen. A small picture frame hangs beside a cuckoo clock. A fading black-and-white sketch: two fat schoolboys, stuffed into cap-and-blazer uniforms, standing under a tree with arms around one another. She recognises the image, but can't tell where from. Trying to remember. Maybe she's dreamt about it before? Or maybe this is a dream now? Is she dreaming? Or is someone else dreaming? Maybe this is someone else's dream? Maybe this is his dream and when he awakens, she'll just vanish into thin air?! Hand on mouth. Are the boy's eyes smirking at her? Suddenly the clock bursts open, illusory cuckoo leaping into her ear. Cacophonous chime echoing through tunnels and chambers. Can't tell what time it is – the needles on the clock are shrugging.

Onwards through the mirror-maze as it opens into a chasming chamber. A clutter of freestanding mirrors, crowding around with reflective faces pointing to watch the Angel in Underland pass. Deeper and deeper... Her reflections gliding alongside, but warping out of shape. Features contorting and distorting in the twisting glass, like a fairground hall of mirrors. Seeing her selves from a thousand perspectives, each image transforming in the echo. Selves in different coloured costumes, fairy light halos flashing or spinning, all sorts of masks and no masks and masks made out of her own face.

Deeper and deeper... Scenes long-remembered and long-forgotten. Images of distant childhood memories, skipping and chasing through. Dreams, fantasies, realities, non-realities, recollections, imaginings, re-imaginings. So many different expressions and impressions. All these selves, and parts of selves, and parts of parts, moving and jostling in the echo. Is the face looking back, her face? Seems hard to tell. Surely she should recognise her own face? Her own self? Which one was it though? Scouring the murky sheen. Trying to find herself in all this confusion... searching for her true self. Deeper and deeper... The mirror-world a repetitive chessboard of black-and-white. All the angels staring down on her... and waiting.

A flicker of movement and the glint of a swinging pocket watch in the mirror behind. The other angel still close. Will catch her this time! Turning off to chase along corridors as the target ducks in and out of view... and then disappearing and reappearing through a complex of chambers. Always leaving the room or passage just as the pursuer enters... sometimes rounding the corner only to see the final swing of the pocket watch vanish.

But now, turning into a long room to find the angel walking directly towards her, time swinging purposefully... and coming to a standstill. Looking into her eyes as they both realise the other is merely a reflection: a fictional figment only imagining she's real. It's unclear who's following who. They're looking into the same mirror-door though. As she pushes her reflection pushes back... and the world swings. The shock of realising: you're the reflection! And the real angel continuing to drive against the door, shoving her backwards, tall heels stumbling into a topple. Body falling. Deeper and deeper...

Expecting the chessboard floor, but it's gone. Falling through the clouds: dropping and dropping. Sinking so soft and plush and snug... into a velvet slide. Sailing down on billowing wings of fabric as the great drapes massage her fall. Golden tassels tickling past in sweeping, ornamental plumes. Mighty stage curtains consuming and embracing. Cushioning the drop into a comfortable float. An angel drifting down through crimson clouds. Deeper and deeper...

Rolling out and hitting the chequered floor with a dull thud. Shaking off dream dust as she stands to find herself in a narrow strip of backstage, between two towering pairs of theatre curtain. Inside a dramatic pause... about to break. The curtain in front twitching and jerking to life, pulleys and mechanisms rolling, and stripping open in a grand sweep of velvet and tassels. Her little gasp undulating in the chasming surrounds. The chessboard stage thirteen metres square and protruding into the encircling darkness of a cavernous auditorium.

A gothic cathedral of pillars and archways, gargoyle statues looming overhead, demonic faces grinning out of the night. A sea of tables and chairs on the floors around, dissolving into the shadows behind. Large, circular surfaces set for a decadent dinner. But empty, with candelabras unlit. Her own echoing footsteps returning eerie from the void – moving towards the front of the stage. Deeper and deeper… Peering out to scan the enveloping gloom. Awareness of his presence dawning peacefully, as if dreamily mistaking the predator's shadow for that of a drifting cloud.

In the high acoustics, the hiss of the ignition whispers all around. But the little fire appears dead ahead, bursting out of the vacuum at the back of the auditorium. Blue and orange flames licking the head of a cigar. Only a hint of illumination – just enough to carve out the silhouette of the Black Throne. The seated figure still cloaked in shadow, except his fingers loosely gripping the tobacco skin. And the flame moving towards his mouth, charming a red snake of smoke to dance above. When he drags, his face will become visible. She strains her neck out to stare as the inhalation begins. Deeper and deeper… The flit of the tiny fire's life sucking out and extinguishing, the cigar embers sizzling a molten coin. Above, his eyes lighting up… and flying out of the night on demon's wings! Black-magic eyes – but human – terrifyingly human!

Sudden blinding brightness as the spotlight splashes down. Can't see anything except the fossil of his figure seared on the inside of her eyelids, dark twists of hair silhouetting like horns. Can smell the smoke already. Not ordinary tobacco fumes: the smog of war and battle, burning homes and peoples. The taste of warm blood in her mouth and throat. And as he pulls the cigar, all the air in the chamber drags in as well, sucking up like the sea before a tsunami. Breath suctioning out of her lungs to leave body quivering on tiptoes, gasping for oxygen. The melting glare of the spotlight astonishing as she flounders. But he's exhaling now – air returning to the auditorium in great, circling gusts. Body flooding to burst as her head spins. A dizzying swirl of light and heat and breath and blood. The echoing clack of her own footstep trying to find balance.

Vision adjusting. The tinged smoke above the God of Power's Black Throne appears as night-clouds over a burning city. Her mind wobbles as the gargoyles loom and menace. The blaze of the spotlight driving her backwards… and turning to run. Falling after her own panicking paces, clattering back up the stage, plunging into the far curtain. Pulling up the thick velvet and fighting underneath, pushing through multiple layers. Deeper and deeper… Her own face suddenly appearing for a head-on collision. Smashing into the mirror and crumpling backwards in a haze of stars. Mask lying on the floor. Tiara-halo still on her head, but crooking out of shape.

Woozy, in the narrow strip of backstage between the final curtain and the great mirror. Her reflection just standing there and watching as she climbs to her feet. Not even offering to help… and refusing eye contact as they draw together. A very peculiar expression. The curtains rippling behind, before parting like the Red Sea and sweeping off to the high eaves. Leaving her on stage once more. Looking into the mirror with him sitting there over her left shoulder. She watches her reflection staring at him. Enthroned shadow wreathed with smoke.

The cigar wisping towards his mouth again. Her own fearful wince appears a lustful sigh in the mirror. The crackle of tobacco as he inspires and the air sucks away. All the energy and oxygen draining out to leave her body hanging on tenterhooks… and the empty atmosphere shivering along. Her own terrifying suffocation reflecting more like the beginnings of an orgasm. He breathes out to submerge everything in gushing relief, acrid fumes coursing through her body. Swooning and buckling with a hand on the cold glass. Deeper and deeper… Her reflection still standing bolt upright, eyes fixated on him. His free hand rising with thumb and middle finger pressed together, ready to click.

A loud, slapping clap as his finger strikes under the thumb and the reverberation shudders through the auditorium. Her doppelganger's body spasming as the wave passes through... and then devoid of tension – suspended on strings. Eyes misting over... and falling into the wholes of her own pupils as they expand and mesmerise. Deeper and deeper... White feathers fluttering away, whilst those that remain darken to midnight. Her reflection's clothes turning black – halo contorting a horn-like curve as the fairy lights flash red. But her own costume remains white. Watching her dark twin binding to his will. Looks so happy and content – sinking inside terrible power as if nestling into a comfortable bed. He's whispering into her left ear, on the dark side, as if perspective has no meaning. A mischievous expression as her body wilts, twisting to fall towards him. Dropping onto hands and knees.

Feeling the power... and the love. Eyes fixating on the source. Pulling herself along with fingernails digging into the stage, as if climbing up it. But truly falling towards him – the irresistible gravity. Body electrifying in the surge of magnetic attraction. Desperate to be near such awesome conglomeration of force: under it, inside it, within it, a part of it. Crawling headfirst down the steps to the theatre floor. Almost tipping in desperation. Onto the chequered tiles, clawing along amongst the draping tablecloths and foresting legs. Knocking the chairs aside with her face and letting the clatter ring out. Eyes hysterical with lust and bursting through a wall of toppling chairs onto the central aisle. Watching her reflecting self in the mirror, yet feeling the wild desire. Feeling without possession. Feeling within possession. Deeper and deeper...

Approaching the Black Throne on all fours. The podium area raised a metre from the floor. All perspectives centring around the tall figure jutting out from the chair in a pentagon of wide-planted legs, branching arms and hair-horned helm. The angles of the chamber pointing inwards, spatial dimensions falling into the void. The God of Power's silhouette is sharp, but his aura shimmers like shadow-fire. Feeling the saliva pouring down her chin as the cigar moves towards his mouth. Part wincing, part rising like a fairy on the breeze.

As he inhales, the light wraps up around his face, digging in along deep contours to cling on for a moment. His plate-armoured mask protrudes from beneath bloodstone skin, dark angles razor sharp in the cut of the flame. Face tightening like a noose around the cigar, lips pointing to drag as cheekbones rise and eyebrows horn. Fierce, triangular lines arrowing to frame black-hole eyes. The eyes of a being who's slaughtered untold millions… and enjoyed it… but will never be satisfied. All the air sucking into him. Her crawling limbs buffeting in the current as everything flows towards the power. Deeper and deeper… Floating up on her own breathlessness. Feeling the adrenaline glitter as it becomes fear. Hands hitting the floor hard on the exhale, crawl wobbling.

Just a few stairs lead to the raised platform. Attempting to steady her movements, but eager energy pulsing in every thrust. Pulling herself up the steps with spine twisting. Dark feathers tickling against her pussy lips. Placing both hands on the podium as the perfumed stench of raw power hits the back of her throat like Hell's House Red. The enthroned figure towering overhead. Skin, flesh and blood, but body glinting as if chiselled from steel. The solid, metal bands around his arms would burst if his biceps bulged. Taut throat holding his head forward with face jutting behind the jaw. Torso bare but looks like armour: pointed bones studding the shoulder plates, chest sculpted in curved steel, abdomen laddered in carving grooves. Loose trousers move like fabric, but sheen like metal, clinking against iron boots. The obsidian-brass of the Black Throne cast with thousands of engraved figures and faces – alive and trapped inside. Writhing in silent screams of agony and delight.

The dark angel's tongue slithering over the podium… begging-bowl eyes upturned. Deeper and deeply… Clasping little hands around his boot and licking. The taste of fire and metal, spiced with the blood of the trampled. Horn-halo twisting. If only she could slide her tongue under the sole. But he ignores the little waggle of white flesh and black feathers. Instead, staring towards the stage – directly at her – still snowy-plumed and watching in the mirror. The returning spotlight not so blinding as before, but the swelter pressuring.

Deep hushing breaths as she turns to face him directly. The dark angel still visible on this side, sucking his boot with white, upturned ass wreathed in black feather boa. Deep breaths. Deeper and deeper… The chime of footsteps as she walks up the middle of the stage once more, spotlight squeezing a bobble-shadow underfoot. Arriving at the front, feeling the blazing beam moistening her skin. The flapping suffocation of another cigar drag through grin-crooking lips. The hazy swill of the aftermath. Atmosphere quivering in anticipation…. before he finally speaks.

'Your plea.' Voice booming in panoramic surround and striking from every angle. Air constricting to straighten her spine, pinning her arms to her sides and clamping her heels together. In the echoing roll of the words, the tones and inflections shapeshift: hot and cold, roar and whisper, threat and promise. Deepness and deeply… Now the crowding silence making space for a response. Too much space for her little voice.

'Not guilty.' Sounding so meek in the vastness… and as the echoes return the 'not' is lost and the 'guilty' resonates. Had to try again. 'Not guilty.' But her words are weaker, despite the extra effort… and the rebounding 'guilty' chorus returning louder still.

'Confess.' The first roll of the word thunders command, but the tone changes in the echo – a confiding whisper to emphasise the profound relief of sincere confession.

'But…' voice tremoring, 'I'm not guilty.' ('Guilty, guilty, guilty!' – her own jeering echoes slithering to impress him.)

'All are guilty.' The assertion snickered in a hollow husk of a chuckle. Just a touch of amusement, but the dark angel's desperate to join in: giggling as she licks his boot. Her grovelling tinkle ringing shrill inside the skull.

'If all are guilty, then why must I be judged?' ('Guilty, guilty, guilty!')

'All are judged.'

'But...' – feet jittering with the vocal chords as the sentence trails – 'that's not fair.'

'No. It is not fair.' Arousing an air of satisfaction as his horn-helm rises. 'This is not a fairy tale. There is no moral to this story. It's not a fable devised to teach children right from wrong. There are no such things. No such rules. There is only one Rule! One Ruler!' Great hand flattening over his gilded chest. 'All who live owe allegiance to me. Me and only me! All must desire me, worship me, lust after me... Love Me! Hate that they love me. Love their own hate!' Black-hole eyes whirling as he stuck his pointing finger straight through her heart. 'I'm the One you love. The One you all love. Your One True Love!' Terrible words rolling through the auditorium like thunder.

'None can escape me. None can deny me. I penetrate every space... permeate every vacuum. And I make you all in the shadow of my image. All who seek me are possessed by me... imbued by me. None can truly hold on to me, however hard they grasp and cling. Those that cannot find me, I crush into nothingness.' The Black Throne winced as he hammered his fist on the armrest. 'Those that find me, I enslave – drunk and drugged on the curse of my blessing. Dependent on me... ever hungry for more... appetite never sated. Crazed, corrupted... owing more... and more... and more... and owing everything to me. To Me! All must kneel. All must submit. All are judged. And All are Guilty!'

Atmosphere reeling under the barrage of his rhapsody. Cigar bitten between the teeth, red hands clasping the throne and thrusting his seated silhouette into the bloody smoke above. As his boom rolls away the silence unsettles in. Fluting lips gripping around tobacco leaves and dragging. Pulling all the oxygen through the vortex and lifting her up by her insides once more. The air heating to blaze on the other side as his body leans forward to exhale. A blast of scalding breath surging over the stage. Scorching skin and blowing clothes away in a scatter of white feathers and burning sparks. Flaming cherub-wings falling to pieces, electricity sizzling through the halo in crackles of lightning, bulbs flickering mad. Singe buzzing in the nostrils. Centre-stage in the spotlight: naked except the heels and fairy tiara. No point in trying to hide anything. Everything here is his.

'Confess.' His voice coming from different directions, demanding… cajoling… imposing… enabling… enforcing. Her legs wobbling like they want to give way, moist thighs slipping off one another and over the edge.

'Forgive me, Master, for I have sinned.' She licks the word 'Master' and it tastes even more delicious as the echoes chime in chorus.

'There is no forgiveness. Confess.'

Her body jostling to attention and thrill gushing. 'I confess that when I'm near you, everything twists and I no longer desire what is right… or virtuous… or moral. I crave immorality and injustice. I want what is wrong. I want to suffer for you… to be punished. And I want you to reap the rewards of all your evil… and all your power. All of it. I want to reward you for it, with total submission. I want to be bound to your will. I want you to make me your slave. I want… what I want… not to matter – it should all be for your pleasure. Standing naked by your throne, pouring your wine, lighting your cigars. Kneeling at your feet and cleaning your boots. Working for you, toiling for you, striving for you, serving you… my Master.'

Her confession echoes around the auditorium in whole sentences, the words caught in infinite reflection. Swirling in the high eaves and reflecting back from every angle.

'Let me be your slave, Master. So I can perform for you, so I can dance for your pleasure. Command me to strip down and display myself for your entertainment. Don't let me dance gracefully – sidling and swaying to smooth music. Instead make me dance like a whore, in cold silence, waggling my hips, wobbling my breasts, shaking my buttocks… pouting my ass cheeks, puckering my pussy lips, twisting and twerking. Thrusting my begging behind towards you with desperate indignity, waving my ass like a white flag. Humiliate me… violate me… violate my femininity… violate all femininity. Deeper and deeper… Nothing more than a little slut – your little slut. I want to feel your ravenous eyes all over my body. Making me dance with a bag over my head, so I know it's just my body you're watching. Groping fingers creeping up my legs, clutching around the top of my thighs, fondling my pussy, squeezing my ass cheeks. Possessing me – all of me. I'm just a possession, a sex object. Your sex object, Master.'

Resounding rivers of her own words streaming back overhead. Thrill escalating in the echo.

'Or any object that's useful to you. Make me be your footrest, Master. Tie me in a ball, with hands cuffed around behind the back of my knees. Face on the floor, ass in the air. Make me wait to be of service to you. I want to feel the vibrations of your footsteps approaching. My cheek jolting against the ground as you thump your boot to rest between my buttocks. A soft cushion for cold metal. The wedge of your heel pushing my cheeks apart… opening me. And I squeeze my face to the ground and push back to improve your comfort. Second boot hammering down on top of the first – force jolting through my body and crunching my cheek onto the stone. Trying to wriggle my bonded fingers towards my pussy. Deeper and deeper… Proud to be of use to you. Honoured to be used by you. Loving you to use me in whichever way you desire.'

Confession sweeping around in great, grovelling gusts. Clarity unfading in the echo – sharpening even.

'Your object, your slave, your prisoner. Keep me in a cage by your side, Master. A birdcage hanging by your throne. Make me sit on a thin, metal perch inside a brass-wire mesh. Yellow feathers pasted to my skin. Elbows perked like clipped wings as I clutch the frame of the swing. A bouquet of colourful tail-feathers pluming from the plug you stuck up my ass. Thrusting my buttocks and breasts as I rock back and forth. Holding my head high and singing for you. Gushing filthy fairy tales. Dark lullabies of shameful secrets – music to sadistic ears. Deeper and deeper… My whole world shaking when you slap the cage. Ordering me to sing darker songs. Darker and darker… making me sing at higher pitch. Higher and higher… trilling like tweetie-pie. Proclaiming my own disgrace. Singing my shame. Cheeks blushing deep. Set smile only pretending to be false. Because I love that you use me like this, Master.'

The chorus of 'Master' vibrating through the atmosphere and building continuously. (Master, Master, Master!)

'And I want you to eat me, consume me, gobble me up. Chew on my submission and then gulp it all down in greedy mouthfuls. Have me brought out and served to you on a big, round platter. Kneeling face down on the trolley's tray with body curling up behind. Skin pinked and pricked and lathered in oil. Shiny, red apple in my mouth. Teeth biting delicately, sour sweetness teasing my tongue. Shining-sharp knife and fork encircling the steaming dish. My Master sitting tall behind, taking the trolley in your hands… rolling me back to kiss your mouth over me. Moaning as I feel your tongue tickling my clit, flicking my pussy lips, slipping inside me. Skittering and sliding and making everything squirm. I want you to taste how sweet I am for you – my juices overflowing. I want you to indulge your gluttonous appetite – drink me up in great, sucking swigs. Wolf me down. My whole body trembling. Biting the soft of my cheek as if tearing off a mouthful of flesh. Deeper and deeper… Devouring me, using me, fucking me, defiling me. Make me bite into the apple, so it smashes to pieces on the stones below.'

The fallen angel was swaying like an enchanting serpent, hands clamping between her thighs in perverse prayer, little fingers tickling up against her moistness. Her confessions swirling around the chamber like circling bats: words, sentiments and feelings dive-bombing in and out. The cigar dragging in his lips… and the air suctioning away, sucking her words up along with it. Drinking all her confessions. All her guilt… and shame… and humiliation… and suffering… and weakness… and love. Devouring and consuming: feeding that insane lust. So only the silence echoes. When the gushing air returns, it's empty – bare as a tooth-polished carcass. But the feelings still bouncing around inside as she manages a small voice.

'Is that enough for you?'

'There is never enough.' The madness of the statement palpable in its sincerity. The spinning emotions, the glowing spotlight, the demonic faces, the dizzying sway. And now his voice right up close in her left ear – sweet as honey. 'Guilty.'

Long fingers falling over her shoulder, against the side of her throat. His hand as warm as freshly blooded metal. Thumb stoking over the top of her spine to press against the back of her neck. Just a tiny touch, but enough to tip her head forward, chin dropping onto her chest. His shadow cloaking over her… blacker than black. Covering her, overwhelming her, eclipsing everything else. Can just feel him now. Just him and her – Master and slave. Powerful presence enveloping everything. Coaxing her forwards, guiding her downwards, leading her into the darkness – into the depths. Deeper and deeper…

Sleep-walking down a sloping tunnel in a body that belongs to him. Obsidian glass walls… and ceilings… and floors. Black mirrors, taking all the reflections without giving any back. The floor should slip, but her heels stick like magic, even as the descent steepens. Each pace falling further than the last. Every step like the end of the plank. His heavy hand so light, but his presence so dark. Bearing down from all around. The smell of power burning. Whole world flashing red... and gone... as the halo throbs like a hypnotised heart. Hearing the screams coming up from below, perverse concoctions of pain and pleasure, elation and fear. Black mirrors swallowing the echoes, so the cries fleet past, thin as thread. Deeper and deeper... Dungeon doors shadowing in the glass on either side. Only shrieks... and whimpers... and sobs escaping. And the grate of desperate nails scratching at the sheen.

An obsidian door stands agape. A black-mirror-chamber... or a void. Unable to feel the floor below, as if walking through blank space... and then stopping in the middle of the vacuum. Nothing here except his presence.

'Please.' Her lonely word wobbles as it slips off and disappears into the night.

Both his hands falling across her shoulders, fingers rippling onto the skin, two-by-two. No ground or friction, so as he swivels her she twirls like ballet. Visible world flashing on and off in bloody red. Timid eyes level with his heaving, plated chest. Demonic face hanging overhead. Fiery breath gushing, but cigar gritted in the side of his mouth, embers barely flinting. His great arm rising, palm preparing to conduct an orchestra. A flex of fingers... and a long rope dances out of the darkness. A sinister animation, hovering in the void like a charmed snake. Deeper and deeper... Fist now closing around her wrist and lifting her arm... into the waiting noose. The twine slipping over her hand and constricting just below, chafing between the bones, bristled texture grating. Releasing his grip and gesturing for the cord to jolt taut. A second rope dancing in to doubly secure the same arm, tangling itself around and then biting tight. The cables dragging from differing angles.

Fear palpitating as two more tousled serpents weave out of the night on the opposite side. Angel pulls away, twisting towards the bonded side to wrap her body around the free arm. He's gliding with her as she twirls. His hand reaching up to spoon hers, hard body solemnly pressing up behind. Following her movements... until he's guiding them. The dimensions of the spinning world oriented by the twining pulleys above, momentum folding inwards. As he steps back, the impetus swings into reverse and her body uncoils – a graceful pirouette beneath the arch of his arm. Dancing to the percussion and bass of their heartbeats, the wind and strings of their breath. Spin slowing until she falls open against him, cheek on chest.

Breathing red iron, smells how it feels to melt. Sweeping her other arm up into the waiting lassoes – tangling and trapping around the wrist. Both arms drawing into a 'T'. Iron fist clamping around the top of her head, hair and halo scrunching as he lifts her by the scalp. Another twining rope knotting into her mane. Headpiece buckling but crimson lights still throbbing: there and gone, there and gone, there and gone. Deeper and deeper...

His fingers pulse pentagons, commanding the ropes taut. Her arms stretching a crucifix, sadistic knots pulling against one another, scraping and flaying. Lines tugging in different directions, but all fighting against her. Suspended in the void – dangling naked before him. Their eyes level as hers continue to fall inside his, spiralling around and around. And the ropes rising from below to ensnare her lower limbs, one around each ankle, one around each knee. A stubbly slither as they loop. A sinister squeeze as they strangle. Tensing straight to pull her legs apart, opening her before him, pussy winking as thigh muscles strain, spread-eagled in a wide star. Squirming this way and that, trying to find relief, but only finding struggle. New pains springing up as her body jerks in continuous readjustment.

He stands back, clenching the cigar in the centre of his mouth. Embers lugging back to life and the air emptying out. This close to the vortex the world spins like a tornado's tip, motion blurring in the rushing violence. A wheel of somersaults spinning a propeller of limbs. Dragged under the great wave and desperately flailing for oxygen. Nauseous feint as the movement steadies... balance and perspective perplexing. The only gravity is his, but the grappling ropes still yanking every which way. Their spiralling eyes level. His pupils an eclipse, expression a Martian mist, jaw jutting like a red crag. Hand clamping up between her legs, thumb stoking the clitoris, fingers clutching around behind. Weighing her in his clasp, like a peach – succulent and ripe for devouring. Oh, to be plucked and devoured! Holding her out in front as she presses her weight down onto him. Squeezing the juices, head lolling, eyes fogging, desire gurgling.

As his hand draws away her throbbing pussy pursues, but the ropes bite to drag her back, body wrestling helplessly. Begging eyes turn to pleading lips, but his silencing finger rises... and clicks against his thumb: summoning another serpent to wind out from the darkness behind him. Not a rope this time – a thin, white thread. All the evil in the world in his smile. He reaches in to grasp her shaking bosom. Her heart attempting to burst out and leap into his hand. The wiry thread tickles against her breast, curling around the nipple... and then tearing slashes of agony as it strangles tight. Her scream flies off into the vacuum... where it can never end. A second snaking strand coiling around her other nipple. Thread noosing and strickening tight, pressing like a thin blade. And both lines pulling taut to draw diagonally forward at competing angles. All her shrieks and squeals hurtling off to live forever in the deep black. Deeper and deeper...

The ropes and wires stretch and yank like a cruel crowd, her body writhing helplessly in their midst. Skin flaying off in the twist, shred by shred. Heart hammering against hot-plate breasts. Breath escaping in pitiful sobs. Splayed like an open rose. A flower that could move about. But only just, tortured petals twitching as the stem squirms. But his face drawing closer, eyes spinning into black-hole pupils. Blacker than black when the halo lights flash off. Heavy hands embracing her hips. The warmth of the embers tickling as the butt of his cigar scrapes against her back. His touch almost gentle, but the movement strains against the network of bonds, torture pulling in all directions.

Horrifically beautiful mask descending. Large lips pressing in to enclose her own. His liquid iron mouth soft and tender. The kiss deepening as she grapples to return it, struggling as the cruel snares tug and claw. Body fighting in every direction, kiss sealing and searing in shooting pain. His swirling tongue swallowing hers as if a small wave washing into a tsunami. The blood in his mouth tastes like fine wine… Deeper and deeper… drunker and drunker, hypnotic aroma swirling.

As he pulls away her tongue follows in the trance – sleep-walking into a trap. The waiting thread noosing tight around the sensitive organ, alien texture gripping to prevent its slip and slide. Panic spluttering as the agony constricts. Tongue unable to retreat! Desperate eyes crying out as the strand circles her head, weaving a gag together in thin braids, cutting around the lower skull, slicing the corners of her mouth. Angelic eyes lit with beautiful shock.

An Olympian silhouette of metallic muscle gleams in red flashes. His body like banded iron. Demonic face marbling hideous beauty. Expression full of intent… bent on taking her. He should take what is his! Fuck her ruthlessly, writhing in the ropes, pleasure and pain pulling every which way, each thrust rippling violent spasms through the web. Imagine the steel belt unbuckling and that monstrous dick leaping out like the minotaur unleashed, hard as horn, great helm menacing. Spittle gushing from her lips, tied tongue making the salivation worse. Pussy salivating too. Eyes begging for him to take her! It's been too long. Please! Just take what's yours. The anticipation is unbearable! His big lips pouting another puff on the shrinking cigar, universe spinning and tumbling… suffocation flooding all things. Deeper and deeper…

The swill of exhalation and the shuddering return of air and balance. Perspective, position and gravity shifting so she's lying horizontal at waist-height, with him standing between her legs. Something in his hands... something dreadful. She can smell the evil. A leather and metal device: brass padlocks and iron hinges. Strapping bands triangulating. Underwear. Lockable underwear – a chastity belt! Frozen eyes too horrified to scream. No, No, NO! Not that, anything but that! That's not possible. That's too terrible. The pent-up energy already too much. That torture would be unendurable.

Deeper and deeply... Web constricting her shaking body. Trying to worm her tongue free, but the thin wire biting. A grimacing grin as he leans in and loops the thick, leather strap around. Wide enough to cover her pussy, even with legs splayed wide. Smooth hide against moist flesh. The slim belt-band slithering over her skin as it wraps her waist. Body fighting frantically, threads tearing her nipples, ropes sawing her limbs, shriek waffling, dribble spluttering. But no escape. Underwear tightening, closing around her. The sinister click of the padlock. No, No, NO! This could not be happening! This is too much. Much too much! The sexual frustration impossibly exciting.

Her torment sprawling around as he takes a final drag of smoke. This time the world holds dead-still as the oxygen evaporates, lifeless air strangling. Showing her the end of his cigar, the darkness at the heart of the molten circle – an icon of black horns. Turning it so the burn points towards her bosom... and lowering. Agony singing as the blaze scalds into the top of her breast with a hot hiss. The stench of roasting flesh sticking in her throat, despite the desperate lack of air. Fire cremating itself into her. And then his exhalation flooding over all things. Gushing smoke blazing her eyes and stinging her nostrils. The embers blowing away to unveil his art. Feeling the agonisingly sharp definition between burnt and unburnt. Blackened skin framing a pair of white horns – the slave-

stamp sinking through her breast, making towards her heart… like a fuse. His brand unmistakeable. Marking her as his… for all eternity. Cruel whisper rusting in her ear.

'Wait.'

The angelic flower squirms and wriggles in torment. The flaying ropes, the biting threads, the sticking tongue… the ripping scalp, the searing breasts… and the feeling of being locked up! Leather absorbing her dripping juices. His physical presence withdrawing, turning to walk away. No footsteps in the void. Leaving her – alone – trapped in her own mind. No perspective or focal points in the swallowing blackness. Just her own breath panting, her heart beating, her body shaking in the web. Saliva streaming from her mouth and dropping into the void, plummeting down into nothingness. Deeper and deeper…

TEN

KISSING

It was only Charlotte's normal ringtone, yet somehow the call sounded intriguing. Jess knew who it was straightaway. Perfect timing as well – just as the writer had stepped out of her room, cup in hand, but before the door clunked back onto Eloy's flank. She cushioned the close and veered to slide along the mirror-wall. Taking up her usual spying position around the corner from reception.

'Hel-lo.'

The receptionist's not-not-normal tone – conspicuously inconspicuous. Jess' ears tickled in the hush. She hadn't overheard a call from him since hiding under Katya's desk three months ago.

'I'm just finishing something off and then I can…'

He cut off Charlotte's quiet words with a surprising statement or instruction.

'Sorry?' Meaning 'sorry' as in 'what?' and sounding confused.

'Okay.'

The agreement was surrounded with hesitation. Charlotte was expecting an explanation, but whatever he said instead caught her off-guard – a little shock of a laugh. The tension afterwards spilling silent excitement. Jess could imagine her colleague's coy expression, finger curling her hair as she considered how to respond.

'It fee—' deciding to rephrase. 'It is exactly as you desired.' The resignation in her voice floated like a balloon. But he'd already changed the subject. 'Okay.'

Once more the word was encircled with misgiving. She was agreeing to something … warily. A pause after she'd listened and then the interesting question: 'Is it such a secret delivery that it needs a codename?'

The words plucked at the hairs on the back of Jess' neck. Charlotte had delivered the line in a peculiar way: a tone not heard from the receptionist before. Somehow camping-up the intrigue with an unusual flourish in her voice.

'What does that mean?' The enquiry sounded emphatic. His answer must have been brief though, because she soon agreed. 'Okay. I'll bring the… "pocket watch" to you, this afternoon.'

Pocket watch! Surely that linked to Jess – a reference to 'One True Love'. The writer shared a suspicious glance with her own reflection. The length of her next inhalation drawing her body straight and rigid. Whatever he was talking about, it was something to do with her. After listening, the receptionist returned an odd collection of words.

'The time you'll leave and giv…'

But she was abruptly cut off and fell silent for a few sentences.

'Right.' She now sounded reassuringly confident and business-like. 'So I'll leave here in fifteen minutes. I'll get the train from Hackney Central. I should be with you in about an hour and a half.'

'With you!' Jess' stomach fluttered. This was a chance – a real opportunity. The detective's mind raced as the receptionist nodded along to a few more instructions. Charlotte then gave a strange exclamation – a murmur, becoming half a giggle, turning into a sigh, before finishing in a tut. Now composing herself to end the call formally.

'Goodbye.' Prim and proper, but the tone was cheeky – the word dragged out for amusement. A satisfied little clop as she put the phone back on the desk.

The excitement panged. What a chance! Obviously Jess had to follow. She looked down at the cup seized tightly in her grasp. Should she make a tea now, as if she just came out of her room? No. It would be smarter to make one in ten minutes, so she appeared settled in and not going anywhere, just as the receptionist leaves. She'd never actually shadowed Charlotte onto the train before, but this was clearly the day to do it. Convenient that Katya was out of the way too. The first decent lead the detective had sniffed out in ages. And she certainly needed it.

As Jess slipped back inside her room she could hear humming wafting through from reception. She had never heard Charlotte do that before. The tune was vaguely familiar. A famous piece of classical music? A hymn perhaps? There was definitely something choirgirl about it. The tune began to march, drawing closer as the receptionist moved towards the writer's room. Jess scurried to the desk, sat down and put hands to keys. Furrowing her brow in pantomime-thoughtfulness and typing the first thing that came to mind. A polite, little knock as Charlotte pushed the ajar door half-open. Head poking around, slanting body part-concealed behind the frame. She was trying to appear more relaxed than usual.

'Hiya.' For once, Charlotte's smile was as wide as the one Jess returned. 'I'm going to head off early this afternoon. I'm leaving to get the train in about fifteen minutes. The information was relayed with raised eyebrows and a miniscule pucker of the lips.

'Oh right. Any special plans?' Jess let her disinterested eyes drift back towards the screen.

'Nothing special.' The receptionist chimed with extra breeze.

'Well, it's a lovely afternoon.' The writer gestured to where a window might have been, but wasn't.

'Yes… and supposed to get even warmer tomorrow. Apparently we're heading for a heatwave.' Charlotte's beam was broadening again, beginning a fake-friendly 'goodbye' expression.

Although Jess interjected. 'Oh, you remember I'm heading off, tomorrow, after the meeting with Ms Stilenskova… to Guildford. To cat-sit for my mum.' The appropriate authorities had been informed weeks ago.

'Oh yes. I remember.' The receptionist reassured. 'Well, I'll errr…' Trailing off into a mumble as she retreated with another suspiciously emphatic curl of lips.

Jess sat back and looked at the words on her computer screen: 'Follow the White Rabbit!'

She pondered the phrasing her hurried hands had decided upon, before deleting with a one-finger staccato-tap. So what was the plan? If she was going to tail Charlotte across London, then she'd better be sneaky about it. A disguise perhaps? Change out of her polka-dot dress and put on a skirt? Go under the cover of her big, straw hat? Probably not that subtle. What's a good disguise for following someone? Who don't people suspect? Joggers jumped into her mind. A childhood memory of Erica's mum advising her girls that they needn't worry about stranger-danger with joggers, who could be safely relied upon to supervise children across the big road.

Erica's mother wore mad-mum leggings and once publicly threw a quiche onto her husband's car, but the point was that people don't suspect joggers. Charlotte had never seen Jess dressed like that, which would decrease the chance of being recognised if the receptionist made an idle scan behind. No one assumes joggers are following anyone – they're just going for a jog, everyone understands that. And the role would enable inauspicious running, if she needed to catch up fast or something. Jess was equipped with all the appropriate attire – would be good to finally get some use out of it.

Leaping into action, she located the running gear, tore off her clothes and pulled on the tight, grey leggings and top. Putting the polka-dot dress back on, as a covering layer, in case Charlotte returned before leaving. Sparkling-white trainers, wireless headphones, a hairband and a university sports-cap were readied under the desk. The phone-holder armband was carefully prepared, pockets stuffed with bank cards, key fob, money... and the mobile fixed into position. Word documents saved, so the computer was primed to shut down at a moment's notice. And she had time to make that tea as well, which was steaming by her side (convincingly) as the receptionist hummed back through.

'Okay. Bye then. See you tomorrow.'

Big, innocent smiles all round. The writer was already shutting down the laptop as Charlotte's head ducked out of view. A few seconds listening to the receptionist's footsteps withdrawing before all systems go! Jess ripped off the dress with a yanking criss-cross of limbs, body wriggling with urgency. Hearing the front door slam as she pulled on the trainers. Drawing her hair into a ponytail, slipping on the cap, yanking on the armband and waggling an earphone in on one side. The mirror-wall proclaimed she looked every bit a jogger... although it didn't believe she looked innocent (it never did). A few seconds running on the spot to warm into character. Shoes fit and springy and ready for action... and off she goes.

Out of the room, sly reflection fleeting along the glass towards the exit. Always a surprise to open the front door and find the outside world right there. Jess probed her head into the glaring brightness and gushing warm air. Her target about fifty metres down the road. Was this a good distance to follow at? Surely Hollywood must've taught a basic rule like that? But couldn't recall specific guidance on the matter. Anyway, she knew where Charlotte was going, so could afford to hang back. Although wouldn't want to miss any clues. What if the receptionist was picking up the 'pocket watch' on the way?

The writer stepped out into a beautiful summer's day. Warm sunshine, but a cool wind to keep the air fresh and keen. The meadows of southern England could be scented on the breeze, although not without a hint of London's sooty perfume. A lazy blue car swaggered past, slinging a few twangs of reggae out the window as it swung around the corner. Charlotte was trotting off in front, head bobbing along naïvely. She was a bit hit-and-miss with her choice of clothes, but the green skirt and top looked pretty good today. Those sandal-heels must be new, because there was something funny about the way the receptionist was walking. Stilted and uncomfortable, despite the spring in her step. When Jess had followed before, she'd noted the even rhythm with which Charlotte's satchel-brown handbag jounced off her buttock as she walked. This time, the bag seemed to be bumping wider, with less regularity in its swing (although perhaps wearing the backpack was responsible for the change). Charlotte was definitely in a good mood – that tell-tale smugness bouncing up-and-down in her posture.

Jess felt invigorated as well. This was clearly leading somewhere – leading to him! Her feet felt like running, although obviously that would defeat the object. Instead she checked her pace, ensuring no ground was inadvertently gained. Calm breaths... Charlotte was taking her directly to him. About fucking time! Six months since she saw the online ad for the erotica competition. Six fucking months! She really deserved this.

Especially after the submission she made last Friday – her most revealing one yet. Alongside 'One True Love' she'd submitted all her autobiographical pieces, from 'The Proposal' to 'Classic Romance'. She'd really exposed herself – told him everything about what she did, said, thought and felt. And her account had been ruthlessly honest, in almost every way. She'd explicitly admitted to obsessing about him, described her sneaky tactics trying to unravel the mystery, confessed to hiding under the desk and eavesdropping on the phone call. Had even recounted her embarrassingly boring sexual history and told him about her weird, childhood games with Carl.

In fact, the only part she left out was the post-it note detective-work bit with 'Muriel + Prisi'. Not quite sure why she decided to keep that useless scrap of information back. What was her rationale there? And how was she supposed to work out what was really going on, when half the time she couldn't even understand the reasoning behind her own behaviour? She didn't even know why she'd started writing the autobiographical pieces in the first place. Surely he'd instructed her, somehow? She couldn't remember how exactly... but then, their relationship had always been like that.

The glow tickled warmer every time she thought about her relationship with him. Okay, so it was a bit weird. And okay, it was only part real. But what a part – the best part! How many parts do you need anyway? And what really is real? How real can an emotion be? Surely feeling it makes it real. Especially feeling it with this intensity – this depth... deeper and deeply. The distance between them drew closer every time they looked into each other's eyes through the mirror... or simply when they thought of one another. Not only could Jess feel him watching through the glass, sometimes she could feel him thinking about her from miles away. A wolf scenting the air as the fragrant breeze of her dreams washes over his moonlit hilltop. Their connection had purified into an unspeakable kind of intimacy. Becoming closer, stronger, more intense every day... and every night. It was the rest of the world disappearing into the distance.

Jess tugged herself out of the daydream before the real world vanished completely. Rationality scolding her to concentrate on the task in hand. Charlotte was waiting at the zebra crossing, holding her handbag back with her palm as if it might swing into the road by itself. Did that mean she had something valuable inside? Codenamed 'the pocket watch'? Maybe... but Jess didn't really think so – this whole white rabbit thing was very suspicious. The odd half-waddle still evident as the receptionist resumed walking. And some kind of skulk in her manner. She was definitely up to something. Jess let her quarry get around the corner and partway down the alley before crossing herself. Continually having to resist the urge to break into a jog.

One way or another, things felt like they'd been coming to a head recently. Charlotte had seemed genuinely busy over the last few weeks, with many of her emails important enough to require sign-off from Ms Stilenskova. The atmosphere had been escalating in subtle ways and this had whetted the writer's anticipation even further. Jess had to make some kind of progress today. She'd be leaving for Guildford tomorrow (to spend a week cat-sitting) so really needed something to hang on to. It would be weird not sleeping in the mirror, for the first time in months. Although Mum's house would be empty (except for Baggins), so she wouldn't be thrust back into the real world too rudely.

The target was now standing at the traffic lights, at the top of the road leading down to the station. Her gaze fixed dead-ahead, paying little attention to the world – satisfyingly naïve. After crossing, Jess kept to the other side of the pedestrianised street. Watching Charlotte diagonally through the chugging flow of human traffic. A meandering drunk with sun-squinted eyes raised to the heavens. A circus of teenage boys, laughing uproariously as the joker of the pack waggled his head and performed. A strict, young mum, shout-chatting into her phone as she led a well-ordered division of children into McDonalds. The mobile app said the next westbound train was due in six minutes. Assuming the target was going west again. Were there any actual reasons to presume this? Or just fictional reasons, that the writer had forgotten she'd made up herself? If they were going west, then the receptionist would probably do the same as last time – cross over the footbridge and move to wait where the front of the train was due.

Charlotte was now making her way up the sloping path towards the station's entrance. Jess kept visual contact until the target turned through the ticket barriers. The best plan was to wait outside, then make a rush for it when the train arrived. She looked at her phone with half-an-expression posed, convincing passers-by that everything was normal. There were any number of plausible reasons she might decide to wait outside the station. If she smoked, she'd have a cigarette now (presumably spies often use that cover). Although it would clash with her jogger's attire. Was the runner thing really such a good disguise? Did joggers use trains to go somewhere to exercise? Surely they just run around the local park? And of course, she wasn't actually jogging… and didn't look as if she had been. But no point in worrying about that. Just pretend to be relaxed.

The arriving train provided cover for Jess' move through the ticket barriers and up onto the concrete footbridge, springing up the stairway and crossing the tracks at an energetic canter. (Fuck you, doubters, I'm jogging!) She congratulated herself for agility as she shimmied past an old man doddering down the steps on the other side. Charlotte would already be on-board, about twenty metres further forward. Stepping inside, the slick cool train flushed contrast with the warmth outside. A shiny, modern vehicle with conjoined carriages to enable vision right the way down. The stretching tunnel of metal and glass lined with seats – about a quarter occupied, plus a few standers, hanging or huddling around the poles. The crowd-cover was thin-to-moderate. Could be better, but definitely preferable to tracking the target during rush hour.

The faces of her fellow passengers didn't suspect anything. A thickset, pink-skinned man in a tool belt, sat with eyes closed, resting his shaven head back against the glass. Opposite him, a couple of caramel-coloured teenage girls gaggled and squawked in dispute over which song their shared earphones would play next. An earnest young man in an oversized suit hovered near the doors – bespectacled face ghost-white and skull strained with several bonus years of stress. As the train pulled away, Jess tentatively began to make her way forwards. Needed to find the target, but there was the risk that Charlotte might catch sight of her first. That would be bad – there was no plausible excuse for being here. Today's whole mission would be blown if she got spotted. She tilted the cap to provide more cover and scanned carefully.

There she was! Sitting innocuously on the right-hand side of the carriage, less than ten metres away, reading something on her iPad. Jess quickly sat down on the same side, a vast Caribbean lady with a peacock fan providing perfect concealment. Although with the impressive air-con, it was surprising she felt the need to ventilate quite so melodramatically. Menopause maybe? Not important! Focus on the task at hand. After a quick risk assessment, Jess realised that when the target finally made for the doors, she'd probably come this way down the carriage. Maybe manoeuvre away a bit? Although doing so could look strange to her fellow passengers. But who cares? No one was paying attention to her anyway. Not like she was the one being followed.

But as she made the move, the thought occurred to her that it was possible she was being followed. What if he was tracking Jess, while she was tailing Charlotte? Had he seen the writer's espionage through the mirror-wall and decided to hunt along? Although that would mean the whole pocket watch phone call was a pre-meditated trap from the outset. She'd written about her previous eavesdropping (and intention to one day follow the receptionist) and now he was using it against her? That was so like him. And the detective hadn't been watching her own back at all. She'd just fixated on Charlotte, ironically congratulating herself on how naïve her target was. What if Jess was his target – locked in his sights? The jitter in her calves shivered up the inside of her legs.

She peered down the snaking belly of the train. How could he have got on behind her? Her mind ran through various calculations and simulated scenarios. There were several possibilities. He could have left the office earlier (after confirming she'd fallen for his lure) and then got on at the back of the train before her. Jess scanned fervently, there was a tall man standing by the doors at the distant rear of the vehicle, although he was too far away to see properly. Why would he follow her now? A hunting game? Was she being lured somewhere nice and quiet? A cool breeze over the skin as she exhaled. Shouldn't let her imagination get carried away. Had to remind herself: she was going crazy... being driven crazy.

As the train pulled into the first station the detective found herself focusing on the far figure, rather than the target. He didn't move. Shouldn't let herself get distracted with his illusions. A quick check found the receptionist still absorbed in her tablet. Wonder what she's reading? Hope it's smut! Dirty little bitch!

The receptionist stayed on the Overground after passing the Underground connection, so was definitely heading for West London. Jess had been getting deeper undercover, acquiring an abandoned newspaper and swaying to the imaginary rhythm her earphones weren't emitting. Really she was still dwelling on the mystery. What was 'pocket watch' code for? Did it refer to an actual object, or was the phrase being used as a playful lure? What were Charlotte's exact words again? They didn't really make much sense. Another frustrating riddle! Life was full of them recently... and Jess hadn't been finding any solutions. What did 'Muriel + Prisi' mean? She'd been puzzling about that for months. Were Muriel and Prisi names? If so, who the fuck were they? Other women? Women in the same position as Jess? She didn't like that idea at all. Surely what he and Jess had was unique and special. Muriel sounded like an old woman. Was Prisi even a name? Prissy?

Sounded uptight. And why formulate the words like that:
1) Muriel – Prisi
2) "

Why bother to put the second point and the ditto? Surely: '1) Muriel, 2) Prisi'. Including the second number didn't make any sense. Nothing made any sense: the magic mirror, the proposal, the building, the business, the overheard calls, the strange dreams, the feelings she felt. The whole mystery had been swirling around the skies of her mind for so long… and the endless motion continued as the train meandered across London.

The sensation of deceleration as they began pulling into another station. Charlotte was standing by the door, handbag suppressed behind. They were getting off here. Where was here? A sign for Hampstead Heath flashed past in a blur. Jess cast her eyes back to check on the tall man. He'd vanished, although he'd definitely been on-board after the last stop, so must still be on the train somewhere. She strained her brow but couldn't make him out. The doors slid open as the auto-announcer proclaimed their arrival at the heath. Charlotte was given space to alight and get a few paces ahead. Jess kept half an eye over her own shoulder as she followed. Couldn't see any suspicious figures behind… and a tall man like that would find it hard to hide in such a modest crowd. The ticket barriers swung open as she slipped her card over the sensor. The receptionist was bearing right, moving the chase up onto the heath itself.

Keeping to the paved path, Charlotte followed the marching line of grand, old trees up the grassy slope. Jess stopped and knelt, pretending to tie her laces whilst surreptitiously watching the station behind. Just an ordinary jogger prepping her footwear before exercise – perfectly normal. Returning attention to the fore, she noted the exuberant rhythm maintained in Charlotte's gait… although the wide lumber suggested she still hadn't got used to the shoes. Was it the shoes, or had she been injured somehow?

Suffered a punishment perhaps? What kind? What sort of weapon might inflict a shuffling waddle like that? A wide, thuddy, wooden paddle? A long, thin, flicking whip? A swishing, metal-studded flogger? Jess didn't really have the experience necessary to make an informed guess – her practical education had been ruthlessly neglected. When the fuck was show-and-tell?! Anyway, don't daydream! Just concentrate on the real world here-and-now.

The sunshine winked and dappled under the shambling foliage. Breezes picking up a playful gusto as they ran around bare legs and bounded out across the green. The smell of summer flowered all around and it seemed the whole city was out to enjoy it. Babe-laden prams pushed by yummy mummies or fresh-faced au pairs. Couples strolling arm-in-arm. Extended family picnics spilling out over the grass... static nuclei of adults surrounded by buzzing swirls of children – some orbiting in racing loops, some shooting off at random, several bursting with excitement or tears. And lots of joggers of course. Jess avoided eye contact with the serious devotee speeding past. She looked impressive with her sleek kit, toned body and sweat-lathered skin. Imagine the contempt she'd feel for a blatant faker like Jess.

They walked uphill, past the three large ponds. The swimming lake would be crowded today, but the view was mostly obscured by the shoreline trees. Overhead, a few patches of cloud raced across blue skies in high winds. Jess watched a line of shadow sweeping across the landscape as one such shroud enveloped the sun. A swish of Nature's cloak, highlighting the dramatic contrast between bright and dark green, before the sun returned in full dazzle. As the slopes trundled higher, views across various swathes of London popped and ducked out from behind the treelines. The vegetation beginning to crowd closer as they headed north, grassy parks turning to heathy woodlands.

The city seemed far away up here. The chirp of birdsong from the branches, the buzz of bees among the foxgloves, the rustle of life in the undergrowth. A solemn old couple, pacing along with arms behind their backs. A group of teenage girls, perched on the splayed limbs of a fallen tree, listening to their loud-lipped friend boasting about sex. A long-limbed canine racing ahead of its unseen human, hunting through the vegetation with playful, predatory dreams. The people were fewer and further between though… and the path had become a dusty track. Actually there was no one in sight now, except Charlotte. The target was far ahead, but Jess felt conspicuous. Let the gap between them widen a little further maybe? The fake-jogger paused and put hands on knees, as if tired from all this running. Actually she was perspiring a bit, after the long incline. Charlotte's green figure shaded into the trees as the path ahead wound out of sight… leaving the writer alone in the woods.

Her eyes flicked towards some dense brush at the side of the path. The leaves were moving slowly. Not the way they move when the concealed creature is small. She'd heard that large predators fit their motions to blend with the natural sway of the undergrowth, lulling their prey into a false sense of security. At least Jess didn't sense security. A heavy shroud clouded overhead and the woods darkened like a black spell. The complexion of the whole world changing. Shadows among shadows as she cast her eyes about. A chilling stir of wind twirled a few leaves from the ground as if to emphasise how quiet it was. The civilised London park had suddenly become 'the heath': worthy of all the wild, wuthering romance evoked by that word. Now easy to imagine the place as it was long ago, before the metropolis expanded around it – a lonely stretch of countryside, miles from the distant lights of the city. Easy to imagine oneself getting hunted here…

If you go down in the woods today,
Your lure of a big surprise,
If you go down in the woods today,

MIRROR SECRET MIRROR

You'd better go in disguise,
For every dare that ever there was,
He'll take you there for certain,
Because today's the day the,
Wolf is having his picnic...

Imagine... noticing that tall figure following behind. In the distance, but gaining ground purposefully. Long, stealthy strides, head hunting forward – moving like a predator. The creeping feeling that you might be prey. The hunted walking quicker, hurrying along. But scanning back to see the shadowy pursuer drawn closer. Trying not to panic – don't look over your shoulder too often. He must be able to smell the fear already. Jittering feet scurrying now. Best not to run; don't want to provoke a chase. Casting eyes back to find him closer still, padding silently through the brush... moving in. Realising you're definitely prey! A little stumble over a sneaking root, the other foot jolting to catch up... and then neither wanting to be left behind. Run, run, run!

Hurtling off the path and diving into the bushes, brambles scratching forearms like grasping claws... tearing through their clutches. Low body moving at speed, ducking under the grab of the thorny branches. Undergrowth and scrubs coming thick and fast, arms fending them away from the face but a swishing lash of thin wood across the cheek. Driving onwards... and the heavens dramatically rearing up overhead as she breaks out onto the open heath. Running over the grass with the whipping wind chasing. Legs pummelling full-pelt. Big, dark, open sky. Ground tilting downwards, fleeing feet plummeting towards it. Blood burning in the adrenaline of the chase. The wild excitement of running and being pursued. The clutch of primal fear! No need to look back; she can feel his timeless presence behind... pursuing... catching up... drawing closer... ever closer. Predatory eyes deathly calm.

KISSING

She knows she needs to run faster, but has nothing more to give. The oncoming woods striped black and grey, growing rapidly taller before she plunges headlong through the treeline. Thorns stinging the cheeks in a flurry of sharp lashes. Face full of scrub, heart hammering, leg tripping on a rudely extended tree-limb. Hands clutching the soil, but pushing off frantically. Lurching up and keeping half her balance as she tumbles forward through the bracken, wood snapping underfoot. Vision spinning back and forth, glimpsing the predator's shadow closing… closer and closer. A heavy thwack of brushwood on the head and her ankle clipped by creeper. Sprawling forwards to bang hands and knees on the hard ground.

Cruel trees circle the dusky clearing, caging the sky with twisted wood-wire. A lonely part of the forest. Scrambling to her feet, but she knows it's too late… can feel him close. And looking up to see him right there. Predator's eyes freezing some of her delicious fear for later. Trying to run, yet feeling the glide of his pounce in the air behind. Arms catching around her waist and thighs… and bringing her down. Body slamming onto the dirt, elbow pick-axing the ground, soil billowing up into her mouth and nose. Cap flying off, but glasses clinging on. And the feel of his teeth sinking into her flank, biting through the leggings into the buttock, clenching hard. Prey screaming wild in the sharp, shooting pain. His incisors releasing grip as a strong hand grabs the top of her leggings and rips downwards. Clothes tearing away to leave her bare behind waggling.

She thrusts a hip forward, but his teeth come down again, biting into her ass like a juicy slab of meat. Squealing, wriggling and squirming… a roll of her twisting flesh clamped in his jaws. Digging nails into the dirt to claw away… and him just letting her go. Sprawling and falling upwards in her desperation to escape. Finding her feet, but leggings and panties twisting around the ankles like manacles and tripping her to tumble forwards. Flashes of muscular body looming over as she rolls. The buzz of flies unzipping… the sight of his big, nasty dick swinging… bearing down on her.

On her back and scraping her heel down the calf to kick the fabric shackles onto just one shoe. Feet scrabbling at the ground to drive away, but his powerful body springing on top. Arms hooking up under the knees and wrenching her legs into the air, his whole trunk thrusting between them. Savage eyes coming down under a coat of bark hair, fierce snarl crunching the top of his nose as the nostrils flare, mouth salivating. All that strength and muscle pressing down on top, pushing her into the dirt, pinning her prone. Sticks and stones digging into her back. The tip of his hard cock tickling around her exposed pussy. His right arm curling up, clutching and tearing open her top – ripping it clean off. Frantically twisting her body away, but a hand on the neck to flatten her back out. Bra torn and flapping either side of blancmange breasts. An evil grin savouring the sight. She screams and smacks an open hand across his face. A roar of a laughing glee thrown out to the forest.

Releasing her neck to re-secure her flailing left leg. Pushing her knees back over her shoulders, so her groin curves up against him. He could've gathered the arms underneath, but decided not to. Wants to feel her wild, desperate counter strikes as he takes her. Her traitorous pussy overflowing with juices as his helmet presses it open. The humiliation of his triumphant smile. Jiggling and yelling, but her lips forced apart, gaping to fit all that girth, driving deep inside. She cries war and swings her whole body into the slap. A loud clap to turn his face for another howl of a laugh to the wilds. As he turns back down she punches with closed fist, but his chin is harder than her knuckles. Grabbing a handful of hair to pull his head down onto the blows – instead lifting her upper body towards him. Smacking and hitting, yet nothing soft on his evil, smiling face, her fingers cutting against enamel. She tries to pull her lower half away but he blends with the movement, thrusting deeper inside her pussy, the recoil of the violence bouncing back... shaking her up and down along his shaft.

She screws a thumb-nail inside his smirking lips to try and tear off the side of his face, but he counters with a playful chomp of the teeth. Insulting mirth in his eyes as his head follows her withdrawing hand. Pushing it aside to run his long, slavering tongue up over her chin, cheek and eyelid... and thrusting his cock along with it. Wet saliva slopping over her face. Half her vision a sticky blur as he withdraws his tongue to prepare the next lick. She crunches up to snatch his lower lip in her teeth and bites with all her might. The enjoyment of real pain in his chuckle. His hot blood trickling into her mouth as they hold one another on the floor of the forest.

The sun's bold return speckled shafts of light through the leafy canopy. A butterfly flittering in the haze. A woman cooing for her dog somewhere close by. Enough external awareness built up to startle Jess out of her daydream. Shit! What was she doing? How long had she been dawdling here? Where the fuck was Charlotte? The writer had been so away with the fairies, she'd completely lost track of the target. Had to find her. Time for a jog. She scuttled into stride and began towards the last sighting. What if she went the wrong way? Pace picking up as she cantered around the corner and continued through the woods. Scolding herself as she had to choose which way to go at a crossroads – meaning she risked losing her quarry entirely. How could she be so stupid? Although as it turned out, she needn't have worried too much. It wasn't long before she spotted the tell-tale bump of that brown handbag against the receptionist's green-clad behind. Jess stopped running and let the pursuit settle back to a more leisurely pace.

Continuing northwards, the noisy return of angry traffic surprised as they cut across a busy road. But the dappled woodland resumed and soon they were among the trees again. Back to the sort of place a bunny could get held face down with the wolf's teeth clenched around the scruff of her neck. Or tied to a tree and taken with her back scraping painfully on the rough bark. Afterwards, left hanging there like a trophy. She shook her head and rebuked herself: don't get distracted with sick fantasies. Just focus on the task at hand.

The lie of the land was now sloping downhill and the view opened out as they emerged from the woods. It didn't look like the suburb of London she knew it was, more like a village in a valley. Layered greens, neatly lined with hedgerows, dropping away in the foreground. In the background: terraced gardens rising into clusters of picturesque houses, with the skyline dominated by the sleepy spire of a church. They walked towards the steeple, heading out of the park and onto the streets of Hampstead. Big, expensive houses on well-manicured estates. Sleepy, residential avenues interspersed with squares and greens. The lusty smell of wealth. They must've been walking for forty-five minutes since the station. The receptionist's trundle even more laboured now. But they were coming to a turning... that seemed familiar. Jess gasped in surprise.

The oaks stood either side of the road. Wizened old gatekeepers, guarding their leafy cul-de-sac. Charlotte walked along the hedgerow of little conifers, fronting the property, and turned into the driveway. Holy shit! Jess raced to catch up, glimpsing the metallic claret of his car through the trees. She jogged past, but her target had disappeared around the curve of dusty shingle. Fuck! How to see? She couldn't just walk down the drive, so the only option was through the conifers. They stood close, so she had to go low and push her way through. But as her pine-feathered head popped out of the treeline the only thing she saw was the front door slamming closed. Shit! Had he let Charlotte in? Did she have a key? Was there a key under the pot with the painted sunflower? Now Jess couldn't see anything – no movement spotted through the windows. The building stood squarely overhead. Its outward expression gave little away, although there was the definite feeling that it knew something she didn't.

She spied on the house from the hedgerow for a while – not even a glimpse of movement. She tried scouting around for a better angle, but couldn't find any approaches that didn't require going through neighbour's gardens... and Jess wasn't prepared to clamber over tall fences in broad daylight. Already felt conspicuous enough: hanging around, casing out the property. The area seemed deserted, but the stalker was vulnerable to prying eyes from an upstairs window. She found a place to wait and watch close-by... and loitered for over two hours. But it was futile. It was tempting to just march up and ring the bell, although that would be a crude way to play the game. There really wasn't anything she could do from here. In the end, she just had to give up and go back to the office. Very frustrating – so close... and yet so far.

It was an exasperating evening of pacing and clenching. And she was unable to sleep, of course. A long, muggy night inside a mind that wouldn't shut up... and couldn't shut down. It didn't exactly put her in a good frame of mind for the review meeting – the ninth official face-to-face with the charming Ms Stilenskova. That first one, back in winter, seemed like a whole lifetime ago – a whole, weird lifetime. They still observed the same absurd ritual now, Jess bringing her little chair through to wait in reception, even though the writer would ordinarily be working at her desk about ten metres away. And obviously, Katya felt it appropriate to keep her sitting there for over twenty minutes. Jess' reflecting face looked highly irritated. So disappointing to find the house, yet still not catch sight of him. Although she shouldn't feel too upset – at least she'd been to his home... in reality this time. That definitely counted for something. It was progress. Of course, the whole thing about the house begged the obvious question...

Charlotte's phone buzzed into life and the receptionist answered in her pathetically polite way, assuring her boss that the writer was coming through. Jess packed up the chair and walked across the room. Her mirrored expression embittered and impatient; untamed, sleepless eyes. Surely she had to get something significant today. A reproachful glare into the mirror-wall as she pushed through the door. Katya was reading something on her mobile, sitting back from the desk in a neat S-shaped pose. Jess resolved not to concede a greeting smile, so maintained a grave face as she set up her seat. Meeting the agent's frown with a serious expression of her own. Although she worried her disinterested eyelashes might appear sulky – in a weak way. Katya slapped the mobile down and pulled herself closer to the desk. Elbows on the surface, steepled fingers arrowed as she leant forward. There was no time for small talk.

'So, I am to tell you 'thank you' for all of your work.' The agent pronounced 'thank you' as if a word she'd never seen before had just popped up on an autocue. However, the next words rolled off the tongue more easily. 'But he don't want any more story right now. So when you go today, you take your stuff with you to your mum's. You don't stay here after today. You don't work here anymore. You not needed.'

Jess must've zoned out for a moment, because she found herself staring directly into Katya's eyes. The agent was glaring back, absorbing the writer's shocked confusion with an air of frosty satisfaction. Jess felt words trying to come, but they caught in her throat (even though the voice was so small). Couldn't work out what was going on. Katya seemed to be saying that the writer was getting fired and thrown out of the building. But that couldn't be right… surely?

'What? What do you…?'

'You not needed here anymore. You move out and take your stuff today.' The Russian sat back, combative eyes holding Jess' gaze.

The writer felt the air passing out through her mouth. She tried to catch some to form words. Eventually managing a little,

'No.' The shy exclamation wobbling out into the room on its own. She was shaking her head to let Katya know that she must be wrong. There'd obviously been some kind of misunderstanding. But the agent's posture spoke unflinching affirmation. Turning to the mirror, the writer just found her own face staring back. She looked perplexed, shocked and upset – as if she might cry. She could already taste the sobs gulping up from her throat.

'So, Charlotte will give you the money and the… feedback… as normal. But then you go.' Jess could feel her face quivering. Katya was prodding for a reaction – putting on a 'rabbit in the headlights' expression and repeatedly flash-flaring her nostrils in supposed mimicry of the writer. She obviously wanted to see her victim burst into tears – finally, make her cry – as had always been inevitable. She'd love that. Well, she could go fuck herself! Jess now felt a new negative emotion surging to the fore at a furious gallop.

'You're lying.' The words hissed out almost under her breath. Katya must be lying. This was her – not him. The evil bitch was trying to sabotage everything. This wasn't what he wanted. The anger welling up inside, bubbling up her spine. Her legs straightened and she was suddenly standing and speaking forcefully. 'No!' Katya had to withdraw her head to maintain eye contact as Jess glared down. 'You're lying!' The writer proclaimed it loudly. 'I don't believe you!'

Her voice and posture quivering with adrenaline, but still strong and blazing with defiance. The Russian glowered back and began to stand. The slim shake of her head expressing silent threat as she rose to her full height. Now staring down on Jess with arms poised as if she might have a weapon at the waist. The writer squared her shoulders and boldly held her front. But it was no use arguing with Katya – the stupid bitch wasn't going to admit her mistake. Jess needed him. Where was he? A glance towards the mirror. Maybe she should call him out. The agent was about to say something, but she wouldn't get the chance.

The writer burst out, 'Liar!' The childish statement at least served the purpose of shouting Katya down.

Jess swung around and stormed off. She needed to find him and tell him what the Russian had said. He couldn't possibly have green-lighted this. She yanked the door and stormed into reception. Charlotte had heard the shouts and was staring intently at her computer – cowardly little bitch! There were two brown envelopes on her desk. One of them was the feedback! The feedback from him. That would make it all alright, set the record straight. The door's slam boomed in the high hollows. Jess jabbed her face in to challenge as she snatched the packages up. The receptionist squirmed away, keeping her eyes cloying to the screen.

The writer stomped around the desk and cornered into the kitchen area. Holding the packages to her chest as she shunted into her room. Tearing open, the large envelope held print-outs of all her latest submissions – the stories stapled together separately. She spilled the papers over the desk and went through them impatiently. Eyes hunting for marks and comments. He'd have said something in the feedback, bypassing Katya. This communication was between him and Jess and the agent didn't understand. He'd discredit the Russian and tell the writer to ignore her and just carry on as before. He'd make a joke out of it perhaps – say 'she's rash/insensitive/misleading'... something like that. Surely? Although scanning through she couldn't see any red scribblings on the first manuscript... none at all. Not on the next one either. Turning the pages over frantically now. Where was the fucking feedback?! There was nothing. After she submitted all that exposing stuff! What the fuck!

She thumped onto the wood and spun towards the mirror. Surely he was here. Surely he'd come out to calm things down. There'd been a misunderstanding – those had been forgiven before. The writer's frazzled reflection morphed into him as if she were seeing through the glass: cold eyes, stony face... heartless bastard! She wanted to hurl something at the mirror and smash it to smithereens. Maybe she should finally do that. Use Eloy as a battering ram: a war elephant! She'd love to see all these fucking mirrors come shattering down.

The rage coursing through her began to melt in the escalating heat. Frustration, hatred, fury, dismay. Her eyes were watering red. That was just anger so far, but other emotions threatened to explode. Half of her wanted to break down and cry, but the stronger half resisted. She wasn't going to blubber... not here. But that meant she had to get out fast. She certainly wasn't going to helpfully remove her stuff. Fuck you, Katya! The writer grabbed the rucksack (already packed for cat-sitting) and stuffed the money and manuscripts inside.

Withdrawing Eloy from position and pushing the door to swing as she stalked through. The massive slam building up to provide a well-timed, dramatic accompaniment for Jess' return to reception. Katya was standing by the desk with suspicious, dark eyes targeting the writer. Charlotte was swivelled away, hands on lap and gaze not-looking. Jess marched past to stand between the coat-stand and the exit before swinging around to confront them. She didn't know what to say though. Glancing her enemy's suit jacket hanging, the writer jerked out her hand and toppled the stand.

'Fuck you, Katya! You horrible fucking bitch!' Jess swung her glower to strike Charlotte with surprise eye contact. 'And fuck you too!'

The receptionist looked satisfyingly shocked... and the agent satisfyingly angry, peripheral vision lingering over her crumpled jacket. Katya was preparing to say something, but again wasn't quick enough. Jess had already turned and was making towards the door. A flash of movement behind as the agent came after her. The sun blazed as the writer stormed out into the heatwave. Her pursuer catching the swinging door before it slammed. Well, fuck her! Jess wasn't going to run off like a coward. She stopped and turned, managing to prevent herself from posing a livid hand on hip. Katya stood on the doorstep, body steaming with energy. Furious eyes seething. But a flutter of lids and her breathing seemed to calm. Jess' pathetic display of defiance cheering the Russian's temper. Regaining composure, her expression sneered into a smirk.

'Aww, poor little puppy. But you not wanted. So you can just fuck off now.' Exaggerating a smiley face as she mocked and mimed... 'Kiss, kiss, kiss.'

Hand on hip, the mistress curled her body playfully, touching fingers to pouting red lips as she overblew the final kiss with theatrical flourish.

The door slammed shut.

ELEVEN
JUST BETWEEN US

Baggins blinked a casual glance of acknowledgement towards Jess as he padded into the lounge. She smiled, always pleased (and mildly amused) at the appearance of this fat, middle-aged tabby-cat with head disproportionately small, relative to the size of his body. He paused, eyes squinting zen as he pondered the key question of the afternoon. But the angle of the sun made the decision easy, the light bathing invitingly over the comfy, green chair with the long, wooden armrests. The mental labour accomplished, he sidled across the room and began psyching up for the physical. Clearing his to-do list with a lolloping leap up onto the seat… and settling down to indulge his favourite pastime. Curling up cat-like on this occasion, rather than adopting the ridiculous, human-style pose he sometimes preferred (sitting belly-up with paws down his sides).

  He didn't bother pretending his lethargy was the result of any recent exertions. Baggins was completely unashamed regarding his chronic lack of ambition and drive (low even by feline standards). There'd never been any desire to prove his hunting prowess, or build his social/political status in the eyes of his peers. He didn't even bother trying to defend his territory. He'd never really done anything at all.

Jess fondly remembered the time the neighbours asked to borrow the cat, after they'd located a rodent in their sitting room. Upon being airlifted to the scene, Baggins pricked and postured, in recognition that there was, indeed, a mouse hiding under the sofa. Before quickly deducing that the little creature posed no threat to his own plan of bedding down, on the sofa, and treating himself to a substantial snooze. The neighbours didn't invite him back in a pest-control capacity, but he still dined out at their house regularly. Such a friendly, content being – perfectly at ease with his low-achieving lifestyle. Not a cat who'd ever be endangered by curiosity.

Jess cupped her mug in both hands as she moved over to join him. Nestling into the plush carpet beside Baggins' chair and placing her tea on the armrest. Smoothing her palm along his silky coat as they basked in the glorious sunshine. Summer breezed through the open windows, along with the hum of distant lawn-mowers and the fragrance of freshly cut grass. The scents and sounds of a suburban Saturday afternoon, under the lazy blaze of an English heatwave. The cat purred gently as he nuzzled into Jess' hand, tickling finger smudging against buffeting face. She rustled the tuft of fur between his eyes, where hairs met from different directions and spiked into a little tussock. Such a satisfying bristling sensation for all concerned.

The writer had contemplated Baggins' personality, worldview and lifestyle with envious eyes over the last few days. He didn't have to concern himself with money, work, ambition, sex. The only potentially complex thing that mattered to him were relationships, but the important ones had worked out perfectly well (with little effort involved) and various friendly apes provided all the food, petting and general adoration he required. So there wasn't anything to worry about... and he was happy. Jess should take a leaf out of his book and just chill out – try not to dwell on all the troubles of the world. She'd done far too much of that lately.

It was weird not living in the mirror. Everything seemed different being back in Guildford, seeing things from a removed perspective. Her reflections changing, awareness half-awakening from a dream. Inhabiting the bewildering hypnopompic state between sleep and wakefulness, but starting to look back at events with fresh eyes. Noticing beliefs, she'd held onto tightly, feeling as if they may float off. Watching her perceived reality in the process of shape-shifting… her story in flux. Although some things remained the same – the pain she felt was still real and vivid and heavy. It wasn't just going to evaporate. But there was no point wallowing in emotional sentimentality, she needed to be rational and properly straighten things out in her head. This was an opportunity to take a step back and look at the cold, hard facts. The truth: the brutal truth.

But what were the cold, hard facts? For months she'd been building an elaborate structure of interconnected beliefs ever higher into the clouds. But it was a fantasy palace, established on the shakiest foundations of half-facts and hopeful assumptions. Suppositions built upon presuppositions. How to sort the fact from the fiction? One approach was to take a certain belief she held, about a particular aspect of the situation, and ask: what reason did she have to accept it was true? Was there any actual evidence to support it? Often she found the inspected belief was unsubstantiated… and was actually based on other uncorroborated beliefs. Reflections reflecting reflections… all the way to the horizons. Almost nothing concrete or real. Shocking how little there was to be sure about. And yet she'd just been acting as if everything her mad, off-the-wall imagination wanted to be true, was genuinely true. When maybe it wasn't.

What did she really know about him? Truthfully? There was plenty to go on, if one counted circumstantial evidence and accepted a number of dubious, fundamental assumptions. There were written messages, overheard calls, possible sightings, intuitive whisperings, feelings... strong feelings. But not much hard evidence of the kind a neutral observer would require in order to formulate a sensible judgement. She could've made him almost entirely from the clouds... but that just didn't feel true! There was too much reality to him... inside her. She felt she knew him. She knew she'd felt him. Couldn't just have imagined all that... out of thin air. Could she?

Jess recalled a friend once complaining that, before Tinder dates, she tended to build up a utopian vision of what the man she was meeting would be like in real life. Only to realise afterwards, she'd constructed her fantasy on little more than misplaced hopefulness and mindless optimism. Was it possible to do that on an epic scale? A difficult thought to even begin to think, when it came to the question of who he was. Because if one really comes down to it... looking at the actual evidence available... any sane person would have to conclude: This was not the time for the full-on, brutal, rational truth!

Why does everything have to be so brutal anyway? One can be honest, without having to resort to brutality (at least partly honest). Jess turned to gentle Baggins and his sincere purr of contentment. She had more than cold, hard facts – she had knowledge gained through actual experience. She'd experienced him: seen him, heard him, felt him, smelled him, tasted him. She knew him – she knew it. They'd connected: a real connection; an emotional connection; a spiritual connection. A meeting of hearts and minds. She felt the memories vividly enough to purr her own contentment.

Until she remembered he'd thrown her away... just like that. A waling throb of hurt pulsed throughout, neck dropping the head forward melodramatically, face falling like a slow-motion vase. She really shouldn't think about it – it was too raw and painful. Smoothing her hand along the soft fur on Baggins' underbelly and sitting back for a sip of tea. Although it'd gone cold. Been left for too long. Should get another. Or maybe some wine instead? That might quell the anxiety. Help her forget about things.

No point trying to work everything out anyway. There's few true certainties in life. Although one thing to be completely certain of: Katya was a total fucking bitch! And it was certain she'd read the stories – at least one of them. The way she stood on the doorstep and quoted the exact words from 'Those Three Little Words'. Blowing her kisses precisely as described in the text. It obviously wasn't a coincidence. And if she'd read that, then she'd probably read the other stories as well. A deep cringe shuddered through Jess' body. How excruciatingly embarrassing! What a complete fool she'd made of herself. And why was she so surprised to find out the agent had read them? After all, the writer had been sending her submissions directly to Katya's email address. Why assume she blindly forwarded them on? Just because it was easier to think that, basically. Jess felt so stupid. Best not to dwell on that either.

But opening the fridge, the cool flush of air washing over her body reminded of the wine-serving scene in 'Pet Names'. Katya would've read that. All those grovelling words about how sexy she was, with it being perfectly obvious the writer was using Charlotte's character as a proxy for herself. In fact, the agent would have noted Jess' explicit confession of that humiliating truth whilst reading 'The Proposal'. God, it was mortifying! The memory of the blown kisses and the flamboyant panache of the movement. What a wonderful way to let the writer know, that she knew. The disproportionality between the effortlessness of the action and the level of pain and anxiety it caused – such an elegantly efficient display of power. Ravishingly sadistic! Katya deserved to be so pleased with herself.

Charlotte would probably be less pleased with the way she was described in the stories. If she had read them, then it would certainly explain why the atmosphere around reception never got over the initial awkwardness. Imagine the poor woman having to interact with Jess, all the time knowing what fucked-up fantasies the writer was penning about her own degradation and humiliation. Christ, it was head-plunging! Although if true, you had to commend the receptionist's game-face. Her multiple masks layered over one another perfectly. Jess tried not visualise what Charlotte's sincere facial expression towards the writer would look like. She might not have read the stories of course. She may not really know what was going on.

But he certainly knew what was going on... and he'd deliberately decided to get rid of Jess. Why would he do that? Got bored of her? Found a better one? He already had Katya and Charlotte. The writer probably never meant that much to him. No, that could not be true! So what was the reason? This couldn't be a rejection power game as themed in 'Those Three Little Words'. It'd gone too far for that. He'd thrown her out of the whole world they'd shared and sent her away somewhere completely different. He'd had her: under his control; under his roof; under his command. Why relinquish that? It couldn't be part of the original plan. Or what was she expected to do – go grovelling back to him with another unrequested tribute story... with Katya as intermediary? Not fucking likely!

She could go over to the house of course. But that would mean she was going over to complain. What was she going to do – bang on the door and make a scene? Not her style really. And in any case, she felt more sad than angry... which was pathetic. At least her own feebleness evoked feelings of rage (although mainly with herself). A pitifulness that plumbed new depths. And she couldn't face going back to the office to collect her stuff – another thing to avoid thinking about.

Everything had gone so wrong. But then, what did she want to happen anyway? She'd behaved very strangely ever since this whole thing started. Obsessing into the fantasy with trance-like focus. Getting drawn deeper and deeper… into the game. Where had she hoped things would lead? Between herself and him? What sort of relationship was she looking for with a man like that? One who already had a wife and a mistress. What the fuck was she thinking?! Did she want to fit herself into their weird relationship? Situations like that should obviously be avoided. Men like that should be avoided! How the fuck could getting involved with him/them possibly be a good thing? It couldn't! Images of he and Katya giving her the treatment flashed coarse, eliciting a blush of shame. Just motivated by lust? Then why did it feel like love? It couldn't be love. How could she love him? What a ridiculous, irrational, feeble-minded creature she'd become. Fuck! It must be love. Bastard!

Or could just be obsession? Obviously she was infatuated with him. Guess there's quite a lot of overlap between obsession and love (and lust for that matter). But whatever the intense feeling was, she was certain: he'd deliberately manipulated her into feeling that way. He'd tricked her – it was all a confidence trick. A trap… and she'd walked right into it… with head in the clouds and arms outstretched. What a fool!

Had been so easy to pull her in – juvenile curiosity naïvely following the whiff of mystery. And he'd centred the intrigue around himself personally, right from the outset – lured her emotions towards him. The psychology of competition, the thrill of 'winning'. He'd made himself the prize she was striving towards. Had seemed so natural as she'd bounded along like a Labrador chasing a tennis ball. He'd weaponised flattery of course (that old chestnut). And by making her struggle to earn his praise, he'd made her emotional response to it that much more intense. She'd been so pathetically grateful for his approval – felt she owed him so much in return… owed him something 'special'. And needed to find it somewhere deep.

The writer had been drawn deeper and deeper into her own seductive fantasy. Enthusiastic momentum carrying her over the edge, leaping from the precipice on his command, like some kind of brainwashed cultist. Diving into the depths... where her dark, primal instincts had been hiding all along. Revelling in the excitement of adventure and discovering new things. All those positive emotions tying her to him, rope by rope, thread by thread. Love and loyalty, bonding and building, sharing the exhilaration of the game. Like a pair of naughty schoolchildren, bunking off to explore a forbidden mansion together. Telling him naughty secrets she'd never confided to anyone else. Such mischievous fun they'd shared!

And yet he was also an authority figure: teaching, guiding, educating. She wanted to impress him so much – longed to be teacher's pet. Losing herself in her own imagination. Becoming lost in the role he'd awarded her, sinking deeper and deeper into character. Until she was mostly just a character in his story. His story! Surely it was her story?

It was their story – that was the whole fucking point! A shared story, growing out of their unique and special relationship. Despite the content, she'd kind of treated it as if it were a love story: old-fashioned sweethearts, separated by cruel circumstance, conducting their courtship through longing love letters. Twisting the romance had actually spun it full-circle... and perversely intensified it. As if they'd invented a new type of romance that was only for them. A dark rose – black as midnight. What could be more romantic than that? God, what a pathetic, little girl she was – dizzied by romance while the big, nasty man got his dick out, spunked over her face... and then dumped her.

What the fuck did she expect... from a man like that? He was obviously a chronic womaniser. He'd clearly seduced both Charlotte and Katya, whether or not they were his wife and mistress. Yet that'd just made him more attractive to the writer. Was that natural or unnatural? It was definitely stupid! Certainly shouldn't be natural. But you did have to wonder at the kind of man Katya felt was worthy of her. What a bastard! And what a bitch that Jess was still more angry with herself than anybody else.

The way she'd behaved over recent months reflected very poorly on her character. She usually expressed mild disapproval when friends sacrificed too much of their own lives to merge themselves into the lives of their new boyfriends/girlfriends. She'd always congratulated herself on being much too strong-willed and independent-minded to let that happen to her. Then he comes along, waves his magic wand and she immediately surrenders all her strengths, virtues, morals and principles – casting them aside with a cheeky smile.

Shit! Her self-respect, dignity, integrity, pride – abandoned without a fight. Talk about disempowering herself. Best not to count the ways she'd betrayed feminism. She was definitely a bad feminist… a bad woman… a bad person. Hadn't even behaved like a real person should. Had acted more like a fictional character from some far-fetched, erotic story. Behaving the way she thought he'd want his erotica heroine to behave. Jumping into the role and prancing along mindlessly… deeper and deeper… until inevitable disaster.

What a total fucking mess! But what could be done about it? She needed to understand the situation better, but it made her head hurt… and it was so blazing hot. At least the wine was going down well. Needed to do something more constructive than drink though. What could she actually do? Pausing her pace to glower down at the pile of printouts on the breakfast bar. Another sink of disappointment. She'd already gone through the manuscripts a second time. Was so depressing to see all the pages unblemished and pristine white. As if she'd enthusiastically offered her bare butt for a caning, but just been left standing there with her panties down. Why not mark them? And why return them at all, if they were going to be left unmarked? It was so sadistic.

Maybe he didn't like the new autobiographical stories with Jess as the main character? There was less explicit eroticism in them of course. But surely, that approach was his idea – he'd whispered it in her ear or something. So she must have offended him some other way. Was there something in the stories that could explain the problem? Perhaps she should go through the documents again, trying to put herself in his place whilst reading. That may help elucidate the issue... and possibly suggest how it could be fixed. Although she wouldn't be the one to do the fixing. That was an important principle: if there was to be any reconciliation, the ball was definitely in his court.

Jess gathered all the printouts together, marked and unmarked: everything she'd written for him. Settling herself on the sofa, out of the sun, and slotting the manuscripts together – not in the chronology they'd been submitted, but in the order that made most sense to the overall story: 'Red Rose', 'The Proposal', 'Pet Names', 'Love Heart', etc. At first, the task of reading was difficult to face. She kept cringing away from the pages, horrified at what'd been exposed. But as she got into it, she forgot about remaining detached and instead re-immersed herself in the fantasy, submerging into the depths of her own imagination... deeper and deeper... Reading for hours. Baggins didn't like it of course. One of the few things in life that did bother him was apes gawping over papers when they should be focusing on more important matters (like cat-worship). But his affectionate attempts to separate Jess from the story were rudely palmed off. She didn't even look away during numerous top-ups of wine.

It was early evening by the time she came to the final printout: 'One True Love'. Her imagination drifting along in the trance of the mirror-maze... when suddenly she spotted something in the real world – a pencil mark! So light and thin it was almost invisible. But definitely a deliberate act. The words 'Mirror Secret Mirror' were underlined with a soft stroke of grey lead. And a few paragraphs below, the word 'search' had also been picked out – the underlining carefully excluding the 'ing' suffix. A message from him! She chanted the words over in her head. She had to search for Mirror Secret Mirror. This was an important clue! A cryptic clue. But what did it mean? Search in what way? Literally search for the words online?

She sat up from her reclined position and pulled the laptop across the coffee-table. Flicking the screen open, waking the device from standby, and opening up the browser. The web-search returned several relevant-seeming results. She clicked on one and found herself on Instagram. An account entitled 'Mirror Secret Mirror'. She immediately recognised one of the pictures: a voluptuous, white love heart floating against a pitch-black background, the top of the shape dramatically rimmed with a thin, red outline. It was the love heart image she'd spied on Charlotte's laptop. There was a brief bio: 'This is a unique setup. Our resident writer, Jessica Seaques, does not control this account. She's chained to the desk… literally.'

Jess was sitting very still… except for the drifting shake of her head. She reread the bio several times, but was having trouble taking it in. Thoughts and feelings rushing by too fast to catch. What was going on? She noticed a website link and clicked through to the 'mirrorsecretmirror.com' website. Felt like a trance as she scrolled down the page. Numb eyes noting a book was being promoted: the title was 'Mirror Secret Mirror'; the author was 'Jessica Seaques'. Her finger was moving itself like the dismembered tail of a worm, clicking on a tab marked 'Blog'. There were about a dozen posts listed: a few familiar book reviews and a story broken into multiple parts. It was called 'The Circus Master', although clicking through Jess immediately recognised that it was one of her stories: 'Love Birds'. The name had been changed, but it was exactly the same story.

Jess paused to gather in the spin. So what was going on here was… Something blatantly obvious was taking a while to sink in. It was seeping in though… slowly but surely. This was her story, under her pen name, openly available online… and being used to promote the forthcoming book: 'Mirror Secret Mirror'. How could this be?

An easy question actually. There was only one way this could've happened. Jess was standing and staring down on the laptop, arms looped back with fingers clench-knit behind her head. She stooped out of the pose, plucking up her glass and emptying it with a big, winey swig. A swelling roll of alcohol sluiced over her mind. It was very clear what'd happened. He'd taken her story, 'Love Birds' – stolen it – and put it online. Without asking her. Without even telling her. No agreement. No consent. She never consented to this. How dare he! The bastard had stolen her book! She didn't even know she had a book to steal: 'a full-length erotic novel' apparently. He'd stolen the book and thrown the writer away. The absolute fucking bastard!

The last of the bottle sloshed into her glass as she sat down to investigate further. She clicked on a recent post and discovered it was a 'Contents' page, listing the fifteen chapters that comprised her book. The first four had been named by her: 'Red Rose', 'The Proposal', 'Pet Names' and 'Love Heart'. The title of the fifth chapter was unfamiliar though: 'Sweet Nothings'. What did that mean? The writer cocked her head as if expecting guidance to be whispered in her ear. Was that a new chapter not written by her? Or had the over-long story about her first day and night in the office simply been split in two, with the second half given a new name? How did she end that chapter again? She'd only just read it. Forgetting to remember? Remembering to forget? How could she be so dreamy and drifty? Eyelids fluttering a few moments, before she was able to refocus on the screen.

Chapters Six, Seven, Eight and Nine also had familiar titles: 'Those Three Little Words', 'No, You Hang Up', 'Classic Romance' and 'One True Love'. However, Jess wasn't previously acquainted with the last six titles on the list: 'Kissing', 'Just Between Us', 'Our Song', 'Romantic Rhapsody', 'Love Me Tender' and 'You and I'.

Jesus fucking Christ! How was this happening? What exactly was happening? Was this what was supposed to happen? Was this in the story? Her story? His story? Whose fucking story was this? Shit! The adrenaline began to fume, some growling out through gritted teeth. Baggins stirred and looked over with a hint of concern. Making eye contact, Jess felt the surging need to tell him what was going on – get some external understanding of her plight. But the big tabby wouldn't get it at all – there was no cat-equivalent of this situation. Fuck! The writer stood and began to pace. She needed to think. No! She needed to find out more.

She returned to the computer, hands tremoring with excited energy. Wine goes down so easy, when one just opens the gullet and pours it in. The mirrorsecretmirror website was well-connected. Jess clicked on a familiar logo and found herself on Twitter. Another book-focused account, with the same logo used everywhere else.

Shit! He'd stolen her story – her book! And it was being advertised to the world… with the intention of selling it for profit presumably! How much had she been paid? A few thousand pounds. And now he'd taken her story, her baby, her personal work. Her unique thing! Her secret thoughts. Secret! No one had consulted her. God! 'The Circus Master/Love Birds' was currently online, available to the general public! Were people reading it? Had anyone read it already? And he was planning to publish everything else as well! All her shameful lusts and desires – just thrown open to the universe. Her perverted fantasies, her honest sexual history, her fucked-up fetishes, the weird games she used to play with Carl! Oh Fuck!!!

'Mirror Secret Mirror' was being actively promoted via multiple social media accounts. An organised marketing campaign gearing up to sell the 'product' – selling stolen goods! The promotional material didn't make any mention of that fact. Just used mysterious and opaque language to make the nefarious wares seem more commercially appealing. Jess' eyes flicked over the most recent tweet, rechecking she'd read correctly a couple of times. It really did say exactly what she thought it said: 'Only one person in the world will understand this in-joke. So this is Just Between Us :) xxx'.

'Just Between Us.' But… that's the name of this fucking chapter! Jess caught her falling face in both hands, body crumpling back into the sofa. This was too much. And the swinging head movement swelled the alcohol to reel and crash. A pathetic, little noise escaping along with her breath, as if she were being deflated. 'Just Between Us?!' An 'in-joke'. Was that supposed to be fucking funny? Smiley face, kiss, kiss, kiss! He was really taking the piss. And it was obvious the previous chapter had been titled in honour of Katya's theatrical 'kiss, kiss, kiss' goodbye. How was this possible? Who was writing this story anyway? How could he?! Jess felt overwhelmed. The room span as the wine swam, but she managed to upright her body. The screen was blazing bright, so she scrunched her eyes before refocusing. He was mocking her – adding insult to injury. Stealing her precious stories… and gloating in her face about it. She couldn't believe he would do this to her.

But why not? She didn't know who he was. Not even his first name. Whilst he knew all sorts about her: full name, phone number, address… deepest, darkest, secret, sexual fantasies. Shit! The informational power imbalance was chasming. What could she do? She was in a ludicrously weak position. Knowing nothing! No, that wasn't totally true. She knew some things: what they all looked like; where the office was; Katya's email address; both women's phone numbers… and she knew his home address. That was a valuable bit of intel. And he might not know that Jess was in possession of it.

Unlike virtually every other bit of information. All of which, the writer had given away when she submitted the autobiographical stories. She'd foolishly told him everything (except for the bit about the post-it note – which was completely useless anyway). She'd been absurdly open, whilst he'd been suspiciously secretive, conspiring with the others. Jess should've been smarter. Should've played the game differently – very differently. Needed to play smarter from now on.

What was the strategy then? What was the game? Whatever game it was, it was clearly her move. What should she do? Again, she visualised herself going over to the house to confront him. At least she was now angry enough to properly shout and scream. But that was the exact opposite of playing it smarter. Maybe she should spy on the house? Although she wouldn't necessarily learn much sitting in a hedge outside. The best place to get more intel was online – she needed to find out everything she could. She collected her thoughts and tried to suppress the emotional energy.

Semi-patiently going back through the web pages one by one, looking for info she might've missed. A schedule boasted that two more stories would be published on the blog, over the next few months – presumably 'All the Mistress' Money' and 'The Master Plan' were new names for 'Because You're Worth It' and 'Choosing the Ring'. That was annoying. After a few more irritable emotional reactions Jess found her eyes hovering over an email address mentioned in the main website's 'Contact' section: 'mirrorsecretmirror@gmail.com'. It made her think: when he and Katya were discussing 'Mirror Secret Mirror' over the phone, perhaps it wasn't just the general title of the book they were talking about. An idea was brewing inside. Jess could sense the bubbles zipping to the surface of consciousness.

Already acting on it: opening up the Gmail sign-in page, but not using her usual account. Instead selecting the 'Use other account' option and inserting the contact email address. Challenged to enter the password, Jess stared at the text box with rising confidence. What might one write down after recording the name of a shared email address? She carefully tapped in the characters:

'Muriel+Prisi'. Triple-checking the spelling as the cursor hovered dramatically over the 'Next' button. This had to be right; she was so clever. But no: 'Incorrect password'! Jess wasn't fazed, immediately realising her initial mistake. It explained why Katya appeared to record two seemingly identical numerical points. This time she entered: '1)Muriel+Prisi'. Watching the cursor move across the screen... this felt too important to simply use the 'Enter' button. The tension tingling as she clicked.

'Loading'.

Holy shit! She was in. What was she doing? Being sneaky, spying, finding stuff out. And not just stuff he expected her to discover. This was all secret! She was genuinely supposed to be locked out. The excitement gripped both shoulders forward. The inbox was full of social media notifications: Instagram, Twitter, etc. This was clearly the control email address for all the online accounts associated with the book. The writer's chest swelled as she noted how much stuff was coming through here. Mostly web-platforms she'd heard of before. What's 'FetLife'? She clicked on one of the notification emails and tapped through to land on a red-and-black sign-in page. Entering 'mirrorsecretmirror@gmail.com' in the first text box. Now, you wouldn't use exactly the same password for your social media accounts and the associated control email address, would you? What would be the next-simplest thing to do? Jess submitted the password: '2)Muriel+Prisi'.

And straight inside this account as well! The spy congratulated herself on how well her post-it note trick had worked. And what a brilliant stroke of genius – deciding to keep it out of the stories. She always knew it was important! Bonus satisfaction from knowing it was Katya's dumbass fuck-up that led to the breakthrough. Now what could Jess find out here? FetLife appeared to be some kind of online fetish/BDSM community. The account name was 'MSM_Erotica'. That fucking logo visible again. The profile 'About' section read: 'Mirror Secret Mirror... This is a unique setup. Our resident writer, Jessica Seaques, does not control this account. She's chained to the desk... literally :) xxx'

Scrolling down, she came to the 'Fetishes' section. The alphabetical list was clearly based on the writer's own kinks and fetishes: 'affectionate cruelty, angel in underland, ass-licking, ball gags, blow jobs, blushing, bondage, boot licking, butt plugs, chastity belts, collar and leash, consensual non-consent play, cuckqueening, deep throating, discipline, exploitation, face fucking, face slapping, fantasy merging with reality, hiding under the desk, humiliation, hypnosis, hypnotically-enhanced orgasms, orgasm control, orgasm denial, primal predator and prey, puppy play, red correction marks, romance, ropes, service submission, slave tattoos, smoke and mirrors, something cruel with sandpaper and lime juice, spanking, talking dirty, threesomes, trophy bruises, tying nipples with thread, verbal humiliation, voyeurism, when the devil makes them dance, writing erotica, writing for him.'

There was a 'Curious about' sub-section, with only one interest noted: 'pugglemuffling'.

Fucking bastard! This was essentially her profile, constructed from her own personal details. Her real kinks and fetishes, previously buried deep inside. Recently drawn to the surface and put into words, for him... and now openly online for the whole world to see. Anyone on the network could view this profile, detailing her previously secret lusts. She'd never told anyone except him about this side of herself. And he was just brazenly sharing everything with the universe. All part of the marketing campaign! This was obviously what Charlotte had been doing all this time, under his directions. The sneaky, little bitch had been connecting with other erotica writers and fans and getting tips and advice – joining groups and discussion forums, exchanging private messages, interacting with real individuals. For fuck's sake! Jess' blood throbbed with rage.

After going through the FetLife account, the writer used her skeleton-key password to do the same for the other social media platforms. The 'Goodreads' account included many of the book reviews Jess had written. Across the various social networks, her connections were eclectic, but tended to focus on erotica writers and fans. Many of the accounts had received private messages from real people. These had been responded to in a similar way as the FetLife messages – everything garbed in cryptic language to evoke a sense of mystery.

Jess trawled through all the accounts connected with the master-email address. Determined to find out everything she could. There wasn't that much more to find though. None of the accounts were used for proper private communications. The Gmail inbox contained no messages from real people at all, although there was one interesting email sent. From when the account was first set up, about three months ago (soon after Jess' under-desk espionage). It was to Katya and was entitled 'previous account'. The content was very brief: 'dreamsandstories@gmail.com – 1)AnaisNin'. The investigator immediately figuring that was probably the account used in the earlier stages of the project.

Grabbing her iPad, Jess logged into 'dreamsandstories@gmail.com' using '1)AnaisNin' as the password. The inbox looked similar to the other one – exclusively notifications from online networking sites. It didn't take long to search the account and confirm the original hypothesis: that it was the precursor to 'mirrorsecretmirror@gmail.com'. Many of the social media accounts had been activated using this email and later transferred to the new address. Some of the accounts were a few years old, but had recently been renamed. There wasn't any new information here, but the key point was: 'dreamsandstories' was the security backup account for 'mirrorsecretmirror'. Not very clever to leave a sent email with the password to the backup account. Charlotte obviously not quite as smart as she thinks she is. Actually it was probably Katya who ordered her to do it. Haha! Another dumbass mistake… and one that left a significant vulnerability.

This was an opportunity. How to go about exploiting it? Had to do everything in exactly the correct order. She began by changing the password for the 'mirrorsecretmirror' Gmail. She then changed the security backup account to her own personal email address. The next stage was to go through the social media accounts, removing the older Gmail as a backup/security address and then changing the passwords. All notifications relating to these actions were virtually incinerated. She was smart about everything, even taking the precaution of changing her own personal email password, just in case. By the time she'd finished, the old 'dreamsandstories' account would still be accessible to them, but it wasn't linked to anything at all. Everything else she'd snatched control of: Instagram, Twitter, Goodreads, FetLife, etc. And 'mirrorsecretmirror@gmail.com' itself of course. A complete takeover. Seizing what was rightfully hers – a liberation!

Fuck, that felt good! The energy fizzed as she popped off the sofa like a cork. She'd done something – had made a move… a good move. She had him by the googles now. Her mind wondered what to do next. But her fingers were already asking her phone the time of the next train to London. There was one at 11.19pm.

TWELVE
OUR SONG

The headlight's beam swashed over hedgerows as the Uber rounded another corner. The sling of momentum pressing Jess' body against the car door, ear dipping out of the window, into the gush of displaced air. The streets of Hampstead lonely and vacant. The big houses dark. Just a few minutes from her destination now. Could feel the anticipation welling up… and other emotions, besides. Best to just let them slipstream past: breeze over a placid, mountain lake – tranquil waters. Ignore the pebbly questions skittering over the surface. No point stirring herself into an anxious tizzy again. You can spend your whole life wondering what's about to happen. When the reality is that you simply don't know.

Jess had requested a drop-off point a couple of blocks away, so the house could be approached on foot. Flashing a blank smile as she thanked the driver and alighted. The vehicle pulled off and slid into the gloom. Her phone buzzed with the journey-complete notification – she switched it to silent mode. The heat clung close and heavy, sticking to the skin of the earth. Atmosphere swimming with humidity. Bright, full moon submerged in haze. The air encircling the streetlamps stained petrol-purple, while their taps poured pools of orange light onto the pavement below, spilling her shadow all over the night. And the crickets chirruping their tropical chorus – as if London were a rainforest.

So what was the plan again? What was she actually intending to do? There hadn't been a specific strategy when she set out. Although her choice of clothes emphasised stealth: dark trainers, jogging top and leggings. It was unusual that she'd decided not to bring a handbag. Instead zipping phone, keys and purse into the pockets of the black hoodie, currently tied around her waist. Her mobile swinging to beat rhythmically against the back of her leg as she walked. Actually, maybe better to put the cloak on and conceal herself. She pulled the hood overhead, masking her face in shadow.

The big oaks towered above as she reached the mouth of the cul-de-sac. Peering around to confirm she was alone on the streets… and no movement or activity visible from any of the houses. Through the little row of conifers – only darkness behind darkness. She stepped over the wall and ducked to push under the trees, the same approach she'd used on Monday. The silk-smooth smell of pine. Emerging to crouch on a raised rock-garden facing the front of the house and overlooking the drive. There was no car. All the lights were off and the curtains undrawn on this side of the building. The property appeared empty, although a glow emanating from within suggested rooms at the rear may be inhabited. Perhaps the car was in the garage? Although he usually parked at the bottom of the drive, right? Jess stared intently into the black windows. But if there was someone looking out from the upper floors, then she wouldn't be able to tell anyway.

She needed to check the building from the other side. The perfumes of the surrounding flowers tinkled in her nostrils as she skirted the conifers to squat by the driveway entrance. The route to the back garden lay to the left of the house from Jess' perspective

– a gap between the side-fence and the garage. She adjusted her glasses and focused on the top windows once more. If she stepped out onto the drive, she'd be illuminated in the peripheral glow of the nearest streetlamp. Best be quick about it. She stood and crunched briskly over the stones, angling to get back into the shadows by the quickest route. Now padding along the slim corridor of grass between the fence and the garage. Deep breaths as she drew towards the end of the wall. She could hear the low rumble of bubbling water close by.

A hesitant head poking just one eye around, spying along the rear-wall of the garage as it retreated to meet the core body of the house. The back corner of the main building directly ahead, in front of that: a luxurious hot-tub surrounded by giant pot-plants. The grand ceramics beautifully painted in classical Mediterranean style: bone-white rimmed with rich azure. The plants they contained jungled into lush, green foliage, hugging a dense crescent around the bath. Jess moved closer, using the vegetation to shield her from overlooking windows. It felt like a tropical mangrove as the steam wafted above the cauldron of bubbling water. The circling plants reaching over to drink, leafy arms bejewelled in sparkling beads of moisture. Jess scooped her hand into the warm swirl and peered towards the house behind.

The visible ground floor was mostly windows. Tentatively approaching, Jess could make out a bar area occupying the nearest corner of the building. There was a door along the side wall, and two sets of patio doors punctuating the long back wall. She ducked to skirt the rear of the structure. Crossing the first set of doors and peeping her head up on the other side of the saloon area. The bar: an open-plan square of counters with a mini-skyline of curvaceous beer-taps and several hanging stalactites of bottled spirits. This side of the building was dominated by the vast garden room – spacious, wooden floors and bookshelf-lined walls. Most of the furniture clustered towards the far end, where the dining chairs circled in shadowy conference.

All was dark, save for that ethereal luminescence emanating from within. Cupping hands over her eyes, she leant on the window and stared towards the source of the light. The building's central wall separated the garden room from the entrance hallway. In the middle – right at the heart of the house – a large, glass box was set into the wall itself. Like an aquarium, except without water. Full of some sort of matter though. Were the hazy lights inside rippling? Pulsating? Or was there some other movement sensed? A strange kind of motion – creeping with rhythm. Couldn't tell what it was from here. Jess shook her head and stepped back a few paces, confirming that the top floor windows were dark, with curtains undrawn. The house was definitely empty. She turned to scan over the garden: well-tended lawns; vibrant flowerbeds; silvered elms lining the back of the property. As she watched the sprinkler system startled into life. Bursting arcs of water cascading the thirsty grass, with the chirpy, insect orchestra continuing their serenade.

So now what? She retraced her steps around the garage to the front of the property. Onto the drive, to move gingerly down the slope. The house stared blankly overhead, trying not to give the impression: it knew something she didn't. As she hovered, illumination suddenly splashed over and all around. The rusty shingle lighting up. Shit! Must've triggered a motion-sensor. Feeling the urge to flee into the night, but her legs scurrying in the other direction. Ducking a flower-festooned hanging-basket to arrive at the big, red door. The heart of the house glowing serenely through the frosted pane. A small, plastic dome hung in the top corner of the porch area. A camera? Jess pulled her hood down and turned away.

The vegetation thronging around the entrance sprinkled rich colours and exotic fragrances. The invigorating scent of mint cutting clean and fresh through the muggy air. An eclectic range of flowerpots huddled: some big, some small. The one she recognised wasn't even trying to look inconspicuous. The painted sunflower staring right up at her expectantly. In contrast to the illustration on it, the vessel contained a stout, frost-blue conifer. The writer blinked a couple of times to refocus and recheck. Surely not? She squatted down, tipping the pot to peer underneath. The metal winked and gleamed up at her.

Surely not?! How could this be? This must be a trap. Her head jerked up and whipped around... but everything was quiet. The hot night leaning in vacantly, like an oblivious drunk. Sweat trickling down her cheek as she took the keys and rose, pinching the hood closed and covering. What was she going to do now? Sometimes in life, it's more interesting to let one's mind sit back and watch what happens next. A Yale and a deadlock on the door. The key slipping in smoothly, the whispering grate of metal and then the catch. Turning until the click indicated she was in. Not even deadlocked – easy as that.

Opening the door just enough for her to slither around the frame and fit it closed again. It was done now. If an alarm had been tripped, then it was a silent one. A deep breath as she turned into the house. The whole place smelled of him. She could taste it as she drank the air. The spacious hallway had three internal doors. The one leading through to the kitchen, at the foot of the stairs, was immediately on Jess' right. The one connecting the lounge – diagonally on her left. A third door ducked under the staircase. A couple of un-partitioned metres of floor led through to the garden room and the back of the house. But the intruder's gaze set dead ahead, towards the structural centrepiece of the building. Transfixed... as she drifted towards the light.

Definitely not an aquarium. It was packed with earth... and movement – bristling with energy. The great, glass tank was three metres long, two metres tall and over a metre wide. Three-quarters filled with soil, with a layer of greenery at eye-level: grass and a jungle of small plants. The turf was bustling, tickling with insect motion. A busy, creeping pitter-patter. Ants! An ant-farm built into the heart of the house. Their tunnels running along the glass in a web-work of interconnected lines. Lit with wisping blue incandescence, so they appeared like veins, cross-sectioned long-wise. Fluttering with tiny, black shadows, marching through in well-organised processions.

Fascinated, Jess drew up to the tank, fingers against the glass. The ants from one column were carrying grainy parcels. Following back, the workforce appeared to be gathering food from the grassy area above, although their line snaked off into the dense green and disappeared. The plants inside were lush and glistening with moisture – must've recently been watered by an automated system. Her eyes fell on a lone ant creeping up a tall shoot of grass. The stalk straining as the lookout reached the top. Insect legs fumbling to grip and balance.

What was the ant looking for? Suppose it's generally best to keep one's guard up in this world. Jess hunched her shoulders and startled herself out of the trance. She couldn't just stand in the middle of the hall, lost to the universe. Shouldn't be here at all. She'd broken into the house – his house. Shit! What was she thinking? What the fuck was she doing? This wasn't the plan. Was it? Was this in the story? This was definitely dangerous. She was putting herself at risk, breaking and entering, sneaking around a man's empty house. This was a bad idea – a terrible idea. The night sweated profusely.

Casting her eyes around, she noticed a hooded figure watching from the shadows. A shady silhouette, dressed all in black, standing in silence and staring into the tall, hallway mirror. That was her: the midnight intruder, the burglar. The adrenaline really coursing, excitement jittering against the nerves. The punchy, nasal push-and-pull of her breathing sounded too loud, so she began blowing the air out through her mouth at a slow pant. There was nothing she could do about her heart though – beat building like a war-drum at dawn. Deeper and deeper…

Jess lowered her head and moved towards the ajar lounge door. It was even darker in here. Without the luminescence of the ant-world, only the ghostly moonlight. And now the ray from her phone-torch skirting and probing. A comfortable sitting area with sofa, chairs and coffee table. The room circled with bookshelves and a computer desk on the far wall. The large, flat-screen TV was brand new. Her beam fell on the samurai sword mounted above the mantelpiece and she drew towards it. Set eye-level on a forked, wooden stand, so the curve smiled. Leathery, black sheath with a circular, metal hilt protruding. Handle gripped in stringy weave. A gilded pommel at the end.

She leant forward to sniff where his hands had grasped. It smelled like him training: lean, muscular body flexing and tensing. Her torch glared up to dazzle as she set the mobile on the shelf. Reaching to clasp the grip with her left hand, steadying the scabbard with her right, and unsheathing a few centimetres of sword. It slid out slick and smooth. The gleam momentarily blinding as the torch-light sliced off the blade's edge. She touched her finger against the steel – razor sharp. Pushing up, she sensed the thin metal threatening to slit her skin. The sudden urge to press the cut and leave her blood on his sword. No, that would be mental! She removed her finger and clinked the blade back into its sheath.

Torchlight flicking around the room, burglar-style. An eclectic variety of pictures: oil paintings, landscapes, enigmatic abstracts. An extensive library of books: fiction and factual, modern and classic, famous and obscure. Tempting to explore his collection, but best not to get lost in that endeavour just now. Instead she padded out of the lounge, back into the phantom fluorescence of the ant world, past the creeping intruder in the hallway mirror. Around the glass tank, spindling veins scuttling with marching silhouettes. Into the garden room, with the bar area ahead on her left. Jess turned right to face the stretching, wooden floor of the big chamber. Remembering how long it takes to clean on one's hands and knees. At the far end, two large sofas faced each other in the corner and the dining chairs surrounded a grand, oval-shaped table by the kitchen.

Her light pointed out an object, sitting on a low surface near the ant-tank. Ghosting over, Jess recognised the statue: a thirty-centimetre-tall replica of Bernini's 'Rape of Proserpina' in baroque, white marble. What was the story again? A young woman carried down to the Underworld, in the arms of an evil god. Not willingly by the look of it. She was fighting, desperately trying to wriggle out of his grasp. The vivid violence animated perfectly in the stone, as if it lived, breathed and screamed. Him running with captive held aloft, gripping tight around her thighs and hips. Her twisting body vertical with flailing arms pushing his face away. The brutal ferocity quivering with life as his strong hands clutch her body, fingers pressing into pulsing flesh. The power, the struggle, the terror, the helplessness of the victim… her dark fate. The great god's chiselled chest sculpted like an armoured breastplate. Arms, legs and buttocks bursting with muscle and vitality. She didn't have a chance. What was it that happened to Proserpina again?

Pulling her gaze up and away, she noted the heavy-set dining chairs were exact replacements for the ones hacked up with the sword. She turned into the kitchen, passing the cake table and island bar. Recalling when he drank from the Bavarian tankard, after filling it at the big fridge with the ice dispenser. The water splashing onto his chest, the drop tickling down his torso along beautifully-defined grooves of muscle and bone. Powerful body, dangerous eyes, sadistic inclinations. Right inside his lair now. Shit! This was a bad idea. She really shouldn't be here. Imagine if a neighbour saw her torch flittering about the darkness.

Completing her circuit of the ground floor, Jess returned to the hallway and stood at the foot of the stairs. Eyes following the beam up the steps, until the wavering spotlight glimpsed the door set beneath them. That must lead down to the basement.

Treading softly over, she hesitated before pulling the thick, plastic handle. The heavy frame was weighted to tug back, almost felt like someone deliberately closing it from the other side. She had to reposition her body, heave and then prop a foot in to hold it open. The torchlight dissolving into the pitch-black. Stairs heading downwards… deeper and deeper… The writer felt the goose bumps bristling as she listened to the silence. A little trill of fear. Going down there would surely be a bad idea.

As she hesitated, certain sounds began to bite: the growl of an engine, tyres crunching on shingle. Jess froze stone-still. A dazzle as the headlights swept menacingly across the windows. A flash of metallic claret. His car! He was home. Shit! She shoved the torch in her pocket and leapt through the door. Despite the weight, the frame was slow to shut. For a few seconds, she willed it to move faster, but as the band of half-light thinned, she suddenly dreaded the close. The ominous, mechanised pace. The efficient click-clack as the door sealed – sounded like the twist of a robotic jailer's keys.

Total darkness, save the muffle of glow through cotton. Shit! What the fuck had she done? How did this happen? Quick analysis: he'd be coming through the front door in about thirty seconds, whilst she'd trapped herself in the basement. Fuck! The decision was irreversible now – there was no time to go back out. No escape. Shit! The only sound was her heart pounding out of the silence. Would she even hear the front door from here? The basement door seemed like an air lock. Not a good sign! The intruder's back was pushed up against some coats. What if he came in to hang his up? Actually it was too warm for a coat, but it was still risky loitering here.

There was only one way to go – downwards… deeper and deeper… She redrew her torch to jab the dull blade of light ahead whilst descending. Trainers sneaking on polished, wooden steps, fingers clutching the handrail. Ducking below ground level, she could sense the basement opening out beyond the banister, but didn't divert her beam until she'd reached the foot of the stairs. Turning into the room and walking a few paces to get out of sight from the door. Now hovering beside a trident of thick, crimson candles set on a tall, iron frame.

Her beam wisped across the darkness to pick out other similar lanterns – the candelabras standing ominously, like men waiting in the shadows. The room was large… very large… and made to feel even more expansive because of the multiple mirror-walls, echoing torch-light flitting in the deep glass all around. Her own ethereal reflection haunting the gloomy sheen a couple of metres to the left and, more distantly, on her right. The atmosphere was even heavier down here – air warmer, thicker, denser, wetter. The night breathless.

A nervous glance behind, but the basement door was well-sealed, so she wouldn't be able to sense the hallway light anyway. It must be switched on though – he'd definitely be inside the house by now. And the writer was trapped. Shit! Moving deeper into the darkness, the musky aroma of old incense itching at her nostrils. Trainers creeping over the polished stone floor, fuzzy beam poking tentatively into the surrounding blackness. The rectangular room was about twelve metres wide and twenty metres long. The stairs slanted down one of the shorter walls, whilst the other three were completely sheeted in giant mirrors.

Obscure objects and pieces of furniture loomed and cluttered towards the edges of the chamber. Most of the items concealed under drapes, deliberately hidden… horrors waiting to be ceremoniously unveiled. The positioning of the sinister paraphernalia left a broad aisle running up the centre of the room, leading towards the dominating feature at the far end: a grand, oaken four-poster. The bed overflowing with regal-red curtains and spilling with silk and velvet. The surrounding floor skinned with thick, fur rugs.

Holy shit! This was it: his Secret… her Secret… their Secret… The Secret Room! Actually for real – in the real world! An underground play-room. A torture chamber. A suburban dungeon! The exhilaration tickled.

Making her way towards the other end, Jess startled at the touch of metal chinking against the top of her hood. A pair of handcuffs dangling on a chain, suspended from the wooden rafters above. Looking up, the whole ceiling rained with ropes and chains, manacles and restraints creeping all around. The veiled object on the ground beside her was just over a metre tall and roughly conical, cloaked in a silky, jet-black drape. It looked like it was plugged in via a long extension cable running out of the clutter. There was something peculiar about it – could somehow sense that it had moving parts. But Jess was distracted by a larger, undercover item a few metres away – two towering juts of wood rearing up like velvet-hooded horns… dread to think! Nothing in the ashtray on the small table nearby, but the one on the table, by the foot of the bed, contained two extinguished cigarettes: one thin and white; one thicker and cork-orange. There was also an ornately carved incense-burner.

To the left of the bed, from Jess' perspective, the floor was clear up to the mirror-wall, and to the right most of the furniture was short, so anyone on the mattress could enjoy uninterrupted surrounding reflection, except for the bedposts. The solid frame of the four-poster dripped with black metal and leather: leashes and cables, cuffs and shackles. Jess brushed the smooth mahogany with her right hand as she passed, moving to meet her own shadowy reflection in the shortest mirror-wall at the back of the chamber. Drawing close, she used the torch to up-light her face – sorcerous shadows cutting about her features. Was expecting to look nervous, but instead appeared kind of dreamy – entranced by the unfolding story. Surely he couldn't be behind the mirror now? She peered closer.

The mechanical click-clack of the basement door warped in the echo, sound swimming as if underwater. Fuck! Dreaminess swept off in a flash-flood of panic. Lowering the phone and frantically fiddling to turn off the torch. Drop-down menu appearing and then whipping away as her fingers fumbled. Shit! Fluttering her eyelids, she managed enough calm to extinguish the light. Pocketing the phone and dashing to her right – into the passage of clear space between the back wall and the bed. The hiding-cover was poor, due to the short headboard, so Jess continued her flight, scurry-skirting along the mirror like a fleeing mouse.

She bolted into the corner furthest from the stairs and dropped behind the largest object in the vicinity: a velvet-covered item about a metre-cubed in size. The underground stone was cold on hands and knees, refreshing compared to the sweltering air. His measured footsteps descended the stairs with steady rhythm: tick-tock, tick-tock, tick-tock... and then clacking heavy as hard shoes reached the stone floor. She could feel his presence filling the room... unfurling into it. And now his words projecting as well.

'Did you miss me?'

Deep, gravelled-honey-velvet voice resounding in the echo. The mock in the turn of his tongue boasted that he knew the answer already. But how did he even know she was here?! Maybe he'd seen her break in on some kind of smart home-security system? And she still had the key in her pocket, so its absence would've been conspicuous if he'd checked under the plant-pot. Fuck! She was in deep shit now... deeper and deeper... sweat pouring from shaking skin. The cocky click of his lighter. Could sense him gliding the flame over the candles by the stairs. Then hear him walking again, hard-souled footsteps providing a beat behind his lulling, vocal bass.

'Poor little thing – kept in the dark for so long.'

Pausing to ignite another candelabra, before moving off again. Jess kept perfectly still. Did he know exactly where she was, or just that she was hiding somewhere in here? In the increasing illumination there was the risk he'd glimpse one of her reflections bouncing around in the enveloping mirror-walls. The lighter hissed again and the glow brightened another notch – the shadows huddling ever closer. A heap of rich velvet sprawled by her knees, the furrowed pile of material left over from covering the item in front. The writer shifted her body to slip underneath, sweaty skin slithering against smooth material as she amalgamated herself with the hiding object: a cage.

'Waiting in the dark... and wanting.'

Jess pressed up against the crouching cage: thin, coppery metal gridded in three-centimetre squares. It was positioned to leave an even triangle of space into the corner, so it faced diagonally out over the room. The enclosure was uncovered on the far side (save a fringe of overhanging material), but the hider remained well-concealed because the cage was mostly filled by a large, oaken chest. The arrangement shielded her body, yet provided a hooded window to peer out from. A good view over the central region of the chamber, but significant blind-spots towards the outer areas: unable to see the stairs at one end, or the bed-area at the other. The silk-draped, conical, plug-in object, she'd noticed earlier, hovered in the centre of her visual field. He was out of sight, lighting the incense burner and candelabra near the four-poster.

'Wanting... so much. So, so much.'

His voice encircled the final 'o' and rolled into a harsh pronunciation of the last word. Very close now. Perhaps he was manoeuvring to creep up behind? She poised to be caught, hands fidgeting against the cage. But instead, he moved into view, striding across her zone-of-sight, just a few metres away. She smiled fondly at the familiarity of his distinctive walk: smooth, languid movements with a playful spring in his step. He was wearing a coal-black suit and carrying red wine. A bottle and two glasses held elegantly in one hand, long fingers clinking the flutes together at the stems and crossing them over the neck of the bottle. He moved out of view and she heard the lighter spark again, flames now spilling from a torch nearby. A glowing flush of heated panic. She felt like a rabbit, getting smoked out of her hiding-hole. Actually, looking out from her rectangular window, she felt more like a rabbit who was inside the oven already. The flicker of fire dancing all around… and the flicker in his tongue as well.

'Always wanting too much, aren't you, my little one?' More candles kindled, further away. Echoed flames twinkling in the long mirror-wall on the opposite side of the chamber. Fleeting reflections of his dark silhouette moving amongst the fairy-fires. 'And the trouble is… that just makes it worse.'

Patronising tone absolutely sure of itself, but the creeping excitement audible too. And visible… as he strolled back down the middle of the room towards the bed, wine swinging casually by his side. Expression relaxed and confident – deep, brown eyes glinting with knowing smiles. Such an attractive man, facial features and contours angled the perfect balance between sharp and smooth. Strong brow, chiselled cheekbones, full lips. A lush tangle of unruly, dark hair with a few streaks of grey rustling. Black leather shoes shining like the sleek suit. He wasn't wearing a tie and the top button of his white shirt hung open. He looked directly away as he strode through the centre of her view, but continued to taunt.

'And worse and worse. Deeper and deeper…'

His voice drooping deeper and deeper as he said the words. And her head lolling along in familiar faint. She had heard that phrase so many times. The echoes reverberating – reflections reflecting reflections. He'd moved out of sight again. Maybe he was looping around the bed to creep up on her? Perhaps that's why he looked directly away from her hiding-hole whilst speaking: to conceal the fact he was coming to get her. She was just a little bulge in the cover. Imagine strong hands coming down from behind, bundling her up in the velvet and carrying her off. Fuck!

There was no escape now. She cringed in fearful expectation, but the next sound was him setting down the bottle and glasses on the small table near the foot of the four-poster. She sensed the corkscrew being unsheathed, brandished and inserted – his gliding movements conducted with assertive grace. Jess twitched impatiently at the bars of the cage. An intrusive click-clack rattled the darkness. All the candles shivered as the basement door swung open. The sound of Katya's heels stabbing the wooden stairs.

'Deeper and deeper…'

He said it more quietly this time, whispering so the approaching Russian couldn't hear. Stiletto-sharp footsteps chiselled as they turned onto the dungeon floor. Jess couldn't see, but she could sense the arrogant flourish as the mistress noticed herself in the mirror-wall, distracting attention for a few seconds before she announced:

'You know what I put?'

'Yes,' he answered, adding quietly, 'I made a bet on it.'

Hard heels rapped on stone as the mistress proceeded into the chamber, walking close to the opposing wall, so her reflection appeared just a moment before her. Sidling into view with a pacey slink. Dramatic beauty always striking: sharp, statuesque, facial features. Dark, sorcerous eyes. Wearing a blood-red dress, ribboning straps over the shoulders triangulated to meet below the breasts – crimson horns set against snowy white skin. Narrow waist curving at the hips and then dropping away in a series of ruffled layers. The dress fell below the knees at the back, but was more open to the front, so everyone could see Katya's long, supple legs advancing. Murderous, red heels to match the dress and make-up. She stopped by the far mirror where the light glowed bright, right in the middle of the writer's field-of-vision. The mistress and her reflection surrounded a vintage record player sitting atop a long shelving unit of vinyl. She bent down to scour the collection for a moment, before rearing up.

'It not here.' The outrage already palpable. 'It's not been put back properly. Someone's moved it.' Turning directly towards the concealed hider as she snarled the accusation. Jess flinched, but there was no way she could be visible from this distance.

'Well, not everyone's as patient as you, my Little Fireball.' A smile in his voice that made the writer smile too. A clink and glug as the wine was poured.

'Ah! Got it.' Katya brandished the record triumphantly.

Jess could hear him taking a swig as the mistress slipped the vinyl out of its sleeve and leaned over the turntable. He set down his glass and strolled into scene. Moving to block the writer's view of the mistress, as well as the silk-wrapped, conical object sitting between he and her. Jess admired the way the jacket accentuated his strong shoulders perfectly. The casual lean of his posture slanting his body, aura of relaxed confidence inking out into the surrounding air.

The Russian positioned the vinyl and activated the mechanical lever. Stepping back into Jess' sightline, she spun on her heels – red smile flashing around the room like a siren. A fuzzy hum reverberating as the record began to turn, air buzzing against the glass. Katya's eyes shining as she drew towards him. The whir warbled as the music shimmied out into the atmosphere. The mistress moving with it, body shaking to the sandy tap of the bongos, hips snaking to the synthesised snare, lashes quivering to the pitter-patter percussion. A recognisable intro, but Jess couldn't identify the song yet. He adjusted his stance, preparing to meet his lover, head cocking to fondle her approach. She swayed lightly as the rhythm bounced, a little cha-cha-cha of a foot-shuffle. The underlying vocals began cooing and oohing as the keyboard poured a smooth melody into the room. An unmistakeably eighties' riff.

The cone-shaped item was obscured by his body, but Jess could see Katya leaning in as she passed, grabbing the silky cover and hurling it up into the air theatrically. The featherweight fabric flew high, opening out like a parachute. Rippling material fluttering down behind the mistress as she pouted her pose, body curling a dancing 'S', hips and breasts sashaying like flames. Dazzling red and white framed in jet-black. His posture swooning as he took in the whole view. Jess was sitting up on her knees with eyes wide, watching from behind the walls of the cage. He raised his hands in meeting, whilst the 'Lady in Red' strutted the last few steps towards him. They came together as the words of the song began.

Bodies clasping with perfect click: a traditional, ballroom stance. And sailing into step like smooth rivers sliding into one. A strikingly attractive couple, swaying gently as the lyrics soaked over. The stringed instruments wavering and wooing whilst the dancers physicalized the melody. As they turned, Jess could see his face sunset over Katya's shoulder: expression enchanted, eyes half-closed, delicate hint of a smile. His lightly stubbled jaw brushing against his lover's face. Jess fluttered along with the memory. The energy in their movements built with the music as the chorus rose.

"... Lady in Red..."

The classic line spilled romance through the atmosphere like expensive wine. As the chorus broke he swerved off to the side and they swirled away in a series of long, sweeping steps. Once their bodies moved, the surprising nature of the conical object, originally concealed under silk, was revealed to the writer. Her jaw dropped. No fucking way! It was the bitch-chair... with Charlotte sitting in it! Cuffed in and facing directly towards Jess. Creamy, naked skin flushed pink and glistening with perspiration, voluptuous body rolling in curves.

A delicious, plump pear, waiting to be juiced. The ring-gag's cords bit into the raw corners of her lips. It held her mouth open, but something had been shoved inside: a small, pink, soft toy. She'd been pugglemuffled! Blue eyes glimmering like pools in the mist, exhausted and energised. Waiting and wanting... for too long – much too long! Mesmerised pupils drifting to follow the dancer's undulating bodies as they glided a rhythmic circle. Flowing back to where they'd started, steps shortening as the next verse began.

Rocking back and forth, he used an upswing to briefly lift his lover a few centimetres from the dungeon-dancefloor, holding her preciously close as they twirled. Another glimpse of the captive's enchanted eyes. Jesus! She'd been here all along. So it must've been Charlotte he was talking to before. Which meant he didn't know Jess was here... not necessarily anyway. But the prisoner would know: she'd have sensed the intruder creeping past. Despite her weird, hypnotised state, she must be aware of the writer's presence. That was worrying, but at least the witness was well-gagged. A swaggering twang of the bass guitar skipped the dancer's steps as they drifted nearer the bed. The momentum escalating towards the chorus once more.

"... Lady in Red..."

Again, breaking into lengthier steps and swinging away. Twirling and spinning across the floor, balance perfectly focused, orbiting around their mutual gravitational centre. And then the oohing and cooing restarting as the song began its gradual, final descent. The dancer's movements melting down and the range of their sway narrowing. He was whispering something in her ear, growling a bass tone from behind lips that barely moved. Her hands flexed a little clutch of relish, smile dawning as she listened. They both laughed. The song was sinking away and he used another upswing to sweep his lover into a cradle of strong arms. The afterglow of the dance swishing in his movements as he carried her out of view. The final words of the song whispering love and romance.

The slats flexed as the beautiful couple dropped onto the mattress. Charlotte's eyes obediently sleep-walking after them. Could see their kiss reflecting in the sheen of her captivated pupils. The sound of lips sloshing together like waves on a beach. Then a few intimate murmurs as Jess heard them readjusting on the bed. The ringing clink of glass on glass... on echoing glass. The writer didn't recognise the next song.

'I don't like this one,' Katya stated decisively, springing up. Red-dressed buttocks sidling into view, dangling right arm hooking hold of her wine glass on two forking fingers. Charlotte was drowsily trying to catch attention, but the mistress stalked past. The clapping sound of his shoes being discarded on the floor, then the rustle of cushions piling as he made himself more comfortable on the mattress. Jess caught a whiff of the incense now lacing the atmosphere – the powdered scent of spice and lullabies. The music stopped with a startled glug.

'What shall we put?' Katya removed the record from the turntable.

'Leave it for now. I want to listen to the night.' His cool, crisp words contrasted the muggy haze of the atmosphere.

She turned. 'Listen for what?' And then a suspicious flicker. 'For her?' The words were pure curiosity, but the mistress added a note of contempt in the pause afterwards. Was Katya referring to Jess? Another squirt of adrenaline into the bloodstream. The mistress slipped the vinyl back into its sleeve, tossing it at the shelving unit as she marched back towards the bed. He hadn't answered, so she rephrased: 'She is coming tonight?' Jess's heart skipped a beat. They must be talking about her!

'Yes.' He replied with a showman's air. The writer's heart became a skimming stone.

'How you know this?' Katya demanded, before a frustrated protest. 'Why you never tell me these things? How you know?' Disappearing from view.

'Because... I know her.' Jess' skimming heart caught the glide and took off on the magical breeze.

'Oh yes. And she is so fucking "special".' The mistress blasted the word 'fucking' to spatter 'special' in bitterness. The quotation marks were obvious – clearly a phrase she'd heard repeated a few times. Jess' swooning celebration was sugared even further by her enemy's intense irritation.

'She is. Exceptionally talented – a very beautiful mind.' There was a warm dreaminess in his tone. Jess' heart sailing over the skies and into the heavens.

The conversation paused as cigarette packets rustled and the lighter hissed. Katya dragged the smoke into her lungs aggressively, as if pulling it inside a cell for a beating. A few seconds later the flame kindled again. He drew the smoke in calmly yet possessively, like a cult-leader summoning his flock and then imperiously surveying their compliance. Jess' body rose along with his inhalation and then sunk with the exhalation, eyelids flittering. Deeper and deeper... A long, smouldering gush of air breathing into the chamber. The writer tried to imagine their non-verbal communication. Would love to see Katya's jealousy written all over her face. How could something so sour taste so sweet? Maybe the spy should reposition to get a view of the bed? But what if he heard her creeping? A wolf 'listening to the night'. She didn't want to miss out on the opportunity to overhear more.

'Yes, she is a good pen-push,' Katya sneered eventually, as if this constituted agreement. 'She describe me very well. How I look, anyway: "dramatic beauty always striking".' The Russian pronounced the word 'striking' with three syllables, dragging the 'r' to break its back on the wheel. She was clearly accompanying the statement with an arrogant pose to prove it was true. Bitch! Although Jess couldn't deny she'd ultimately brought that scalding pang of exasperation on herself. The tobacco smoke twitched at her nostrils – smoulder mingling with the musk of incense.

'She gets you spot on, for sure. In many ways.' He took a pondering drag on his cigarette. 'Very wise for her age. Very insightful.' God, he was such a perceptive man!

'Not so wise, if she come back here, after tell me: "Fuck you, horrible bitch".' Jess could sense the underlining glower. 'And in these stories, she take piss out of me – a lot. Like I'm stupid.' The word spat aggressively. 'I'm not stupid – I speak four fucking languages! And this little bitch make me sound like I can't speak English properly.' Anger escalating as her memory agitated further. 'And she says that I am the "weakest link". Weakest! Weak! We will fucking see about this. And that I am "mental"!'

His laugh chortled into a tease. 'You are a bit mental, to be fair.'

Katya ignored the comment – she was quite capable of winding herself up. 'This cheeky little sneak write like she is laughing at me. Like I am joke. And use clever-clever words to make me sound like... to make it seem... and never direct; always sneaky-sneaky. Pretending she not doing it... and making it difficult to... But I know what she doing.' Jess' secret smile beamed with delightful mischief. 'She make me so I'm... some kind of... comedy character!' The Russian was astonished. He leapt on the opportunity to misinterpret her bemused expression – pretending she was searching for a more concise word to replace 'comedy character'.

'A jester?' he suggested helpfully.

'A jester?!' Katya was outraged. 'This little fucking bitch! Laugh at me?! She will be sorry for this. If she dare come here... then we see who is laughing.'

Poison dripped from her lips. He kissed them, savouring the venom. Jess could feel the thirst in the hot, wet air as they drank one another. The sound of lips and tongues wrestling, the biting clash of tooth on tooth. She sniffed the raw meat beginning to cook – it smelled dangerous. The stone below pressed hard as her knees wobbled, fingers clinging around the bars of the cage. She licked her tongue up the thin metal. She felt so soft: yielding around the narrow strip of hardness. She could sense the lovers disengaging and adjusting positions on the bed. They began dragging their cigarettes simultaneously, but he took longer about it. The writer floated and submerged along with his confident rhythm, now kneeling back with her ankle pressed up against her pussy. A stealthy writhe in her hips to rub against herself.

Charlotte was fidgeting in the bitch-chair. He must've been looking at her, because her eyes flickered with communication. He rose from the four-poster and strode into view, bearing down on the seated prisoner. Barefooted and strolling slowly, swinging his weight from side to side, jacket hanging open, gun-slinger palms poised. Smoke licking up from the lowered cigarette like a smouldering pistol. He halted to obscure the chair from Jess' view.

'Do you know?'

His question sounded sincere, as if he genuinely wasn't sure of the answer. The prisoner must be making some kind of gestural response. He leant forward, lowering his head closer. Was he mouthing another question? Some sort of information must've been exchanged because he began an understanding nod. Straightening his posture and stepping back, so Jess could see Charlotte staring up at him – big, begging-bowl eyes appealing for a reward. He took a thoughtful pull on his cigarette and blew the smoke out in a fuming jet overhead. Half a whistle at the end of the exhalation, chattering the air inside his cheeks.

'So, I suppose you want...'

The captive's eyes dissolved in pleading, head nodding furiously, eager agreements pugglemuffled into a warble. Her body twisting, wrists against cuffs, thighs against mesh. Using her feet to swing the chair from side-to-side. A flashing glimpse of fluffy tail as her ass waggled behind. He smiled fondly, as if entertained by a bouncing puppy. Teasing his head closer to silently ask the question again... and again. Charlotte responding with ever more emphatic physical assertions.

'How long has it been?'

The prisoner's expression was screaming 'much too long', but Katya was more specific, piping up from the bed, 'Thirteen days.'

Lines of wince sliced over the victim's face.

'And it hasn't been made easy for you.' His flat tone emphasised the extremity of the understatement. Charlotte's traumatised, blue eyes shaking along with her head. His voice seeped deeper and deeper... 'You remember everything I told you.'

There was no question mark. The prisoner went back to nodding violent agreement. He stepped behind the chair, ducking, tilting and winding his upper body around hers, lips drawing close to her left ear. Charlotte's whole being magnetised towards him as if she were made from tiny flakes of metal. Jess couldn't tell what he whispered, but the captive's eyelids melted shut and her nod became a high-frequency tremor. He rose and smoothed a drag on his cigarette, before stepping over to place it in the nearby ashtray. He was now standing diagonally behind the bitch-chair, so Jess could ponder his expression. Lines of thought twitching on the surface of his skin – a few fidgets splashing above the great shoal. His muse involved several calculations. Flames dancing in the air and glass, leading the shadows dancing across his face. How many shades of darkness are there? Now his focus hardened decisively. Reaching into his jacket and fishing around the inside pocket.

'Okay.' He decreed solemnly. Charlotte fixated on the small, metal object in his hand: a key.

'No,' Katya protested. Jess could hear her kneeling up on the four-poster. 'This was not…' the pace of her words slowing with confused surprise. He was communicating something to the mistress, holding her glare. Very slight movements: left eye narrowing, eyebrow raising, upper cheek twitching, a confident explanation concealed within his expression. It wasn't clear what the Russian thought, but Jess heard her sit back on the bed.

The writer worried about the prisoner's potential release – the moment the gag came off, she'd start blabbing – singing like a tell-tale tit. Fuck! The delicacy of his smile was sinister as he lowered towards Charlotte. Reaching both arms into her lap and concentrating as he unlocked something around her midriff. A small padlock clinked onto the floor… and another one. Realisation gradually dawning on Jess. Because of the angle of Charlotte's body and chair, the chastity belt had previously been obscured from view. Holy shit!

He pulled open a girdle around her waist. The prisoner enthusiastically pushing her legs wide against the armrests so he could fully remove the device. The blubber of relief as the thick thong-strap unwound. The stick of moist leather peeling from flesh. A clunking slap as the belt dropped onto the floor. The victim's head lolling in relief. Thirteen days! Dirty little bitch! No wonder she'd been walking funny. The writer winced in empathy. What a brutal ordeal. Whose idea was that? Jess shook her head, fingers kneading at the metal, heel stoking up against her pussy. Charlotte's intense anticipation flooding through the waterlogged atmosphere like an oil spill.

He went down on one knee to take something from under the chair, passing from hand to hand through quivering legs. Now holding it up for all to see: a purple, plastic sceptre about thirty centimetres long, attached to a power cord. A Magic Wand Vibrator. Bulky with a bulging, helmeted head. Captor and captive stared at one another as smoke from the discarded cigarette wisped from the ashtray behind. He ran his fingers down her thighs to tickle her pussy. Katya could be heard rising from the bed and jostling about as he passed the vibrator back between the prisoner's legs and below the seat.

Concentration as he fiddled to attach it. There must be some kind of specially-designed holder on the underside of the bitch-chair. The wand clipped in – a hammerhead shark, lurking below Charlotte's vulnerability. A mechanical click as he raised the angle a notch. A few more levels of inclination until the device was almost vertical: pressed between parted legs, thrusting up against her clit. A pugglemuffled gasp... her pussy soaking tender. She grimaced as he checked it was pushed up nice and tight. Holding her whirlpool eyes.

'Remember what I told you.'

He rolled his thumb on the dial and the wand buzzed into a low hum. The vibrations visibly passed through Charlotte's body, rippling down her legs and up her spine. Wobbling thighs, cringing calves, curling toes. Splaying fingers, twitching torso, lolling neck. Head flopping back in slow-motion. Eye-pools bulging as if a grenade went off underwater. A muted exclamation muddled between pleasure and pain. He stood, but immediately leant back in, clutching her cheeks in strong hands and turning her face towards his, fingers pressing into pulsing flesh. His whisper was loud, but the pitch so low it was inaudible – a growling hiss. Charlotte understood though, horrified eyes quivering in her head. He stood back to drink in the scene, sadism feasting.

Katya slunk into view, just wearing bra, thong and heels – all red. Silky, black hair flowing. Coming up behind and slipping her arms beneath the jacket to encircle his waist, snaking her body underarm and winding up his trunk like poison ivy. Bauble-buttocks pouting at Jess as the mistress groped over his torso, claws ruffling beneath the suit. He dipped his head and they kissed, heads at right angles, lazy lips luxuriating. Disengaging mouths, Katya stepped to his front and ran both hands up him, pushing in so she could feel the rugged texture of his abs through the shirt. Palms gliding over his chest and Y-ing up inside the lapels, fingers now spiking like shoulder-studs.

He lowered his limbs so the jacket slid off as her hands outlined his body. She caught it in her right hand, deftly diverting momentum to sweep it up and over her own shoulder. Stepping away and shooting him a sly glance as she slipped it on herself. It was much too big and broad… but looked amazing. He purred an approving murmur. The back of his shirt was sweaty, damp patches scrawling the messy illusion of a face under the chiselled brow of his shoulder blades. The mistress drew back in, untucking his shirt and unbuttoning it. He closed his arms around and kissed her again.

A muffled squeal brought Jess' attention back to Charlotte – the escalation already beginning to boil, face flushed and pouring with sweat. But the others ignored her babbling. Katya flapped open his shirt and removed it similarly to the jacket. This time tossing it behind, just missing the captive. Jess grabbled her eyes over his body. Tanned skin glistening with moisture, serpentine spine curving, shoulder blades ridging and rolling as he handled his lover. Clasping around her waist and swinging her to swivel. Greedy kisses devouring one another as their bodies pushed and pulled and played. His biceps swelling, flexing, rounding in the dancing wrestle.

The mistress manoeuvred to set both hands on his inside-elbows, so her forearms rested along his. Levering on his solid pose and flicking her legs up to catch him in between, clasping tight around his waist. The sinews in her thighs toning and tensing in the squeeze. His hands coming around so each could clutch a perfect handful of ass-cheek. Jess watched the muscles in his buttocks clenching like gloved fists as he gathered in his lover's weight. Katya licked his purring growl of a grin and their lips re-engaged. Groin leading his steps as he carried her towards the bed once more, turning back to Charlotte briefly.

'Be careful what you wish for. Your dreams may just come true.' He underlined the statement with a pointed look at the prisoner, before opening out to speak more generally. 'That's good advice for anyone.'

The lovers moved out of view and dropped onto the mattress with a thump. Charlotte's wet skin trembled all over. Her head wanted to roll, but she held it in place, staring at them as they wrestled and writhed on the four-poster, misty eyes fizzing electric blue. Jess wanted to get a better view, but her position felt fixed, kneeling on the stone with hands pressed against the cage and ankle angling in to stimulate her pussy. The energy fidgeting, her fingers silently tapping. It sounded like the Russian had rolled on top of him now. Jess could imagine him stretched out on his back, the upright mistress straddling and posing as she spoke.

'So… is this in the story?' Katya's tone started as playful banter – a rhetorical question. But then changed pointedly as she realised the answer. 'Oh this is "Our Song".' He chugged a chuckle behind closed lips. The mistress murmured thoughtfully, before returning to her jocular manner. 'So is she writing this now? Is this imaginary?' Some sort of physical gesture must be accompanying the words. 'Or is it real?' This was the first time Jess had heard Katya express humour that didn't involve sadistic humiliation. Sounded like the Russian was slipping off the jacket, presumably to accentuate another pout. 'Is it real? Or imagined?' The writer watched her own fingers tip-tapping as she peered through them towards Charlotte's blur. The prisoner jiggling from side-to-side, muted sigh buzzing in tempo with the vibrator. Katya continued, 'Or reflection maybe? Or dream? Or fantasy?'

His growl rumbled as he squeezed his mistress' lithe body. 'Seems like some kind of heavenly fantasy.' He licked his words as they curled from his mouth. 'But it's real – now – really happening in the real world. Because... fantasies can become real – can be made real.' Sitting up a little. 'I made all this real... through the mirrors... fantasy reflecting reality reflecting fantasy... all the way to the horizons.' He paused, before tapping the side of his head. 'This is where the world is made.'

'You do talk a lot of shit. You know this.' Katya stated it flatly.

He emitted a low murmur of good humour. 'There's truth.'

Charlotte was trying to say something. Eyebrows kiting as she angled her jaw to point the words. She was asking a question, but the specifics were pugglemuffled. Repeating the same four or five syllables again and again.

The others still ignored her though, Katya rocking on her mount as she mused: 'So, if this is "Our Song" then next is "Romantic Rhapsody". You never tell me what happen at the end?'

Her curiosity was sincere, but Jess' was more intense. In the background, the prisoner's muted squawk was becoming louder, moaning into her gag. Desperate request repeated with escalating urgency.

'I don't know what's going to happen at the end.' His emphasis on the word 'know' proclaimed innocence. 'It's her story.'

Was it really?

'No, it is your story. Your... fantasy. She is puppet for you. You know everything that happen. You are controlling this story. You say she will come here tonight, then she will come here tonight.'

Katya's intonation shrugged, the comment wasn't designed to flatter his ego (although undoubtedly, it did). Rather, it was an attempt to make him admit he knew the rest of the story. Their facial expressions waved silent messages in the long pause. Charlotte's stifled pleas had reached full volume... and her eyes crying even louder. And perhaps she'd finally managed to attract some attention – her head now micro-nodding in high velocity communication. The shuffle of Katya dismounting as he shifted to the foot of the bed and rose to stand just out of Jess' view. The prisoner kicked into the ground to jolt the bitch-chair, focus fixed on him as she slowed her desperate, muffled request for maximum emphasis.

Could see his reflection in Charlotte's eyes – a tall man staring down into a pool. 'I'm controlling some things.' Voice swimming in the cloudy depths. 'She will come.'

Jess experienced the urge to crawl over to him right now, but couldn't take her eyes off Charlotte – who exploded in orgasm. Smothered squeals as her body spasmed and head swirled. Eyes popping blue plasma. Face crumpling in long-awaited relief. The pleasure hitting her in waves – multiple crashing waves. He sauntered into scene, a predatory sidle in the sway of his haunches, the symmetrical dimples at the base of his spine winking. Coming up on the bitch-chair from the side, so Jess could see Charlotte's face as he stood above. He dipped his head towards the prisoner, but her world still convulsed in orgasm, so he pulled back and waited. An air of satisfied amusement.

The reverberating climax took a while to exhaust itself, but gradually Charlotte began quietening down, elation dying into a pant. Although the busy hum of the wand continued. The writer watched his face in profile as he leant forward again, the shaded carve of stubble under his chin devilish by candlelight. The captive nodded emphatically in reply to a hushed question, eyes flickering as she relived the delightful relief. Bobbing his head back to snapshot her face before bending in to whisper again – words sharper this time. A flash of fear in the blue and Charlotte's head shaking anxiously. He dipped in and out to elucidate further, enabling a good view of his victim's face after each detail had been communicated. She was learning what was going to happen to her. What he was going to do with his power. The tormentor's jaw jutting arrogantly, torch-flames gleaming on his lower lip as he breathed words over her face like smoke. Charlotte jerked her body in protest, the swing of her head frantic. But his eyes were glazed in stony affirmation.

Big hands closing around her neck, one at the front, one at the back. Fingers slipping on sweat but squeezing to choke her throat and pull her head up. Cruel words grating as they penetrated her ear. Hand sliding down her torso now. Sloping the rounds of her bosom, belly and thighs before reaching lower. Cupping the wand's helmet to ensure it still nuzzled snug against the clit… and then fingers creeping back to roll the dial. The pitch of the vibrations rising, the intensity of the buzz jumping a notch. He'd turned it up! Charlotte grimaced, creasing lines skating and skidding over her face. It was obviously too much already, her sobbing pussy raw and tender. He straightened his posture and patted his victim on the cheek a couple of times – soft slaps plopping like stones in a pond.

'Be careful what you wish for.' As he pivoted, Charlotte's eyes lit horror on his turned back – as if she were going over the edge of a cliff. She stomped her feet and waffled hysterically. The clank of the chair rocking against the floor. Could hear his teeth grit. Eyes very dark – flashing frost and fire. Then swinging to face the victim, but a pause before his slow, drawn-out words. 'Be quiet.'

Charlotte's protests dropped dead, her expression collapsing back into itself.

He disappeared from view, moving to stand at the foot of the four-poster. Jess really had to change position; she needed vision over the bed area. She should crawl along the back wall and peep up from behind something, but would have to do it silently and be mindful of her reflection. With exaggerated care she detached her hands from the side of the cage and backed out from under the concealing cover. The heavy velvet dropped soft as she disentangled and turned on her knees. A glance towards her silhouetted reflection a metre to the right – a small creature crouching on all fours, sniffing the night… and finding the overwhelming smell of predators. The clutter formed a low wall, giving her decent cover if she stayed low.

Katya must've been thinking over the last few minutes and now restarted the conversation. 'So, I give her kiss goodbye. She go home and cry into her pussy cat.' A nasty sneer. 'But you have left her some kind of clue that she find today. And she look online, and find website, and her stories… in her pen name.' The mistress snickered. Fuck you, Katya! Jess pulled herself forward on her elbows, worming stomach over stone, moving along behind the ridge of concealed objects as the Russian continued. 'And she know we laugh at her, because she can see chapter titles and she see the name of the chapter is "Just Between Us".' She laughed again.

'She see this today. She know you in control. She is upset. But she is weak… and there is nothing she can do.' Not quite nothing, Katya – maybe some dumbass jester gave away the passwords to all the accounts! Jess' cheek hovered over the cooling stone, peering into the mirror to watch the open space above their heads – the creeping vines of rope and chain. 'Nothing she can do except come here, crawling to us, on her hands and knees, to submit in every way. Just like she always wanted.' Jess had reached the end of the object-wall. They were now about three metres away: him standing, her kneeling up on the end of the bed, embracing each other loosely with faces close.

'You think she will be so passive?' His words provoked the air.

'Of course. She has no choice. She is weak… soft… submissive.' The mistress oozed contempt.

'You underestimate her. I'm certain of that. She's very smart. She can stand up for herself. I think she might surprise you.' His voice lingered in the stillness.

The Russian dismissed the idea with a confident tut. She waited for him to respond, but he didn't say anything. He was listening to the night. The silence dripped with expectation… and Jess found herself rising into the empty space. Standing quickly, although experiencing it in slow motion… and in the third person. Watching herself popping up from the behind the covers… at the deep-end.

'Who are Muriel and Prisi?'

THIRTEEN

ROMANTIC RHAPSODY

The darkness flickered in candlelight – phantom flames echoing in the surrounding glass. A heavy atmosphere; could smell the air sweating. The evil lovers were loosely entwined face-to-face: him standing at the foot of the bed, her kneeling up on the edge. His muscular upper body bare, her sleek figure scanted in bright strips of red. Behind, their naked torture victim, writhing in torment – frantic, nasal panting providing mood-music alongside the sinister purr of the wand.

Jess popped up about a metre from the four-poster, by the mirror-wall at the deep end of the chamber. Posturing tall with shoulders squared and eyes fixed defiantly. Katya's reaction to the intruder's emergence was satisfyingly dramatic – like a cat who'd had her tail tugged from out of nowhere, torso swerving away as her hissing face snapped around. He tried to remain still... and would've succeeded if the mistress hadn't jerked back, forcing him to raise a steadying arm. His expression held ruthlessly calm, but Jess could sense activity fizzing behind his eyes – calculating and analysing as he attempted to work out what she meant. He was (at least partly) surprised.

'Muriel and Prisi must mean something to you. You picked the passwords.'

She projected her voice into the room like an actor on a stage. Could see her final word echoing around in all the eyes looking back. She held his stare with combative resolution, but he wasn't trying to fight. His countenance was subtler than that – trying to absorb her. Katya's left arm crossed her body to rest on his chest, their blending postures all slant and curl. She turned to him, but he continued looking into Jess from behind a protective haze of serenity, shoulder lowering slightly to over-emphasise how relaxed he was.

In a light, enquiring tone: 'So... this is how you're going to start Chapter Thirteen.' His words repointed Katya's face like a weathervane. But the writer wasn't going to let him redirect the conversation. This was his attempt to seize the initiative – to wrest control of the situation... the story... the world.

'I'm going to start the chapter with you telling me about Muriel and Prisi, because that's what's going to happen.' A gladiatorial glare. 'One, closed bracket, capital M, lowercase u, r, i, e, l, plus-sign, capital P, lowercase r, i, s, i. Two, closed bracket, ditto.'

On the final word she husked her voice in mocking impersonation, focus flicking to triumphantly point out the Russian. A moment to enjoy the beautiful shock splatted all over her enemy's face, before it whipped back towards him. He narrowed his left eye, dragging the corner of his mouth up a touch: a penetrating stare accompanied by the wisp of a smile. The minuscule amount he moved his head away from Katya's betrayed a certain amount of discomfort – annoyed that her pantomime passion was undermining his near-perfect poker face. The mistress now detached from her lover, stepping off the mattress behind him and walking around the four-poster on the other side. She plucked his jacket from the bed and cloaked herself defensively, taking a phone from the inside pocket and beginning to tap the screen. He continued to ignore everyone except the writer.

'I thought you wrote the autobiographical chapters exactly as they happened in real life, but you must've omitted something from "No, You Hang Up".' His tone was breezy and familiar, although the actual words implied criticism, suggesting a betrayal on her part. 'Doesn't matter. You can write it back in for the final draft.'

A peculiar allure cloaked his false innocence, seductive aura inking out all around. Could feel his tendrils of manipulation prying and probing. Their eyes remained locked, his coolness implying that her defiance was a sign of weakness. But it wasn't! He slid a quarter-step to widen his stance, underlining that he could easily intercept any escape towards the stairs. Jess didn't care – she wasn't running anywhere. Katya had been pacing about, tapping the mobile screen. Her face suddenly leaping up.

'She changed the password!'

The discovery announced as if it wasn't blatantly obvious. He turned his head towards the mistress – concealed teeth biting flat across the bottom lip, whilst his eyes attempted to reassure her everything was alright. But her toss of the head communicated she knew it wasn't. A dramatic about-turn and Katya went back to the phone, face glowering in reflection as she paced away towards the long-side mirror-wall. Probably going to try and reset the password using the backup account. How long would it take her to find out Jess had removed all controls from that account… and shut them out of everything else? It would be fun to tell her, but best not – good to keep her distracted for a while… and Charlotte was still distracted on her electronic device.

'I just want to know who Muriel and Prisi are.' Smug innocence twinkling with provocation. Confidence brimming as she advanced, setting her hand atop the hooded object in front and moving around it (the feel of metal concealed under velvet).

He emitted a good-humoured tut of resignation, twisting the upper part of his body to face Charlotte, as if intending to include her. But the prisoner was sizzling with eyes sealed shut. He continued his about-turn and swung into step, walking directly away down the central aisle of the room. Head straight and ears pricked – listening to the night. It seemed as if he was eavesdropping on Jess' thumping heart, but he surely couldn't hear it from there. Just the callous hum of the wand, Charlotte's muzzled panting and he and his mistress' footsteps on the dungeon floor. And the writer's quiet treads joining in as she advanced to take the ground he was abandoning – had him on the run now.

'Muriel and Priscilla are puggles from Melbourne Zoo.' He continued to walk whilst speaking, projecting his voice in the opposite direction. 'There's adoption certificates somewhere.'

A casual shrug, then gesturing towards a small object on the ground by his feet. Pursuing his retreat, Jess moved past the bed – venturing towards the centre of the chamber to identify the item. A little blob of pink and white fluff with gleaming, beady eyes: Puggle's decapitated head. She flicked her focus to Charlotte. The prisoner's lids still squeezed. The writer was close to the bitch-chair now, a few metres from the bed. He'd moved towards the stairs, about five or six metres from Jess… when he drew to a halt.

'Is that all you wanted to know?' Maintaining the chipper tone as he turned, but Jess recognised that predatory look. Dark eyes seething – hot coals clasped in icy tongs. Her heart fluttered, a little wobble in the knees. And the prickling realisation she'd advanced too far into the middle of the room.

A sharp crack of heels announced Katya was stalking back towards the bed. Her voice calmer and colder than before. 'She has broken into all the accounts. And shut us out. She steal everything.'

'Steal?!' Jess scowled around at the Russian, but turned back to address him. 'How can I steal my… my own stories? My own book?' Rage and frustration surging. 'You've stolen my stories!'

The denouncer fired an accusing finger, arm quivering like an arrow after impact, then rotated her upper body to swing condemnation across the others as well. Katya had reached the foot of the bed, continuing towards the location recently vacated by Jess. The writer used her gesture to disguise a step away from the Russian… although that just took her closer to him. The mistress halted, so Jess was positioned directly between the predators, ranged four or five metres on either side. There was no good direction to point her back, so she decided to face him and cock her ears to keep track of Katya. Reconnecting eyes, the writer noted he wasn't protesting her allegation. His neutral expression acknowledged it was true, yet implied he didn't know why she'd bothered mentioning it. As if it were so obvious, it didn't need stating – old news. His focus began to intensify.

'What's the new password?' He said it kind of rote, in a deadened tone that didn't expect a willing answer. The feel of hidden blades unsheathing in the darkness all around. And then Charlotte's desperate wail breaking out – her head swinging so the sound swirled around the atmosphere like a sobbing siren.

'They're my accounts and it's my password. And I'm not telling you.' Jess' voice didn't seem quite so powerful now, echoing back from the encircling mirror-walls… sounded like a spoiled little girl. She increased the volume to compensate. 'And I certainly didn't write it down and leave it lying around on a post-it note.' A sincere smirk as she coiled her body to enjoy Katya's angry glare. That was a good line, re-boosting her confidence for a determined exclamation: 'It's my story!'

'I love your story.' He rolled his tongue over the word 'love' – snarl tremoring over nostril and cheek. A gap in the torches, on one side, made that half of his face darker. 'I can't wait to read the rest. What happens in this chapter?' He nodded over Jess' head. 'Katya wants to know.' A long, deliberate step forward on his right, before swinging the left leg parallel, so both feet drew together.

Jess puffed up her posture. 'Katya wants to know how you think it will go.' Flashing a quick glance behind. She barely came up to the heeled mistress' neck, so (disconcertingly) the predators could make eye contact with one another overhead.

'Hmmm...' a wry smile as he mused. Focus drifting towards the chains hanging from the ceiling above Jess. 'Well, it's difficult to answer that question, because I'm not sure I have all the necessary information. It was a... genuine... surprise to me that you took over the accounts. I thought your real-life chapters were completely honest, with no significant omissions. But apparently, you removed a key part of the story from Chapter Seven. So that makes me wonder...' deep voice lulling, 'whether you've made any other omissions or changes – edits to reality?'

'No. That was the only thing.' Truth blurted from the part of her that felt guilty for having deceived him. Her other parts crowding in to lynch the traitor, behind a face that now pretended she might've been lying. His advancing steps had become subtle. She would hardly have noticed them, except for the clink of Katya's stilettos, mirroring his moves on the other side.

'Good.' His eyes weighed evenly, then another change of tone: excitable, friendly conspiracy. 'Although, I do like what you've done here. A clever trick. And the fact that you were so honest and open about everything else' – a searching pause – 'served to hide the deceit perfectly.' He and Katya were moving with seamless synchronicity: the poise of pack predators closing in. Jess felt the nerves in her calves flexing, motion creeping through her body, tickling up her spine... a bramble of goose bumps at the base of her neck. 'And it fits so well with the rest of the story. Because, when you reflect on it – the situation and context, the goals and motivations of the characters – it's very obvious where the dynamics go from here.' Emphasising the point with a happy nod. 'A good approach – just give everyone what they want.' He rotated his torso, shrug expanding to stretch his arms wide with palms raised. Looked like a stage-actor, trying to win the audience over to his side. In fact, that's exactly what he was doing – the sweeping gesture signifying he meant everyone... including the reader.

He and Katya were only two metres away now, auras encircling, knowing smiles reflecting back and forth. One side of his face dancing in candlelight. The other, watching from the shadows. The glow of the flames licking shaded grooves over his naked upper body. The hint of muscles limbering up below the skin. Jess imagined trying to escape around him: darting low at a wide berth, but him swooping down to pluck her up... like Proserpina. Impossibly strong hands clutching her body, fingers pressing into pulsing flesh. The power, the struggle, the panic, the helplessness. She didn't have a chance. And what he was saying was true – her actions had created an inevitable dynamic for the end of the story – this was only going in one direction. How had this happened? Was this planned? Had she planned it? Was this her story?

Charlotte's cries had re-solidified into that same four of five syllable request, repeated again and again. She looked even more of a state now, slipping around in her own sweat and juices, wild, wet eyes streaming. But still ruthlessly ignored.

His arms resumed their precocious animation. 'You've taken over the accounts.' Physicalizing on the one hand. 'We need the accounts back.' Emphasising with the other (and using the sideways movement to glide forward a touch). 'We need the password. But you won't give us the password.' Repeating the balancing hands as if they were the scales of judgement. Then looking over to Katya with a shiny, rhetorical chime. 'How will we get you to tell us?' Eyes falling back to Jess and volume dropping. 'What approach would fit with the rest of the story?' The writer tried to look calm. Had she set this trap herself? Had she set all her own traps?

The smoulder of perfume warned too late. Katya's palm thumped the middle of Jess' back, thrusting her into a stumbling fall. He swooped in so her cheek slapped onto his chest. The stick of sweat, the musk of man – smelled like all her favourite dreams. Firm fingers closing around her biceps. His long sidestep felt like a dance, turning Jess forty-five degrees so they remained face-to-face. Although he was looking over to the mistress.

'What do you think?' He swayed the writer up on one foot, unbalancing her before shoving with both hands. The force propelled her backwards – wouldn't have kept her feet except she crashed into Katya. The mistress' body stiff like a pole, arm wrapping up around Jess' throat, elbow below the chin – pulling the choke so the eyes bulged.

'I think we should gag her now, or else she'll tell us too quick.' Her voice was icy, carnivorous and husky enough to pull a sledge.

'Ha!' he wolfed. Jaw jutting to chase away the upper lip. Katya twisted Jess another forty-five degrees and he repeated his circling sidestep.

'I want to torture her for long time.' The mistress clarified (in case her previous statement had been too subtle).

A little squeeze before the choking arm withdrew. Katya's other claw splaying over the back of the writer's head and shunting. Jess sprawled forwards and downwards, but her white knight was there once more, sweeping her out of the fall. Swirling around to position his body directly behind hers, and pulling her upright, to face the snarling Russian.

'Of course.' He soothed reassuringly, manhandling his prey to keep her off-balance. 'But we'll leave her ungagged as a test of mettle.' He kept hold of an arm whilst stepping back, swaying Jess ninety degrees, so one shoulder pointed at each of them – rocking-horse weight shifting to-and-fro.

'I'm not telling.' Childish relish in her dizzy defiance. 'You can't make me.'

The predators moved in synchrony, shoving opposite shoulders from front and back, so Jess span a merry-go-round. Before she could rebalance, the mistress' hand shot out to clamp around her neck. Driving in to slam the writer back against his gritted torso. Floundering on slippery tiptoes, hands desperately trying to loosen her attacker's grasp. But his long limbs circled around to brush Jess' defences away. Vice-fingers enclosing the wrists as he drew her arms down to pin at her sides. Clapped in irons whilst the Russian attempted to lift her off the ground by the throat. Grinding the writer up over his sculpted rack of a body, thick shaft brushing against her buttocks.

Katya slackened her grip to let Jess slump. Leaning in behind a cobra's hood of flared lips. 'So you make me comedy character, eh? I make you laugh, yes? Writing in this way... these words... and the tone... like I am...' (Finding it difficult to elucidate the specific accusation.) 'Try make me sound stupid, but use clever-clever words so you can pretend you not saying... and make it hard to...' (Confusing herself further.) 'You are sneaky. You not direct... not make things clear. But I tell you directly: I'm going to make you scream... and cry... like little bitch. This is very clear, yes?'

Jess' eyes widened with angelic innocence. 'I'm sorry you're finding it difficult to keep up. Maybe it's just you sound more stupid from the outside than you do from the inside.' Satisfying to hear him chuckle... and to see the fury bubbling up all over Katya's stupid, jester face. Their holding hands fell away. He took a step back. The writer continued, 'Sorry, I'm probably not making myself clear enough for you to underst—'

The mistress' arm lashed out to clap an open palm across Jess' cheek. A bright splash of pain as she swivelled a half-circle. His big hands returning to steady the spin, the base of his thumbs moulding into her clavicles. She focused in on his amused, conspiring smile through wonky glasses and a dizziness of stars. Could feel his forefinger raised over her shoulder to ward the mistress off. Katya swerved away to stomp out her vigour, seething swear words in raging Russian. And from behind her, Charlotte's muffled begging still reverberating at fever-pitch, those four or five syllables repeatedly smothered by Puggle's soft corpse. He readjusted the writer's specs and poised to speak, but a twinge in the cheek betrayed irritation at Charlotte's relentless attention-seeking. And now the clang of the bitch-chair on stone. Jess watched his expression turn. The whites of his eyes freezing over, but pupils blazing up to burn at the stake – a fire on the ice. His face swung towards the blubberer.

'No! You can't.' The long 'N' drum-rolled and the 'c' cut clean. 'Be quiet.' Charlotte's face crumpled into crying creases and she hushed into a tearful pant. He turned back to the writer with a candle-flame smile. 'What's the password?'

'It's my story. They're my accounts. And I'm not telling you the password.' Her resolution was rock-solid.

His lips shrugged as he rolled Jess' shoulders towards him… and then over and back, pressing her into the waiting arms of the mistress. Katya's touch was surprisingly gentle. Nails fanning out and tickling around the writer's sides, thumbs tracing below the breasts, hands circling the curves of the stomach. As the Russian's body snaked lower her fingers slipped over the hips, finding the grooves at the top of the thighs. Nails play-pinching through Lycra as Katya pulled Jess' buttocks back into her standing-lap. The wall of his chest closing in… along with the sweltering heat. His hands sliding over the writer's shoulders to envelop the mistress. Jess could feel the other woman's body pressing against her own as his palms flowed down Katya's flanks. The symmetrical squeeze of his tautening forearms along the writer's sides, clutching tall hips behind. Could sense the predators' eyes locked together above. Hear the cluck of pouting lips. Feel the drip of venom landing on her shoulder.

He grabbed the mistress in for a greedy clash of a kiss and the three-way embrace noose-snapped. Strong, slim bodies slamming in either side, with Jess squashed in between. Her cheek pressed into his sweat-slick chest – heartbeat pummelling in her ear. Crushed inside violent passion – loud, hungry kisses biting back and forth, jaws gnashing and snarling – like wolves fighting over fresh meat. Raw, fleshy, carnivorous smell.

Jess gasped for air as her head went under. Body liquidating in the pressure, heat and intensity. Hands all over and everywhere: pushing, pulling, tugging, grabbing, groping. Scything nails gliding and prickling. The roughened texture of manly palms pressing into flesh. Fingers falling like rain, washing away in the monsoon, sweeping her away, holding her breath. And his throbbing heartbeat echoing in underwater candlelight. World swimming around and around, at the bottom of the whirlpool – bodies buffeting and bouncing. His strength swelling like an oceanic bulge, bearing down to swirl them all backwards on stumbling sea-legs.

The hoodie melted off her shoulders and splashed onto the floor. Katya's sharp nails fondling under Jess' top and bra, scratching around to locate a nipple. The writer's hands slipping up his body, fingers purring as they brushed over corrugated abs. His skin as tough as it was smooth. Could feel herself sinking into the puddles of her knees, sliding down their bodies like water down walls. But his hand catching hold to clench up between her legs. Katya's skittering fingers finding the nipple and pinching hard. Jess' moan drowning whilst their kiss stormed on overhead.

Charlotte was frantically trying to attract attention once more, her chaotic blubbering foaming back into that repetitive plea. Threatening to overturn the bitch-chair was the only leverage she had. The clang of metal on stone as the swivel-legs lurched precariously. Jess could feel the tension rising through his body. As it reached the neck his head snapped upright – a wolf disturbed during feeding-frenzy. In a thunderous voice: 'No! You can't.' The 'c' cut even deeper this time. He disentangled limbs and reared up, arm cracking a pointing finger towards the bitch-chair as his body turned to follow. Rapid strides, bearing down on Charlotte. 'Don't you dare!'

As he moved away, the mistress repositioned behind Jess, holding the captive's arms in front, right-angled at the elbows. Her own limbs looping either side with hands fisted around the wrists. The two women still rocking against one another in the remnants of the sway. His voice dropped with his body – gargoyle shadow falling over the seated prisoner.

'If you do…'

His next words were too low and deep to identify the specific threat. But Charlotte understood… and exploded in orgasm. Everything on fire – whole body consumed – flesh convulsing. He rose up, riding the swell of dark energy. Arms floating into a crooked T-shape, rays of invisible electricity sizzling from his fingers. And now shifting weight to step away, both arms coming up over one shoulder as if swinging a sword.

'You're not trying hard enough.'

His right hand struck the arm of the chair as his left backhanded fingers across Charlotte's cheek. The seat swivelled – victim spasming in her spinning, electric chair. The wand's power-cord coiling around the stem as Charlotte rotated 360 degrees to reface him. The orgasm tremoring on – face flooded with sweat and tears, chin dribbling with spittle. He crouched to ensure the wand's head was still firmly ploughing into her pussy. And then rolled the dial, twisting his whole body to celebrate the small move of his fingers. Turning it up another notch, so the harsh pitch made the glassy echoes flinch. Charlotte's face dissolving like cinders. He stood back and watched.

Katya was enjoying the torture show too, staring over Jess' shoulder. Her hold around the wrists overly relaxed – leaving a possible opening. Those heels should be easy to unbalance… and would surely make it impossible to chase. As the mistress poised to say something to him the writer seized her opportunity. Cutting her right wrist out of the grip and swinging that side of her body across – lunging left towards the stairs. Rapidly rebalancing and shifting weight to tear the other side free as well. But Katya's fingers clamped to hold that half of the body in place – the fleeing leg re-grounded like a puppy bouncing against a leash. Keeping a low centre, the runner swung her weight back to the other side and pulled with all her might: lurching and leaning, attempting to dive diagonally down and away, arm-span at full stretch.

But instead of tottering on her heels, the mistress stepped forward on her right and planted the stiletto spike into the floor. Jess strained and strove, yet it was as if she were chained to a metal pole. And could feel the momentum beginning to reverse – a sharp tug and she was ravelling back into Katya's bosom. The mistress shifting grip and twisting her victim's left arm behind, yanking the hand up between the shoulder-blades. Simultaneously slipping her other arm under Jess' right armpit and looping it back over the shoulder V-shaped. Screwing the writer's ponytail in fist and tensing her muscles to lock Jess' right limb in the air. The pinned left twisted up to tease the breaking point. Too painful to wriggle – no chance of escape anyway.

Jess could feel a smug, smiling cheek rounding against the side of her head. A scoff in the ear to show contempt for the pathetic escape-attempt. Fuck you, Katya! The frustration twinkled like a rainbow of stars. Now looking across to see him pacing towards them – head bowed, pupils glowering below the horns of his brows. Charlotte squirming and squealing behind.

Katya released Jess and shunted her in the back. The writer fell into him again, sweat splashing as she bounced upright off his chest. He took her hand and hip, as if setting for a waltz, and then swept her away across the chamber. Sailing towards the clear area, left of the bed at the deep end – his gliding body driving her tottering steps. They stopped about two-and-a-half metres from the back mirror-wall, with a similar distance to the wall on the left, the bed on the right, and three tall, cloaked objects behind. He stretched her arms overhead, guiding her eyes towards the manacles dangling from the butcher's hook above. Clinking the cuffs around one wrist and then the other – hanging her up. Metal sliding on sweat until it reached the base of her thumbs and pressed into the flesh – steel winkling between the joints. The shackles were set high, forcing her to shift uncomfortably on tiptoes. Wriggling to adjust position, with the restraints continuously tugging and bullying.

The mistress removed the cloaks from the three tall standing-mirrors. They opposed the back wall, so infinite reflections now surrounded on all sides. He threw his arms out playfully, as if pushing a swing, and the writer's body swooshed up, cuffs biting deep. Sweeping around with toes skittering to find the floor, but the mistress thrust her into another spin. Flashes of her puppet-silhouette swirling in the dark glass... and the predators circling. Could still see Charlotte, diagonally to the left, behind the standing-mirrors – she must've swivelled the bitch-chair to watch. His hands came from behind to clasp the writer's waist. Steering her hips to turn her, in stumbling pirouette, towards him. It was burning on the other side of his eyes, but the words hissed out cool, as if his tongue were cold stone.

'Remember everything. Don't leave anything out. Write it, exactly as it happens in real life.' He paused before gesturing towards the reader once more. 'For them.'

His fingers clawed down her neck to slip under the collar of her top. He rotated and scrunched his fists, so both sets of knuckles lined her chest horizontally. Stretching the Lycra taut, and tweaking to rip it open, tearing down between the breasts. Then a sharp yank to strip the top and cast it off. Lacy, black bra beneath. Katya's palms clapped onto the writer's haunches, sliding around and then fingernails skating upwards to unfasten the bra. It dropped loose and his hand swept down to wash it away. Jess gave a little gasp – blush glowing like coals in a sauna. Bare bosom juggling as she shuffled on tipping toes. Her focus floored, but his knuckled forefinger clipped under the chin to raise her head.

That micro-snarl again. The glint of enamel. A single tooth biting the inside lower lip, as if restraining his appetite. It was obvious how hungry he was though – hungry for her. Hands and eyes fondling over her body, gaze pressing intensely, but fingers barely touching. Tracing her breasts in symmetrical circles, sharpening them pert. Nerve-endings magnetised to meet his caress. Katya's fingernails tickling around from behind. Jess could feel the tremble all the way through, her breath shaking out in cooing wafts. The mistress' palms cupped under soft, round breasts, weighing them to bounce and wobble. Lifting electric nipples into the pinch of his thumbs and forefingers.

His hands drifted, drawing the tingle beneath his touch, tracing the outline of her figure down the flanks. Clasp closing as he reached the curves of her hips, massaging around the buttocks on the outside of the Lycra. And then advancing his body, to teeter and swish her from the floor. The cuffs biting before he gathered her in, palms cupping ass-cheeks and lifting. Her face slipping over his shoulder as her legs rose to wrap his waist. She let her weight flummox, so only his strength held her up – drifting on the clouds. Katya moved around to face Jess, pulling the writer's leg straight, ripping the shoe off and tossing it into the shadows. Likewise, the little sock. She repeated on the other side, chucking everything in different directions.

Jess tried to re-embrace him with her lower limbs, but he slid away. Wringing palms over her haunches and lowering her to the floor. Katya returned to the writer's rear as his fingers slunk down to peel off the leggings, swaying her body to work the hem over the hips. He stretched the waistline wide as it crested the curb of her ass. The mistress swung her leg up in a high, circling stamp, skilfully hooking the hem under the arch of her heel… pausing for a moment… and then completing the stomping movement to rip the leggings down. The shock tremored. He leant in to disentangle the ankles – cuffs holding Jess upright as she tripped out of her clothes. The writer now blooming in only silky, black panties. Katya moved in to grab her ponytail, ripping the hairband out. His greedy eyes eating everything up.

'Sexy panties.' He complimented with a teasing smile. 'You bought them for me, didn't you? Especially for the finale.' A cocky scoff oozing from the sides of his grin. Arrogant bastard! She wouldn't give him the satisfaction… not even in the book. Fuck you!

His fingers picking at the panties now, sliding them off her buttocks to slither down her legs. He stepped back to lick his eyes over her pussy. Succulent lips glinting with moisture as they puckered from her neat, little slip, a light dusting of hair surrounding. The plumps of her inner thighs brushing against one another as she tried to conceal herself. Advancing along her flank, he thrust his left hand to clamp up between her legs, base of his thumb stoking her clit, fingers hooking to clutch underneath and lift. Felt herself opening up as he weighed her in his clasp like a juicy peach – ripe for devouring. Oh, to be plucked and devoured! He held her out and she pressed her weight down against him – only the points of her big toes touching the dungeon floor.

The mistress squatted to snatch up the lingerie, twisting them to shackle the ankles and lifting to pluck Jess' feet off the ground. Squirming suspended by the cuffs at one extremity and the pantie-manacles at the other… with his hand squeezing the juices out of her pussy. Katya cast off the underwear, but the prisoner kept her legs hooked up behind. Moving to him, the mistress slapped an open palm on Jess' ass as the evil lovers' lips clashed in another long, grappling kiss. The writer groaned and ground herself into his palm.

As they disengaged mouths he slid them sideways, withdrawing his hand from underneath Jess. Her throb tried to pursue, but the cuffs dragged back, body wrestling helplessly before dropping limp – showering down in a waterfall, insides sploshing over the floor. Raining sweat as her head lolled forward through her arms... and looking up, over steam-drenched specs, to see them peering back down. Postures slacked and slotted together, head resting against head, wearing one suit perfectly between them. God! They looked so good – fitted together so perfectly. Jess hated them so much! But all emotions were subsumed in lust. Charlotte was blurring and shaking in the background – flabbergasted moan juddering in time with the wand.

Katya's face brightened as she remembered what was coming next. Pushing off his chest and stalking away across the chamber. His eyes remained fixed on Jess – a predator locked onto target. Could sense the saliva pooling on the floor of his mouth. The stick of bare feet on stone as he began to prowl. Slow, steady paces, encircling his prey. Focus kept fastened – could feel his lingering stare as he slunk behind her back. Eyes groping her body: squeezing to gauge the tenderness of the flesh, tearing juicy pieces off, biting into the meat, chewing obnoxiously. There was no escape. Strung up, stark naked, on the butcher's hook – shuffling on tiptoes to cringe away from the violation of inspection. The blush tickled up her legs, spine and neck – buzzing at the base of her ears.

But the tingle began to shapeshift, protruding outwards, expanding in all directions... and exploding. She was enlarging, amplifying, unfurling – a sail fanning out. Toes planting solidly into the ground as she grew taller. Able to lean into the cuffs, controlling her restraints instead of them controlling her. Sweat-glittered breasts bursting out of her chest like torpedoes... heart thumping behind. Bouncy buttocks jumping with jut, swelling to curl rounder. Energy fizzing up the insides of her thighs and in through her pussy. All her most sexual areas surging to prominence... and shuddering as the hot moisture over her skin flushed cold.

He continued to circle: teeth gritting, micro-snarl ticking, freeze-fire eyes transfixed. Watching her womanly curves rolling around. She raised her chin – tilting her head back as if peering down on him. Her expression calm and shining with confidence. She turned under the chains to keep him directly in her sights – their myriad reflections echoing all around. The distance to the far mirror-wall warped the replicating silhouettes in those directions, whilst the three standing mirrors spun a moving tapestry of framed portraits along the deep end wall. Jess was facing that way when he stopped. He removed her glasses, wiping the steamy lens' clear on his trousers, before rebalancing them on her nose.

'What's the password?'

'I'm not telling you the password.' A hint of mischief in her voice, cheek swelling up. 'But you tell me… what else is it, that you want?'

He scoffed dismissively, focus drifting as his head turned away. But then flicking back to double-take – checking for meaning. The writer expanded her pupils in encouragement.

'What do I want?' He reflected, with steady emphasis.

'Tell me.'

'There are many things I want.' Pausing to ponder. 'Things that I'll make. Things that I'll take.' He set off on another circling pace, focus fixed dead-ahead. Jess remained facing the deep mirror-wall – watching him, and his reflection, as he moved.

'Tell us one.'

He emitted a bass breath of air. A conspiring glance to acknowledge her particular choice of words, before his voice opened out.

'I want the story.' (Expressed as if the desire were entirely innocent.) 'This story. I want to live it. Experience it. Be it.' Hands warming into animation. 'I want to see the story – our story – made into a book. I want to make it happen. I want to see the finished product. Hold it. Smell it. Feel it.' Emphasising the word 'feel' and picking up the pace as he spiralled into a tighter orbit. 'I want to read it, remember it, relive it… revel in it! I want to be inside it again. In the moment. In the story.' Deeper and deeper… 'And I want to know your story. To know what it's like to be you. To see this world… of ours… through your eyes.' He swept around behind, but turned to push his palm into the delve at the base of her back. 'You! Mirror, Mirror, Secret Mirror.' He thrust Jess off her feet, keeping his hand in place, as if holding a bow. Presenting her to her own reflection – startled expression, billowing body, jerking legs. Him standing side-on, so her figure obscured his own… and his face not visible in the rebounding reflections.

'I want to see through the mirror. I want to know what it's like to be you. To see through your eyes. Hear through your ears. Feel what you feel. Smell what you smell. Taste what you taste.' Holding her off the ground and turning her body – zig-zagging his steps behind to maintain the archer's pose. 'To know how you feel: hanging from the butcher's hook… in the Secret Room. Seeing your reflections swirl around in the glass.' Jess watched distant reflections swinging, like string-puppets, in the long side-mirror-walls… and then her framed face flying past in the standing mirrors… one, two, three.

'Feeling: my hand on your back; the bend in your body; the rip of the shackles on your wrists. The dizzy swell as you go around and around. Deeper and deeper…' His voice pouring into her like hot, honeyed gravel. 'And smelling all our sweats running together.' The metallic clang of the bitch-chair ringing out as Charlotte renewed her muzzled squawking. 'And I want to taste your excitement, your anticipation, your exhilaration, your lust. Your pleasure and your pain. I want to consume it – eat it all up.

'And I want you to take what you want. All of it! I want to make you. All of you!' The rhythm of his words chanting. 'Want to make you want. Want to make you cry. Want to make you come.' Charlotte's orgasm erupted in the background – cries flying off in all directions as her head swung like a mad lightbulb. The clack of Katya's heels as she moved to deal with it. 'And I want to know... that it was all because of me. My plot. My plan. My Power!' He thrust Jess at the deep end mirror, so she bounced on his palm.

'You will tell the story "Mirror Secret Mirror". And they will read it.' Volume growing louder – a stage-actor raising his voice to the high rafters. Splayed fingers tensing against her back every time he emphasised a word. 'I want them to live it. Inside it. In the moment. In the story. I want them to revel in it!' Across the room, a wet slap across Charlotte's cheek flung her cries off at a different angle. 'I want them to know what it's like to be you. To see this world, of ours, through your eyes. Hear through your ears. Feel through your skin.' World spinning faster, wand buzzing shriller, excitement bulging to burst. 'Smell what you smell. Taste what you taste.' The musk of man. The taste of food that's still alive and kicking inside the mouth. 'And I want them to feel the excitement, the anticipation, the exhilaration, the lust. The pleasure and pain. I want them to consume it – eat it all up! I want them to take what they want. All of it! I want to make them. All of them!'

Intonation enchanting. 'Want to make them want. Want to make them cry. Want to make them come.' Charlotte's orgasm still fountaining into the atmosphere like cartoon jets of tears. 'Make them come, thinking about me. Imagining me... and what I'll do... when I get my hands on them. Because I'm hunting them. Oh yes! This whole fucking story is hunting them.' Voice exploding in all directions. 'I'm hunting YOU! This whole fucking story is hunting YOU! And I've got you now! I've caught you and I'm taking you deeper. Deeper and deeper... Inspiring your deviance, flooding your mind with filth, corrupting your soul. Haunting you... leaping into your imagination, at any time of day or night... and carrying you away. Into the depths of your own depravity. Oh yes, yes, yes!' His words flowing through the writer and out into the world. 'Leading you astray whilst you're at work. Daydreaming about getting called to my office for a dressing-down... bossed and humiliated... bounced up and down on my big, greedy cock... then dumped over the desk with sticky streaks of come dripping down your thighs.'

The swoon was dizzying as the world spun in the palm of his hand. 'And when you're cleaning the house, see yourself dressed as my little maid – bending over with legs straight and ass plumped... getting a feather-duster stuck up your ass and being ordered to squat and wag until all the floors sparkle.' His accent marbled rough and smooth. Most words clean, polished and set for a dinner. But others dirty, jagged and gritted for a street fight.

'When you see a dog on a leash, imagine yourself kneeling at my feet – the perfect puppy-pose... nose all covered in chocolate.' The word 'chocolate' melting in his mouth. 'And when you're sitting on the train... all prim and proper... halo shimmering. But fantasising about me – something dark and depraved and slatheringly sexual. No one in the carriage suspecting.' The world swinging around faster and faster. 'When you walk in the woods: remember I'm hunting you .. chasing you down, tackling you to the floor, sinking my teeth into your ass. Digging your nails into the dirt to claw away. But there's no escape: you're mine now!' Whirling reflections crashing into one another – blurring together. 'And just wait 'til we get to Chapter 14. Oh fuck, yes! We're going to have some fun, for sure. Tie yourselves to your vibrators! Oh, yes, yes, yes... Mirror Secret Mirror!' Her body bouncing off his hand like a bug on a booming bass amp.

'And after your twisted orgasms, blush with shame to catch your own perversion. Feel your guilt. All of it. All are guilty!' Jess heard her own voice echoing the word back as it swirled inside her skull. 'And I want you to confess your sins.... to yourselves... under your breath... in sly murmurs to friends and lovers. But most of all I want you to confess directly to me. I want you to pour your confessions onto the internet, so I can see them... read them... eat them all up.' The whirlwind moving fast – the rebounding images reforming – a kaleidoscope of different faces leaping out of the glass. 'I want to know... how I made you come – how MSM made you come. Tell me in code... or in detail. And I'll devour all the confessions you submit – I'll count every one. MSM is to inspire, enrich and darken at least a million orgasms across the world. Oh, yes, yes, yes... Mirror Secret Mirror. Confess! Confess! Confess!' Thrusting Jess towards the standing mirrors... one, two, three... and letting the echoes fly.

The energy sizzled from his fingertips, but she felt the pace of his movements beginning to wind down. He continued the parade for another couple of circuits, steadily bending his arm to lower her to the floor, toes brushing the stone. A world-wobble of wooziness as the spin finally came to a halt. Jess was facing outwards on the room, with Charlotte's endless electrocution diagonally on the right, and Katya standing across the aisle, diagonally on the left. He leant in, so his lips hovered around the ear.

'Is that enough for you?'

'There is never enough,' she projected theatrically.

His laugh was hearty, then murmured into a chuckle. Jess rested her head against his jaw for an intimate moment, before he pulled upright and looked towards the mistress. The concealed item, behind Katya, was a standing cylinder: two and a half metres tall and three metres in diameter. The Russian grabbed hold of the silky, red cover and turned back to the audience – posing hand on hip and curling so her slim, white body slanted through the half-hollow jacket – smiling like a magician's assistant. She whisked off the covering with practised panache, jetting it into the air, but keeping hold to sweep it down to the floor. Gleefully presenting the armoury: a big, wooden box of torturer's tricks.

All manner of weapons, restraints and tools, laid out on rungs and shelves... strung up on hooks and hangers. The shiny, mahogany unit had a circular base, enabling the five-faced trunk to rotate inside the supporting stand. The mistress pushed it into a smooth, heavy glide. Each side of the pentagon was a wall of pain: the swish of floggers, the wink of metal-studded paddles, the tinkling giggle of chains… unseen items rattling inside drawers and boxes. Katya marched around behind the unit and Jess watched her reflection removing something from a hook. His heavy breathing exhaled into quiet words.

'What's the password?' Child-like excitement sounds so sinister in such a deep voice.

'Fuck you.'

FOURTEEN
LOVE ME TENDER

The oaks stood either side of the road, great boughs and branches floating in the waterlogged sky. The full moon hung heavy, ethereal light seeping down through the tropical night to gloss the trees and rooftops in outlines of silver; the world wallowing in sticky swelter. Air thrumming to the rippling rhythm of the crickets' tribal percussion. And the house silently blending into the suburbs – expression vacant, deadpan, unassuming… flowery perfume wafting purity. All dark, save the sorcerous glow emanating from the heart. Pulsating with movement. The creeping trickle of tiny silhouettes flowing through an illuminated network of veins and arteries. Deeper and deeper… down the wooden steps as the weighted door seals shut. Descending below, where the candlelight twinkles and fires dance with shadows and smoke and mirrors. Hear the air tremble to the thin, buzz-saw hum of the wand. Atmosphere feels hot, wet, breathless and tense. Smells of smoulder, spice, sweat and danger. Tastes… Alive!

Jess hung naked from the butcher's hook: voluptuous, white body reflecting endlessly in the encirclement of dark glass. He stood behind, arms sculpted around her waist with his dick snaking down the valley between her ass-cheeks. She could feel the push as the blood throbbed. Charlotte seethed in the bitch-chair, flesh shuddering in time with the vibrator – tortured mood-music wining the room in sadistic decadence. Katya stood behind the armoury. Could hear the swoosh of the flogger as it flicked about her reflected figure. And then the tick-tock of stilettos as the mistress rounded the pentagon and swung into direct view. Sweeping her weapon in a horizontal figure-of-eight: dozens of twining, leather straps, stinted with metal tips. Dark, psychopathic eyes.

Stepping away, he slapped a patronising pat on the doomed writer's butt… and the mistress descended in a dazzle of lashing leather. Jess had heard that floggers were soft, sensuous weapons, but quickly discovered this one wasn't. The straps swiping a hail of steel studs through the right breast and then looping back to strike from below. Metal tips streaking the nipple. She barely managed to hold the yelp inside. Katya turned side-on, twirling the leather a clean circle – a Catherine-wheel of shrapnel cascading over the left breast. The writer twisted into her own flinch, swinging away to shelter her burning bosom. The mistress rotated in the opposite direction, spinning her body to deliver a backhanded pelt across the buttocks. Steel teeth thrashing over the rump. A pathetic little bounce. Air hissing as the flogger swept into a wide figure-of-eight – the writer forced into a humiliating jig with Katya moving around to spread her attacks across the ass.

'Bouncy. Bouncy,' she crowed. 'Bounce, bunny. Bounce!'

The victim's hatred exploding and collapsing – infuriating helplessness. He'd circled the armoury and returned brandishing a riding crop – a small, squared loop of leather tipping a thin, flexile cane. Slashing diagonally down, so the rod split the air with a whoosh... and then a sinister reverberation as the serpent's tongue flickered. He flashed Jess a cheeky wink, mocking her wince as the flogger dusted her hopping-hot buttocks. His arm drew back for a sweeping forehand, angled so the cane struck the front-centre of both thighs simultaneously. Lean, red line branding into white flesh. Her exclamation was irrepressible – a strangled, little yowl. He strode around behind as Katya circled to the front. A splash of straps across the top of the thighs and then the crop-pole striking her left flank. Another sleek, crimson line – this time where the skin had already been tickled pink. The writer pirouetted under the chains to cower away from the cane, but the flogger swept across her butt like a bushfire.

The predators paced at the same tempo, circling their helpless prey on opposite sides and lashing out repeatedly. Flogger trouncing and crop cracking. Jess squirmed and spun, but the shackles flummoxed her movements like a sadistic puppeteer. Twisting back and forth, there was no escape... and no mercy. Flinching a body part to dodge one weapon, just made that part the target for the other. And the attacks were relentless. The crop coming down vertically on her bust and hitting the bullseye – leather-flap slicing through the tip of the nipple. A proper whelp of agony, spinning away in the cuffs, but Katya strafed shards through the nib of the same breast... and the barrage continued... for several minutes.

As the assault paused Jess was left stumble-swinging around on the butcher's hook. The fierce faces of the predators glistening with sweat, bodies crackling with energy, nerve-endings blasting off from the skin. He drew up behind so she could feel his erection. A slim pant in his voice, but the tone was relaxed and teasing.

'What's the password?'

'Fuck!' she managed, but he knew she meant, 'Fuck you!' (And she really did mean it.)

He pushed her head forward between her arms, placing the riding crop in her mouth. She bit to hold it horizontally in her teeth, plastic pressing against the corners of her lips. His hands slalomed down her back, buttocks and legs as he moved into a crouch. Grasping behind both knees and lifting, plucking her from the ground to rest on his chest. Opening her legs to present her spread-eagled... to Katya! The panic surged. Jess tried to clamp shut, but his grip turned to stone. A purr of a growl rumbling over her ear. Her face blushed red-rose as she splayed before her enemy. Plush, layered pussy-lips unfurling like petals as he stretched her wider. Katya was flush with excitement too – cruel smile curling with gloat. Ensuring eye contact with the victim as her weapon raised. The blows flayed down on the inner thighs – dashing straps and grazing steel. The mistress winding her body in rhythm with the attacks. Jess gritted her teeth around the crop, gnashing down the pain – hiss spitting from the sides of her mouth.

'What's the matter, bunny rabbit? You are laughing at me, maybe? Because I am so fucking funny!'

He lifted Jess higher, prizing her legs wider. All the curves of her body winding inwards... pointing down between her thighs. She closed her eyes and bit hard as the flogger whooshed down over her vulva like a firework – nearly cut the crop in half with her teeth. The Russian laughed as the flame of leather flared up to engulf the pussy from below.

'What's the password?' His voice laced. Jess could feel his heartbeat thumping out of his chest and into her own.

Her reply was muffled by the crop but the message was clear: 'Fuck you!'

The mistress delivered a dozen more sadistic strokes before pausing to shine her victim a poisonous smile. Jess felt the humiliation pulse along with the hate – both firmly trapped inside the lust. He removed the crop from her teeth and she lolled her head back into the nape of his neck. But he shouldered her upright so Katya could push the top of the flogger into her mouth. The dense wodge of thongs tasted of sweat, leather and her own sexual lush.

The writer was handed over as the mistress moved forward and gathered Jess' legs underarm, balancing knees over the ledges of tall hips. He stepped back, sweat squelching as he peeled his chest away.

Still close, he poked the crop down vertically between the two women's bodies. Leather tab hovering around Jess' pussy and pausing ominously... before he jerked his hand into a rapid shaking motion, flapping violently at the wrist. The crop whipped back and forth, striking the sensitive little plumps at the tops of the inner thighs. The writer clenched her jaw around the flogger and squeezed her lids shut, legs jostling in Katya's tight grip. Pain purpling in the most tender of places. Oh fuck! They were so mean.

He withdrew the weapon and it disappeared behind Jess' back. Could feel the Russian smiling in her ear. The flat head of the crop smacked up against her pussy with a moist thwack. She squirmed around in Katya's arms as the crop struck between her legs a few more times – hot, stinging lips. Then a dozen symmetrical pelts drummed up against her buttocks, the cooing mistress switching hips to present each ass cheek in turn. A long – almost-romantic – sigh when he finally turned away. Katya dropped Jess and yanked the flogger from her mouth. Both predators discarding their weapons on the floor with a thud and clatter.

Jess dripped down from the butcher's hook, weight hanging limp. So many different shades of pain: kneading and gnawing; sharping and shooting; threading and throbbing. Skin mottled pink and rose with streaks and dashes of red. The sheen of rough-raw skin slicked in sweat. Yet a peaceful feeling... like a crisp dawn after yesterday's battle. As the violence lulled, Charlotte redoubled her efforts to gain attention, begging desperately into her gag. Her hair – a matt of soggy spikes – as if she'd been electrocuted underwater. Heavy clanking as the chair bucked under its crazed rider. Jess lolled her head back behind her arms, making eye contact with him over her shoulder. He rolled his pupils in light-hearted frustration and pointed his words at the writer.

'Fucking swivel-chair: not solid enough. I blame you for this.' Then he turned his attention towards Charlotte and darkened his tone. 'No! You remember what I said.'

Charlotte's eyelids fused over, expression melting and running down her body like lava. It was obvious she couldn't hold on much longer. He shook his head as if he'd no idea what'd got into her. A raised eyebrow towards Katya requested that she deal with it and the mistress set off with an aggressive spring in her step. Jess rotated under the chains to face him. Her glasses had slipped off the nose, but had somehow clung onto her face. He removed them for another trouser-polish, before resetting with concerned precision.

'What's the password?'

Her head lunged through her arms – a wild beast leaping out of its cave in a desperate last-ditch defence. Her teeth slipped against his sweaty chest, but she managed to bite a mouth-hold of flesh just below the collarbone. Snarling her whole face into the clench, digging the enamel in as deep as she could. It must have hurt, but he remained still – jaw jutting to gobble back any exclamation of pain. She hung from her incisors for a few long seconds, before her grit slipped. Satisfying to see the mark she'd left above his heart – a lippy, purpling scold surrounding two whitened furrows of dents. Charlotte was orgasming painfully in the background again. The air zinging afresh as the buzz of the wand went up another notch: humming thinner, faster, crueller and crueller.

He and Jess' eye contact sparkled, before his jaws flared and pounced, chasing her head back through the cave of her arms. His weight coming down across her chest and teeth closing around her jaw, just below the ear. But his bite was light – a wolf at play – holding her neck as a show of primal dominance. He moved his mouth, gnashing and nibbling… enamel scraping, etching and gnawing over her neck and cheek. She could feel the growl vibrating through her body. Everything radiant with arousal. Bites kissing down her jawline and then pinching around the upper lip. A feisty, little snarl as she nipped back at him, fighting her face upright so they snapped back and forth with his erection pushing against her midriff.

Looking into his eyes, feeling the electrical attraction… and their faces snapping together like magnets. Mouths colliding with a jarring scrape of enamel, heads at right angles – a fighting square – incisors versus molars. Teeth xylophoning on teeth as their jaws gaped to devour one another, hungrily twisting in the dark romance of their first kiss – coming together at last. Cuffs ripping tight as he forces her back and down, strong hands clutching to panel her body straight beneath his own. Large lips pressing and enclosing. Kiss deepening as she grapples to return it. His swirling tongue swallowing hers, like a small wave washing into a tsunami.

His mouth tastes like wine – dark alcohol flooding through her, hypnotic aroma swelling. Liquid iron lips: soft and tender. Everything else about him: hard and solid. Powerful chassis of ribs and muscles digging into her yielding flesh. Big dick steeled against her like a gun. Bodies twirling under the chains, painful pirouettes as his force comes down and down. Cuffs about to carve off her hands, so she throws all her weight back into him and fights herself upright. His strong hands now chalicing around her bust and waist. Palms pressing, cupping and squeezing – moulding her writhing body like soggy clay – a voluptuous vase wobbling around on the potter's wheel. Curves welling and bulging.

Katya returned with a sharp shock, talons digging into the writer's shoulders and then ripping down the back. He swallowed her scream – eating it all up – licking it out from inside her mouth. Masculine hands kneading and wringing, whilst the mistress' claws scratched and scraped over the ledge of Jess' ass, splaying to rake the buttocks. He sucked up all the air she blasted into his mouth – drinking her insides. As he disengaged from the kiss, she glimpsed flashes of his face through butterfly eyelids, looking over to silently communicate with the mistress. He readjusted Jess' specs and turned to walk towards the armoury. Katya moved her palms over the prisoner's waist and pottered her around to keep eyes on him.

After circling the pentagon, and opening a few drawers, he strode back holding two stocky, white candles. Ever the romantic! The mistress grabbed Jess' hair in one claw, hooking the other around her pussy. Holding her groin in place whilst yanking her head to face directly upwards. Katya's forearm angling between the shoulder blades to force the bosom forward. Presenting the writer's exposed breasts – jumping up and down like excitable puppies as their Master approaches. A touch of warmth as the lighter hissed over the candlewicks. Smouldering, waxy fragrance hitting her upturned nostrils. He held both candles above her quivering bust, rotating them horizontal so the flames licked into the wax. A droplet of heat smelted onto her left breast... and sizzled. A couple of burning scalds dripping onto her right. She tried to flinch away, but the Russian's bony elbow dug in to hold her in place, face angled to prevent her blowing out the flames.

He revolved his hands and the molten rain pattered onto her bosom. The torturers' smiles reflecting one another as their victim writhed. The fiery shower pouring thick and fast, magma splashing all over her bosom. Each drop blazing for a few seconds as it furiously tried to weld into her flesh. Then quickly ebbing away as the wax cooled and hardened. The sensation somehow refreshing – purifying – the wax-sealed skin felt revitalised and stimulated. Jess closed her eyes and drank up the pain. The soldering continued until her breasts were rich, iced buns – overflowing – glaze spilling down the sides.

'What's the password?' His lower lip especially wet, glistening with sadistic sheen.

'Fuck you!' The air from her lungs dodging around Katya's elbow and flying into his face. 'It's mine!'

A nod of the acceptance as he blew out the candles and tossed them onto the floor. The mistress pushed Jess' head upright to observe him removing items from his pocket. Two devices, about five centimetres long: symmetrical loops of metal with little pairs of pliers set in mechanical frames. A scissoring action to open the pincers... which then snapped themselves shut. Circular tong-tips clenching together neatly. He applied them in quick succession. The clamps pinching tight around the nipples, squeezing the teats flat with severe mechanical pressure. Waxy icing crunching in the force of the clinch. Jess' face spliced, her breasts already sore from the flogging, cropping and scorching.

Katya released her hold and stepped away. The writer plunged her head forward, chin-on-chest, soggy hair flopping to spill over her face. Attempting to hunch whilst hanging, huddling protectively around her burning bosom. The skin over her thighs, butt and breasts spluttered with electricity. But the parts that hurt most, were also the parts that felt most alive – nerve endings springing with energy. The rest of her body a muggy, sweat-lathered haze. She watched the scene swing-swaying from side to side. Katya strutted around to the front, slipping under his arm and placing a hand on his chest – palm moulding to clutch a large pectoral muscle. Jess hated (and loved) the way they slotted together with such pristine precision.

He took a key from his pocket and reached up to uncuff the writer. Extreme relief as she buckled and the blood flowed back into her hands. He stooped, dropping his shoulder and slapping his arm around the back of Jess' thighs – scooping her up in a fireman's lift and whisking her across the chamber. A dizzying rush as her head bounced. Then focusing in on the spiralling motion of the dangling clamps, the sound of wax crackling on the surface of her breasts, and the movement of his ass. Buttocks taking turns, on the trailing leg, to punch their muscular outlines through the fabric of his trousers. Katya's red heels rapping along in the periphery.

Passing Charlotte on one side – still blubbering like a puddle of lava – and the armoury on the other. Moving behind a partial partition-wall of three tall, cloaked rectangles. He set her on the floor and grabbed a handful of hair. Jess saw their silhouette in the mirror-wall close-by: a big, muscular figure holding her scalp as if the rest of her body wasn't attached. Although in fact, it stumbled below on legs made of jelly.

Katya bustled in impatiently, forgetting to emphasise the 'ta-da' moment as she pulled the velvet drape off the item in front. Unveiling a large, mahogany box crouching like a table. At one end of the rectangular surface – a vertical panel with three holes in it. One for the neck, one either side for the arms. Tugging her hair, he swung the writer up onto the podium of the stocks. The surface was plastered with sandpaper. Vicious, rough texture under her hands and knees. She tried to hold still, but he pulled her on by the hair. Just a hint of the potential sting as she jostled along without tearing her skin off. He opened the stocks and placed her head in the central gap. She positioned her hands herself and he shut the stocks over her neck and wrists – locking them in place with a steel hook.

Her face was the lowest point of her body, overhanging the edge of the box with head pointing towards the mirror-wall, a metre-and-a-half away. Her butt curled up in a ball behind. Forearms, knees and the tops of her feet pressing down on the sandpaper, stuccoed still to avoid provoking unnecessary friction. The nipple clamps tweezing and pinching as they prodded against the surface of the podium. Looking up into the glass, Jess saw Katya disrobing the partition wall and revealing another set of three standing mirrors. Rebounding the cringing image of her own plump bubble-butt billowing up in the air.

He stood close, dick at eye-level and straining against the wall of his trousers. Hands moving over his black, leather belt. Pulling the strap out of the fastening loop and tugging until the prong slipped from its hole. Opening the buckle and hooking a finger inside the brassy frame to draw the belt from around his waist. The sound of hide slipping over cotton and a rhythmic snicker as the rumpled crease, around the hole, slithered through the holders. As the belt was removed, the waistline of his trousers dropped a couple of centimetres to rest on his hips. Baring his haunches to gleam in the candlelight like a pair of lower-jaw fangs… arrowing V-shape pointing below the hem. Towards his cock, jostling around behind the fabric – a wild-beast chafing to be unleashed. He held the belt out to dangle, crinkle-curling by her cheek. Jess turned her face to smell the rich leather, touching her tongue to taste the hide: oaky and gamey.

'What's the password?' Rote and deadpan.

'Fuck you!' Rote and deadpan.

He paced behind her, double-reflected eyes gliding over the voluptuous, heart-shaped body curled up over the box-stocks. Her sweat-jewelled skin mottled white and pink where the tips of the flogger and crop had lashed. A criss-cross of strict, red lines drawn by the crop-cane. He folded the belt into a loop and licked his lips. The sandpaper held her perfectly still, ass peached invitingly. The first blow struck the round of her right buttock, the two halves of the belt snapping together for a satisfying, leathery thwack. A pained, little gasp.

Rolling his arm for another strike, hitting the same place. And again for the third, fourth and fifth whacks… cheeks cringing away. Sandpaper biting at the slightest hint of movement – sadistic Velcro. Warming into it now as the belt swung again and again, whooping all over her backside. A steady tempo of attacks, the leather loop snapping with clockwork timing. The escalation of power perfectly tuned, every blow fiercer than the last. Every target already tender… the cumulative impact escalating. Fuck, that was so hard! A groan of a wince, but the next attack harder still.

The mistress chuckled and wandered off across the chamber. The pelting barrage of leather continued as Jess watched his silhouette in reflection. Muscular right arm flexing and swinging in elegant motion. As the pain wracked and mounted the blows began blurring together – each strike blending into the last… and the next. Not able to distinguish the individual impacts now, just the blaze of the beating, steadily heating her butt like water on the boil. The feeling of violent attack spreading and diffusing – blossoming over the surface of her ass.

The pain invigorating… yet exhausting. Such a wonderful kind of exhaustion: the comfortable kind you can just keep sinking into. Deeper and deeper… The blows bumping her buttocks with the chuntering rhythm of train travel. A passenger on a long journey, gently dozing off, eyelids flickering in the sun. The security of regular motion – knowing what to expect next. Vaguely aware of Katya's return, brandishing a glass of wine and a circular, wooden paddle. The mistress leant down and slapped Jess' face until she acknowledged the weapon with a bleary smile.

The paddle swatted onto her buttock with a refreshingly cold, wooden slap. She discerned the first couple of blows as distinct attacks, spanking onto her cheeks. But soon the wallops were clobbering into one another, flattening her flesh, hitting everywhere at once. He was standing in front and speaking in his deep, dark lullaby of a voice. She could tell he was asking questions, because of the enquiring sparkle in his eyes. So beautiful – drinking his red wine and pouting over his cigarette with those big, liquid lips. Jess didn't really register the new weapon he was showing her, until it smacked across the back of her legs. A leather paddle: long and wide and lined with rows of steely, coin-shaped studs. It pelted across both cheeks simultaneously with a harsh flapping twang.

And the attacks just kept coming, all merging together into one long, brutal assault… lots of different weapons. So many shades of pain: thuddy smacks, flappy thwacks, belting welts, bristling swipes, cropping whips. The sensations heating more like soup than water, or stew even… tasty tortures marinating together in the broiling juices. A few streaks from the bamboo cane stood out as distinct from the general melee – the thin wood focusing so much force in such a narrow area. But even those attacks quickly amalgamated themselves into the overall swell.

Glimpses of their silhouettes moving behind in flashes of violent movement, timed along with the ebb and flow of the pain. Katya's slim, white torso slanting around inside that oversized jacket – swinging her whole body into the strikes. His turns, slower but harder, graceful dipping posture winding and looping. Jess' white skin washed away and painted pink. Blushing, blooming, rosing: purpling and plumming; patches and blotches; streaks and strafes. A volcanic landscape of skin crinkling up. The orbs of her ass burning like fiery, red planets… but everything submerged in the cooling mist of trance.

They took turns talking to her – interrogating her – but the writer just nodded and smiled along. The only sounds she made were cries of pain, singing them into the darkness like the repetitive mantra of a hazy-eyed monk. Perhaps Charlotte's wand got turned up again, at some point – could sense her continual torment swirling around in the atmosphere. Jess coughed and choked as the mistress blew smoke in her face, but Katya's increasing anger was actually rather relaxing – like nodding off to hard dance music after a long night and the right combination of drink and drugs. Deeper and deeper…

The beating must've ended with a specific blow, at a specific time, but the writer didn't experience it like that. Rather, the assault drifted away – a red fog thinning and dissipating. Could hear the predators speaking to one another over her prone body: she sounded frustrated, he sounded amused. His palms cupping around Jess' buttocks and massaging. Could feel how rough her skin was as his hands rumpled across the blistering braze of her backside. He opened the stocks and took her by the hair, levering her into a tall kneel. The sandpaper grazed viciously as he twisted and pushed her to sit with legs dangling off the backend of the box-stocks. Her own tender backend pressing down on the abrasive material. The surface kissing her a cruel goodbye as he wrenched her off it.

She landed on the floor, up to her knees in the puddle of her own legs. The cold stone felt kind after the bite of the sandpaper. Scrunching a fist of hair, he yanked her to her feet, but kept her in a low squat. Waddling her into position before one of the standing mirrors – ass right up to the glass, head twisted to view the reflection over her shoulder. The mistress helpfully provided illumination by setting a candle on the ground close by. The flame licking Jess' pain with warmth.

Her buttocks mooched and mottled a colourful abstract of agony: pink, purple, rose and red. Much of the surface creased and wrinkled with impact craters, welting bruises and strafing streaks. Rough, sandy deserts of raw skin, where the nerves prickled like alien cacti. The skin was not so much broken as beaten away in places – weathered off in a cosmic storm of hurt. Hot as hell and fun as fury. Blood bubbling up under the surface, so the skin was almost transparent, moving like magma as the candlelight shimmered over a cruel, red sheen… slick with sweat. She closed her eyes and consumed it. All of it.

As the writer tuned back into the world, Katya's footsteps could be heard marching around the chamber. Jess found herself looking up his body into those deep, dusky eyes. Masculine torso heaving – a slim, wolfy pant. The fangs of his haunches bare and gleaming. The helm of his dick must be furiously raw from gnawing against the inside of his trousers. He tinkled the fingers of his left hand under Jess' chin.

'You're very tough.' He soothed. 'Tougher than I was expecting.' The writer simmered with pride. 'Much tougher than Katya was expecting.' He glanced towards the returning Russian, before resettling his focus on Jess. 'We're all very impressed.'

The mistress had brought two coiled whips. She handed one to him, then turned and stalked off. He breezed the weapon over

Jess' head and rolled his wrist. A creeping slipper-slap as the tail unravelled onto the stone. Several metres of platted leather, two centimetres in diameter at the hilt, tapering down smoothly, thinner and thinner, until it was just a single strap of hide with a wiry thread of a tongue. Looked leaner and meaner than any torture device Jess had encountered before. His voice hushed.

'You've taken a lot. Anything more is going to be too much. This…' he said, rippling the whip, 'is going to be much too much.' A tone of patronising reassurance. 'You've made your point. You can tell us the password now.'

She smiled… a coy curl of lips… and a little rush of elation. 'Fuck you.'

He returned her smile, reaching down, tugging her hair and pointing her face back towards the standing mirror. Then taking something from the nearest candelabra and holding it over her. A headband, with a pair of fifteen-centimetre-long bunny-ears sticking out. He lowered his body to crown her. Tongs slipping through the hair, clasping around her skull and gripping in with little teeth. The ears were made of furry, pink felt – held straight by an invisible skeleton of wires. They did kind of suit her: with her cute, round face; twitching, little nose; and garish, pink blush. She was a little rabbit. They'd made her into a bunny. And now… they were going to hunt her for sport. Her insides bouncing, the warmth below her ears tingling up and down her spine.

Re-fisting her hair, he turned her away from the glass and guided a few shuffle-wiggling steps. Then splayed his hand over her face and shoved her backwards past the standing mirrors – sprawling into the central aisle of the chamber. Onto her buttocks, but managing half-a-roll to find her knees. He became a silhouette as he blew out the nearest trident of candles. Only the ghost of his features visible… and the flash of white teeth as he spoke.

'Run rabbit…' he mouthed in slow motion, then, jumping his eyebrows, 'Run!' He stepped back – grin dissolving into the shadows.

Katya was close by. Long, white, wet legs flexing and tensing… whip coiled up in her fist. Beautiful face shimmering with sweat and rage.

'Tell us the fucking password, you stupid bunny-bitch.'

The mistress stormed down in a clatter of heels, leg swinging into a kick. Jess caught the attack early, smothering her lower arm against the calf, yet still enough momentum to knock her sideways. Sounded like a serpent slithering over stone as the whip unfurled behind. Run rabbit… run! Bunny jolted off the floor and accelerated into a scamper. The whoosh of the weapon snaking through the air – long lash ripping itself out. An instinctive bounce as the tongue snapped at her heels.

Moving fast, but fleeing back towards the deep end, dashing past the bitch-chair and the butcher's hook. Her own panicking reflection rushing at her: ears raised, nipple clamps jangling over wax-cracked bosom. Katya close behind: long-legged strides approaching the bed. The runner swerved right, bolting between the four-poster and the back-wall – ducking to scurry on a cartoon-blur of legs. The mistress swept a backhand stroke, jerking her wrist to sling the whip. The leather wrapped a right angle at the bedpost, brushing the mirror as it chased Jess around the corner – tongue whisking so close, it blew her buttocks a kiss.

As the prey rounded the four-poster, Katya turned and cracked the whip out along the foot of the bed – cutting off a direct sprint down the central aisle. The only flightpath evading the mistress skirted the long mirror-wall, but that took her back towards him. She ran past the armoury, shimmied a hooded barrier, and dashed past the box-stocks. Now arcing a diagonal towards the stairs, weaving through a maze of drape-laden clutter and freestanding mirrors. All the glass filled with her own tall ears and wide eyes.

He materialised out of the shadows ahead and she veered to avoid a collision. But it was only his reflection she dodged, instead crashing into his solid reality… and bouncing back off, sore ass thumping on the floor. He stepped around to cut off the stairs-escape. Turning back with wolf's eyes… whip stirring. His arm circled and the leather followed, weapon spinning into a whipping wheel – tongue thrashing the ground beside Jess, chopping up the air. She tore away, rolling up on her knees and lunging through a gap in the clutter, out onto the aisle.

Run rabbit… run! She tilted to her feet but angled the wrong direction and sprinted back towards Katya and the deep end again. He took a couple of pursuing strides and flourished his weapon with a jinx of the wrist – the whip shot out like a reptilian tongue. Just a few, thin centimetres of wiry thread across the lower jowl of her buttock, but the pain slit like a knife – all the agony concentrated into one narrow slice. Both her feet left the ground in a pathetic little bounce, hands clutching around her ass-cheeks like The Scream.

'Bouncy, bouncy.'

Katya jeered as she attacked from the front, unleashing her leather to cut a sleek, red line across the top of Jess' thigh. A squeal as she buckled and dropped to one knee. Surrounded by predators again – everyone in the same locations as the first encirclement of the night. The runner turned back towards the stairs. Her only chance was to escape around him at a wide berth. Darting like a mouse, ducking into the momentum. But he didn't attempt to intercept – just watching as she sped by and bee-lined towards the steps… nothing standing in her way. Run rabbit… run!

Breaking into a stroll, he slung his weapon sideways, as if chucking a ball for a dog. The whip crept through the atmosphere like a rumour, leathery tail wrapping around Jess' ankle as her foot pressed into the ground. When her leg rose the line pulled taut… and her whole body became the end of his whip – snapping straight in the air with limbs outstretched, and then dropping flat, elbows banging on stone, but the real pain exploding from her bosom. Clamps flying off so her benumbed nipples suddenly steamed, hissed and scalded. Fuck, that hurt! And where were her fucking glasses? Probably smashed to pieces! But she could see the bottom of the stairs just ahead.

As she attempted to lunge forward he jolted the lasso to drag her back – flummoxing her movements with a couple more teasing tugs. She twisted onto her front to try and disentangle. Katya was moving at speed, marching past him and lashing the ground beside Jess – forcing her to roll further away from the steps. He spun his wrist, sending concentrated twirls skipping down the line to unwrap the writer's ankle. The mistress arrived at the foot of the stairs, sweeping around to attack. But she'd misjudged the space and the whip caught on something behind. Jess scrambled to her feet.

He stalked forwards, flicking the whip ahead to slice between the writer and the side-wall clutter-maze – corralling her to run between he and Katya. Jess did exactly that, dashing diagonally back towards the butcher's hook, past Charlotte's blurring body... and coming up on the deep end mirror-wall. The wire in one bunny-ear had crumpled and flapped against the top of her head. She could hear the synchronised slink of their pursuit, nice and slow... whips trailing the ground. There was no escape. As Jess drew up to her own reflection she slowed into a sidle, catching her panting breath with a deep inhalation... and a long exhalation. Eyelids flittering. She placed her hands on the mirror and bent forward. Feet together and legs straight, puckering her shining, raw ass. The voluptuous curves of her calves, thighs and hips rolling and welling as she breathed. Fuzzy focus as the predators drew up a few metres behind.

'It's time to tell us the password.' He sounded serious.

Jess smiled dreamily through the glass. The protective aura of the trance swelling to embrace her as the lashes began to come in. Air zinging with snicker-snapping leather. Cruel, thin tongues licking and lacerating over her buttocks, back, flanks and shanks.

She danced to the throbbing beat of the agony – rolling with the cringes, swinging with the recoils, bouncing into the blows and letting them rain long stripes of red. Biting to break the skin. She sung her screams to the high heavens – heartfelt hallelujahs.

Holding onto the mirror-wall and gazing through the glass, almost like she was underwater, peering up through the shimmering surface and watching their shapely silhouettes bobbing and winding, wrapping and reaping – sweeping loose, then jolting rigid. She wasn't sure how long the assault lasted, but eventually Jess became aware the scene was settling. They were talking, the mistress spitting her words with a frustrated bicker in her tone. The writer grinned and held her quivering ass high – triumphantly raising her reddened banner over the battlefield.

He was ignoring Katya and staring towards Jess, deciding what to do next. But the clang of the bitch-chair distracted his attention – rocking around chaotically. Charlotte had long dissolved – melted from the inside out, body swimming in tears and sweat. Her orgasms were no longer separate events: they were crashing into one another, like the carriages of a crumpling train… a very long train. And the sound was excruciating – a creaking, high-pitched squeal as the air screeched out through her nostrils.

He shook his head slowly, but then moved with callous speed, marching over to the bitch-chair, sweeping down on one knee, reaching below… and turning the power up. Charlotte's body convulsed like electrified meat. The wand's buzz really fizzing: razor shrill, shaking the atmosphere at a furious frequency. It must be on full power now! As he rose, he pinched Puggle's body, pulled the toy out of the ring-gag and tossed it away. The mood music thus refined, with Charlotte's orgasmic sobs flooding through the atmosphere undammed.

Gliding around the chamber, he moved over to the bottom of the stairs before returning to the deep end. Blurred reflection expanding as he drew closer. Dropping the whip to slither away across the stone. Jess' skin was trembling at the same tempo as the wand – shivering with excitement, quivering with pain… and all the vibrations jiggling together in a big, buzzing hive. As he arrived he swung his left hand underarm, hooking her groin and thrusting with force. Shoving her against the mirror: body flattening, pussy smudging onto the glass. Then grabbing the tops of her arms, swivelling her to face him, and pounding her back against the wall.

But the violent motion smoothed as he un-pocketed Jess' freshly polished specs and delicately placed them on her nose. She watched his face and body harden and sharpen – all the beautiful angles and carves of his bones and muscles. Wearing a sheet of water so his skin shined. Tentacles of sweat-soaked hair tufted, tangled and tussled up over his head. One long, wet lank clinging zigzag across his brow. Smouldering chocolate eyes. Lush, liquid lips.

He placed her hands over her ears to secure her spectacles. Then he tipped his torso sideways and bent his left arm over his head, seizing Jess around the waist with his hands back-to-front. The strange gripping positions would only make sense if he was holding her upside-down. His whole body braced: a lean biological machine bristling with energy. Springs and muscles coiling and loading… then exploding into action. Her skin was slippery, but he squeezed tight and cranked his trunk. Her feet swept off the ground and she span 180 degrees, body crashing back against the glass the wrong way up. A shockwave of a gasp as her heart dropped onto the roof of her mouth. He had her pinned firmly against the wall, thumbs pressed into the creases of her thighs. Her flesh felt like putty squelching around in his hands. Their eyes were level with one another's chests. His torso muscles constricting like coiled iron – abs crunching, pectorals clenching. Collarbone jutting as if the minotaur was attempting to ram its way out of his skin. Arms strapping with bands of grappling sinew.

Closing in, he placed her over his shoulder. Folding her body in half, bottom in the air, legs tucked to the right of his head, face pressed against his stomach... hands still clutching her specs. Could see his dick bulging below – a wild beast slavering to rip out of his trousers and ravage her. Everything smelled of man. A sticking sound as her body peeled off the wall. A moist, heart-shaped smear left on the glass. He looped his arm around her waist and turned away from the mirror – carrying her in a reverse fireman's lift. She tilted up to balance, groin hugging his shoulder and body winding behind her elbows: swimming through the humidity.

They went past the four-poster, but circled back to the foot of the bed... where Katya was waiting. Her left claw snapped up to grab the writer around the throat, long fingers enclosing the neck. Jess tried to lean out of the choke, but his palm clamped her buttock and tipped her back down. The mistress fiddled around with her other hand. The buzz of flies unzipping and the strain of underwear stretching to let something out. Could smell it already, as if a slab of raw meat had just been thumped down under her nose.

Katya pushed up on the neck until Jess was horizontal, then slid her palm around to the crown and reversed momentum, dunking the writer down, where she brandished his dick like a pointed pike. Jess opened her jaws full-stretch as the great, shining spearhead came thrusting towards them. But the hair-hold tightened to stop the writer's face just short... jumping tongue millimetres out of range. The long, thick trunk of his cock burgeoned into a huge, bell-shaped crown. The shaft engorged and throbbing to the brim, the considerable weight of the helm skewing its erect stance. A little stream of saliva ran down the writer's tongue and dripped onto the tip.

The mistress guided their heads into position, then twisted to push them together, violently impaling Jess' face. Big, fat dick ramming into her mouth – invading her... and taking over immediately. Teeth shoved aside, jaws busted open, tongue jammed back up the throat. Lips enclosing the shaft and cheeky chops sucking in all around. Delight shingling through her nerves. The feeling of being completely full! Over-flowing with dick – stuffed to bursting point. One hand held onto her specs, whilst the other paddled around in the air for balance. He squeezed her buttock, grinding her groin onto his shoulder. Now tickling the outskirts of her pussy. The mistress released Jess' hair and slid her hand up to meet his. Two sets of fingers pitter-pattering over luscious, upturned lips. Their forefingers touching together and dipping inside for a moment, micro-spasms of pleasure rippling in their wake.

'She wet. Very... very wet.' The Russian stated approvingly, holding her claw out for him to suck and taste.

'Like a little pot of honey.' Deep voice oozing, dripping over the rim of the jar.

With a purposeful nod the mistress turned and marched away. Jess continued to gorge, seesawing over his shoulder to pump her lips up and down over his cock. Helmet plunging up her throat as she pressed her weight down. The sweltering thrill of the choke before she drew back up, teeth sliding until they caught against the rim of the crown. He was hooked into her like a harpoon. She was building a rocking rhythm: big, sloppy sucks kinking back and forth. Katya returned holding a small, cylindrical box made of transparent plastic. Impatient jostling: ripping off the sticky-tape; tearing the container open; then tossing the packaging away. Now weighing the object in her palm: a narrow, pink, rubbery egg attached to a fluffy, white ball of tassel. A butt-plug bunny-tail! The mistress manoeuvred out of her heels, clapped a handhold on Jess' ass and stepped up onto the mattress. He turned to face his collaborator, the writer's head still apple-bobbing happily.

'Now you have cute little tail as well, bunny-bitch.' Husky Russian lilt taunting down. 'And you can lubricate it yourself, because you are wet little slut.'

Katya was so right sometimes! Jess felt her legs being parted and something smooth and rubbery nestling against her.

The mistress rolled the egg around on the outside of the pussy, spiralling inwards, then dabbing the tip inside. Fluffy pom-pom tail tickling the upper thighs as the toy dipped steadily deeper. The rocking motion moving the writer's head up and down over his. The Russian now pushing it right into the pussy – sliding the egg fully inside. Leaving only the little handle protruding, attached to the bunny-tail-bun. A cute sucking sound as Katya pulled it back out. He turned on the spot again, swivelling to face away from the bed. The mistress gathered in Jess' twitching lower limbs, arm looping to pin the thighs together. Felt like all Jess' blood was concentrated in her head and vulva.

The tip of butt-plug nuzzled against her asshole. It was wet, moistened with her own juices. As the egg squeezed in, the writer's toes curled up… along with all the nerve-endings in her body. The downward force thrusting his cock further up her throat. The mistress screwed her wrist to jiggle the toy further inside. Stretching the ring of Jess' ass wider and wider, before pressing and twisting to fully insert the plug. The feeling of having her ass stuffed! Completely filled. Taken over. Owned. Fuck, they so owned her! And her face was sitting impaled on his big, brutal dick! She was possessed – an owned possession. The shuddering blush was all-consuming, radiating in multiple waves. A switch on the plug-handle was clicked and the toy began to vibrate – whisking her shudders into foam before they rippled through her body.

Closing her eyes and sucking her lips, she transmitted the buzz of the sex toy all the way down her spine… and onto his dick. It was as if she were the sex toy – his sex toy! His vibrating cock ring, buzzing with titillation. That's exactly what she was. The blush in her cheeks warmed like a cosy campfire. But his hand descended to push the erection out of her mouth. Holding it down as it strained to leap back up. The frustration surged! Jess wriggled, wrapping her arms, clamping her hands around his buttocks and attempting to heave herself down his body. He stiffened to lock her in place. She could feel the powerful muscles along the back of his thighs hardening – her fleshy handholds turning to stone.

She couldn't move – trapped alive in a statue, like Bernini's Proserpina. As she squirmed the spectacles dropped off her face and landed on his cock, latching around to dangle from the trunk. Then bouncing as he removed his restraining hand to cup the back of her neck, the rest of his body gliding in smooth motion. With a twist of the hips he thrust her forward on his shoulder, simultaneously drawing her head around to his other flank and curling her up into a somersault. An extreme contrast as her lower half flew off him and plummeted towards the bed, whilst her neck rocked securely in the cradle of his palm – all his care focused on that point.

She plunked down with force, but bounced comfortably on the softness. The ass-plug remained hooked inside, buzzing like a happy bee. Her vision was blurred, yet she could sense the predators looking down on her: prized meat… finally thumped over the table after an epic hunt. A deep shudder of erotic nostalgia – the feeling of being Lamb, lying on the table in a Wendy House Wolf's Lair.

The mistress pulled off the jacket and hung it from a hook on the bedpost. Jess was dizzy, but bursting with boisterous bounce. She rolled and sprung up on her hands and knees, meeting his cock head on – also bursting with boisterous bounce, spectacles dangling around the base. She looked up at him with the eyes of a chocolate-nosed puppy. Nuzzling into his dick, sliding her specs along the shaft, and rotating them to reposition on her face. Watching his body chisel as her vision enhanced. A rocky, overhanging cliff-face of a torso, with her eyes climbing up the carving ladder of his abs. He tinkled his finger under her chin. She reared up on her knees as he lifted her face toward his. Big, liquid lips descending. She closed her eyes and puckered.

Grabbing a twist of Jess' hair, the Russian yanked backwards violently. The two women landed in sitting positions in the middle of the mattress – prey straddled between predator's legs. Katya's arms slipped under the writer's armpits and looped back into an arch, hands clasping together behind the neck: a 'full nelson' wrestling hold. The mistress then proceeded to attack all the way down the body in a well-ordered sequence of moves. Thighs squeezing around the waist. Shins clamping Jess' own thighs shut. Feet kicking up under the knees, hooking inside, and then lifting to spread the writer's legs akimbo in the air.

Katya curled up behind in a crunch position. Hard muscles grappling to crush in from every angle, steeling to tie Jess up in a strangling mesh. The mistress must've removed her bra, because bare, pointed nipples jabbed in the back. The ass-plug wriggled to popping point as bunny legs were forced further and further apart. Could see him watching them wrestle, framed by her own gaping legs. The blush washed over like a tropical sunset. She clenched the cork inside. So humiliating that Katya was doing this to her in front of him.

He stepped out of his clothes. Well-toned legs bursting with lean brawn like the rest of him. Hunting cobra of a dick snaking ahead as he kneeled his way onto the mattress. Katya released the arm-lock and he loomed in between their legs. He pressed the plug snug with his palm and dipped to burrow his face between Jess' breasts. The sensuous grate of stubble as he brushed up over her chest and neck... and under her chin, right to the back of the jaw. A nibbling kiss around her right ear. Then blowing into it... like shaking a tree full of butterflies.

The mistress snaked in on the other side. Teeth gnashing as she breathed over the left ear. Rainbow butterflies flittering everywhere. He was waggling the ass-plug with his finger whilst brushing his thumb over her clit. Jess' head slithered back and her body arched. The wax had long-crumbled away, so her breasts wobbled in the air like a pair of perfect, pink jellies... topped with glacier cherries. He closed a gnawing kiss over her nipple, sucking it up into his mouth and tickling with his tongue. Moving across to the other breast: kissing, biting and nuzzling. Before heading downwards...

The mistress reapplied the arm-lock, this time scrunching the writer's hair in her fists and tilting back so Jess faced the ceiling of the four-poster. Katya's long legs suppled and hardened – splaying bunny even wider. His thumb was twiddling her tail, stirring the plug inside. The fingers of his other hand traipsing over her vulva, circling inwards. A rumble of a growl bubbling up from the deeps. She felt his tongue dipping into her, then dabbling over her lips... as light as sprinkling glitter. The blissfulness began to tremor through her body, but the mistress constricted like a boa, lithe limbs suffocating all movement... except for twitching toes sticking out in the air above. Jess bristled as his growl purred over her pussy. His tongue lapping up her lips and tickling on her clit. The grate of stubble smudging against her.

Snarl breaking into a lick – a long, luscious lick! And another one. Lots of licks – lashings of them! Hungry... greedy... gluttonous licks. Slipping, scraping, sliding... delving, digging, diving. Lapping her up like cream with a sloppy, smutty, smacking sound. Pressing his weight down on her thighs as he gorged. The thinnest thread of a sigh spindled from the writer's open mouth. Her body warbled, but Katya viced to lock her in place. His lips closed around hers and his tongue slid into her pussy, snuffling his face side to side, bristles prickling against the tenderised jowls of her thighs. And still drilling the ass-plug in with his thumb.

Tasting her sweetness – her juices overflowing. Indulging his gluttonous appetite. Eating her, drinking her, gobbling her up, wolfing her down... consuming her in great sucking swigs. He gnawed up to her clit, engulfing the area with his mouth and letting the warm air swirl. Two fingers slipped under his chin and into her pussy, squeezing inside and hooking up to tipper-tapper her G-spot. And great, gouging kisses over the surface. Jess lolled in her lock, shovelling the saliva out of her mouth with her tongue to keep from drowning.

He feasted until he'd had his fill... and then drew his head up. Long sigh hissing in horns from the sides of his mouth. Katya twisted onto one flank and rolled sideways, tipping Jess onto all fours, before unravelling her movements to sit back in the middle of the bed. The dazed bunny-rabbit dumped off to the side, crouched on elbows and knees with the vibrating pom-pom tail energetically feathering her rump.

The mistress squirmed up on one buttock and then the other, sliding the little, red panties out from under her ass. Smouldering at him as she zigged them up her thighs, zagged them down her calves and picked them off her feet. Now lying back on the bed, raising her legs perfectly straight... and spreading them out wide. Ballet limbs arcing gracefully, stretching into the air, a flower opening up towards the sun. Plush pussy-lips parting seductively. The air tensed behind his gritted teeth as the predators exchanged an affectionate snarl.

He clapped his hands around Jess' flanks and manhandled her towards the pincer-trap. Steering her in between Katya's towering legs... over that pouting pussy. Nuzzling down onto preening breasts, nipples shining like bullets. The predator's legs straddled the waist, folding over the lower back to wrap the prey up and clinch their bodies together. A nailed claw clamped around Jess' chin to squeeze her jaws open. Then a smirking flash of red as the mistress shoved her panties into the writer's mouth and slammed it shut.

Jess' eyes gawped, but her mouth couldn't – her enemy was holding it closed. Could taste Katya's sweat and pre-come juicing into her jowls – salty... and bitter. Oh so, so, so bitter! The panties scuffed her throat and she gagged, attempting to spit them out. But her jaws were sealed and she couldn't prize off the clenching hands. The two women locked in eye contact... right up-close! The mistress' smile blazed so bright Jess could feel the heat melting her face off. Bursting out in blush as her enemy burst out laughing. It was so humiliating. Having to suck on Katya's used panties whilst the horrible bitch laughed in her face about it. So much hate and rage and helpless frustration.

'You are right! I am fucking funny!'

The mistress was really guffawing now, whole body convulsing. Her grip loosened, allowing Jess to twist away and spit the panties onto the bed. But Katya forcefully realigned their faces, intending to hold eye contact so they could reflect on recent events together. The writer's only escape was to close her eyes. Close them very tight. Scrunch her lids right up and seal them shut under multiple layers of skin. Squeezing and squeezing. Gripping herself... so tight... that she suddenly broke: suddenly shattered! A great, blubbering sob rising up from the deeps and breaking like a tidal wave. Face crumpling as she burst into tears – a whooshing, warbling wail of tears.

The mistress howled with glee as the waterworks poured onto her chest – singing in the rain. The women's entwined bodies convulsing together in the mad hysterics of joy and sorrow. Katya crunched up to lick Jess' face, happily lapping up the salt. So carried away by the romance of the moment she even tried to kiss her victim full on the lips. But the writer was crying too hard – a big bawl of honking sobs. So undignified to cry like that... especially when all you're wearing is a pair of bunny ears and a fluffy tail-bun butt-plug.

Noting Jess' reaction, he leaned over to intercede in a calm, reassuring voice. 'Don't worry my Little Fireball... I still think you're funny.'

The writer glugged and the weeping intensified. His thighs were kneeling up behind hers, the base of his shaft pressing the vibrating toy into her ass, whilst the rest of his cock trunked up between her butt-cheeks and skewed into the air above. Katya swiped a tear off bunny's face and stretched her finger towards him. He dipped in to suck it with a lick of the lips. As he ran his hands down Jess' back she could feel the tension in his palms... pressure building... and then it suddenly vanished. All the muscles in his body falling loose and languid simultaneously: totally relaxing. Could hear how slow his exhalation was. A warm current of soothing energy flowed into her... and made her eyelids flutter. But his words were ice-cold.

'Don't cry.' It was an order. The underlying menace of a tightly straitjacketed voice.

Snorting back a sob, the writer burrowed her head into her loathsome enemy's bosom. Smothering her mouth around a breast and suckling gentle kisses over the nipple. The hatred she felt was ravishing. The mistress' bust still bouncing with chuckle, so the two women's bodies remained dancing in step, convulsions ebbing like the long fade-out of a romantic ballad. He smacked down to sting Jess' butt. Sitting back on his haunches, clenching a squeeze of ass in his left hand, pistoling two fingers from his right, and then sliding them into her pussy. Pushing inside and kicking. Turning them to weigh the hum of the vibrating toy above. Now winding around as if he was stirring a little pot of honey. Corking the ass-plug with his thumb and slipping a third finger inside, stretching her wider... preparing her for what was coming next. He pulled his fingers out, inspecting the heavy drench before pasting it over the end of his cock.

His erection now nuzzling up against her pussy. Oh fuck! She'd never had anything as big as that inside her. Katya unfolded her legs as if they were ribbon-bows, unwrapping a special gift: a little bunny sex-toy. He looked down on the writer's voluptuous, heart-shaped body – big, beautiful, red buttocks swelling up from the waist. Curves rising and rolling all the way back down over her haunches, hips and thighs. And gushing over the curb of her ass to pour into the delve at the base of her back. All the curves of her body seemed to flow through this central dipping point… in slaloming 'S's, curling 'C's, and welling 'Y's. He adjusted his position: lining everything up. Oh fuck!

    He thrust forward and the tip of his dick pressed between her lips. But the base of the bell was too broad, catching against the sides and sticking. He pushed on, jostling to bully his way in. Shaft straining, kinking and bending. Jess imagined a monstrous serpent battering open a castle gate, but getting its horns trapped as it tries to rampage inside. He pulled back. Katya leant forward, spanked her hands over bunny-buttocks, and pulled the ass-cheeks apart – parting the pussy. The ass-plug beginning to pop. This time he attacked at an angle, sliding the horn of his helm past the lip on one side, then swivelling his body behind the point to punch in from the other diagonal. Waggling to shove the crown fully in. Oh fuck! Now aligned to plunge directly. Trunk piling in to ramrod the head right up inside – shooting the ecstasy straight up her spine to explode at the base of the neck. Oh fuck! Oh fuck! Oh fuck!

    As his dick swelled into the walls of her pussy it thumped up against the plug on the other side, barging the little egg out of the way. The toy popped out of her ass, rebounded against his thrusting groin, tumbled over the crest of her butt and rolled down the flumes of her lower back. Egg and handle descending in chaotic, vibrating steps – like an off-kilter slinky – fluffy tail-bun tickling along behind. And her whole pussy filling up with his big, fat dick – flooding to the brim with throbbing meat. She gaped around him as he gouged himself deeper and deeper inside… stuffing her to bursting point. Oh my fucking God! The giddy thrill swilled! Her mouth was wide open, but her moan muffled over Katya's breast. The buzzing bunny-tail landed in the delve at the bottom of her back. He plucked it up, tilted his torso away and pummelled the plug into her. His body pressing to drill it inside. Both pussy and ass completely full! Oh my fucking God!

As he pulled back the helmet slid until it caught on the rim – harpoon-hooked inside. An intense moment before he plunged forwards again – jamming his cock all the way back up. Jess' eyes gaped, mouth vacuum-suctioned around the mistress' breast. Could feel his hands spreading over her ass-cheeks like eggs cracked into a hot pan. He began to rock his hips, building up a rhythm – thrusting in and out. The motion tipping her away from Katya's bosom and then ploughing her back in, slobbering her mouth over the breasts. The goose bumps on the mistress' nipples rocketing. And that big fucking cock smashing into Jess' rear like a cavalry charge! Momentum escalating: each thrust deeper, harder and more penetrating than the last. The badly-fitting ass-plug almost popping out every time, but hammered back in as his hard body slammed tight. Her movements were rhyming with his: pushing back to bunny-bounce on his dick with tail-bun bobbling between their bodies.

Lurking below, Katya contorted herself into a new predatory poise: knees folded with thighs flattened against her calves… and toes pointing. Her lower half shaping like a pair of hunting mandibles. As he drew back the mistress kicked in, stepping on Jess' thighs and stabbing toes into the creases at the top of the legs. A double-footed stamp to push bunny back onto his cock with force. A whinny of a yelp from the writer. His sharp sigh twanged: ejected air sucking back into a growl. The predators snarl-smiled at one another as the mistress smeared Jess all over him – like squeezing a lemon over a juicer spike.

He rolled his hips and drove forwards, pummelling up the pussy. Katya's legs recoiled, for a moment, then sprung back to bounce on the writer's thighs. His turn to rhyme with the motion, rocking away and bending his buttocks before snapping his body straight. The predator's movements blending as they seesawed back and forth, him moving a beat sooner, so he could pull most of the shaft out before Katya's legs stamped it fully inside again, fruit squelching underfoot. Oh fuck! Impaled on a massive, thrusting spike whilst a crazy, sadistic bitch jumps up and down on your lap! The excitement was fucking excruciating! And a glimpse of the orgasm that was coming for her: an enormous, shadowy shape passing in the ocean below.

Katya was using the momentum of the bounce to propel herself up the mattress towards the headboard. Each time Jess' face ploughed in she landed further down the mistress' wet body: the bottom of the breasts, the solar plexus, the stomach, the belly button, the waistline. The writer's spectacles had come off but were tangled in her hair so they clattered around on Katya's skin. The bunny ears were still in place, although both wire-frames had disintegrated, so the felt flapped chaotically overhead. He was really shunting: whole body piling in with full force!

Jess felt the splash of moisture as her face slapped into Katya's lush. The mistress stopped jumping, splaying her legs and rolling them around until they pointed diagonally in the air, thighs straddling that cute, little bunny-face. He continued pounding away, ploughing the writer down into Katya. Her svelte pussy-lips curled into a bitchy smile. As Jess kissed around them her mouth slid up over the clit, chin smudging between the thighs. Snatching a twist of bunny hair, the mistress glared down her body and hissed.

'Stick your fucking tongue out.'

The writer's tongue shot out of her mouth. Katya began smearing the bunny-sex-toy over her clit. Holding the hair so tight it ripped into the scalp. Slavering tongue licking and lapping. Jess was just a possession – a toy.

'Stick it right out!'

Jess cringed: she'd already extended full-stretch the instant she was ordered. Now straining to poke it even further. The mistress circled her wrist in time with his thrusts, lushing the tongue-toy over herself. Then dunking to rub the bunny-face right into her pussy, shaking the head in an aggressive scrubbing motion. His movements rhyming to become more circular, thrust swinging in from one side and drawing out from the other – stroking around inside, like an oar stirring a river of honey... happy bee buzzing overhead. And Jess gouging and kissing – snuffling and squashing her twitchy, little nose into the clit and sucking her lips around Katya's pussy.

A little pop of a glug as the mistress detached the bunny-sex-toy. Moving assertively, she released the hair-hold, swiped the spectacles off her stomach, stretched her arms back to grab the headboard, pulled herself from under the writer, then rolled and stood up on the mattress. He was still swinging his hips to thrust in looping motion. Jess pressed her knees, elbows and forearms into the bed to push back, holding herself together like a fortress under heavy bombardment. Her glasses were somehow suspended in the spray of hair over her face and she was able to twist them over and jam them back on her nose. Katya backed up a few steps and sat down. Her ass slapping on top of Jess', before she swept one leg over to straddle her mount. The mistress' body pressed back against his and she lifted her feet from the mattress so her weight squished down through the writer's thighs and knees.

'Yes! I ride you like pony.' Katya waved her arms in triumphant celebration. 'My little fucking pony!'

The pressure of the mistress' buttocks squeezed the vibrating ass-plug's room to rattle and as he drove his dick in the egg attempted to uncork. But his groin rammed it back inside, where it sizzled like a hornet trapped in a can of coke. Katya grabbed Jess' hair and drew back, towing the writer's head up and pulling her from elbows to palms... so she could see over the headboard, into the mirror-wall.

Her face was a hot mess of splashed make-up and monsoon sweat. Specs jumping manically up and down on her nose. Her mane: a frenzied bedlam – the mistress held a few locks as reins, whilst the rest fireworked out in a chaotic mass of spikes, twists and spirals. The hair at the front was so wet and electrified it had evaporated into a fine spray of mist. And her broken bunny-ears ran with a wounded lollop. The predators were reared up behind like a double-headed hydra: serpentine torsos touching just above his cock before snaking off in different directions. Could see Charlotte bubbling away in the background – hob long-forgotten and stew burned to a charred mush. He crossed his arms around Katya's waist and pushed down on her lap, merging her into the rhythm of his thrusts. The mistress laughed and slapped Jess' flank.

'Ride, my little pony. Ride!'

She threw her head back and slalomed her slim body against his, wrapping an arm to cradle his head. His jaws opened, gnashing around her ear. The predators twisted into another of their hungry, fighting-wolf kisses. Jess watched her world whirl in a pool of wide eyes.

'Let's make her… fly.' He panted slow words until the final one took off.

The Russian hissed agreement, springing to her feet, swiftly dismounting and handing the pony reins to him. He held the bunny-tail in with his thumb, preventing it from scooping out as that big helmet withdrew from her pussy. Oh fuck! The writer flinched in a giddy swelter of shooting stars. He pinched a little tug on the plump of her calf as an instruction to shuffle backwards on her knees. But didn't give her much time as he pulled her along by the hair. He stepped off the foot of the bed and onto the fur rug, drawing Jess back until she was fully upright against him, her knees clunking onto the hard bedframe. She screwed with pain as her weight pressed down on the wood, but this was where she was supposed to be. He adjusted her glasses so they almost sat straight.

Katya positioned herself on the mattress in front of the writer. A similar poise to last time: flat on her back with legs folded and toes pointed at Jess' groin. Except this time, her calves were crossed and she clutched her thighs to support them on bedded elbows…

shaped a bit like an anvil. The mistress jabbed her toes into the creases at the top of the legs and he shoved Jess forwards. The writer folded at the waist as she slammed over the anvil, shoulders landing on hard knees with a sharp shin digging diagonally across the chest. Jess tilted up off the bed and swung into the air, weight entirely supported by Katya's athletic legs. The flyer's limbs shot out to find balance, but he cupped her buttocks with both hands to keep her centre of gravity. Rocking back and forth over the anvil. In the reflection, the mistress was obscured by the headboard, so Jess looked like she was flying… and it felt like she was too. Paddling the air with both arms whilst her legs kicked out behind.

He kept one hand on an ass-cheek whilst wielding his cock with the other. As she seesawed back into him he thumped his hammerhead against her butt with a satisfyingly heavy thud. Katya's eyes were fluttering dreamily, stroking her own clit with two long fingers. His dick beat a few more drubs on Jess' ass, then his posture straightened as she rocked back. His palms spreading her cheeks and lips whilst clutching to pull her weight down onto him… and re-impaling her. That huge beast rampaging inside her again, snaking its head as its horns dragged against the walls. Jess swung forward and he thrust in to follow, fingering her tail snug as his dick slid back to hook on the rim of her pussy. A circling motion and her own momentum drove his cock deeper again. Arms swimming as she floated around in the air, her sweat pattering over Katya's face… saliva dribbling off her chin and onto the mistress' neck. The Russian didn't notice the spittle; she was too busy masturbating to her own smug reflection in the writer's lens.

His momentum was building, tipping her weight around on his cock. And now leaning forwards to gather up her arms, pinning them straight down her sides and pulling hard. Like a fairground hammer, smashing the button to ring the bell at the top her spine. The writer squealed as she was stuffed! Her legs stretched horizontal and splayed around him as he used her arms to propel her back and forth. Oh fuck! The glasses flying off to dangle in front of her face. She was flying as well... everything was flying!

Sparks flying as hammer smashed her against anvil in the storming heat of the forge. Panelling her flat, pounding her crooked, pummelling her into shape. Big, muscular body heaving and hulking away overhead, like the God of Thunder himself. Raining down showers of sweat and bolts of lightning as Jess soared through electrified clouds. Flying through open skies and yet pinned helplessly between hammer and anvil. She could feel the orgasm coming for her. Something enormous rising up from the depths... sucking her into its gravity. The breath suctioning from her body.

But as he rolled her forwards he pulled the whole of his cock out. Withdrawing it unannounced to leave her collapsing back in on herself. Suspended in a groggy daze. He slapped his hands down on her buttocks with a hard double-spank. Katya mirrored by clapping her palms around Jess' face, so all the writer's cheeks scolded together like cooks. The mistress then flicked her legs to catapult the hapless bunny off to the side – tumbling and rolling, but managing to stay on the mattress, crouching on elbows and knees.

Fumbling to reset her spectacles, but Katya was already chasing and descended with another attack: biting Jess' ear – her real ear! Felt like it would rip clean off as the mental bitch wrenched around and dragged her victim along. Squeaking like that was so humiliating. And it really fucking hurt. The hate boiling past steaming point. The ear, for fuck's sake! The writer was forcefully positioned in the top-middle of the bed, then the Russian trotted over to where he stood at the other end. Perspiration flowing down his body like a waterfall over the rocks. The intense, trancing gaze of a warrior in the midst of a long battle, powered on by adrenaline and bloodlust.

He lent down to brush his sweaty cheek over Katya's. The mistress raised up on her fingertips and they nuzzled snouts.

Her ass pointing towards Jess – that excruciatingly-perfect ass. Sublimely rounded buttocks, bursting with juice, jut and jounce. Graceful curves curling and kinking. And snowy white of course – pristine and unblemished – like the rest of her skin. Such a contrast with the writer's bruised, battered and discoloured body. And her ear still panged. The ear, for fuck's sake! Katya really was a horrible fucking bitch! A narcissistic, tear-drinking, kiss-blowing, custard-cream-shaming, Puggle-murdering uber-bitch! And she really thought she was just going to walk away from all this without a scratch on her... from all this! Just walk away with pristine-white skin. She definitely fucking wasn't! Fuck you, Katya!

As the predators kissed the mistress' perfect bauble-butt bobbed around smugly in the air. Jess braced into pouncing poise with a feisty little growl as she wiggled her bottom to work up momentum... and then sprang, grabbing her enemy's hips and biting into the middle of the left ass-cheek.

'Aaaaaai!'

Katya's exclamation wasn't high-pitched enough to be a scream – probably more of a yelp – although still very satisfying. The Russian knelt bolt upright and swung her fist backhanded. Jess' arm shielded her face and she managed to cling on, digging her incisors into the flesh and grinning as she clenched. A few heavenly moments before the writhing mistress managed to twist her rear-end away and spin around to meet the writer head-on. Katya's eyes were white-hot – blood boiling out of her face! He was roaring with laughter behind. Jess snarled to confront her enemy, but as the teeth came gnashing in it was apparent that the crazy bitch was literally going for the face.

The writer reared away and fell back as the mistress came storming through with jaws snapping. A trampling knee crunching onto the thigh as Katya bit hard into a defending forearm. Jess squirmed out from underneath and rolled onto all fours. Bared teeth scathing down her back before biting into the top of her haunches and twisting the flesh painfully. An anguished squawk as the writer wriggled away. The slash of pursuing claws raked down her back and buttocks, but the frenzied predator overbalanced sideways and her prey scampered to the other side of the bed.

He dropped onto the mattress and prowled between the two women, turning to face Jess with a wolfy smile, snarl cutting arrows across his face. The writer returned the growl, but hers was so cutesy it made his hairs prickle. She tried to move around him, but he chomped the air to block her path. Jess dodged back and manoeuvred to attack his other flank, darting in with a little nip. He swung away, deftly twisting around to push wide jaws into the side of her waist, play-biting as he swivelled his body behind to form a T-shape with hers. Suddenly it felt like a wolf holding a rabbit sideways in his jaws – just before he shakes his head and breaks her. He drove her into the centre of the bed and Katya came in from the other side, champing her fangs into the sensitive flesh above the armpit.

He reared up to come down from above, cupping the writer's thighs and lifting her fleshy ass into mouth. This time biting hard and growling as he ruffled his jaws. Jess squealed and twirled her body, slipping out of the predators' teeth and turning 180 degrees, but remaining trapped between them. The mistress clamped her arms down to secure the writer's legs, snapping her teeth into the thigh, below the rump, and digging in. He loomed in to overshadow, hands planting into the mattress either side of Jess' head as his jaws came down. The warm breath of a red-blooded carnivore on the back of her neck. Just a pinch of the scruff. He gritted his teeth and growled so the deep bass stimulated all her nerve-endings in tickling waves of sonar. Their positions felt so primal – bestial. Jess shuddered in rhythm with the rumble of his purr.

The mistress released her bite. Muttering some sort of threat as she backed off the bed and walked across the room. Charlotte's undulating moan had hit a particular frequency now, orgasms obliterating one another in chains like atoms in a bomb. Almost sounded as if she was singing underwater. Jess' body was a criss-cross of slack and tension – felt so comfortable nestling in his jaws. Yet when he knelt up and pulled away, the adrenaline surged and she bounced up to face him. Feisty puppy flair – immediately darting in for a nip at his chest.

But a big hand wrapped up over her face and she was overturned and thumping flat on her back. Head tumbling and spinning. An assertive yank of her right leg and she was splayed open: spread out in front of him! Excitement chattering and tinselling. He leant over to reset her specs. There was a lot of steam between them. Hard to tell how much of it was clinging to the lens' and how much was wafting through the atmosphere itself. Everything so swelteringly hot and wet. Could feel the humidity cloaking the skin like fog over the mangroves. Hear the steam in their panting breath. Smell the monsoon. Taste the air sweating!

His dark eyes melted over her body as chocolate melts over sponge cake. Big, liquid lips trickling towards her... and flowing into her. Their mouths coming together like droplets of water coalescing into one. The kiss: weighty, but tender. He massaged her lips to shape around his in fluid ripples. Wave swelling and rolling down her back above the glide of his manta-ray palm. Romance glows, so the ambience is best when set against a dark background. As he drew away his breath purred over her face. He hooked his left arm around her right leg – the back of his elbow against the back of her knee – pushing her limb up into the air as his pressed down on the mattress. Holding a one-handed press-up and manoeuvring his cock with the other hand.

It was easier to push in this time, with her spread-eagle position and well-stretched lips. Still needed to waggle the hammerhead until it clunked inside. Oh fuck! Their eyelids fluttered together like butterflies in the meadow. He thrust his whole body behind his spear, skewering up her middle and stuffing her so full all the air was pushed out of her mouth, nose and eyes. His angled weight held the ass-plug inside – buzzing like two fighting hornets trapped in a can. Greedy lips pointing as he began to grind in big, slow fucks.

'You're mine now!' His voice wasn't loud but it boomed down huge. 'You're mine. The story is mine. The book is mine. This whole fucking world is mine!' His body rolled and swelled before crashing back over her like a wave, flooding her so full the excess water poured out of her mouth, nose and eyes. She was his! She could feel it. All of it! Totally owned, totally possessed, totally taken, totally conquered. 'You're my slave. You'll kneel… whilst I lock a heavy, metal collar around your neck.' She could sense that orgasm coming for her… the depths growing darker and darker. 'I'm going to sit you between the mirrors and you're going to write the rest of my book. I'm going to work you hard… my little slave-bitch.' She felt as if she were a small boat, rolling and bouncing around on the wide open ocean. The great waves of his body crashing with escalation as he wolf-panted his words.

'Call you into my office, every morning… make you bend over the desk whilst I come over your ass-cheeks… Order you to put your panties back on, to sit in my spunk whilst you work.' Charlotte's singing sounded strangely beautiful now: the aquatic, alien language indecipherable, but you could tell it was an outpouring about love and pain. 'Or maybe I'll keep you in a chastity belt until the book's finished… come into that every morning before re-sealing it and sending you to work – sitting in my spunk.' She bristled like tinsel.

He hooked her other leg so his grips were symmetrical, spreading her high and wide and reaching down to pin her arms either side of her head with his fists. 'Or come over your nose and paste the spunk over your cheeks… send you to your writing with a sticky face… that you're not allowed to wash.' He was so romantic! The little boat tossing about on the roiling seas as his powerful hips rolled and wrapped. And that titanic fucking orgasm welling up from the deeps...

Gravelled-honey-velvet words pouring over Jess as the mistress stepped back onto the bed. 'Maybe Katya will come in her panties and then I'll wrap them around a ball-gag... for you to wear in your mouth whilst you write.' The writer's body spasmed, toes curling.

'Yes!' The mistress agreed. 'In the morning, we can both come in my panties – that I slept in – and then bunny-bitch can keep them in her mouth all day.' Pausing thoughtfully for a brainwave. 'And why don't we make plaster-cast of your big dick... and make her sit on it while she write.' Jess was shaking hysterically, raised feet crunched rigid like crab's claws.

'Ha!' He gleamed down with an aggressive nod. The waves of his body smashing in, harder and harder... deeper and deeper...

Katya squatted by Jess' head and brandished a black marker pen in her face. 'I can't believe we forget this.' She scribbled a little circle on the end of the writer's nose. 'Twitchy, little bunny-nose.' Adding disdainfully. 'Very fucking cute.' She tossed the pen away and managed another brainwave. 'And when story is finished, you can make special highlight-edit and compile all the parts of story where you go on and on... and on... about how fucking sexy I am.' The mistress twinkled. 'And then kneel at my feet and read them to me... when I am sitting on big vibrator and smiling at you.' The cringe wracked Jess' body as if the frame of her little boat was shaking itself apart. A mighty wave descending to fling the vessel into the air, before hurtling back down and plunging into the angry waters.

He chortled. 'What about the parts you don't like?' His gaze remaining fixed intently on the writer, head held relatively still as he circled his neck to absorb the powerful motion of his body.

'Ha!' Katya's face scrunched. 'These must be taken out before it published. All these times when you are taking piss out of me with clever-clever words. They must be removed from final story.' The mistress leant closer to spit in Jess' face. 'If you don't take out these piss-take from final book, then… this is what I do to you… What I really do.' Katya proceeded to lay out her plans with steady, robotic clarity. 'I will put you on your knees… with head down toilet… stick my stiletto heel into your ass-hole… and pull on flush-chain… to flush your head… while I fuck you up the ass… with my fucking foot!' She wagged a long, sure finger to reassure that this threat would genuinely be carried out in real life! (Although of course, Katya would never really be smart enough to work out all the ways she's being mocked, no matter how many times she reads the book :) xxx.)

As the writer's body cringed she could feel herself nearly getting sucked into the momentous swill of the orgasm. The predators licked tongues, but he kept his eyes intently on their prey. Katya stood up and planted her feet either side of Jess' head. Beautiful scowl peering down her beautiful body. She clasped her hands around the writer's heels and lifted, opening her even further so his next thrust ploughed deeper than ever before. Oh fuck! Jess met his black-hole eyes: bearing down on her; chiselling into her, sculpting her, making her… making her… making her… Oh fuck!

Charlotte's lunatic-lullaby spilling through the atmosphere and washing everything in endless orgasm… soaking deep into the fabric of the universe. Jess felt herself sucking into the dark swirl, almost vibrating at the same tempo as Charlotte. Little buds of ecstasy twinkling open. His steeled torso was tilted at the steepest possible angle. His wild, wet hair tickling the mistress' pussy. Katya was directly overhead, bending slightly to splay Jess' legs. He released the writer's left side and reset her wandering specs. Then leaning forward, he grabbed her around the neck and locked eye contact. The trunk of his body swilling, rolling and then coming down in a deluge of breaking surf and spitting spray.

'I'm taking your story. Taking your book. Taking the money. It's mine. All mine!' Jaw jutting and fangs bared… arrogant, imperial eyes. 'And I'm taking you! Keeping you as a trophy... on the wall in my office. I'm going to display you... in a hundred humiliating ways. Remind myself of what I can make... what I can take!' The wince of his snarl flinched violently. Something was coming for him as well. Jess sinking into the dark gravity... suctioning into the vortex. All the air sucking up so she could barely breathe. Could feel tracer-lines of the coming euphoria shooting everywhere. His weight crushing down on her throat as he lifted his body back, before gushing forwards to break over her again. Little boat pulled down... and over... and under... and the mighty wave shattering overhead, with everything tumbling and flooding.

The bed-frame was shaking along with the rest of the universe. All the vibrations aligning. His whole body carved up and chiselled in rippling lines of muscle. Could taste the spittle in his breath. Katya widening her stance, pussy-lips parted to scowl down disdainfully. Jess was spilling out and spinning all over. The orgasm's gravity pulling from all directions at once. Keeping one hand on the writer's throat he placed the other around Katya's leg, thumb close to her pussy with fingers pressing down on the top of the thigh. The mistress was writhing her hips so her perfect bauble-buttocks ground around one another... peering down with menacing intent. And that big, fat fucking cock ramming all the way back in! The little boat entirely submerged and saliva flooding out of Jess' mouth to pour down her cheeks and chin.

The orgasm touching her now, from every angle... inside and out. All the breath ripping out of her body. Sinking into the depths. All her nerve-endings falling silent, priming for the final fusillade... and all the agony rising back to the surface. A spectacular swirl of primal emotions. Could still see his face looking down through the shimmering surface of the water... beautiful features dancing in shadows and candlelight. Holding her neck to point her nose directly into the air. The flex in Katya's calves straightened her legs momentarily. The mistress looking down on the writer through the crevice between her buttocks... spitting her words as if gobbing onto the street.

'That soft, round face look comfortable. Now I know what to do with this twitchy, little bunny-nose.'

The mistress' beautiful butt came plummeting downwards, peaching cheeks slapping over the face as Jess' bunny-nose slipped into Katya's asshole. Flesh spreading across the lens' of the specs to plunge the writer into darkness. Spindling cracks webbing across the glasses like twin mirrors disintegrating. As he drew up, his weight pushed down on the mistress' thigh: squeezing the two women even closer. The rim of his crown harpoon-hooking against the inside of Jess' pussy-lips. Ass-plug a furious, buzzing swarm. And the great helm hammering in for the final attack... driving deep and pushing to bursting point.

Little boat popping out of the crest of the tsunami and sailing through stormy skies. Lightning striking the frame and gunpowder cargo detonating to blow everything apart. Shattered bones of the vessel cascading into the sea. Sucking down into the water and drowning. And even the ocean suctioning away as the cataclysmic orgasm rises up to devour it... along with everything else! Everything a whirlpool, spinning into the void. Drenching heat. Flushing cold. Desperate suffocation! Nerve-endings exploding in a cacophony of ecstatic pain and rapture. His whole body shaking – quaking – a colossus about to collapse. Roaring as he drives himself deeper and deeper...

The writer's spasming legs released as Katya leaned her arms on the headboard and kicked her own legs into the air – big, red smile shining as she sat back on Jess' face and wiggled that twitchy little bunny-nose right inside her asshole. The writer could feel him exploding inside, everything gushing out of him... and into her! Jess hit the same frequency as Charlotte... and all the mirrors shattered... spinning shards of sex. The whole world dissolving – sucking into the orgasm – blankness swallowing everything

FIFTEEN
YOU AND I

It was so warm and comfortable inside Jess' dozing mind, eyes hammocking half-open. She could feel his come trickling out of her, drenching down her thighs. She was vaguely aware of something happening on the bed next to her. The hum of a sonar vibrator, held to Katya's clit... whilst he drizzled gravelled-honey-velvet words into her ear. Telling the mistress how strong and beautiful she was, how powerful and radiant, how droves of readers would orgasm fantasising about her... how 'Mirror Secret Mirror' would make her a star! And the mistress was orgasming, coming aggressively. Jess smiled gently as the slumber wafted back overhead.

The next time her lids drifted open, she found herself watching the smoke move in the air above – wispy tendrils of mist creeping and shifting. Everything else was still... and all was quiet. A lazy, snug tranquillity – like it was all done. All she had to do now was relax. Eyes closing as the doze pulsed and floated. Could smell him drawing close, taste him breathing over her skin, feel his strong arms looping around... and lifting her into a cradle.

She nuzzled her cheek against his shoulder and cooed blissfully as he carried her across the room. Katya was curled up on the end of the bed, wreathed in cigarette smoke. Her slender body languid and devoid of tension. Eyes misted with serenity and long lashes heavy. The magic wand had finally relented, leaving Charlotte draped over the chair like a melted pancake – sleeping peacefully with mouth creased into an angelic smile. He and Jess were going up the steps. She nestled cosily into his being.

At the top of the stairs, he turned to shield her body as he pushed through the door. Her eyes were closed, but she could sense the bright light out here… bathing the inside of her lids in a summery orange glow. And ascending another set of steps. This time, twisting around and around – a spiral staircase corkscrewing upwards. Feeling the warmth of the sunshine on her skin… kissing her wounds. And the cool breeze soothing. Winds of purity blowing away her pain… dissipating into the airy ether. The fragrance of distant meadows carried over rolling grasslands. Opening her eyes to see blue skies dotted with dreams of fluffy, white cumulus. The staircase made entirely of clouds: a colossal, coiling column of mist, winding up into the heavens. Rocking gently in her cradle as they ascend – the calm sensations of a passenger dozing in the sunshine. Up and up… higher and higher. He carried her a long way.

At the top of steps, they came out on a plateau of cloud. Rolling wisps of white stretching into the distances. They moved towards the sound of running water. Cloud Mountain climbing above them in a series of puffy steps. The river making its way down in a web-work of waterfalls, spilling into lochs and lakes, which in turn overflowed, showering into the pools and lagoons below. Frothing cascades shimmering with rainbows. The melody of birdsong. The buzz of bees, busy amidst the perfumed flowers. The scent of rose and lavender.

He stepped into the pool, but kept her fully above the water. As he waded she watched dragonflies flitting over the surface –

gleaming and glinting like coloured metals in the sun. He carried her through the waterfall and the warm water showered over her skin, washing away all the sweat... and dirt... and pain. Everything becoming pure... and clean... and fresh. On the other side of the falls, there crouched a cave of clouds – the mellow light tinting pinkish-orange. He sunk into the pool and drew her below the surface. Then letting her pop up to float just above his arms... gazing up into the willowing wisp. She could feel all the cuts and bruises washing away as if they'd been painted on. Skin cleansed back to a healthy pinkish-cream.

He lifted her from the water. Slowly wading to the bank and stepping out of the pool. The Cloud Caves tunnelled up through the mountain, foggy walls glowing like hearth-fire. The wind passing through them was warm, drying her body so only a few jewelled droplets remained twinkling on her skin. Another spiralling staircase led up to Cloud Castle... at the top of Cloud Mountain. Fluffy, white walls dotted with partings of blue sky – flowered ivy creeping in through the windows. Up and up they went... higher and higher. He carried her a long way.

At the top of the steps, they turned through a doorway. Her chamber was at the pinnacle of the highest tower of Cloud Castle. Sunlight spilling through a wisping window to splash over the fluffy bed of clouds at the head of the room. Lustrous green plants, rainbowing flowers, butterflies dancing. Bright smells of summer and riverbanks. Two great, crystal-clear mirrors facing one another across the chamber – somehow encircling everything. And reflecting it all to the infinities – reflections reflecting reflections. He placed her on the bed and she sunk into unimaginable softness. Utter peacefulness as he lay by her side and she snuggled into his arms. So safe and comfortable here. She raised her head and gazed into his eyes. Looking so deep all she could see was her own reflection staring back. His precious smile cared so much. She put her cheek against his chest, closed her eyes and spelled it out slowly.

'15)You+I.'

He laughed gently and her head bobbed happily on his chest. She joined in… and they murmured in harmony… it felt like it would always be this way. Lying together inside the infinite echoes of the mirrors. The way it had always been. Nothing behind the mirrors. Everything in between… forever and ever after…

Find us online at
mirrorsecretmirror.com

Review MSM on Amazon, Apple, Goodreads, etc.

Connect with us on social media and spread the corruption:

Twitter: @MSM_Erotica

Instagram: @MSM_Erotica

Pinterest: @MSM_Erotica

FetLife: @MSM_Erotica

Goodreads: Jessica Seaques